TERRIFYING FREEDOM

LINDA ANNE SMITH

TERRIFYING FREEDOM

LINDA ANNE SMITH

Terrifying Freedom

Scriptural quotations cited in Part One are from the King James Version Bible.
Scriptural quotations cited in Part Two are from the New Revised Standard
Version Bible, copyright 1989, Division of Christian Education of the National
Council of the Churches of Christ in the United States of America. Used by
permission. All rights reserved.

Terrifying Freedom is a work of fiction. Names, characters, places, and incidents
are the products of the author's imagination or are used fictitiously. Any
resemblance to actual events, locales, or persons, living or dead, is entirely
coincidental.

Jacket and interior design: Erik Mohr

ISBN: 978-0-9949295-0-1

To all who seek the truth in love.

PART 1

CHAPTER 1

"**A**hem!" Claudia Woods cocked her head, raised her eyebrows and then continued on her way. Rebecca clicked her nails on her desk, rose with a sigh, and began to walk through the labyrinth of cubicles. She hated staff meetings.

"Our first event with the new HR manager," Sally said as she quickened her pace to catch up with Rebecca. Ever since Mike Tuttle resigned, Sally had eagerly awaited his replacement.

"Event?"

"Well, yes. Wanting to meet all of us. It's so good of him."

"He'd make better use of his time finding a replacement for Enrolment," Rebecca replied.

"He's probably looking for ways to build up morale. . . ."

"Increased production, more like it."

Sally and Rebecca worked on the same floor of a Midwest centre for Secure Star Insurance Company. Their building, on the outskirts of the downtown business district, faced a park that wound through the city of Verloren alongside a rambling river. The late summer sun poured through the windows of the offices and meeting rooms that bordered the front and side of the building. Determined shafts of light found their way to the earth-toned cubicles, highlighting niches that nestled a ficus or palm tree.

Rebecca worked with several other women in the enrolment department, processing new clients, maintaining policies on the established, and creating reports that were passed to the executives for their consideration or consternation.

The enrolment cubicles were at the rear of the building, with Rebecca's wedged between the back side wall and the unoccupied cubicle of a recently retired Ms. Masters. The office of the enrolment manager, Claudia Woods, was in the same area, separated from the enrolment cubicles by a small, open meeting area with a kitchenette.

Claudia held regular department meetings for the enrolment representatives; however, interdepartmental gatherings were rare, generally reserved for the roll-out of a new service or the annual Christmas party. The recently hired human resources manager, Andrew Covick, wanted to change that. According to his initial memo, interdepartmental exchange promoted understanding and collaboration. *Unity of purpose . . . , ownership . . . , pride in belonging to Secure Star Insurance . . . providing security to thousands of businesses and families . . .* He arranged this "event," as Sally liked to call it, to *introduce myself and meet all of you* with the hopes of fostering *increased communication, participation, and initiative.* Rebecca smirked when she read his memo and tossed it in the recycling basket. She wondered how many websites he had plagiarized to compose it.

"I can hardly wait to see who this Andrew Covick is," Sally said.

"Well, you only have five minutes to go."

Keeping up her quick pace, Rebecca passed a group of employees waiting for the elevator and headed up the staircase to the large meeting room two floors above, Sally at her heels.

"Heard he's going to make some changes. About time Tuttle moved on: hire, fire, retire—those were his only concerns," said Sally, repeating an oft-quoted complaint about Tuttle.

"Suited me just fine," Rebecca said under her breath.

For any meeting Rebecca chose a chair in the last row. Securing this spot was her only motive for arriving slightly ahead of time. She hesitated as she entered the room, causing Sally, who followed close behind, to bump into her. Usually, the chairs were set in rows facing a podium and screen at the front of the rectangular room. Today, the chairs were arranged in a broad horseshoe with just a few rows running lengthwise. The podium was pushed into a corner and a couple of chairs were placed in the centre of the horseshoe formation. Rebecca recoiled against the imposed informality of the setting.

"Isn't this great! It's so casual and inviting," said Sally, looking over Rebecca's shoulder.

Rebecca remained silent and chose a seat in the last row off to the side, hoping Sally would find another companion. However, she happily plunked herself in the next seat.

Rebecca marvelled at Sally. Her naivety combined with her softly curled hair and protruding eyes gave her an air of perpetual amazement. She continued to survey the newly arranged meeting space with astonishment.

"The women's Bible study is set up like this—not so large, mind you. . . . I can see that Mr. Covick's going to create a real family spirit here."

"Money will still be the bottom line. Great foundation for a family."

"Yes, we have a great foundation for family spirit," said Sally, distracted by the arriving employees who were squeezing around the knees of those sitting, to reach an empty seat.

James Haverstock, Secure Star's director of this Midwest centre, strode through the door. Surprised by the new layout, he threw out his arms in jest, getting a chuckle from the assembly, and walked to the centre of the horseshoe. Andrew Covick followed nonchalantly, smiling and nodding at the employees to the left and right. He was tall and attractive, his brown hair seasoned with grey.

Accustomed to a more formal setting, Haverstock quickly adapted, although he didn't sit down. He faced the employees, glanced at his watch, and began to introduce Andrew who stood next to him. After presenting Andrew's background and experience, Haverstock stated his hope that Andrew would "revitalize the Human Resources Department to meet the needs and expectations of the wonderful people who make Secure Star the most reliable, efficient insurance company in the nation." Then, apologizing for another pressing engagement, he turned the meeting over to Andrew and left.

Andrew sat on one of the chairs, crossed his legs, and slowly gazed at the faces of the employees before him. Rebecca sank into her chair, lowered her head, and rubbed her forehead. This was going to be a long meeting.

"I'm very happy to be a part of Secure Star and at the service of the employees who make up this company," he said at a slow, reflective pace. "During the next few weeks I plan to meet with each of you and you'll have a chance to discuss your ideas and concerns." Sally nudged Rebecca, smiling broadly.

Rebecca closed her eyes. She really missed Tuttle.

"While Secure Star has always encouraged employee initiative, I would like to see that increased—more extensive. We have to enter this new millennium, meeting the needs of the people of today. . . ."

"That could be done with higher wages," quipped a man from the side. The group laughed and Andrew as well.

"One of the issues we can look into . . . Yes, well, through my personal interviews—and that will be happening very soon—and through various surveys and meetings, we'll work together to improve our service, to move claims along more quickly—after all, these claims could be ours. And as we know, our best advertisement is the good experience of our clients."

Rebecca gazed out the window to the blue sky and the treetops swaying in the breeze. Birds darted from the branches, circled, and returned again. She decided to walk home instead of taking the bus.

" . . .Yes, we'll see how we can make this company more sensitive to family issues and, as you suggest, possibly incorporate daycare." There was a rustle of approving whispers.

The daycare proposal jarred Rebecca out of her reverie. Daycare? Was this guy a politician or a dreamer? Did he realize in building up hopes, he would have to deal with deeper disappointment when he couldn't come through? A daycare . . . at Secure Star?

Andrew looked at his watch and wrapped up the meeting. Sally squeezed Rebecca's arm, "This man is a blessing from God!"

Andrew remained at the door and shook hands as the employees left the room. By the time Rebecca and Sally reached the door, he was engaged in an extended conversation with another employee, so, with Rebecca leading the way, they walked out unnoticed.

Sally, ever perceptive of wedding rings and the singles in the office, nudged Rebecca. "He's not married. What a catch he'd be."

"Too bad you're already married."

"Of course," she stammered, "and happily married. I'll always be grateful for Don who brought me to the Lord. God has blessed us with three children. And just the other night, Rev. Martin said . . ."

Rebecca regretted her remark. Silence was the best antidote for absurdity.

~

Though disappointed to have missed her personal introduction to Andrew as she left the meeting room, Sally knew Andrew couldn't enter the second floor without greeting her. The doors from the small elevator lobby opened to a circular divider with Secure Star's logo. In front of it, an attractive desk with an oval counter created a compact reception area from which Sally observed all the comings and goings. Although visitors and clients were seldom on the second floor, Sally's position assured that the lost were redirected and the solicitors who managed to squeeze by the main reception desk on the ground floor were turned away and escorted out. Her reception duties were in no way a full-time task: Her principal job was clerical work for the claims department. Her pastime was keeping track of the regular inhabitants of the floor. She knew who came to work and who didn't, who left early and who came late, and, if they ordered in, what they ate for lunch. Simply by getting up for a glass of water or to pass on a file, she was able to note much of what happened beyond her reception desk.

Sally was not disappointed in her wait for Andrew. The next day he walked toward her desk before she even rose to introduce herself. He remained chatting for a few minutes, coming to know her entire family through a framed photo Sally kept on her desk.

CHAPTER 2

The midweek service had just begun at the Centre City Christian Fellowship and Sally sat next to her husband, Don. Although generally content, in one area Sally remained disheartened. All her efforts and invitations never drew a new member to their assembly.

Sally had quit work when her first child was born. However, when her youngest was ready for kindergarten, Don found a suitable house for sale and they needed extra funds. So Sally took on a clerical position at Secure Star. She imagined that within the large office on the second floor she would be able to witness to Christ, testifying to his mercy and salvation. The women's group at church had listened to a CD series on how to befriend women in order to bring them to Christ, and she was eager to apply what she had learned. Devotionals and tracts were always in her purse. On the bus and frequently at lunch she opened her Bible, ready to chat with anyone even remotely curious about what she was reading. Surely there would be those struggling with doubt and shame who, noting Sally's conviction and desire to share her faith, would be drawn to Christ in the Centre City Christian Fellowship.

No one ever came. Worse yet, no one even asked for her testimony. Her tracts, scuffed and dog-eared, took on the contours of her purse. Sally's affability prompted conversation with many at the office. But as soon as she broached the topic of her faith in Christ, the exchange cooled. Gradually, other than extending conventional pleasantries, most people avoided conversing with her. A woman in the office advised Sally to ease up. She felt like a quitter. These were dark times, as Rev. Martin often told them. People needed to accept Christ and be washed in his precious blood. As for believers, they had to be in the world, but not of it, holding fast to the Word of God.

There was still Rebecca. As Sally sat in the pew, holding hands with Don, she thought back on her repeated attempts to befriend her. It was difficult. Rebecca rarely left her cubicle, and when she did, she walked rapidly to her destination without pausing to converse or even pass a greeting. She replied when spoken to but gave no encouragement to continue. However, as Sally observed, Rebecca was like this with everyone. And she *had* managed to meet up with Rebecca at the HR meeting. . . . Starting that evening, Sally decided to pray for Rebecca every day and to take whatever opportunities she found to befriend her. When the time was right, Sally would invite her to her church where she would be embraced and welcomed. Rebecca's sorrows would melt in the mercy of Christ. Sally's had. How well she remembered it. The image brightened up her frame of mind as she joined in the hymns and the prayers.

CHAPTER 3

A few weeks passed before Andrew appeared in the enrolment department. Equipped with a list of names and corresponding years of service, he met with each person, inquired about their families or hobbies, listened to suggestions and difficulties if they came up, and jotted down notes. He gradually made his way past the empty cubicle of retired Ms. Masters and walked to the back-corner cubicle of Rebecca Holden. As he looked inside he was struck by its starkness. Generally, the offices and cubicles were adorned with family pictures, children's drawings, inspirational posters, enlarged comic strips, Bobbleheads, sports paraphernalia, and the like. A few even hung works of art and had ornaments and plants aesthetically arranged. But in Rebecca's cubicle there was nothing, absolutely nothing, except the work at hand. He knocked on the metal rim of the cubicle.

"Hello, I'm Andrew Covick."

Rebecca startled. She had not seen him.

"I believe Claudia informed you I'd be around today." He paused.

"Come in. Have a seat." Rebecca stood and extended her hand. "Rebecca Holden."

Rebecca was as cryptic as her office décor. Average height and slender, her brown, shoulder-length hair was blown back and curled slightly around her ears. She wore a classic black blazer and slacks with a blue top. Everything in her manner, her voice, and expression was cool, sharp, and quick. She made eye contact with Andrew—large hazel eyes, intelligent, perceptive, yet with an impenetrable barrier. She didn't smile, nor did she frown. As Andrew settled in his chair and opened his notebook, Rebecca toyed with a rubber band and, under the desk, her crossed leg began to spontaneously jiggle.

"You enjoy your work here?" Andrew asked.

"It pays my bills and it makes Secure Star money—a win-win relationship."

"And the rest of the staff"—Andrew gestured with his hand—"you enjoy working here in this department?"

"I'm here to work and I respect people who do the same," replied Rebecca without a change of expression.

A gush of water and a series of thuds sounded through the wall. "What's that?"

"Paper-towel dispenser. I'm neighbour to the bathrooms."

Andrew looked at the adjoining walls.

"The entrance is in the lobby, near the elevator."

"Does it bother you?"

"I have a private corner cubicle."

Another pause. Rebecca straightened some papers on her desk.

"How long have you worked here?" Andrew already knew but grasped for anything to get a conversation started.

Rebecca picked up a pen and clicked it a few times. "Four years. . . . Have we become sufficiently acquainted? I have plenty to do."

"Well, yes . . .yes," said Andrew as he began to rise. "We'll continue our conversation another time."

With that, Rebecca turned her head toward her monitor and was already typing as he left.

Andrew went to the kitchenette and poured himself a cup of coffee. He took a few sips, watching Claudia at work: one elbow on the desk, her thumb and forefinger propping up her forehead so all Andrew could see was her close-cropped afro as she reviewed a report. Claudia was middle-aged, known for her professionalism and smartness in attire. She and Andrew had already met on a couple of occasions. Andrew liked her. She was down-to-earth, frank, and wore great perfume. Andrew knocked on her office door and Claudia offered him a chair.

"I was just in to see Rebecca Holden." He took a sip of coffee. "What an attitude."

"Attitude or not, Rebecca does the work of three and does it well." She picked up a glass of water and leaned back in her chair. "And she minds her own business."

"Yeah, I definitely got that impression."

After a few moments he asked, "Who is she?"

"She works here, Andrew. She does her work well."

He stood to leave but remained there, gazing at the floor. Then, looking at Claudia, he asked, "You're OK with that? 'She works here. She does her work well.'"

"That's all we need to be OK with, Andrew."

Andrew turned and left the room. As he passed by the office two doors down from Claudia's, Joe Blate, the underwriting manager, called to him.

All the offices that bordered the windows were enclosed in glass from the ceiling to about three feet from the floor where a solid wall continued to the floor. Although blinds could be pulled for privacy, many were left open, so Blate easily spotted Andrew as he was passing by.

"Coming from the North Pole, are you? So, did you meet 'the Berg,'" he said with a grin.

Andrew gave a blank look.

"You know, the Berg. As in iceberg? Holden."

"Oh, oh . . . Rebecca Holden."

"Little slow on the uptake, Andy. Have a seat. Now regar—"

"You ever try talking to her?"

"What?"

"Rebecca. Ever try talking to her?"

"The Berg doesn't talk. Now regarding the proposal I sent you yesterday . . ."

~

Andrew pulled open the filing cabinet in his office and began to hunt under H—Holden, Rebecca. To his surprise, there were only annual evaluations and compensation records—no application form, no references, no interview notes. "They must be in Claudia's office," he mused. He pulled out the evaluations and began to read.

CHAPTER 4

"Your turn for the kitchenette this week," said Claudia as Rebecca passed her office.

"Oh, hell. I forgot."

"Don't tell me you almost dropped the ball." Claudia laughed. She occasionally nudged Rebecca's reserve but never pushed it. A mutual understanding existed between them and on Rebecca's side there was something else—gratitude.

"Any sign of the replacement for Ms. Masters?"

"The interviews are done. It won't be long now," Claudia replied. "And as a senior enrolment rep, you'll be training."

"Whoever it is better be a quick learner," said Rebecca as she turned toward her office.

Later that day Rebecca gathered up the torn, empty sugar packets and sticky stirrers left on the kitchenette counter and threw them in the trash. She put the dirty mugs into a sink of hot, soapy water to loosen the lipstick and petrified sugar-milk residues before transferring them to the dishwasher. *People can be such slobs*, she thought. Taking a damp cloth to wipe off the counter she noticed Andrew leaning on the wall near the kitchenette entrance. *What's with this guy? He's around when you least expect him, moves at a turtle's pace, and the effort it takes him to formulate a thought is painful.* She was grateful she had something to do while he got wound up.

"You've got quite a work record. You could easily apply for advancement. There are internal postings."

"I'm not interested." Rebecca finished the counter and began cleaning the coffee maker.

"Your wages could increase by a third—at least."

Rebecca stopped what she was doing and looked at Andrew. "I have no desire to bid on another position."

Several moments passed. Rebecca began to rub stubborn remnants off the mugs before placing them in the dishwasher. To her surprise, Andrew opened the dishwasher and began to load the mugs she had ready.

"Do you have anything else you want to discuss?" she asked.

"No . . . no. I've covered everything."

"Then I can handle this. I'm sure you have more pressing matters."

Andrew wiped his hands on a towel and walked away while Rebecca continued washing.

By the time she finished with the kitchenette it was almost time to leave. She began to close down the computer and organize her work for the following day when Sally appeared at her cubicle. "Hi, Rebecca."

"Good afternoon."

For a while now, Sally seemed to be passing by the back corner more frequently, commenting on the weather or something just as trifling. But today her comments took a different turn.

"Our church is having an open house service this week for newcomers. Rev. Martin will—"

"I'm not interested," replied Rebecca, bent over application forms.

"If you only knew how much Jesus loves you, Rebecca. Just think . . ."

What's with these people today? Is there a full moon? Rebecca lifted her head, looked directly at Sally, and said, "With every word, atheism becomes more attractive. I. Am. Not. Interested. Please don't bring this up again."

CHAPTER 5

Sally looked up. Toward her walked a tall woman in a bright red dress, black blazer, and heels; hanging from her shoulder was a black designer tote. By no means slim and trim, she was one of those fortunate women whose extra baggage fell in all the right places and her clothing accentuated them all. She had olive skin, large brown eyes, and long black hair layered and curled in a dazzling array of soft waves.

Sally smiled at her. "Can I help you?"

"Ms. Woods is expecting me. First day on the job."

Sally's already protruding eyes opened wider. *The replacement for Ms. Masters?*

"Your name, please?" Sally reached for the phone.

"Well, how many new employees is Ms. Woods expecting?" The woman grinned. "But go ahead and tell her Gladys Belen is here and ready to roll."

On second thought, Sally put down the phone. "It's quiet. I can take you to her office myself."

Sally chose a round-about route to Claudia's office. With a leisurely gait and Gladys's open character, she discovered that Gladys was currently unmarried with three children.

~

Rebecca walked swiftly into Gladys's cubicle and set a stack of files on her desk.

"These are the applications you'll be working on today."

"God, if you're not a bitch," Gladys said with a laugh.

After only a week, she was quickly mastering the processing procedures.

There was no doubt about her competency. Rebecca maintained her reserve and kept strictly to the training. Gladys apparently found her cool, crisp manners amusing and had recently bestowed on her the affectionate nickname "bitch."

"Knock, knock," said a voice at the entrance to the cubicle. Both Rebecca and Gladys turned to see Sally holding a small plant. The pot was wrapped in brightly coloured foil gathered at the rim by an array of curled ribbons, one of which anchored the *Welcome!* balloon that floated above it.

"Hi, Gladys, I just want to bring you a little something from the Centre City Christian Fellowship."

"Why, thanks, sweetie, that was thoughtful of you," replied Gladys as she rearranged her desk to find a spot for the plant. It was obvious to Rebecca that this was not their first encounter.

After setting down the gift, Sally remained half-leaning, half-sitting on the edge of Gladys's desk, smiling. "Violets are my favourite."

Looking at Rebecca, Gladys said, "I'm waiting for *you* to bring me a plate of homemade cookies." Then turning back to Sally with a grin and a teasing tone, "You know she hasn't even given me a goddamn card!"

Sally started. "Gladys, that kind of language is offensive and unprofessional."

Gladys looked at Sally from the top of her eyes. "Your ass on my desk is unprofessional," she said in amusement, "so why don't we just call it even?"

Rebecca watched, amazed.

Sally didn't know how to respond. She straightened up and moved away from the desk. Regaining her composure, she said, "I'll be seeing you later, Gladys," and walked out the door.

Gladys caught Rebecca's eye, then raised her eyebrows.

CHAPTER 6

Through a stroke of good fortune, Andrew discovered an international food court several blocks from the Secure Star offices. A couple of weeks before, he had decided to take a walk through the downtown district before going home and happened across the eatery. Most Secure Star employees preferred the convenience of the local food joints and the park across the street. Andrew enjoyed the international food court's quality and selection so, when possible, he made the trek.

Today he took his iced tea and custom-built pasta to a small round table and was just beginning to enjoy his meal when he looked up and saw Rebecca in a line. Their tête-à-tête over a month ago had gone so poorly that he'd decided to take Claudia's advice and leave well enough alone. Now, without any attempt on his part to meet her, there she was. The food court was busy and he was off to the side near a knot of small, leafy trees. Most likely, she wouldn't see him, and even if she did, she would be even less likely to share a meal. So Andrew settled just to savour his pasta and observe the live tableau around him.

A wail rose up in their section of the food court. The crowd hushed and turned in the direction of a sobbing toddler. Rebecca was the first to make a move. She left her place in line and approached the child, glancing around to see if there was anyone who looked like his parent. No one came near the little boy. He had golden brown skin, curly black hair, and appeared to be about three years old. Tears streamed down his cheeks and his nose was running profusely. "Mamma, Mamma," he cried.

Rebecca gently touched his shoulder and squatted down to meet his eyes. "Are you looking for your mamma?"

His only reply was sobbing "*Mamma*s."

"Hey, hey . . ." Rebecca stroked his hair. "Your mamma's here. I know she's here and she's looking for you." By this time Rebecca had her arms around him. "Let's go find her. Let's go find your mamma."

The little boy's sobs began to subside. "You'll have to stop crying because I'm going to lift you real high so you can see your mamma, OK?" She took out some tissue from her jacket pocket and began to wipe his eyes and nose.

"Are you ready?" He nodded. "What's your name?"

"Car-los," he said through his after-sob heaves.

"Well, come on, Carlos, let's go find Mamma."

Rebecca stood up and lifted Carlos onto her hip, kissing his cheek as she did so. Carlos sat easily on Rebecca's hip and wrapped one arm around her neck. Both began looking through the crowd.

Andrew's pasta remained untouched from the time the scene began. Rebecca's tenderness, warmth, and naturalness—her ability to relate to this unknown child—were striking. Her demeanour was widely divergent from what he had previously experienced.

The search didn't last long. "Carlos, Carlos!" a young woman cried out. She carried a number of large bags filled with recent shopping and wobbled on her high heels as she half-walked, half-ran to her little son. She set down her parcels and reached for Carlos who was already leaping from Rebecca into her arms. He snuggled against his mother. "I told you not to run. You see what happens when you run away from Mamma."

Carlos's mother turned to Rebecca, flustered. "Thank you so much."

"He's a beautiful child," Rebecca replied, gently ruffling his hair.

Another woman rushed up to the mother. "Oh, you found him!" After kissing the toddler on both cheeks, she said, "Carlos, Carlos, you scared us!" She picked up the mother's bags and then both women and the child walked out of the food court and were soon swallowed up in the throng.

Rebecca looked at her watch and left.

When Andrew returned to Secure Star, he sat down at his computer and sent out a memo to all managers.

CHAPTER 7

Departing Secure Star employees crowded into the elevator. As the doors closed, a large, aqua shoulder bag swung in, forcing them to reopen. Many occupants muttered impatiently.

"Ah, just in time," said Gladys as she squeezed in, forcing the others into the walls and onto each other's toes. On the ground floor, the elevator emptied and Gladys stepped aside to button up her coat. She noticed Rebecca moving toward the main entrance and caught up with her. "Well, well, didn't see much of you today."

"Lucky you."

Outside Gladys took out a pack of cigarettes and offered one to Rebecca.

"I don't smoke."

"Oh, I thought all bitches smoked."

"Allow me to break the stereotype."

"Allow me to reinforce it." Gladys laughed and lit up. They walked on in silence. "You take number 48?" asked Gladys as she approached her stop.

"No, my bus is further up."

Rebecca kept walking. She was glad to be free of Gladys—of all people. Ever since the incident at the food court, Rebecca felt unsteady. She didn't understand herself. The foot traffic lightened. She had long since passed her bus stop, walking on and on, slowly making her way home. Carlos's distress, his trust, his ease on her hip, the mother's relief, and his joy at their reunion—all of this unsettled her profoundly.

There was a time . . . The memories had become black and white, silent stills, intellectual acknowledgements of the past. Memories on which she never dwelt were now forcing themselves to awareness, and with the awareness, the pain she believed to be gone. She quickened her pace, almost running.

Her disillusionment had initially left her angry, confused, and frightened. But that gradually passed into detachment, with Rebecca moving through life, expecting nothing. She observed life through a thick glass pane and gave heed to little more than what was essential or imposed upon her, interpreting her muted reality in isolation. Her disengagement silenced her emotions and dried up her dreams.

Previously, when circumstances were tough or the future uncertain, Rebecca had taken refuge in her imagination. Worlds and relationships were conceived and embellished, transmuting and morphing into alternative realities in which she flourished. They eased the present and brought hope for the future. Now her imagination was, at best, a blank wall. More often it was a pit that conjured up images and prophecies that threatened to drag her into a darkness from which she feared she would never emerge. So she never rambled there as she had done in the past.

Rebecca turned the key to her apartment and flicked on the light. It was small but sufficient for a single woman with no intention of receiving guests. The door opened into a combined living room/dining room. On one side were a desk, TV, two folding wooden trays, and a glider with its ottoman; on the other, a round pine table with two matching chairs. Off from the dining area ran a compact galley kitchen that abutted the bathroom and a bedroom that ran parallel to the living room. A few Impressionist and Asian paintings softened the arrangement out of austerity.

In the bedroom were two pictures, and two pictures only. One captured a smiling couple with four children—her brother and family. The other was an enlargement of a snapshot—Rebecca in an evening dress with her father's arm around her shoulder. It was taken shortly before his death. There was a bed and an end table, but the bookcase dominated the room. It revealed the two interests of Rebecca's outside of survival—how people learn and mystery thrillers. As to the first, Rebecca had an insatiable curiosity; as to the second, an insatiable appetite. She made frequent excursions to the library and always had a novel on the go with a couple waiting on the side. During the weekends, she scanned books on various learning theories. Some caused her to snicker, others she cast aside in disgust; but there were authors who captivated her. These she would purchase and study. Over the years, her personal library gradually increased.

Except for news, the odd documentary, or an occasional mystery, she rarely watched TV. Besides reading and research, her one other source of enjoyment was nature. She often took extended walks through parks and tree-lined neighbourhoods. During vacations and occasional long weekends she would drive off to a picturesque area. Only in these solitary excursions did she feel some form of wholeness or anything resembling peace.

~

Rebecca set down her handbag and glanced about the room. The incident with Carlos upset her. She couldn't close it out. She couldn't stay within the confining, constricting walls of the apartment. Rebecca kicked off her shoes, quickly changed, and left.

CHAPTER 8

The next day when Andrew arrived at his office, there were several envelopes on his desk. The managers had read his memo. He poured a cup of coffee, closed his office door and began to open them. A pile formed on one side of the desk. On the other lay a file from Claudia Woods. He took the solitary file and opened it. Rebecca Holden. He felt a twinge of . . . was it guilt? Rebecca's work record was great. She had no desire to advance. So why read her file? Even he couldn't explain his concern for this woman. But he had a right to the information, a right to examine it, and so he began.

There were no details related to her initial interview, just a note that read: "R. Holden was interviewed and found qualified to fulfill the tasks of the position." It was signed and dated by Claudia. Illuminating, thought Andrew. He searched further and found Rebecca's resumé. She had a master's in education, and from what he could gather, her entire work experience had been in that field. Any administrative duties were only part of a role directly related to teaching. She joined Secure Star as a junior enrolment rep with no previous experience in clerical or insurance-related work. Due to her stellar work record, she moved quickly to her current position—senior enrolment rep. Her teaching positions, at least those she listed, had been in the East. What drew her to an entry-level position at a Midwest branch of an insurance company—a field so different from her training?

Andrew had hoped her file would shed some light on Rebecca. It only deepened the mystery

CHAPTER 9

"Bitch, you OK?"

Rebecca clipped around her office with her usual efficiency, yet there was a sombre quality that even Gladys couldn't toy with.

"Fine," replied Rebecca in a low voice, continuing her work.

"You want to go somewhere for lunch?"

"No."

"Well, if you need anything, you just let me know."

～

Unlike Rebecca, Gladys did not restrict herself to the back-wall cubicle. Her gregarious character and good-natured laugh were known throughout the second floor. In the kitchenette, at the copy maker, coming up the elevator—she had a story, a quip, a laugh. At times, when she returned to her desk, she was still laughing to herself. She wished the camaraderie with a couple of men would transpire into dates—she was eligible now. But Gladys was beginning to realize that with three young children, her eligibility was sorely tried. As her mother said, "Smart with numbers, unlucky with men. Your three children will help men be more discerning where you are not." Well, she wasn't going to give up trying. And she had just stumbled upon a new possibility.

～

A couple of weeks later in the Secure Star lobby, Rebecca met up with Gladys as they were leaving for the day. "You'll never guess what I have planned for the night," Gladys said.

Rebecca just looked at her.

"I'm going to Sally's prayer meeting."

"What!"

Gladys smiled to see that she had managed to crack Rebecca's general indifference. "Maybe that's my problem. Maybe I don't have enough religion. And who knows, I might find myself one of those good, Christian guys who's willing to stay with a woman."

Rebecca couldn't imagine Gladys in a prayer group, let alone with Sally. "Gladys, you don't go to church to get a man. Religion's not a dating game."

"So the bitch is an expert in religion." Gladys smirked. "I say, whatever works."

~

Gladys decided to dress down for the church service but anyone seeing her for the first time would never have guessed. Her grey top, black suede jacket, and form-fitting slacks seemed subdued to Gladys, a little too subdued, she thought as she looked in the mirror. She changed into a fuchsia silk blouse and matching jewellery. Her mother, pleased with her fledging inclination toward religion, willingly looked after her children.

Now Gladys just had to find the church. She stepped off the bus and walked down the street. The click of her high heels on the cement sidewalk echoed in the quiet residential neighbourhood. A block up she noticed a concentration of parked cars and people walking toward a lighted building. *Must be the church.*

Gladys tried to remember the last time she had ever thought about going to church. As a child, she had been marched to Sunday school every week by her God-fearing mother. During her teen years, Gladys drifted away. She tried to recall the name of the church but it had vanished along with her attendance.

Two divorces, three kids, single mom—her run with men had not gone well. Stanley, number one, had been a great guy and a lot of fun. But when their son arrived, he wasn't ready to take on any of the baby watch or redirect the fun money to the needs of the family. Their arguments became even more intense when their daughter arrived a year later. Stanley left shortly after.

Gladys could now admit that she had been a bit desperate in the choice of her second husband. He was more than happy to look after the children and pitch in around the house—when he wasn't enjoying his ale and watching baseball . . . and football . . . and basketball. Gladys called it quits when she came home and found her preschool son and daughter unattended on the front lawn. However, by then she was expecting her youngest daughter.

Nine, eight, and five. She wanted a decent man—someone she and her kids could count on. And they were good kids. Maybe she just needed religion.

~

A few doors down, Gladys could make out Sally standing in the well-lit church entrance, looking in one direction and then the other. As Gladys came within the range of light, Sally hurried to her, gave her a hug and, arm entwined, brought her inside the church. The music had just started when Sally stepped into a pew near the rear and quickly introduced Gladys to Don. He acknowledged her with a nod and a handshake. As the congregation sang the hymn, Gladys took in the scene. The building was small; maybe two hundred people could squeeze in. About sixty were spread throughout the church tonight. She had heard enough about Rev. Martin from Sally to surmise that he was the sombre minister behind the lectern at the front of the church who belted out the hymn despite his sagging shoulders and drooping jowls. Although tidy, the pews and other furnishings showed signs of age and wear, as did many of the attendees. Gladys could feel her disappointment creeping in.

"Looks like the regulars are busy tonight," she whispered to Sally.

"Oh, Wednesday nights are quieter. The larger crowd comes on Sunday." Gladys was growing wiser by the minute. Well, she was there now, so why not make the best of it?

Rev. Martin opened the Bible.

"Isaiah 64:6, '*But we are all as an unclean thing, and all our righteousnesses are as filthy rags; and we all do fade as a leaf; and our iniquities, like the wind, have taken us away.*'

"Filth and rot. It is not in our nature to do good. St. Paul in Romans 3:10 through 12 tells us, '*As it is written, There is none righteous, no, not one: There is none that understandeth, there is none that seeketh after God. They are all gone*

out of the way, they are together become unprofitable; there is none that doeth
good, no, not one.'

"We are all bent toward rebellion. Your thoughts and desires are prone from
birth toward disobedience and chaos. It is only when Jesus comes into your lives
that you learn to submit your deviant wills to God, for Jesus, '*though he were a*
Son, yet learned he obedience by the things which he suffered,' Hebrews 5:8. And
with submission comes the promise of eternal life. Blessed be God! Praise his
holy name! Jesus, the Son of God, who stands sinless before the throne of God."

Then, pointing at everyone in the congregation, Rev. Martin continued,
"None of you would ever be worthy to come before God. But Jesus, praise his
holy name, the sinless Son of God, paid the debt of your sin with his precious
blood. Through his death on the cross, Jesus washed you from your guilt so that
you can stand forgiven before the throne of God."

Rev. Martin looked at each person as he reiterated his message. The
seriousness of his tone impelled Gladys to look around and see how the others
were taking it. Everyone was as grave as the pastor. She also noticed that she alone
had long, thick black hair and olive skin. Her eyes wandered to her shoes. One,
she noticed, had a scuff, and as she polished it off on the hem of her pants, she
saw a streak of dust on her black slacks. Damn bus, she thought, as she brushed
off the dust. She checked both shoes again for scuff marks. What a good deal she
had gotten on these shoes. They were comfortable as well as stylish—not an easy
combination. She had to go back to that store. A surge in volume from Pastor
Martin brought her back to the sermon.

"Luke, chapter 21, verse 36, '*Watch ye therefore, and pray always, that ye may*
be accounted worthy to escape all these things that shall come to pass, and to stand
before the Son of man.' God is coming to judge the world, but will there be any
righteousness when he arrives?"

His voice rose to a crescendo as he lifted his arms emphatically. "Despite
the waves of opposition, despite the persecution, despite the filth that bombards
us from movies, newspapers, TV, magazines, and every other sort of devilish
invention, let us not lose heart. Let us lead lives of godliness so that when Jesus
comes, we will be there, standing tall, standing firm, ready to enter his kingdom.
Amen. Praise the Lord, our Saviour, the sinless Son of God."

Whuu! Gladys felt as if her hair was being blown backward by the force of his
message. Another hymn broke out. Sally smiled at Gladys. People were leaving

their pews and moving toward the podium to reconfirm their commitment to Christ and to state their petitions. Pushed ahead by Sally, Gladys gathered with others. Sally prayed for Gladys and all those searching for the Lord. Gladys, instead, searched the faces and in the end was constrained to accept reality—there was no husband material here. And the preacher was so goddamn serious. This wasn't the place . . . but maybe a step in the right direction. She just had to find the right church.

CHAPTER 10

The rain turned to drizzle as Andrew pulled in front of an expansive brick building. He drove to the end of the parking area, stopped the car, and double-checked the address. Definitely the place. He pulled out the keys, clicked off the seat belt, but continued to sit. This was really going over the line, tracking down a reference on Rebecca's resumé. On the other hand, Secure Star had sent him to a national HR convention just a half-hour drive from Slandail. What were the chances? He opened the car door and walked leisurely toward the main entrance. An elderly nun swept the walkway in front of the building, clearing it of the autumn leaves that had just begun to fall. She paused and smiled sweetly, her plump, sagging cheeks brightened by the cool breeze.

"Is this a school?" asked Andrew.

"No, it's our motherhouse. Would you like to enrol your children in one of our schools?"

"Is that a possibility?"

"Why, certainly!"

"Would I be able to speak to Sr. Maureen about the process?"

The nun paused and looked up more closely. "You know Sr. Maureen?" Then buoyed with recognition, "Are you her nephew—her brother's son?"

"I'm a friend . . . of a friend. . . ." He extended his hand. "Andrew."

"Sr. Candida." She shook his hand warmly.

"Wonderful place you have here." Andrew scanned the extensive grounds landscaped meticulously with gardens, lawns, and copses of the ancient trees that towered overhead. Then, nonchalantly, "Do you know Sr. Maureen?"

"Oh, yes. We taught together for years in a little place called Whitewaters. She was the principal." Sr. Candida bent to pick up a withered leaf. "It's closed now."

"Does Sr. Maureen still teach?"

"She's been over at St. Peter's lately. An emergency. One of the teachers had surgery. Ruptured appendix, they say. Nasty business, nasty business."

~

The unmistakable school smell brought Andrew back to his childhood. Then the sounds: teachers imparting lessons, the muffled rumbling of children involved in a class activity, and an intercom message that broke through it all. A group of students in plaid jumpers, dark pants, and white shirts left the library across from the office and walked two by two down the corridor to their classroom. Jesus and the saints, looking down from large devotional pictures that bedecked the walls, admonished the pupils to follow in their footsteps.

The school was, without doubt, a long-established, prosperous institution. The foyer, front office, windows, and doors had been cleverly renovated to preserve the architecture of an earlier era.

The receptionist returned from a back office to her post but Andrew didn't notice, absorbed in what he could see of St. Peter's Academy.

"May I help you?"

"Oh, yes . . . yes, you can," said Andrew, turning around. "I came to see Sr. Maureen. Is she available?"

"Is Sr. Maureen expecting you?"

So she is here, thought Andrew. *Good.*

"No, no . . . I went to the motherhouse and was told I could find her here." He extended his hand. "Andrew Covick. Remarkable school you have here. Right in the city and yet you would think you're in the country."

The receptionist smiled. "Yes, that's one of the features parents like about our facilities. I'll see if Sr. Maureen is available." She typed a few keys on her computer and referred to a chart. "She's in class . . . due to end in fifteen minutes for recess."

"I can wait. Would you let her know I'll be outside—it's a wonderful day and I'd like to see the grounds."

"Certainly. I'll give her the message."

Andrew wandered about the building, but always within view of the front entrance. Before long, he heard the hooting and hollering of children released for recess coming from behind the building and he slowly made his way closer to the entrance. Soon an older nun appeared, looking about. Andrew quickened his steps, waved, and the two approached each other.

"Thank you for making time to see me." Extending his hand, "Andrew Covick."

Sr. Maureen shook his hand. "Do I know you?"

Though garbed exactly like Sr. Candida, Andrew sensed instantly that he was dealing with a very different person. Sr. Candida was a marshmallow, both in personality and stature. In Sr. Maureen's gaze, Andrew discerned perception, prudence, and depth.

"We have a mutual acquaintance."

"I've been teaching for over forty years and have met a lot of people," Sr. Maureen said with a smile. "You're going to have to refresh my memory." She pointed across the parking area to a stand of trees in a grassy area. "There's a bench close by. Do you mind remaining outside?"

"Not at all."

"It would be a pity to go inside on such a lovely day."

As they sat, Sr. Maureen said, "Your name is Andrew—? I'm sorry, I don't remember the last name."

"Andrew Covick."

"So, Andrew, where are you from?"

As he searched for and passed his card, Andrew told her about Verloren, the insurance company, and his position in human resources.

"And your family? Are you originally from the Midwest?"

Andrew began to feel uneasy. While he had come to discover more about Rebecca's life, he never anticipated that he might have to share some of his own.

"No, no . . . originally from California."

"You moved from California to cornfields?" Maureen's voice rose in disbelief. "Whatever for?"

"Work opportunities."

"Work opportunities . . ." Sr. Maureen looked at Andrew and cocked her head. "You don't look like the kind of person who would have to search too far for work opportunities." To Andrew's relief, she did not pursue the issue further.

"So, who's our mutual friend?"

"Rebecca Holden."

All conversation and movement came to a standstill. Sr. Maureen peered intently at Andrew. "Rebecca Holden . . . You know Rebecca Holden?"

"She works at Secure Star. I know her through the HR office."

"So why are you here?" The initial casualness was gone. Not once did Sr. Maureen let up on her gaze. Andrew felt scrutinized, but at the same time, Sr. Maureen showed no antagonism.

"How well do you know Rebecca?" Andrew responded.

Both were on a tightrope now, each testing the other regarding their intentions, debating how much to trust. Sr. Maureen took the plunge.

"How much *did* I know Rebecca? We taught at the same school. . . . I haven't been able to contact her since she left." Then, shifting her body to look fully at Andrew, "Why are you interested in Rebecca?"

"I wonder about her."

"You *wonder* about her?"

"I'm concerned about her."

"Andrew, let's be frank here. Just what is going on?"

It was retreat or total revelation. "I wonder why a woman with an MA in education, and whose work experience has only been teaching, is now alone in a back cubicle entering data for an insurance firm."

"God."

Andrew thought he saw tears beginning to well up in Sr. Maureen's eyes, but she turned and put her hand to her forehead.

"You know she used to be a nun."

A nun? Rebecca, a nun? "No, I didn't. I knew she taught. She had you for a reference." *A nun! Rebecca!*

For a while neither said anything.

"How are you going to use the information we share?" asked Sr. Maureen.

"It's off the record. To be completely honest, I shouldn't even be here."

"So why are you?"

Andrew told Sr. Maureen of Rebecca's outstanding work record, yet how distant she seemed with anything and everyone not related directly to her job. Sr. Maureen looked ahead, listening attentively. Andrew went on to relate the incident of the lost child at the food court.

"After witnessing the way she handled the child—her warmth and kindness—all of it so at odds with her manner at the office . . ." Andrew sighed. "To tell you the truth, I don't know why I'm really here."

"Who does, really?"

After a few moments, Sr. Maureen looked at Andrew. "The food court scene—that's Rebecca. She has an intuitive sense with kids. Sr. Jeanne and I used to call her the child-whisperer."

"So, what happened?"

Sr. Maureen continued to look at Andrew.

"I would never hurt Rebecca or embarrass her. I just want to understand, and help if possible."

"It's not my story to tell. You've already been given a glimpse of her soul and honoured it." Sr. Maureen sat back in the bench and looked at the autumn leaves. "You can offer respect and goodness, but you can't force trust."

"Maybe I haven't done enough."

"Andrew, how do we know what is enough and too much? Look toward Rebecca's good and forget your own desire to fix and save. You'll know what to do. You've cared enough to come this far."

A bell sounded. Sr. Maureen rose immediately.

"I must go. I have class in five minutes." But then she sat down just as quickly, pulled out a pen and small pad of paper from an unseen pocket deep within the inner recesses of her habit, and began to write rapidly. She detached the paper neatly from the pad, folded it in half, and gave it to Andrew.

"When the time is right, pass this on to Rebecca, will you?"

"Of course."

Sr. Maureen put her hand on Andrew's shoulder, "God bless you, Andrew." Then she rose and walked rapidly back to the school. Andrew watched her, blessed and confirmed.

~

Andrew turned toward his car, then paused and pulled out the note he had slipped into his jacket pocket.

> *Rebecca, I'm stationed at the motherhouse. Jeanne is in Birchbark. We remember you with love and admiration.*

I'll always be here for you. Maureen.

He heard the crunch of gravel behind him and re-pocketed the note.

"Couldn't help noticing a visitor from my window," said a pleasant voice. Andrew turned.

"I'm Sr. Miriam Pistós," she said, extending her hand. "The principal here at St. Peter's Academy." She was relatively young, considering the sisters he knew and had just met, certainly still in her thirties. Slender, attractive—everything about her was neatly pressed and well-placed, right down to the tuft of hair that bordered her veil.

"Sr. Pss—" Andrew attempted to repeat the name.

"Oh, it's a tough one. Pistós. It means faithful in Greek."

"So your family is Greek?"

"Oh, no"—she laughed—"it's my profession name."

"A professional name?"

Again Sr. Miriam Pistós laughed. "Profession name. When we prepare to take our vows . . . become nuns, we take on a new name. I asked for Pistós. I wanted a name with meaning, something that would inspire me."

"Well," looking at his watch, "I really must be off. Nice to have met you."

Andrew turned to leave.

"I saw you speaking with Sr. Maureen. When I passed her in the hallway she said you were a friend of an alumnus. Who did you know from our school?"

You came all the way out here for this? thought Andrew with irritation. *Why don't you just ask Sr. Maureen?* He paused and said nonchalantly, "An acquaintance really. . . . If you don't mind me saying . . . I haven't seen many nuns your age."

"Oh," said Sr. Pistós with a broad smile, "our order is blessed with many young sisters—much younger than myself."

"Well, congratulations. And now I really must be off."

And with a brief handshake, he turned and walked to his car. As he pulled out, he could see Sr. Pistós in the rear-view mirror, returning to the school.

～

A few days later, Andrew was walking out of the office of James Haverstock. He had given a report of the convention and exchanged several ideas regarding their division of Secure Star. As he made his way to his office he felt Sr. Maureen's note, now in a small envelope, burning in his inner jacket pocket. He wanted to pass it on to Rebecca, but had no idea when. He knew he had overstepped his boundaries by digging into her past history and meeting Sr. Maureen. His plan could backfire. At times he wondered if he shouldn't just drop the whole idea. He finally decided on the "pending" mode. He wouldn't force the situation. If it arose, he would move on with his plan. If not . . . well, he would see. He wasn't ready to let go. He had gone too far.

CHAPTER 11

I t had been a good year for Secure Star. In addition to a year-end bonus, Andrew convinced James Haverstock not only to recognize employees for their years of service in the company, but to give additional recognition to those who had done so with intelligence and initiative. "These people are gems and the reason Secure Star is thriving. If you want to keep them, recognize them."

Andrew researched persons who had been in the company five, ten, fifteen, or twenty years to determine if, during their time, they had contributed to the company's growth, competency, customer service, community involvement, expense reduction, and the like. Secure Star had employees who put in the time, did the minimum, and lived for retirement—a going-away party would be a celebration. On the other hand, there were the givers: people with initiative and energy who developed their positions, went above and beyond for the clients, and brought their departments to a new level of cooperation and efficiency. They were people Andrew wanted to recognize and reward.

James, an innovator himself, saw the wisdom of the proposal. Secure Star would rent out a ballroom in the hotel down the street. Everyone would receive a bonus, and milestones in the company would be acknowledged. However, those with anniversaries who had also made a significant contribution to Secure Star would receive special recognition and be reviewed for a salary increase in the new year. Claudia was one of the chosen.

In November invitations were sent to all the employees with a date set for mid-December. Rebecca could hear Gladys's shout of excitement. Her boisterous congratulations to Claudia rang through their end of the office floor. Rebecca never attended the company Christmas parties, and never had the desire to do so. Now, she tapped a pencil on the desk and gazed at the burgundy fabric wrapping her cubicle. Long walks over the past weeks had burrowed Carlos in the background of her memory and settled Rebecca in an uneasy calm. The thought of a Christmas party only created angst; however, she could not disregard Claudia's recognition. She had been accommodating to Rebecca when she applied at Secure Star, and Rebecca appreciated Claudia's discretion and support throughout the years. The point of her pencil cracked off. Rebecca picked up her sharpener and watched the shavings curl and fall from the blade as she slowly turned the pencil. She would attend the party, skip the cocktail hour, arrive in time for dinner and leave right after the awards.

～

The Christmas party created quite a stir among the employees. Andrew was singled out as the initiator of this new development and his popularity subsequently increased. Even Rebecca had to give him credit. After their initial encounters, she rarely saw Andrew, let alone spoke with him. From a distance, her opinion of him softened.

On the day of the party, most employees packed up early in order to freshen up, get their kids and pets settled, and return to the party with a spouse, partner, or friend. Rebecca joined the others in the early departure. Having no social life, her selection of clothes for the occasion was rather slim. She slid the closet door open and began leafing through her wardrobe. She stopped at a deep-green outfit, took it off the hanger and held it against herself. She had purchased it for her parent's wedding anniversary a couple years back. It brought back bittersweet memories. At the anniversary party, her dad embraced her, then held her back at arm's length and told her how lovely she looked. He died a month later. She turned abruptly and ran the water for her shower.

～

A couple hours later, Rebecca arrived at the hotel, checked her coat, and made her way to the ballroom. When she'd anticipated the event, this solitary entrance created the most apprehension—moving alone among fellow employees with no business to do, no function to fulfill. Claudia spared her the worst, however. Stopping by her cubicle one day, she invited Rebecca to sit at her table—those being recognized had reserved seating. This invitation made Rebecca's decision to attend ironclad and it saved her from the awkwardness of sitting alone at an empty table until a couple, not finding a space elsewhere, joined her. Or worse yet, sitting with the ebullient Gladys after a couple of drinks. Rebecca felt safe with Claudia; she had worked with her long enough to trust her respect and tact.

Reception tables were set up outside the ballroom doors to gather the reservation cards and pass out tickets for drinks. Andrew was at the door greeting employees as they entered. As he turned to greet the next couple, Rebecca caught his glance. He seemed startled, or was it just surprise. Without a doubt, he remembered her.

The ballroom was elegantly arrayed with round tables throughout surrounding a dance area. Music, coming from a band to the side of the dance floor, drifted among the throng of Secure Star employees. Buffet areas were arranged along the walls and a bar with a lengthy queue provided cocktails.

Rebecca gradually made her way among the tables, keeping an eye out for those marked reserved. She found them skirting the dance area. Claudia spotted Rebecca first and waved to catch her eye. As Rebecca approached, Claudia came to meet her, squeezed her shoulder, and said, "Rebecca, you are beautiful! Why this green suits you so well and the pearl is gorgeous."

"It was a gift from my father."

"Well, the man had taste. Come and meet my husband," she said, leading Rebecca to a table.

Despite all the years they had worked together, Claudia and Rebecca did not know each other beyond their working relationship. Had it not been for Rebecca's bereavement leave, Claudia would never have known of her father's sudden death. This open display of Claudia's admiration and affection was unexpected and Rebecca's reserve wrestled with her appreciation of being welcomed. For the moment, appreciation won out and she actually smiled somewhat.

"Brad, this is Rebecca who I've told you so much about. A real whiz in our department." Brad Woods stood and extended his hand. They were seated, and with just a couple of general questions from Rebecca, Brad began to tell of his work and how he'd met Claudia. With Brad so willing to converse, Rebecca began to relax in the listening mode. She could see that Claudia was genuinely pleased to have her as her guest and, notwithstanding the discomfort that the event initially evoked, Rebecca was glad she had come.

The reserved tables were small, allowing for four people and there was still an empty seat at Claudia's. As they got up to go to the buffet, Rebecca asked if she were expecting anyone else.

"Oh, no. All my kids are grown and out-of-town. So I left a seat free in case you wanted to invite someone yourself."

While grateful for her thoughtfulness, Rebecca could feel the taunt of rising embarrassment. Perhaps they had other friends they would have preferred. However, from behind, Brad was telling her about the great baked clams he had already tasted on the way in. And Claudia, on reaching the buffet, told her she had to try the chocolate cheesecake. And so it went throughout the buffet choices and back to the table. Their cordiality was genuine and her unease subsided.

At a certain point, the music died down and James Haverstock went to a small dais near the band. He welcomed them all, thanked them all, and began the acknowledgements. Rebecca watched Andrew at the rear of the dais, passing Haverstock the pertinent information and gifts for each round of acknowledgements.

"Five years of service. . . . Ten years of service. . . . Fifteen. . . . Twenty. . . ."

Exceptional recognitions followed. Claudia was honoured for fifteen years of service as well as creating a training program for the enrolment department, now in use throughout Secure Star's national divisions. Her step-experience approach allowed new employees with little experience to grow in expertise by refining one duty at a time and, simultaneously, to contribute quickly and accurately to enrolment entry. At the same time, the program did not patronize those coming with experience in similar fields, allowing them to pass quickly through the levels, identifying and honing the knowledge and skills that were weak. Claudia's method had streamlined training and maintained accuracy in an entry-level department with high turnover.

Claudia received a thundering round of applause. Aside from her competency, she was admired for her integrity, professionalism, and the respect that she offered everyone. A few cheers and hoots, distinctively Gladys's, were heard above it all. Brad's smile and hearty applause radiated his esteem.

At the conclusion of the acknowledgments, James invited them to enjoy the continuance of the party, and the music began again. Rebecca was just about to excuse herself when Brad said, "One of our favourite songs!" He took his wife's hand. "You don't mind if I dance with the honouree, do you, Rebecca?"

"Not at all," she replied. But before she could say anything further, they were dancing, and Andrew was crossing the dance floor, coming straight for her table.

CHAPTER 12

As Andrew arrived at the table, he smiled and said, "Mind if I sit a minute?" Rebecca gestured to the empty chair. "This seat is free."

Up to this point, he had noticed Rebecca, Claudia, and Brad pleasantly conversing. Maybe it was just the wine, but Rebecca actually looked like she was enjoying the evening. Her guard seemed down. Andrew almost asked her to dance but then noticed her toying with her napkin. *Slow down, Andrew, slow down*, he thought.

For a few moments they watched the dancing.

"Claudia is a wonderful person," Andrew said

Rebecca added her own praise and coupled it with admiration for her husband. "You did a great job with this event, Andrew. And you were so right to recognize Claudia."

Although hardly loquacious, this little exchange was the longest and most personal he had ever had with Rebecca. Her compliment increased his courage.

The song ended and Claudia and Brad returned to the table. Andrew, who had met Brad briefly at the door, went on to get better acquainted. As this conversation wound down, Rebecca thanked them all and said that she would be heading home. Claudia did not press her to remain. Andrew, however, was not about to let this opportune moment pass.

"Let me walk you to the door." He rose with Rebecca and said good night to the Woods.

Other than the dance floor, tables occupied every available space. People moved back and forth to the buffet or the dance floor, and as Rebecca and Andrew wended their way through the crowd together, Andrew spontaneously put his hand on Rebecca's shoulder. The gesture came so naturally he hadn't given it a second thought, but he grew conscious that Rebecca had not shrugged him off. This was it. He would go through with his plan.

From the far side of the room came a resounding, "You, hooo! Rebecca, over here." Andrew and Rebecca paused and turned. Gladys waved. "You look great, sweetie!" she hollered over the crowd.

~

Gladys! thought Rebecca. At least she had enough sense to keep *bitch* for the office. She waved back as she and Andrew continued toward the door.

As they entered the large corridor and walked toward the lobby, Andrew dropped his hand and said, "Rebecca, before you go, could I speak with you briefly? It won't take long . . . Right up here in the lobby."

They arrived before Rebecca could object and he led her to a set of chairs in the corner. Except for a couple checking in, the lobby was deserted.

"Rebecca, I hesitate to bring up business at this party but I'd like to share an initiative with you that you might find appealing."

Rebecca made no reply.

"From the time I've arrived, there've been repeated requests to establish some form of daycare for the children of our employees. I'm setting up a committee to pursue this project and would like you to be a part of it."

Rebecca could not have been more surprised. "Why are you asking me? I'm not married. I don't have any children."

"I noticed in your resumé a background in education."

Rebecca tensed. "I'm sure there are plenty of people with a background in education who would not qualify as consultants for a daycare centre."

"That may be true . . . However, I've seen you with a child . . . a lost child . . . Carlos. . . . I know you can relate with young children. I was at the food court."

He was at the food court! Rebecca felt the heat of a flush rising in her face. He remembered Carlos's name as clearly as she did. Stunned and confused, Rebecca could make no reply.

"I know you're qualified." With that he pulled the envelope from his pocket and handed it to Rebecca.

Rebecca took the envelope and flipped it front and back. It was blank. She looked up at Andrew, perplexed. "What's this?"

"I went to a conference and met Sr. Maureen."

Rebecca glared at Andrew. "Maureen! You *just happened* to meet Maureen?"

"I can expl—"

"Your conference organized convent tours?" said Rebecca, incensed.

"Rebecca—"

"You've gone through my file, Andrew, and you went deliberately to the convent. Admit it."

"I saw how you handled Carlos."

Rebecca's breathing quickened and her lips began to tremble. "That gives you *no right* to pry into my life." Though speaking forcefully, Rebecca could not keep the tremor out of her voice.

"You have a gift with children."

Rebecca's two worlds collided. With Andrew's note, Rebecca's orbs, spinning in spheres she had so tenaciously isolated, spiralled off course and came crashing together.

Shock and confusion swelled to waves of rage. She had no words. She could not even look at Andrew. She rose quickly from her seat, went to the coat room, then left the hotel.

∼

Andrew remained where he was, watching her go. The encounter could not have gone worse—far worse than he'd ever anticipated. He had mistaken her coolness and distance. He had hoped to draw her out. Instead, to watch her tremble and hear her voice quivering with anger—she had been furious. And to think that he had precipitated it; it was one of the most painful moments in his life. Andrew began to question his own motives, remembering Claudia's words: *She does her job well . . . that's all we need to be OK with.* And Claudia's sensitivity had gained Rebecca's trust to the point that she was here tonight. He had never seen her so relaxed and lovely. And in his determination to go ahead with *his* plans to elicit her talents, to unveil the real Rebecca, he had driven her further within herself and unleashed an antagonism he would likely never overcome. And he had put an even greater distance between herself and her friends of the past.

49

Andrew was lost in reflection when Joe Blate, noticing him alone in the lobby, came over and said, "What! A little party's worn you out?"

Recalled to his duties, Andrew returned to the ballroom to greet the departing guests.

CHAPTER 13

Rebecca closed the door to her apartment. She slipped off her shoes and dropped her coat on a chair, then walked to the front window and peered out. She turned and went to the bedroom where she sat on the edge of her bed. She was thirsty, needed water, and moved to the kitchen. She drank. The walls closed in around her. She had to get out.

In minutes Rebecca was changed and on the sidewalk, walking rapidly nowhere. Her mind and emotions flitted from one topic and sensation to another. The dinner with Claudia and Brad. Their kindness touched her. She had not felt—or had not let herself feel—so accepted in a long time.

And then . . . All the pleasant sensations were shattered within moments. She had no coherent thoughts for what followed. Maureen confiding in . . . *Andrew?* Andrew—prying, digging, going to the motherhouse to peer into her past. What kind of creep was he?

Yet when she came to his proposal regarding daycare, her confusion mounted. He had researched her expertise. He wanted her to explore the possibility of company daycare, to organize it, mould it, shape its focus. But this consideration soured with her sense of betrayal.

Rebecca re-entered her apartment as the indigo sky softened to periwinkle and lay exhausted on her bed. She glanced at the unopened envelope on her end table. The frozen memories of the past were thawing, vivid in colour and sound and pulsing with emotion. Carlos had cracked the seal; Andrew had smashed through. No amount of walking or busyness could quell pain and disillusionment. Rebecca broke down.

~

The phone rang, jarring Rebecca out of a deep sleep. She swore softly and raised her head to look at the alarm clock. It was almost noon. She reached for the phone.

"Thought I'd get you while you were preparing lunch," said the hearty voice on the other end. It was Rob, her brother in California.

"I haven't even thought of breakfast," replied Rebecca in a husky voice.

"What? You're still in bed? Come on, girl. Up and at it. Thank God, you have a brother who makes sure you're not lounging around in bed all day."

"Damn my brother who woke me out of a deep sleep."

"Out on the town last night?" His voice was upbeat and teasing, but now he became more serious, "Are you OK? You're not sick, are you?"

"No, no." Rebecca lay back on her pillows. "I'm fine. Just a little tired."

Rob was Rebecca's only sibling, five years older. Her father was an insurance broker and Rob had successfully established himself in the same field. He'd moved to California shortly after completing a business degree, and was now a finance manager in an insurance corporation. Rob had met his wife in California, married, settled there, and had four children.

"How are Judy and the kids?"

"They're doing well. Caitlyn's getting ready for the Christmas production— quite involved in drama and singing. Which is one of the reasons I called. Judy and I would love to have you here for Christmas. The kids keep asking if you're coming. And if you came the week before, you'd be in time to catch one of Caitlyn's performances. It would mean a lot to her."

Tears began to fall while Rob spoke. Rebecca had always enjoyed her nieces and nephew, but in the past four years, even these relationships had waned. Although warmly invited, she rarely visited, and when she did, it was only for a few days.

"Are you there, Rebecca?"

"Yeah, yeah." Forcing her voice to be stronger, she said, "Let me think about it, Rob. What's Mom up to?"

"You won't believe this. She's going on a cruise."

"You're kidding!" Rebecca leaned up on her elbow. "A cruise? Mom?"

"Yep. Leaves the day after Christmas. Flying out to Florida and moving around the Caribbean. Seems it's a cruise combining fun and religion."

"Oh." Rebecca lay back down. "That sounds more like Mom."

"She is loosening up, Rebecca."

"I'll call you back about Christmas."

"I've done some research regarding flights. I'll email you."

"Tell Judy and the kids I said hello." She hung up the phone and rolled over.

~

The week following the party Andrew walked through his regular routine. On the surface he maintained his usual calm and attentive manner; however, it required a lot of energy. He was continually distracted by memories of his conversation with Rebecca. What he had previously considered concern and appreciation, he now deemed ill-conceived and arrogant. Remembering her anger and distrust, left him feeling defeated. He avoided the second-floor offices while he debated what his next step should be. Set up an appointment? Apologize?

He decided he would make some contact before the holidays. What he would say or do, he would leave to the reaction he received from Rebecca. A few days before Christmas break, Andrew causally wandered onto the second floor and began to greet the employees he met. They were happy to chat, congratulated him on the party, and inquired into his plans for the holidays. He eventually made his way to the back wall and passed in front of Rebecca's cubicle. It was empty. Any hope of reconciliation was dashed.

"Hello there, Andrew. Merry Christmas!" said Gladys as she returned to her desk. "Now that's what I call a Christmas party! I had a wonderful time. And Claudia's recognition was outstanding. Great job!"

Andrew spent some time asking about her family and Christmas plans, and then casually asked, "Rebecca out sick?"

"Out sick? You kidding? Out on the beach more like it—while we're here worrying about snow. No, Rebecca's in California for the holidays."

CHAPTER 14

"Come on, come on, we don't want to be late," Gladys scolded as she came out of her bedroom and into the kitchen.

"Get a move on yourself," retorted Harriet, Gladys's mother. "We've been waiting a half-hour for you to show your royal head."

And royal head it was. Gladys looked gorgeous. So did her children.

It was Christmas Eve and the whole family was going to South Side Christian Assembly for services. Gladys had bathed and coiffed her children earlier in the afternoon then parked them in front of the TV with strict orders not to move a single hair. They didn't need to be told. Her kids were proud of their classy appearance and, after numerous trips to the mirror, settled in to watch their favourite videos until it was time to dress up in their new clothes.

It hadn't snowed for over a week, so the sidewalks were clear and Gladys was happy she could step out in style with her new heels.

"Come on, come on," said Gladys as she pushed her children toward the front door. "The taxi will be in front of the apartment building any minute now."

"The taxi?" said Harriet.

"Mom, it's Christmas Eve. We're not going to freeze our butts off for two hours waiting for the bus. Are you coming or not?"

Harriet finished wrapping a scarf around her neck and began turning off the lights. Nagging aside, she was pleased in her daughter's growing participation in a church. With her mother, Gladys had not been as forthcoming regarding her motives as she had been with Rebecca.

~

The taxi pulled up in front of a edifice creatively forged in brick and glass and glowing with Christmas lights. People streamed toward the numerous entries. "Doesn't look like a church to me," Jeremy said.

"Wait till you see the inside," said Gladys. "Come on, move out. Out, out, out!"

South Side Christian Assembly was a sprawling complex organized around a large worship area. With foresight on the part of the elders, a large tract of land had been purchased in an undeveloped area just south of the city. With time, the city boundaries expanded, developments sprang up, and now South Side Christian Assembly was flanked by an industrial park on one side and suburbia on the other. The worship area could hold a thousand people and easily converted to a theatre for the stage productions of South Side's drama clubs and choirs. In addition to its youth centre and dining hall, there were Sunday school areas for children of every age-level which were utilized for a daycare program during the week.

Gladys's children walked through the glass doors into the atrium. They gazed upward at the ceiling from which large, glittering snowflakes gently swayed, then moved their attention downward to the walls burnished with wreathes, arriving at last to a brilliant poinsettia tree at the centre of the atrium. Off to the side, and clearly a main attraction for the children, was a nativity scene. As the children pulled their grandmother to view the tableau, Gladys was warmly welcomed by members of the church and handed programs. When she caught up with her children, they were inching around the railing, gaping at the figures.

"Let's go and find ourselves some seats before they're all filled," said Gladys. "We'll stop again on our way out. Come on, come on. The seats are filling fast." Harriet just shook her head.

The worship area was tiered and curved around a stage. The lights were dimmed and the hundreds already gathered were hushed. Projected on two screens flanking either side of the stage were photos depicting the Christmas message, in sync with instrumental renditions of traditional carols. Gladys, Harriet, and the children settled into cushioned chairs and continued to take in their surroundings.

This early evening service was geared for families. On regular Sundays, children and teens participated in programs directed to their age and concerns while adults attended the services in the main worship area. Tonight was different. The service would feature children and youth choirs and a theatrical performance of Christ's birth. Gladys read over the program with growing excitement. She was sure of one thing. This was the right church for her personal project.

~

A couple of days later, Gladys greeted Sally at her reception desk on the second floor.

"I thought you were going to visit Don's father over the holidays?"

"That was the plan. Don's sister called at Thanksgiving to say that his dad was going down. He wasn't seriously ill, nothing like that, still living with her family, but she thought it would be a good idea if we spent Christmas holidays with him at her place. Who knew if this would be his last . . . ? Don wanted to celebrate Christmas with the fellowship, so we were all set to go the day after. Christmas evening his sister called—right when we were finishing our dinner. Don's dad had collapsed, they weren't even sure if he would make it through the night. His sister urged him to come right away; however, with the crisis at hand, she recommended he come alone. She couldn't put up our whole family in her home."

"That's too bad."

"Don wasn't that keen on us going in the first place. He and his dad aren't that close. He thinks his sister is overbearing and her kids are much older than ours. Don doesn't trust them. Besides, I don't think his dad is conscious. Don thought it would be better if I came to work and saved my vacation time for the summer as I usually do. The elderly couple next door said they would look after the kids—good people who have always helped us in a pinch. Everything worked out. . . . So Don left early yesterday morning and here I am."

"How's Don's father?"

"He is just hanging on. . . . I'm not sure when Don will be back. . . . How was your Christmas?"

Gladys had already let Sally know that she was changing venues for worship and now she filled her in on the details of her Christmas experience.

"Hey, this Sunday why don't you and your kids come with us to South Side Assembly. You'll love it, I'm sure."

"Well, I don't know. We've always gone to the Centre City Christian Fellowship. I'm not sure if Don would like me going elsewhere. . . ." Sally's voice trailed off.

"He's not even home! Come on, Sally, you can tell him all about it when he gets back. Rev. Martin won't even miss you. Well, maybe he will, but it's only for this Sunday—what's the big deal?"

"I don't have the van. Don drove to his father's."

"I don't even own a car. You call a taxi and get dropped off. It's not much. Besides, you'd have to do the same to get to the Centre City Christian Fellowship. I'm telling you, you'll like this church."

Sally was already relenting. "I'll think about it."

"Just do it."

By the next day the plan was finalized. Their families would meet in front of the church a half-hour before the service so Gladys could give Sally a tour, and then they would go to Gladys's apartment for dinner.

~

If Gladys had been impressed with South Side Christian Assembly, Sally was awestruck. Her ever-protruding eyes were even wider than usual.

"This is only the foyer!" Gladys laughed. "Now who are these kids you've brought along?"

"This is my oldest, Deborah." Sally put her arm around a blonde-haired girl and straightened out some strands that had abandoned her French braid. "She's ten."

"Hi, Deborah, I'm Sasha," said Gladys's eight-year-old daughter.

"And Caleb." Sally smiled down at her son in his Sunday-best, his hair parted and slicked back. She looked at Gladys's son. "You must be, Jeremy."

Jeremy moved in rhythm to the Christmas music piped into the foyer and smiled at Caleb. "I'm nine. Want to go see the nativity?"

"Hold your horses," said Gladys. "We still have someone else to meet." She directed her attention to a small girl standing close to Sally, her brown hair in a French braid identical to her sister's. "You must be Sarah."

She nodded her head.

"Well, I'm sure you will be good friends with Eliza, here. She is five and you are . . . ?"

"Six," said Sarah shyly.

"Now can we go see the manger?" said Jeremy impatiently.

"Just for a minute. I'm giving Sally and her kids a tour. We can stop on the way out."

Jeremy rolled his eyes and groaned.

~

With their children checked in at their appropriate Sunday school programs, Gladys and Sally went to the service. The music and singing were wonderful, the sermon upbeat and inspiring, and the visuals projected on the screen were great.

"If only Don could see this. He would just love it," Sally said as she and Gladys went to pick up their children. "Are you coming for the New Year service?" asked Sally.

"No, I think I'll pass." A singles' party was scheduled at the church the evening before and Gladys had no intention of coming home early. "But we'll be back next Sunday."

On the way to Gladys's apartment the children happily chatted about the games, the crafts, and the things they had learned. Sally glowed to see her children as excited as she. None of them even mentioned the Centre City Christian Fellowship.

Harriet opened the door and, from the smells that filled the house, dinner was well on the way.

"Oh, Harriet," said Sally after they were introduced, "we could have helped."

"That's fine. My church is just down the street. Lovely folks. And I'm able to get an early start on dinner."

"But South Side is fantastic. You would have loved it."

"Honey, I'm glad you enjoyed it. But I'm happy where I am." Then, turning her attention abruptly to the children, "Jeremy, get your fingers out of the mashed potatoes. If I told you once, I told you a thousand times . . . Now all of you, hang up your coats and go wash your hands so we can eat." Jeremy smirked mischievously and skipped off to the bathroom.

"And you can wipe that silly grin off your face, smart ass, or you won't get any dessert," said Gladys as he passed in front of her.

Harriet sighed and returned to the kitchen. Sally had long since chosen to ignore Gladys's choice phrases. She turned and helped her own children out of their coats.

CHAPTER 15

R ebecca dug her toes in the sand and felt the surf wash up against her calves. It wasn't warm enough for a swim but she couldn't resist walking in the waves. The sun was shining in and out of the clouds, the beach empty except for a few joggers. Rebecca gazed out at the ocean. Its expanse and rhythmic motion had always brought her peace. She was ambivalent about God, but could never wholly discard belief when she found herself immersed in the beauty of nature. Standing in the waves, watching the clouds slowly drift across the sky, calmed and soothed her.

Rebecca had attended Caitlyn's performance over the weekend and was staying at a hotel near the beach for a few days' rest before returning Christmas Eve. Rob and his wife, Judy, were genuinely happy to see her as were their four children: Caitlyn, now thirteen; Kristen, eleven; Brian, ten; and their surprise baby, Emily, who was five. It would be fun to be with them now, preparing for Christmas, listening to little Emily chatter on as they baked or decorated a corner of the house or let her nieces and nephew guide her around the neighbourhood to look at the lights.

Rebecca continued to stare out into the ocean. How much she had missed by cutting herself out of their lives. And she was doing it again, now, to avoid her mother.

Margaret had never been able to reconcile herself to Rebecca's departure from religious life. From her perspective, Rebecca had a Call, she had made a sacred vow and broken it. She had severed her relationship with the Church, putting herself in danger of eternal damnation and setting a poor example for her nieces and nephew. Margaret's joy and pride at Rebecca's perpetual profession soured to the bitterest disappointment when Rebecca left.

"You made a promise before the Church to God, *to God*. You don't walk away from that. The children you taught, so you *used* to say, were God's work. And you just walk out on them? Where's all the love and concern you spoke so much about? Pride at its worst. You know more than your superiors . . . more than the Pope . . . the Church which continues strong and sure after two thousand years. Pride is at the root of it all. And if you're too blind to see that, then you are all the more to be pitied."

Pity, however, was not what Rebecca wanted nor what her mother extended. An icy wall of mere propriety grew between them. Not a family gathering took place without Margaret restating her position through a look or comment. Reunions with her mother were painful, and Rebecca avoided them as much as possible. Her father had been different. Although initially baffled by his daughter's decision, he trusted her judgment, respected her position, and tried to help his wife understand. She, however, remained intransigent. With her father's death, home vanished. Margaret moved to California to be closer to the grandchildren.

Rebecca walked through the surf and let her toes drag through the sand. A breeze brushed back her hair and kissed her cheeks. Reassuring, silencing, challenging. She could stay here forever yet, right now, this was not where she wanted to be. She was on the beach to avoid the censure of her mother. Always avoiding. Pushing back, closing off. The ocean ebbed and flowed with memory and insight. Avoidance controlled her life.

~

"Auntie's home, Auntie's home!" Emily jumped around the room then went to Rebecca and hugged her legs. Rebecca was grateful for her outgoing little niece. Emily was enamoured with her aunt, notwithstanding the little time she had spent with Rob's family.

Rob turned toward Rebecca. "We're just finishing dinner. Come on in, we'll warm some up in the microwave."

"Oh, I ate already." Rebecca dropped her duffle bag on the floor and walked into the kitchen-dining area with Emily in tow. "I decided to take you up on your offer and spend this week with you. I haven't prepared for Christmas with family for years."

In the meantime, the children had pulled closer together around the table and Rob brought in another chair. "I've got some tea on," Judy said. "It'll be ready in a few minutes." She reached into a cupboard and pulled out a mug. Emily sat on Rebecca's lap.

Brian reached behind his chair and brought up a Game Boy. "Hey, Auntie, I'm at level five."

"Put that away at the dinner table or it will disappear for a month," said Judy.

"Show it to you later," he said as he slid the Game Boy behind him.

"I'll challenge you tonight," said Kristen.

"You're on!"

Judy turned to Rebecca. "I still haven't figured out the game."

"Auntie, we'll teach you!" said Brian.

"I'm sure your aunt has many other things she'd rather do," said Rob.

"No," said Rebecca, "I would like to learn."

~

Emily followed Rebecca around like a shadow, and when she sat, Emily was either on her lap or snuggled up under her arm. This afternoon Emily had gone with Rebecca to buy some materials for a "surprise project" and now Emily, with her unbounded enthusiasm, was bouncing on her knees to see what it was all about.

Rebecca spread out her supplies in a quiet corner of the basement family room. Brian came over to see what was going on. This was a favourite activity Rebecca did at Christmas with the children she had taught and she smiled when she saw the same enthusiasm in her niece and nephew.

"OK, this is the deal," she said. "We are going to make Christmas angels." Rebecca cut out stiff white paper so that it would roll into a cone with a large base on the bottom and a narrow hole at the top. The shape of their hands became the angel's wings and a round, even thicker paper became the head. These Emily and Brian set out to decorate with markers and glitter glue. In the meantime, Rebecca took out a camera and snapped a few close-ups of the children's faces. Brian and Emily stopped what they were doing to judge them in the display screen and pick out their favourite, which Rebecca printed out. When the angels' gowns and wings had been decorated, Brian and Emily assembled and taped them together. Then their close-ups were cut round, glued on the round head piece, and put in place.

"I have an idea!" said Brian. "Let's make an angel face and cover our own like a flap. Then we can lift it up for a surprise."

"Great idea," said Rebecca. Emily clapped and they set to work.

They were so engrossed in their project that they hadn't heard an arrival upstairs or Margaret as she came down the stairs. Rebecca's mother watched the activity from the bottom step, sipping tea from a mug. Emily was the first to notice.

"Grandma, we're making Christmas angels. But don't come over, 'cause we're doing the surprise part right now."

Rebecca tensed and her enjoyment froze over. Margaret came a little closer. "Grandma!" Both Emily and Brian took their unfinished projects and crouched over them to keep them from their grandmother's view.

Margaret looked at Rebecca. "What a waste."

Previously, Rebecca would have silently walked out of the room, out of the house, and as soon as possible, out of town. Her impulse now was to do the same. But the past couple of months had unblocked another path. She slowly stood and looked directly at her mother.

"To what exactly are you referring, Margaret?" she said in a soft but firm voice. The children looked up.

"You know exactly to what I'm referring. 'Many are called, few are chosen.' You threw it away."

"I 'threw out' my 'divine' calling?"

"Rebecca, the children," Margaret snapped.

"The children didn't stop you from walking down here and making your snide remark, did they?" Rebecca trembled. "I don't understand your God or your beliefs that justify the cutting . . . the disparaging . . . remarks that fly out of your mouth. I don't ask you to understand me or support me. I only ask that you respect me."

Rebecca turned from her mother, and squatted down with Emily and Brian. By sheer force of will, she refocused on the children and their project. Despite her inner turmoil, she said in a brighter tone, "OK, where were we?"

"But Grandma will see!" Emily said.

Rebecca turned her head but kept her eyes down. "It's a surprise." Margaret turned and left the room.

The children looked at Rebecca then returned to their project in silence.

Rebecca switched on a holiday radio station to help dissipate the tension of the unexpected encounter. Gradually, their chatter increased and less effort was needed by Rebecca to be present to the children and their craft. Her trembling subsided, but her cutting revealed lurking twitches of anger. She sat cross-legged, assisting, gluing, cutting . . . with tears in her eyes, anxious, yet strangely giddy— she had passed through to a newfound freedom.

～

"I know. Let's make an angel for everyone without them knowing," said Emily.

"Yeah, I'll make Kristen's—with horns!" said Brian.

"Auntie, you can sneak up on them and take their pictures!" said Emily with growing enthusiasm. "We'll even do one for Grandma."

～

On Christmas Eve Rob, Judy, and the family were busy with the immediate preparations. Festive aromas wafted from the kitchen. Since Margaret was to leave on her cruise the day after Christmas, they were having their holiday meal that afternoon and opening gifts in the evening after Mass. Rebecca was spooning out cookie dough when Rob pulled her aside.

"Look, Rebecca, I understand how you feel about church and whether you come with us tonight or not is really up to you. Just so you know, we're going to the early "midnight" Mass—6:00 p.m. It's a children's Mass and Emily will be one of the shepherds . . . they're acting out the Christmas story. To get a seat, we need to be there at least an hour early."

"I'll think about it. But it won't be an hour early. If I go, I'll walk up later."

"That's quite a hike."

"It's only around ten blocks, no problem . . . and no parking. Don't look for me after Mass. If I go, I'll walk home as well."

～

California Christmas. It was great to be out walking in December with her jacket open. The fronds of the palm trees, backlit by the setting sun, swayed in the breeze. Rebecca soaked it in as she walked to the church. She was getting closer. Overflow from the parking lot packed the side streets surrounding the church.

Her father's funeral had been the last religious service she'd attended. And before that . . . Now here she was, approaching the horseshoe driveway for "Drop-off Only" that lead to the entrance of the church. She joined other latecomers funnelling toward the front and side entrances. A large overhang covered the wide sidewalk encircling the church, creating a huge porch. Toddlers were already running up and down the walkway, exploring the pillars and squatting to look at the flowers and bushes. Parents casually followed them, picking up what they could of the service from outside speakers. As Rebecca neared the entrance, she could hear the "Gloria" warbling out. She pushed the door open and slowly walked through.

The vestibule curved around most of the worship area. Those who hoped for a glimpse of the service converged near the open doors that led from the vestibule to the pews within. The late and resigned either leaned against the walls of the vestibule, sat on anything elevated, or slowly paced, listening to the piped-in service. There was no chance of an empty seat. It was all so familiar and yet so distant.

Rebecca walked to a far-side door whose view of the sanctuary was blocked. The usher posted at this unpopular entrance informed her that the church was at capacity, so she leaned against the door frame. Shortly, the usher was signalled to another door and Rebecca slipped into the church. The lighting was dimmed except for the altar area. She gradually made her way up the side of the church, edging past the diehards who chose to remain in the church, even though standing. As she continued her approach toward the front, she felt like she was watching herself from some point high on the wall, detached and observant.

The reading finished and children began to sing a psalm. Standing next to a pillar, Rebecca was close enough to the front to clearly see the altar and the Christmas play that was about to be enacted. Children dressed in costumes were seated in the front pews, shifting with anticipation, looking toward adult coordinators for their cues.

The priest was at the podium. He began the familiar story, "And Joseph went to Bethlehem to be registered with Mary who was with child . . ." The priest moved back from the mic and the children continued with the enactment of the Christmas story.

"Now there were shepherds keeping watch over their flock at night . . . ," a young narrator read. Little shepherds squeezed out of pews from every corner of the church, wearing tunics and dishtowels secured with strips of cloth on their heads. Several teen shepherds ushered the children to either side of the altar and sat them comfortably on the steps of the sanctuary. Emily went to the top step and began to peer out into the darkened church. Rebecca recognized her immediately. She squinted, looking intently in Rebecca's direction. Rebecca gave a little wave. Emily smiled broadly and waved back.

$\sim$

The Christmas play was coming to an end. As the children sang "Silent Night," Rebecca made her way to the back of the church and out the door. The last strands crackled from the speakers as she walked down the driveway to the sidewalk.

$\sim$

When Rob, his family, and Margaret returned, Rebecca had just finished making the hot chocolate. Brian and Emily ran downstairs. Kristen, Caitlyn, Rob, and Judy were bringing the platters, plates, and bowls they had prepared earlier in the day to the dining/living room. Rebecca was ladling the hot chocolate into a couple of insulated pitchers. Margaret came and stood nearby. "Emily says she saw you at church."

Rebecca stiffened. "Margaret, please, no comments. It's Christmas."

"Emily was very happy. . . . And I'm sorry about the other day. I shouldn't have brought it up in front of the children."

"Alone? In front of children? Does it really matter, Margaret? Until you accept me, sarcasm is going to poison every encounter we have."

Margaret lowered her eyes. Rebecca picked up the pitchers and moved toward the dining area. She nearly collided with Brian and Emily who came bounding into the room, their arms filled with paper angels. They set them on the table between the bowls of nuts, the tray of fruits, and platter of cakes and cookies. "What's all this?" said Judy.

"Lift up the flap, lift up the flap!" Emily laughed as she jumped up and down.

When the family members picked out their angels, Emily came around to

Rebecca and hugged her legs. She held up a paper angel. "Brian and I made one for you too."

CHAPTER 16

Gladys stood within the entrance to South Side Christian Assembly and looked at the sealed envelope in her hand. In one corner was printed a bold "95." *What the hell is this all about?*

"You keep that closed for now," said one of the greeters, raising his eyebrow. "We'll be using it later on." He pointed to a few tables further into the atrium. "The name tags are just ahead."

Name tags? Gladys had chosen a snappy evening dress for the singles' New Year's party and the thought of marring it with a name tag annoyed her. She picked up the adhesive label with a bright green *Hello, My Name Is* and considered where to place it. She folded it in half and carefully tore the label in two, leaving half of its cheery message on the table. After writing her name on what remained, she placed it high near her shoulder and shrouded it with her hair.

Having settled that dilemma Gladys took in the lay of the land. The atrium was transformed. Small tables, draped in red floor-length cloths, were set up along the peripheries. In the centre of each table were arrangements of evergreens and white flowers with a red candle rising from the middle. Spotlights highlighted the poinsettia tree and glistened off the large, glittering snowflakes that hung from the ceiling.

Christmas music ebbed and flowed through the bustle of arrivals and the murmurings and chuckles of people mingling in the centre of the atrium. Gladys moved in and joined a circle of people who were getting acquainted. The rumble of conversation and laughter grew steadily louder.

Eventually the music faded and the MC went to a mic.

"Welcome, welcome," he repeated with increasing volume until the conversations subsided. "All of you should have received an envelope when you entered the atrium. If not, please go to one of the greeters at the main entrance."

Two women waved their hands high and a few people moved in their direction.

"Since many of you may not know each other, we want to begin with a few icebreakers."

Icebreakers, thought Gladys. *Who needs icebreakers?*

"You'll notice on your envelope a number. Someone in this room has the exact same number. You have five minutes to find that person and exchange some information about yourself."

The DJ revved up the music and immediately the atrium became a mayhem of movement and chatter. Gladys flipped her envelope facing out and began to move from person to person. Many couples were forming and chatting together. Unfortunately, they did not move to the sides, which made it harder for the unmatched to locate each other. The minutes were ticking away.

"Hell," muttered Gladys.

"Ninety-five?" inquired a man from behind.

Gladys turned. "Why yes."

"Harry," said the man, extending his hand. "And I see you are . . ." He squinted to make out the largely concealed label.

"Gladys." She smiled, shaking hands.

"You'll have to lower that name tag so we can see it better."

Like hell I will. Gladys smiled. She was grateful it had taken her so long to find 95.

"Have you been in the city long?" asked Gladys.

"My whole life." Harry beamed. His pale, fleshy face was highlighted by his white shirt and pale blue tie.

"My dad has a water filtration business and I've recently been made a partner. What about you?"

"Oh, I've been in and out of town. Just recently returned. You seem awfully young to be a business partner."

Harry chuckled complacently. "I hear that all the time. Actually, though," in a softer voice, "I'm older than you think. Forty-two."

The music stopped abruptly and the MC was back at the mic. "I hope you all found your match. Now I want you to open your envelopes. You'll notice two cards. One has the picture of an animal, the other a color. Take out the picture of the animal. There are others in the room with the same animal. To find each other, begin to make the sound of the animal and move around. You have five minutes." The music started.

Gladys opened her envelope. A red card and . . . *A cow? A bloody COW!*

Action started in an instant. Guys were flapping their arms and squawking, dragging their toes and neighing, oinking, and the like. Some of the women joined in the dramatics. The majority laughed at the antics and circulated among the group making their animal calls. A smaller number of men and women, Gladys among them, walked around, casually listened for their sound, and compared pictures if directly approached by someone else.

Damn kids' game, she thought. *There's no way I'm mooing around this room.* Her eyes caught another woman nearby.

"Moo?" said the other woman softly.

Gladys smiled and nodded.

"Carol," she said, extending her hand. "Can you believe this, a *cow*?" Gladys laughed.

"You here for a guy?" said Carol with a sidelong look.

"You got that right."

"Then let's split and find our bulls." And off she went in the other direction.

Several men squawked and chirped by, looking hopefully at Gladys. She shook her head and they passed on.

"What are you?" said a man at her side.

"A cow. How about you?"

"A pig." He smiled. "That's close enough. The name's Ben."

"Gladys."

"You look great. Where are you from?"

The music stopped and the MC was again at the mic.

Hell, thought Gladys.

"OK, everyone, it's time for your last card. It's either green or red. Those with red move to the far side of the hall. Those with green, move toward me. When the music starts, everyone move toward the centre of the room. The green card holders exchange names with five people holding a red card. The red card holders exchange names with five of the green card holders. Take a few moments to get to know each other. When the music stops, pick up a beverage with your partner and join other couples at one of the tables. Then feel free to get up, mix, dance, chat. . . . Our DJ will then begin the evening entertainment and the food will arrive shortly after. Have a great evening."

Ben looked at his card. "Red, how about you?"

"Red."

Then taking her by the arm and moving toward the "Reds," Ben said, "What do you say that we stand in the rear and when the music starts, get ourselves a drink and find a table."

"You got it."

Gladys found this guy more appealing by the second. Soon they were seated at a table by themselves, the lights were dimmed and the music began. Someone came by and lit the candle in the centrepiece.

Ben was a good-looking man, deep, brown skin . . . perhaps a mix of Latino and Asian. His taste in clothes was impeccable, and best of all, he disregarded the "mixers" to be with her. . . . This was going to be a great night.

CHAPTER 17

Rebecca walked through the lobby, passed the queue for the elevator, and climbed up the stairs. Everything so familiar, and yet, so oddly different. She had been away just over two weeks but it felt like months. She opened the door and entered the second-floor office area. Sally and Gladys were laughing together at the front desk.

"Well, well, well, the sun bunny has decided to come back. How was California?" said Gladys.

"Two feet of snow and more on the way," replied Rebecca dryly.

"My ass, you had snow."

Rebecca continued to walk toward the rear of the building.

"You have to hear the news," said Sally. "Gladys has a boyfriend."

Rebecca stopped and turned toward Gladys.

"His name is Ben," Gladys said. "Real nice guy. Met him at the New Year's party at South Side Assembly."

Gladys gave Rebecca a significant look that was lost on Sally.

"So I take it, you've enjoyed the holidays," said Rebecca. "See you later."

Rebecca stepped into her cubicle and glanced around. She hung her coat on a hook, put her purse in the usual drawer, pushed the power button on the computer, and sat in her chair. She pulled over a pile of files that had accumulated during her absence and began to leaf through. In the background, the computer hummed into life, the paper-towel dispenser thumped rapidly from the adjacent bathrooms, and the sound of increasing activity came from the office area beyond.

Rebecca took out a pencil and a sheet of paper and began to prioritize her work. All so familiar, except for a growing resolution: *I'm not doing this for the rest of my life.* She picked up the phone and made an appointment.

~

The last time she had been on the fifth floor was over four years ago. Rebecca paused at the secretary's desk. "I believe Mr. Covick is waiting for me. I'm Rebecca Holden."

The secretary lifted her head. "Oh, yes. He stepped out for a moment and said he would be right back." She pointed to her right, "Just walk in and make yourself comfortable."

Rebecca stepped through the opened door. In front of her were a few upholstered chairs facing a small coffee table. Just beyond against the back wall was a credenza set up with carafes, bottles of beverages, and a plate of pastries. Rebecca turned and gazed at a striking seascape displayed on the wall behind the polished wooden desk on the other side of the office.

"I was hoping to get back before you arrived," said Andrew from the door. "Have you been waiting long?"

"I just arrived."

"Sit down, sit down." He walked to the credenza and, gesturing to the array of beverages and pastries, said, "May I offer you something? Would you like some coffee?"

"That would be fine." Andrew brought over a mug of steaming coffee with a bowl of cream and sugar packets.

"Just black, thanks."

"How about a Danish?" he asked, extending the plate toward her.

"Maybe a little later," said Rebecca.

Andrew poured coffee into his mug.

"I understand you were out for the holidays. When did you get back?"

"A few days ago."

He stirred in cream and sugar, then settled in a chair across from Rebecca.

"It's been a while since we last spoke," said Andrew. He took a sip of coffee and looked at Rebecca. She sat on the edge of the couch, her hands on her knees, watching the steam rise from the mug she had placed on the coffee table.

"Rebecca, I'm sorry about the incident at the Christmas party. I never intended to hurt or offend you."

"That's why I came."

Andrew looked at Rebecca. *So this is it*, he thought. *What will it be? Two-weeks notice, a month?*

Rebecca picked up her mug, took a sip, and met his gaze. "What's your plan for the daycare?"

CHAPTER 18

"You OK, bitch?"

Rebecca was at her desk intent at her work. She looked up at Gladys. "Why do you ask?"

"I've never heard you listen to a note of music." An easy-listening instrumental played faintly in the background. "Are you in love?"

Rebecca smirked. "I'm not as fortunate as you, Gladys."

"Aren't you going to ask who he is?"

Rebecca set down her pen. "Who is the guy?"

Gladys smiled and left. She was back in moment with a photo—a picture of her and Ben at the New Year's party.

"Hmm," said Rebecca. "You look great."

"Bitch, what *is* up? I mean, this is the first compliment I've ever heard out of your mouth."

"Must be the left-over effects of California. I'll soon be back to my nasty self." She returned to her work.

Gladys glanced at her watch. "It's almost noon. Come on, let's go for lunch. I'll tell you all about him."

"Gladys, I have a lot to do here. Besides, I brought my lunch."

"So did I. You can eat it tomorrow."

Noticing a shred of hesitation, Gladys continued, "Come on, come on, come on. Let's go before the spell wears off."

In that second of ambivalence, Rebecca relented. A few minutes later, they were out of the building and walking down the street.

"Where in the hell are you taking me?" said Gladys after a few blocks.

"It's just a couple more blocks. You'll like the place."

"Yeah, well my feet aren't. Next time tip me off if you plan on hiking across town for a hamburger. God, and there are restaurants hanging off our building."

Rebecca had to smile. She'd forgotten about Gladys's heels.

～

Gladys plunked herself down at a table. "And now we stand in line to get our meal? I pick out our lunch spot the next time."

"Look at the selection."

Gladys crossed her leg, took off a shoe, and rubbed her toes. In the meantime, she surveyed the dining area and the food vendors encircling the dining area. "It is a nice place," she conceded. "Not your standard fast foods. I think I'm going Mexican."

"I'm up for Greek today. Meet you back here in a few minutes."

～

"Great food," said Gladys.

"Thought you might like it."

"And now about Ben."

Gladys relayed the highlights of the New Year's party, "We hit it off from the start and spent the whole evening together."

"What's his line of work?"

"He's an engineer."

"An engineer of what?"

"How in the hell do I know? He's an engineer in an engineering firm."

"That's surprising."

"Shut up. Something to do with electricity."

"How did he wind up at a New Year's party . . . *in a church*?"

"He started going to South Side a few months ago. Heard about their after-school program . . . He has a son, seven years old, Nigel. Has him enrolled in a school close to South Side and not far from his office."

"Have you met him yet?"

"Bitch, we just started going out. Went for dinner last weekend. Still the great guy he was at the party. Our kids aren't involved yet."

Both continued eating and for a few moments neither spoke. "I have to admit, this is delicious." Gladys looked over at Rebecca, head bent, quietly eating her meal. In a softer voice she said, "What's going on?"

'What do you mean?"

"I mean . . . you're different. You're eating with me."

"So what?"

"What's up?"

"Nothing is *up*." Again both ate in silence.

Rebecca said quietly, "Have you ever had the wind knocked out of you . . . totally? You're stunned, caught in the pain. A rhythm you've taken for granted is . . . is ruptured . . . you can't even gasp. Everything is just a blur, out of focus . . . nothing seems right . . . nothing feels familiar." Rebecca paused. "I'm starting to breathe again."

"Wow," said Gladys after a moment. "When I had the wind knocked out of me, I just hopped into the arms of another man for artificial respiration."

Rebecca looked up.

"It didn't work."

They finished their meal in silence, then began to clear the table.

"Thanks, Gladys."

"You'll always be 'bitch' to me."

CHAPTER 19

"**Y**ou did what?" Don put down his fork, clearly irritated.

"I thought we'd just visit another church with Gladys and her family," said Sally with growing apprehension.

"You don't *visit* churches. You belong to one or the other. We belong to Rev. Martin's congregation. We have always belonged to Rev. Martin's congregation. So you don't go skipping off to another church just because a person wants you to try something new. Besides, this is something you should have discussed with me. But no, you wait until I'm out of the house to go gallivanting."

"It wasn't like that at all, Don." Sally blushed with shame and anxiety.

Don's father passed away shortly after New Year's. With the funeral and some business that followed, he hadn't returned home until the end of the first week of January. Sally, captivated with the new church, assumed her husband would feel the same. She and her children had continued to go to South Side ever since Gladys's first invitation. Don called daily, but after prolonged days and nights at the hospital with his father in and out of consciousness, he merely recapped his father's condition, too tired to even think about much else. Sally thought of bringing up South Side but it seemed so trivial in comparison to the sickness and then the death of his father. She let it go. Now Sally realized that she had crossed the line that she avoided at all costs—the anger and displeasure of Don.

"We were invited and we went. It was that simple. If I thought you wouldn't have approved, I would never have gone. In fact," her voice now lifted slightly with hope, "if you come just once, I know you'll feel the same. The programs for the children—"

"I am *never* going to South Side Christian Assembly. *We* are never going to South Side Christian Assembly. From the little I've heard, South Side has turned the Gospel into a playground, and . . . and Sunday service into some . . . some high-tech Hollywood entertainment." He stared at his plate for a few moments. "Christ died for our sins . . . our sins." Sally lowered her eyes and blushed again. "Religion isn't fun and games."

Silence descended on the dinner table. Don had only arrived home an hour before. Sarah, the youngest, eager to relay all that her father had missed, brought up their new Sunday school. What had begun as a lively, happy reunion soured within seconds. The children stared wide-eyed at their father. Sarah started to cry and moved from her chair to her mother.

"You sit right back down, young lady, and finish your supper." Sarah returned to her chair and continued to whimper quietly. Don alone resumed his meal, chomping rapidly. When he had finished, he pushed himself from the table and walked out of the room. Sarah got up and cried in Sally's arms.

"I liked our new church."

Sally, generally quick to defend her husband's decisions, had no words. Tears rolled quietly down her cheeks.

CHAPTER 20

"So when are you coming over with Don and the kids?"

Gladys knew that Sally was expecting Don any day, but when Sally lifted up her head, Gladys could see something was wrong. The large eyes, generally bright and eager, were tired and sad.

"Did Don come home?"

"He arrived yesterday," said Sally.

"Is he OK?"

"He's fine," said Sally with a sigh.

"Well, honey, *you* don't look fine."

Although initially brought together by self-serving interests, a rapport had developed between the two women over the past couple of months. Just the same, Sally had only spoken of Don and her family in glowing terms. She wasn't insincere: it was all she saw. Foreboding now sullied her perception and the lode of devotional reflections she resorted to in difficult times proved futile.

Sally was well liked in her church community. Her friendly, willing disposition endeared her to many, especially the older women: "A sweet little thing," "a dear child." Among the middle-aged women she was held up to the younger generation as the model wife—submissive, gentle, and dutiful—"a rare find in our day and age." Gladys didn't venerate anyone and had already sensed something was off.

"He's really upset with me . . . you know . . . about going to South Side while he was away."

"Good God, girl! He wasn't happy that you went to church while he was away?"

"We didn't go to Rev. Martin's church, Gladys, that's the problem. And, believe me, we won't be going back to South Side."

"He's *that* angry?" Then changing tone, Gladys said, "If all your church services are like the one I went to, I'd say Rev. Martin has a lot to learn from South Side. Just bring Don to a service, he'll see the difference right away."

"I already suggested that. . . ."

"And?"

"He said religion isn't supposed to be entertaining."

"You mean uplifting . . . relevant . . . friendly?" Gladys looked at Sally, head bent down, supported by one of her hands. "Girl, what do *you* think?"

"I don't know."

"You don't *know*? You sure seemed to know a couple of weeks ago."

"Is this the customer service department?" An older woman approached the counter and Sally and Gladys both snapped back to their Secure Star personas.

"We can talk later," Gladys whispered as she turned toward her cubicle.

~

Don was sitting in the pew, midway, right side as he always did. Sally brought her children to Sunday school downstairs and then quietly joined him. Members of the congregation came over to offer their condolences. Often they turned to Sally: "We've missed you too, Sally. How are the children?" She smiled meekly and assured them all was fine. Don gazed off to the side when these comments were made.

No one in the church found Sally's absence surprising because Don had informed Rev. Martin and many in the congregation that he would be visiting his father during Christmas break. And during the holidays, the overall attendance at the fellowship was irregular with travel to relatives. On Christmas night, when their family plans were shifting by the moment, Don told Sally he would inform Rev. Martin about the turn of events. However, amidst the phone calls with his sister, Sally's conversation with the neighbours, and the frenzied packing, Don's intention morphed into completion when, in reality, the call had never been made. Rev. Martin was unaware Sally and the children were home until she called during the week to tell him of the funeral and he apologized for not arranging a ride to the services.

The hymns began. Rise. Sit. Rev. Martin was getting into his sermon. His voice, his themes, his examples—so tired, so predictable. It wasn't just his sermon: the building, the pictures, the people . . . She couldn't close it out or deny it. Why had she never seen it before? She went through the motions, sang the final hymn, and smiled her greetings as she went downstairs to collect her children. The dusty pipes overhead, the dim lighting, the musty, stale odour— where had she been?

~

A couple of weeks later Sally was busy cooking dinner. Her two older children, Deborah and Caleb, were at the kitchen table finishing their homework. Don had arrived from work several minutes before and was changing out of his work clothes. Sarah watched her mother and helped when she could, chatting away. However, the preparations were coming to an end, and since Sally was more occupied with cleaning up than cooking, Sarah's attention wandered to her older siblings. She stood at the table, spread her elbows out on the top, and rested her chin on the palms of her hands.

"What are you doin', Caleb?" she asked, watching her brother form letters into a notebook.

Caleb said nothing.

"When I go to school, I'm not gonna just write, write, write. I'm gonna draw pictures and sing songs."

"Mom-umm! Can you tell Sarah to go away. She's bothering me."

"Sarah, go play with your toys and let Deborah and Caleb finish their homework."

"Yeah," mimicked Caleb, "go play with your toys."

Sarah put her hands on her hips. "You smart ass," and turned to walk away.

Just then Don walked into the room. "What did you say, young lady?"

Sally froze. So did the children. The smirk on Caleb's face disappeared.

"Where did you learn that?" Don demanded.

Everyone else in the room knew exactly where she had learned it and waited for her response.

"I just heard it," whimpered Sarah.

"Well, I don't ever want to hear that out of your mouth again, do you understand?"

81

In spite of herself, Sally could feel herself relaxing.

Don turned to Sally, "Can you believe this? We try to raise our children as Christians and look at the language they pick up off the street . . . and at her age."

Sally just nodded.

~

Since the homecoming meal South Side was never mentioned, yet from Don's irritability with her, the children, and life in general, Sally knew he was still upset. There was no way she was going to address Sarah's comment, especially since Don had unknowingly deflected the blame off the real target.

As she washed the last of the pots and pans, she reflected that none of her children had said anything on the subject. All of them knew that *smart ass* was a common phrase directed at most of humanity when Gladys's feathers got ruffled. Yet her two eldest kept their heads down and dug into their homework. Even little Sarah, who generally blurted out everything, had edited her confession.

Sally's relief began to mingle with guilt. She was holding back from Don. And so were the children. During the afternoons they had spent with Gladys and her family, Gladys had taught them line dancing. Gladys's children were already quite adept and they stood near Sally's children coaching them in the various steps. Even Harriet joined in. Sally's family loved the dancing and picked up the Electric Slide and the Tennessee Twister in one evening. Thinking back, Sally realized that after Don's initial outburst, none of the children brought up the dancing they enjoyed nor did any steps when he was home. She reddened with the realization that she herself had said nothing. No one planned this. It was an unspoken collusion.

"How you doing with your homework, Deborah?" Don asked.

"Almost done, Dad. Just two more multiplications to figure out."

"Done!" said Caleb holding up his pencil.

"Good, while your mother and the girls get the table prepared, we can review your Bible quotes for next Sunday."

CHAPTER 21

A dinner meeting. That's what Andrew called it. Had he not given specific directions, Rebecca would have missed the Dionysus entirely. Located in the city's historic theatre district, the entrance was lower than street level. A neon *Dionysus* shone above the restaurant window, which peered over the sidewalk. Rebecca walked down the steps and opened the engraved wooden door with etched windows. In the subdued lighting, Rebecca's eyes went directly to the tiffany lamp that illuminated the reservation booth. A young man in black slacks, matching vest, and white shirt put down a pen and looked up. His curly dark hair was gelled in style.

"Good evening," he said with a quick smile. "Would you like a table or do you have reservations?"

"I'm with Covick."

He swerved around the booth. "Just follow me."

As she rounded the divider into the restaurant, Rebecca saw it was much smaller than she had imagined. Crisp white cloths covered the tables, napkins transformed into birds with wings outstretched and heads bent in greeting lay atop. Dimmed sidelighting gently accentuated the grotto-like motif and the frescos depicting seaside life. In the occupied tables couples sipped wine, a candle flickering between them. The snug quarters, the Mediterranean music, the air warm and fragrant with freshly baked pita, were soothing. From a corner table in the rear, Andrew rose and pulled out a chair. The young man gestured a greeting to Andrew and backed off to let Rebecca pass.

Andrew took Rebecca's coat and placed it on a chair on top of his own. "So, did you have any trouble finding the place?" asked Andrew.

"Your directions were excellent."

After a few comments on the attractiveness of the restaurant, the weather, and such, their drinks arrived. Rebecca opened the menu. No prices listed. Andrew had pulled out all the stops. When the ordering was done, Rebecca reached into her shoulder bag, pulled out two files, and gave one to Andrew.

"There are a few ways we can approach this project, Andrew. First of all, Secure Star can set up its own daycare. This means that Secure Star would be responsible for program development, employment, safety, and insurance. So, Secure Star would have to know the certification requirements, and also keep abreast of all new legislation and policies regarding daycare centres. They—you—would have to ensure that those hired were equally updated as well as certified, not to mention having sufficient experience and the right personality.

"With this option Secure Star would have complete control over the direction of its daycare program and the people involved. However, Secure Star would also be responsible for continual program development, supervision, evaluation, hiring, firing, and so on. And daycare is not the speciality of Secure Star."

The project was more complex than Andrew had anticipated. Rebecca had given him an inkling of this in their brief meeting a couple of weeks before.

"There is another option," continued Rebecca. "We find a daycare chain that is responsible for all the above and Secure Star is only responsible for providing the space and, perhaps, the initial furnishings."

"And how many daycare chains are out there?"

Rebecca pulled out another file. "I've done research on four." She passed Andrew four stapled packs of paper and began to go through each set, highlighting key points. Andrew noted that each set followed the same format: the mission statement, outline of program, details of program, financial information, et cetera. Essential information of one company could easily be compared with another.

"Your salad," said the waiter. Bowls of Greek salad were placed in front of each and a basket of warm pita between them.

Rebecca and Andrew stacked up and stowed their materials. Both took a couple of bites, then Rebecca began again.

"There is still another option: subsidized daycare. Secure Star pays a portion of the employee's daycare expense."

"What's your recommendation?"

"How serious are you about going ahead?"

"Like I said . . ."

"Are you ready to make a financial commitment?"

"I guess we would have to assess just how much it would cost. A proposal would have to be put together and presented to the board of directors. I want to go ahead and Haverstock is open."

"I would suggest a survey to see exactly how many persons are interested . . . the age level of the children and their needs. That would give a better idea of cost. Subsidizing would be the easiest and parents would have more options."

Once again Rebecca reached into her shoulder bag and placed a slim file on the table. "I've come up with some survey questions I believe are pertinent. Perhaps you will have others to add."

Throughout this exchange, Andrew listened and observed. He knew of Rebecca's thoroughness and organization—it was noted in every evaluation— yet to see it firsthand was impressive. In their previous meeting, Rebecca had simply stated that she was supportive of the daycare project and Andrew offered her the task of initial research. This evening, a few weeks later, she was articulate, informed, efficient, and caring. And they had become partners in a project.

"Andrew, why are you pushing so hard for this daycare project?"

Rebecca's question shook him out of his reverie.

"Well . . . I think daycare makes a corporation more human." He picked at the remnants of his salad. "It acknowledges that employees have lives beyond the company and that the executives are concerned about supporting that life. Besides, daycare is also a benefit for Secure Star. More people may be attracted and stay longer. So it's a win-win situation for Secure Star and our employees."

He took his copy of the survey and put it in his briefcase along with the other files. "Thanks for all the work you've put into this, Rebecca. I'll look over the material and get back to you within a couple of days."

Both Andrew and Rebecca remained silent for some moments as Rebecca finished off the last of the salad. She took in the music playing softly in the background, yet she couldn't relax and enjoy the moment. She dreaded it. This was the point she had played over and over in her mind—what to do after the business finished. When Andrew had suggested a dinner meeting, her first impulse was to decline. It would have been easier to meet in his office, go over the options for company day care, and leave. She had told him she would think about his offer and get back to him.

Awkward or not, Rebecca knew she had to speak with Andrew on more than business. The Christmas party debacle was a thicket through which they spoke. It was there, always between them, preventing any ease in their communication. Rebecca could avoid addressing it, but her walk on the beach had given her insight and a choice. Right now she and Andrew needed to talk as people, not just as functionaries of Secure Star.

Rebecca looked up at Andrew. He was gazing at her reflectively as she had often seen him do.

Escape. Go to the ladies room and walk right out.

Rebecca met his gaze. "How did you meet Maureen?"

Andrew shifted ever so slightly.

"I was at a conference. I knew from your files that you used Sr. Maureen as a reference. . . . Slandail was just a half-hour from the conference site. I drove to the address you listed, on the chance I might meet her . . . and eventually I did . . . at St. Peter's Academy."

The roast lamb arrived, still sizzling on the plate and the pita was replenished. Both ate in silence.

"Why, Andrew? Why would you seek out a meeting with Maureen?"

Andrew picked up a piece of pita and broke it in half. "This is great pita. Would you like some more?" Rebecca reached over and took the other half.

"I looked over your resumé, Rebecca. . . . I wondered why a woman with an MA in education and years of teaching experience would be holed up in the back of an insurance company crunching out data to the rhythm of flushing toilets."

"Those flushing toilets really get to you, don't they?"

She broke off a piece of pita and ate it with her meal.

"Andrew," she said calmly, "it was none of your business."

Andrew lowered his eyes. "You're right. And I apologize. I overstepped my boundaries."

"Overstepped is an understatement. It was more like a crash landing in my living room."

Andrew looked up.

"Why do you even care, Andrew?"

"I'm assuming the meeting aspect of the dinner is over."

"This dinner was always intended to be more than a meeting, wasn't it?"

"I left that decision in your court and you served the ball."

Both ate in silence for a couple of minutes.

"So, why did you care, Andrew?"

"Why did you care about Carlos?"

"Carlos was a lost baby. I didn't think twice about helping him. Anyone would have."

"You didn't have to get involved. A security guard could have been called in to handle the situation. Besides, I was there. You weren't looking around and waiting for 'anyone' to come forward."

"OK, I helped Carlos. What does that have to do with Maureen."

"Watching you with that child convinced me that there was a whole lot more to you than a cool, detached woman with a bent for data entry. So you're right, Rebecca, I could have thought, 'It's none of my business' and moved on. But I couldn't. I wanted to understand." Andrew paused. "There was too much pain . . . and so much goodness."

Rebecca could feel tears begin to well up and turned her head away. Never in her life had she been prone to cry. But since her veneer had cracked in December, tears came easily. She did not want Andrew to see how much he had affected her. It was too late. Without even looking, she could feel his gaze.

"It sounds like you were a kid that brought home stray dogs."

Andrew smiled and Rebecca blinked back the tears. She set her cutlery on the side of her empty plate.

"So what did you find out about me, Andrew?"

"That you were an enthusiastic teacher, that you were great with the kids . . . and that you were a nun."

"That's certainly a sanitized version. Maureen's discretion, no doubt."

"She didn't go into the details."

The waiter arrived and inquired about dessert.

"This was wonderful. Thank you, Andrew, but I really must go."

"I'll drive you home."

"No, I'll be fine," Rebecca said as she rose and reached for her coat. She had no desire to leave with Andrew.

"We need to set up another appointment to go over your proposals."

"Email me at work."

"I would be up for another dinner meeting."

This guy is relentless, thought Rebecca. She didn't care. California had given her distance to reflect. Andrew may have overstepped but it wasn't out of mere curiosity or power. What she had intuited, Andrew confirmed this evening— he had reached out because he cared. Claudia had always given her respect and space—that's what she needed in the beginning. Andrew had broken through her façade and was offering friendship.

"I know a place," said Rebecca. "And thanks again for the meal."

Before Andrew could respond, she was gone.

CHAPTER 22

"How did you find out it was my birthday?" Sally said.

"Your little Sarah has a big mouth, that's how," replied Gladys. "Here comes Rebecca."

"*Rebecca* is coming?"

"Yep, this is going to be a first-class birthday party."

Sally had stood clear of Rebecca ever since she'd failed to entice her to church. Although it was several months ago, she winced when she recalled the attempt—all desire to find new members for the Centre City Christian Fellowship had vaporized. She wished Gladys had not included Rebecca.

"Hi, Gladys. Happy birthday, Sally." Rebecca handed Sally a rose.

~

When Sally had arrived at work that day, she'd found on her desk an invitation Gladys had prepared. Sally's spirit lifted and she was smiling when Gladys walked through the office doors that morning. The birthday outing had been carefully planned a few days before with Claudia and the woman who replaced Sally during her lunch break. Today Sally, Rebecca, and Gladys stayed through lunch, left work early, and met in the lobby downstairs.

"So where are we headed, Gladys?" said Rebecca.

"The Nub."

The Nub was a popular name for the downtown shopping district. Enclosed corridors bridged several streets at the second- and third-floor levels, connecting a few department stores and office buildings. Boutiques and shops of various kinds lined the wide interior corridors, creating a mall in the heart of the city.

As they rode the escalators, Rebecca asked Sally about her children and she began to relax. It seemed there were no hard feelings on Rebecca's part.

With Gladys in the lead, they walked into the women's section of a large department store.

"Sally, for your birthday, Rebecca and I want you to pick out a dress—our present to you. And then, we stop somewhere for dessert."

"What!" exclaimed Sally. Gladys and Rebecca both smiled at her surprise. "No, I can't, I really can't. It's too much. Let's just go for dessert." Sally felt her face reddening.

Gladys put her arm on Sally's shoulder. "Sally, we want to do this with you, have some fun together. It's your birthday! Come on, let's start."

Tears began to trickle down Sally's cheek. "I don't know what to say."

"You don't have to say anything. Just get your butt in gear and follow me. I've already scouted out some great dresses."

Sally laughed in spite of herself and wiped her tears. "Thanks," she said in a soft voice.

Gladys led the way. Among the three, Gladys was the undisputed leader in fashion. She rifted through the racks with a confidence and speed that astounded Sally and amused Rebecca. It wasn't long before Rebecca, the appointed bearer of possibilities, was carrying about a dozen choices. "We're never going to get into the fitting rooms with this many dresses."

"There's three of us, right?" Gladys winked. She and Sally picked out a few more. "We're going to make the most of this trip. Here, let's divide up the goods."

They entered the fitting rooms with several dresses each. The fitting room was practically deserted. "Let's go to the handicap stall. It has wider mirrors and more hooks."

"The *handicap stall*! What if someone needs it?" Sally asked.

"Look around, girl. I don't see a line of walkers. If someone in a wheelchair rolls in, we'll pull you out and shove you into the stall next door." Gladys took her dresses, then those of the others and hung them up in the stall.

"OK, Sally. Rebecca and I will wait outside for you to hit the runway."

Sally giggled. "This is crazy."

And so it started. Sally would come out and Gladys would pick the dress apart. Rebecca leaned against the wall and observed the scene. For the first few dresses, Sally was deferential to Gladys. Then she found one she liked. "But Gladys, I think it fits fine and I like the color."

"What! *Girl*, have you looked in the mirror?" She marched Sally into the fitting room in front of the mirror. "Look at these drooping shoulders and the color—it washes you out. You need something bold. No, no, this will never do. Rebecca, don't even put it among the maybes. Get rid of this dress. The sooner we forget it the better."

Sally laughed and passed the dress over the stall door. "Try on the red dress, Sally," Gladys called.

"I don't know about this one," Sally said after a few minutes.

"Let's see it," said Gladys.

Sally stepped out. "This won't go." She pointed to the V neckline that cut into her cleavage.

"Come on, girl. You dress like you're ninety. You'll get there soon enough. Now's the time to show a little of what you have."

"I could never wear this. Don would never approve."

"Well, if you ask me, Don should be enjoying your assets a little more."

"When would I wear it anyway, at the seniors' fundraising tea or Caleb's soccer practice?" She sighed softly. "It is a pretty dress, though."

The playful banter that accompanied previous outfits began to droop as Sally became more pensive.

"Well, take the damn dress off, Sally. Rebecca, hide this one too. We don't want Sally making the old bastards' eyes pop at the tea party."

Rebecca shook her head.

"Try that black one, Sally."

And so it continued, with Rebecca sent on an occasional trip to find a different size. In the end, Gladys and Sally settled on a royal blue dress with a striking design in red and hints of green and black. The top followed her curves and then hung on her hips, going off in an A-line. It was beautiful.

"You don't think this neckline is too low?" said Sally hesitantly.

"Low? Sally, are you seeing something I don't? Your cleavage starts here."

Gladys pointed two inches down from the corner of the V

"You'd have to be standing on your head for anyone to catch a glimpse of your boobs."

Gladys looked at her and in a softer voice said, "Seriously, Sally, do you like the dress?"

"I love it."

"Then, when you're with Don, wear a sweater and take it off when you come to work."

~

Rebecca took a candle from her purse and put it in Sally's ice cream sundae. Gladys pulled out her lighter and lit it. "Happy birthday . . ." they sang. A group of students at a nearby table joined in, adding a rap rhythm, then clapped and hooted at the end. Sally flushed with pleasure. The three women began to spoon up their desserts.

Sally looked fully at Gladys and Rebecca.

"Thanks. I'll never forget today . . . ever."

The women separated, each going to a different bus stop. Sally, however, made a detour to the office and slipped the shopping bag with the dress into her bottom desk drawer.

CHAPTER 23

"Hi, Rebecca." It was Sally. "Had to drop off something for Claudia. Wanted to thank you again for the other day."

Rebecca looked up at Sally. "You're welcome."

Sally handed Rebecca a thank-you notecard and lingered a moment.

"How's the family?" asked Rebecca.

"Oh . . ." Her tone changed. She paused, then sat on the extra chair. "I suppose Gladys told you about it."

Rebecca had asked the question in a general fashion, never intending to pursue her marital difficulties.

"Not much . . . a disagreement of sorts . . . I went with Gladys to South Side. Everything was . . . inspiring and . . . lively, I guess. I loved it, the kids loved it. I thought Don would too." Sally picked at a seam on her skirt; her voice dropped. "He'll never change."

There was a long pause. The tendency Rebecca had followed for so long was pushing her toward silence—don't get involved, wish her well, and get back to work. And yet, this was not the proselytising Sally with her contrived conversations and plastic platitudes.

"Does it really matter whether a church has the latest technology, a cappuccino bar, and a daycare centre, or . . . is in an old barn in the middle of the country? Sally, the deeper question is: Why are you going to church at all?"

Sally looked up.

"And, God, . . . why does Don call all the shots?"

93

CHAPTER 24

Rebecca stepped off the bus and waited. It was beautiful outside: still chilly but clear and blue. She looked at her watch. Andrew would be coming any minute. She looked down the street as he turned the corner. He had the same stride as the first day she had seen him walking into the conference room: unrushed, looking around him as he moved down the street, smiling at the passersby. So different from Rebecca's determined gait to move from one point to the other. She waved.

"So what's this place?" asked Andrew as they rounded a corner.

"China." They were standing before the Song Kai.

The restaurant was cafeteria style. Square tables filled every possible space. The black Formica tops were partially covered by white paper placemats, each with a set of utensils tightly bound in a paper napkin. Several people were circling the buffet area with plates, a number of others were eating. However, most of the tables were waiting for company.

"It's very busy during the week. I'm surprised they're open on Saturdays but it must pay. They're famous for their dim sum."

"Great. I love Chinese food."

"I was hoping you would. But I figured if you didn't there are always hamburgers."

After their plates were filled and they were heading to their tables, Andrew picked up some chopsticks. Rebecca sat, unwound her napkin, and released her cutlery. Andrew pulled the chopsticks out of their paper wrapping, cracked them apart and began to eat.

"When did you learn to eat with chopsticks?"

"In college. Some of my friends were Asian. It's a great way to eat. Ingenious." Andrew deftly handled the sticks and brought up a dumpling. "No cutting." He took a bite. "No changing from fork to knife." Another bite. "Just pure culinary enjoyment." He finished off the dumpling.

"Westerners are lazy cooks. They set great big hunks of food on a plate and expect the diners to finish off the job. Asians have everything chopped." He looked over at Rebecca. "You want to learn?"

"Well, after all that, I don't think I could enjoy another bite with this fork and knife." She began to push back from the table to get a set of chopsticks when Andrew pulled out one from his pocket.

"I always pick up an extra set."

Andrew began the lessons.

"You make it look so easy," said Rebecca as she attempted to hold the chopsticks as Andrew instructed.

Before long both were laughing as Rebecca struggled to keep her food between the sticks long enough to make it to her mouth. Suddenly, she became self-conscious and picked up her fork.

"That's enough for today or I'll never finish this meal."

Getting serious, Rebecca asked, "So what did Haverstock have to say about the proposals."

"We're going to take it a step at a time, starting with the survey." He pulled an envelope from his jacket pocket. "Here's the revised version."

Rebecca took out the sheet of paper and glanced through it quickly, noting it was substantially the same, except for the last couple of entries.

"Elder daycare. I'm impressed."

"Both ends of the spectrum."

"Do you think there'll be complaints when we circulate the survey . . . you know, from those who don't have younger children or aging parents? People asking for a wage increase instead?"

"I've been thinking about that and brought it up with Haverstock." Andrew scouted through his chow mein with his chopsticks, picking out cashews.

"We have people paying into health and dental plans. Some use them more than others, some not at all . . . but a time can come when the tables are turned. Besides, I think there's enough variety among the benefits—people plug into some more than others. What's more, if employees are satisfied and do their job well, we all benefit whether we're using daycare or not."

Discussion continued on various aspects of the plan—Haverstock's reaction to the different proposals, the probability of its realization. Eventually, the conversation dwindled.

Rebecca was still working on her meal; Andrew was ready for seconds.

"I'm going back for a refill. Would you like anything else?"

"Maybe a couple of pot stickers."

When Andrew returned, he put a plate of fruit between them and from his other loaded plate he slid some pot stickers onto Rebecca's plate with his chopsticks. "Do you want anything else?" His sticks were poised to share more of his selection with her.

"No, that's fine."

Andrew sat down and began to eat.

"How did you find Maureen at St. Peter's?"

Andrew looked up, surprised Rebecca had brought up the subject.

"I met a nun outside the . . . big convent."

"The motherhouse."

"The mother ship . . . OK. Well, a nun outside told me Sr. Maureen was at St. Peter's . . . substituting for a teacher on sick leave."

"Just like that."

"Yes."

"I'm surprised she gave you the information without consulting the superior first."

"Well, initially she thought I was a nephew . . . she seemed to know Sr. Maureen well."

Rebecca tilted her head. "What was she like?"

Andrew gave a brief description. "Sounds like Candida," said Rebecca, more to herself.

"That's it! That was her name."

Andrew continued eating.

"So what happened at St. Peter's?"

Andrew looked up, tentative. He related the significant aspects of his meeting with Maureen, deleting a few details he felt were meant for him alone.

"They called you the child-whisperer."

"Who did?" said Rebecca.

"Maureen and another nun she mentioned."

Rebecca took a couple of bites.

"Jeanne most likely. . . . That was kind of them."

"Sounded like it was based more on fact than kindness."

For several moments neither said a word, Rebecca lost in her own thoughts. "Is she well?"

"She looked OK to me. I mean, I don't really know her. . . . Seemed energetic." He took a piece of fruit from the plate they were sharing. "I met another nun as I was leaving. Rather different from Maureen. Sr. Pie . . . Pes-something."

"You met *Pistós*?"

"That's the one! How do you pronounce her name?"

"Pis—stos. Jeanne called her Pissed-off or Piss-off, depending on the circumstances."

"You got to be kidding!" Andrew laughed with surprise. "In the convent?"

"Jeanne was not your typical nun."

"Piss—off . . . Well, I'll never forget her name again."

He went on to tell Rebecca of their encounter on the school grounds. As he did so, he watched Rebecca's countenance change.

"Pistós, Pistós . . . ," said Rebecca under her breath. "So she's principal of the congregation's flagship academy." She shook her head slightly.

"I better go," she said in a subdued tone. She gathered her jacket and purse. "And this time it's on me."

CHAPTER 25

The children were in bed. Sally looked over at Don. He was reclined in an easy chair watching a documentary on the Christian network. She was ironing in the dining area where it opened into the living room. From her vantage point she could see the TV and Don. She studied his face, intent and serious. It was all so familiar. During the breaks he would comment on what he had seen, pointing out the way the world was becoming ever more deviant; children, the victims of unbelief. He would give examples, some she had heard before; others, fresh observations from work or recent news reports.

The iron hissed as she set it upright and adjusted the shirt on the ironing board. Don was oblivious—totally caught up in the message of stone-faced commentators with menacing chords playing in the background. Who was this stranger? He had been her man of faith, strong and solid in his principles; confident, faithful, consistent, a good husband and father. In all things she had deferred to his better judgment. She had admired him . . . no, more than that. She had revered him. But over the past months her exemplar had transmuted.

She continued her rhythmic motion, back and forth across the shirt. As she lifted her eyes from the steaming iron, she saw a rigid, controlling, temperamental man. She had tried to justify his attitudes; tried to jump-start herself into her previous admiration, but she could not stifle the overpowering evidence. She chafed as he directed household affairs. She suffocated in his embraces. When he put his arm around her or held her hand, she felt shackled. She went through the motions as before, but within she was dog-paddling to stay on top of her surging emotions, confused . . . and frightened.

Sally knew that the program would finish in about ten minutes and she would then be subject to a half-hour rehashing. She took the freshly-pressed shirt off the ironing board and clicked off the iron. "I'm really tired tonight. I think I'll go to bed early."

"Sure," said Don without taking his eyes off the screen.

Lying in bed, Sally's mind swirled to the days before Don. Throughout her school years, and notably in high school, Sally tagged along with the girls who were popular and sure of themselves. She sought to be like them, wanted to be with them. Her parents had the money; she could keep up with the fads.

She had always been a follower, a damn follower. Sally seared with the insight and turned over. The TV droned on. Don was watching another program. Good.

Alicia, Madisyn, and Gaia. They were "in," they were cool, and Sally was part of a group. They had so much in common, so she thought. The malls, the films, the music, the clothes . . . and later, the pot and the "moves" with the boys. After high school, Sally's dad transferred to another state. The move was considered during her junior year; however, Sally was distraught at the idea. She had already been uprooted from several schools due to previous transfers and wanted to graduate with her friends. Her parents relented and waited until after graduation. The moving van arrived a week after the event. Sally decided to stay, clinging to the vestiges of the familiar. However, her close-knit circle disbanded at the end of summer. Alicia and Gaia decided to flee the Midwest and go to New York. They planned to work and pick up training in some field or other after they had a little fun. Once they were settled, they assured her, Sally could join them. Madisyn, who always managed to keep up her grades with minimal effort, was accepted at a university in Chicago with a partial scholarship. The friends promised each other to keep in touch, but with the distance, some months of time, and new occupations, Sally was forgotten.

For a few years, Sally waitressed and took some business courses at the community college. The world was a different place outside of high school. She wanted to replicate her old group of friends, but it never happened. Her parents encouraged her to move closer to their new home but at the time she was involved with a guy, a regular at the restaurant. She actually moved in with him for several months before they broke up. Then Don came in.

He was almost ten years older than Sally, settled in his job, and attracted by Sally's friendliness. He became a regular and they often chatted. One day he invited her to the Centre City Christian Fellowship. It wasn't long before they were dating and attending church regularly. One evening, some months into their relationship, Sally poured out her confession to Don—the guys, the pot, cheating on exams, shoplifting for kicks with her friends. She sobbed, convinced that Don would drop her right there. But he had taken her in his arms and told her she just had to accept Christ as her personal Saviour and she would be washed clean in his precious blood. Her relief and gratitude were intensified a few days later when she professed her faith in Jesus before the whole assembly and was warmly embraced by the members. It was bliss. She and Don were married shortly after in a quiet ceremony, to the chagrin of her family.

The bliss of gratitude gradually wore away but the debt of gratitude was always there. A married, middle-aged woman became Sally's "intentional friend," a mentor to coach her as a newlywed. It began with household management, cooking, and, ever so delicately, her responsibilities as a woman toward her husband's needs. Sally aimed to please, to be the best wife, mother, and Christian, so that Don would never regret his decision. She deferred to him in everything. Unlike herself, Don had never had a misstep. Disciplined and temperate from childhood, he had nothing to regret other than not accepting Jesus as his Lord and Saviour before the age of thirteen.

He was sleeping next to her now. Sally listened for a few moments to his slow, measured breathing, then slipped out of bed. She wanted to be alone. In the darkened living room she curled up on the couch.

Did she believe? Sally shifted restlessly on the couch. She could no longer avoid the question. *Why do you even go to church at all?* She didn't know. Her pat answers were no longer convincing. Her cheeks flushed again. Was her "conversion" just another attempt to fit in, another way to feel accepted and admired?

Someone shuffled into the room.

"I looked for you but you weren't in bed." It was Sarah.

"Come here, baby." Sarah cuddled up to her mother. "What's the matter?"

"I woke up."

"Me too."

As Sally snuggled with Sarah, she was certain of one thing. She loved her children.

CHAPTER 26

The park wound its way through Verloren on either side of the river. At some points, it shrunk to a mere pathway, and in others it expanded into ball parks, picnic areas and play grounds. Rebecca unzipped her jacket. Although it was still March, there was no wind and the sun was up. The outing was Gladys's idea. Having been burrowed in an apartment throughout the winter, she was willing to endure the nip in the air for the first picnic of the year. However, the sun broke through, dispelling the chill if one remained in its rays.

Eliza was walking alongside Rebecca. She was a confident, expressive child—five going on sixteen. From all appearances, one would never have known that they'd just met. During their trek through the park, Eliza amused Rebecca with tales of the various events that make up the life of a five-year-old and she had an opinion on them all.

"Well, today I *finally* get to meet Nigel. Ben says I'll like him."

"You looking forward to it?" asked Rebecca.

"We can play together. That's why we're going to the park." Eliza began to hop. "I can jump *almost* as far as Sasha. She doesn't jump far because she doesn't like to fall down, but I don't care. See." Eliza ran, jumped, and tumbled to the ground. "See, I don't care if I fall."

Gladys was about twenty feet ahead, walking briskly with Jeremy and Sasha. They all carried shopping bags, as did Rebecca. Gladys was dressed casually . . . well, casually for Gladys. She wasn't wearing heels and had on jeans, form fitting and embroidered on the hems and down one pant leg. Gladys walked off the path and cut across the grass toward a picnic area. They passed by a playground on the way and Eliza immediately ran to the swings. Jeremy and Sasha slowed their pace to look over the many climbing structures.

"Eliza, come and see where our table is and then you can go back," Gladys hollered. Eliza rejoined the others and followed along with Rebecca.

Gladys chose a table that overlooked a large pond. In the opposite direction the playground was visible. A perfect spot. They deposited their bags on the table and the children ran back to the play area. Rebecca and Gladys laid out a plastic tablecloth and began to organize the picnic foods.

"Couldn't be a better day for an early picnic," said Rebecca. "Does Ben know where to find the place?"

"He better after all the instructions I gave him." Gladys scanned the park but there was no sign of a man with a young boy.

"Have you met Nigel yet?" asked Rebecca.

"Briefly. Ben and I picked him up from the babysitter after a date and then we went out for ice cream."

"Hey, Mom!" the children hollered from the playground. Rebecca and Gladys looked over and Jeremy was pointing down the path. Coming toward them were Ben and Nigel. Nigel broke loose of his father's hand and ran toward the playground. Reaching the swings, he lay across one of the seats and pushed himself into motion.

Ben walked into the play area, greeted Gladys's children, and called Nigel over to the little group. He put his arm around his son and introduced him. Nigel nestled close to his father and peered at the other children. When his father rose, Nigel ran back to the swing. Jeremy and Sasha returned to a rope wall. Eliza stood for a moment and then followed Nigel to the swings. Gladys waved from the table and went to meet Ben as he approached the picnic area.

"Ben, I told you not to worry about the food."

Ben kissed Gladys on the cheek. "I didn't worry about it. I bought it."

Gladys smiled and took one of the bags. A few steps more and they were at the table.

"Ben, this is Rebecca."

"Heard a lot about you. Good to finally meet you."

"Same here." They shook hands. Then all three were pulling out sandwiches, drinks, chips, fruit, preparing the table for lunch.

Jeremy bellowed from the play area, "Mommmmm!" All three raised their heads. He pointed to the pond beyond the picnic area. Nigel was running, making a beeline for the water.

"Hell," said Ben as he took off to intercept Nigel. He missed and chased his son to the edge of the pond, grabbing him just as he was about to run in.

"Nigel, we talked about this," Ben said sternly. "It's too cold to go into the water today. You play on the playground with the other children, or you are going to have to sit on the grass near me. Is that clear?"

Nigel looked up with his brown eyes filled with tears. He nodded, dropped his head, and trudged back toward the playground.

As Ben returned to the picnic table, Rebecca watched Nigel, his head down, his feet dragging.

"What a kid," Ben said when he arrived at the table. "Just loves water." He pulled out some juice boxes and set them on the table.

Rebecca continued to glance over at the play area. Nigel ignored the other children as he kicked through the gravel to the swing set, lay again on an empty swing and slowly swung back and forth.

"We're pretty much done here," Rebecca said. "I think I'll go and watch the kids play."

She stepped into the play area and unobtrusively sat on the end of the slide. Nigel continued on the swing, only now he twisted it a few turns, then lifted up his legs like a shrivelled bug, allowing the swing to reverse, rocking him from side to side.

Jeremy, Sasha, and Eliza were playing some form of tag with Jeremy dictating amended rules as they went along. Eliza was tagged repeatedly. After a few minutes, as Jeremy and Sasha competed on the monkey bar hoops, she came and leaned against Rebecca's knees, pouting.

"I hate playing with Jeremy and Sasha."

"Look at Nigel. Seems he would like someone to play with."

"He's kind of dumb," Eliza whispered. "He didn't know how to play the game. He ran away."

"Well, you're used to playing together. Nigel doesn't have brothers and sisters." Rebecca put her arm around Eliza. "Why don't you do something that doesn't have a lot of rules, something he likes?"

"Jeremy says he's stupid."

"How would you feel if someone called you stupid?"

Eliza didn't say anything.

"He looks lonely to me. Why don't you just swing next to him. Do what he does for a while."

Eliza seemed unconvinced yet straightened up and slowly approached Nigel. When she reached the swing, she lay on it like Nigel and pushed herself back and forth. After a few moments she asked, "Do you go to school?"

"Yeah."

"Next year I'm gonna be in first grade and I get to ride the bus with Jeremy and Sasha."

Nigel made no reply. Rebecca could just make out the conversation from her perch on the slide. She got up slowly, walked nonchalantly toward the swing and sat down off to the side. She pulled up her legs, wrapped her arms around them, and rested her chin on her knees.

"Do you ride a bus?" Eliza continued.

"No."

"How do you get to school?"

"My daddy drives me."

Eliza swung gently back and forth.

"I don't have a daddy."

Nigel looked over at Eliza.

"Who takes care of you?" he asked.

"My mom. She's over there." Eliza pointed to the picnic table.

Nigel stopped rocking, stood up leaning against the swing seat and gazed toward the picnic table.

"My mom is gone. She's never coming home." He lay back down on the swing seat and alternated between pushing and dragging his toes.

"My mom fixes my hair. She puts polish on my nails. See." She held out her hand to Nigel. He remained on the swing but scooted in for a closer look.

"Jeremy thinks he's so big," said Nigel glancing at the two older kids playing together. "My dad is bigger than him."

"Yeah, Jeremy thinks he's the big boss," Eliza said with resentment. "We don't have to play with them."

Although the day was bright and sunny, the ground was still cold. Rebecca could feel the pebbles pressing into her rear, the chill penetrating through her clothes. She had remained motionless up to this point but her body urged her to shift. Her movements caught Eliza's attention. "Rebecca, come and push us!"

Rebecca walked over to the pair. She looked at Nigel and squatted to eye level. "I'm Rebecca and you must be Nigel." She put out her hand. "I'm happy to meet you." Nigel looked up but did not extend his hand. Rebecca patted his shoulder.

"So what are you up to?"

"Rebecca, will you push us? Come on, Nigel, Rebecca can push us really high."

Eliza sat on her swing and Rebecca began to push. Up she went, higher and higher, giggling.

Nigel sat in his swing and looked at Rebecca. Soon he was up. He closed his eyes and smiled when he felt the gush of wind going forward, oblivious to the others around him.

Jeremy and Sasha came over to check out the excitement. "Hey, it's our turn," said Jeremy.

Rebecca had just met Jeremy but resolving playground squabbles came as naturally as breathing.

"Jeremy, there's lots of other things to play with. Leave Eliza and Nigel on the swings."

Jeremy dug his toe in the gravel. "I didn't want to play with the babies anyway. Come on, Sasha, let's go."

"I'm staying." She climbed on top one of the baby swings and, leaning back and forth, put the swing into motion. Not to be outdone, Jeremy climbed on the neighbouring baby swing and the two began competing with each other to get higher.

Gladys hollered from the picnic table, "Rebecca, it's time to eat."

The swings slowed. The kids jumped off and ran to the table. Rebecca brought up the rear.

Ben called Nigel and with his hand on his shoulder brought him closer to Gladys. "You remember Gladys, don't you?" Gladys smiled down at him. Nigel nodded. "Gladys is the mother of Jeremy, Sasha, and Eliza."

"Glad you're here, Nigel," said Gladys. "I saw you having fun on the swings."

Nigel continued to look at Gladys but didn't say a word.

"OK, kids"—Gladys, resumed her usual commanding manner—"I've got the hand cleaner. Come here, I'll put some on. Now rub your hands together . . . Good God, Jeremy! What the hell do you have on your hands! Rebecca, grab me a napkin. Here, Jeremy, wipe that crap off and I'll put more on. Eliza don't play with it, for God's sake, rub it all around. You know what you're supposed to do."

Nigel looked at the dab squirted in his palm and glanced from child to child as Gladys supervised the hand washing. Ben brought his attention back to the dab. "Like this, Nigel." He had put some of the gel on his own palms and taking Nigel's hands into his own, they rubbed the cleaner around together. Nigel giggled and tried to wipe some on his dad's face.

"Mommy, do it like Ben." Eliza tried to snuggle with Gladys.

"Just get those hands clean, young lady."

Then turning to the other children, "Get your plates, put your sandwich and anything else you want on top, grab a juice, and go sit on the blankets we have laid out for you."

The children approached the table. Nigel took a sandwich half and sat at the end of the picnic table bench. Jeremy gave him a puzzled look.

Eliza said, "Nigel, you have to get your plate and all the other stuff. We're gonna sit on the blanket."

Nigel looked up. All the children were staring at him. Nigel threw his sandwich on the grass and ran off crying. Ben went to catch him.

"What the hell?" said Gladys, bewildered. She looked at Rebecca.

"That guy's nut-so," Jeremy said.

"You cut out that type of talk, young man," said Gladys.

"Well, he is," Jeremy said under his breath.

"He's not used to so many people," said Rebecca.

"I like Nigel," said Eliza. "And his mom never comes home," she added for reinforcement.

"His mom probably took off, just like our dad did," Jeremy said.

"Enough," Gladys interjected. "Get your food and go eat on the blanket."

As the children were getting settled on the blanket, Gladys stood near Rebecca. "What was that all about?"

They both looked over at Ben talking to Nigel some distance away from the picnic area.

"I don't know."

"Do you think he is a mental case?"

"My guess is, he's not used to the other kids or us."

"He has a problem with me?"

"He's out of his element, Gladys. You're going to have to give him time."

Ben approached the table with Nigel. "OK, Nigel, let's start over."

He gave Nigel a plate and they began to make their way around the table. Nigel had his head down and just gave little nods when Ben asked him what he wanted.

"Now you can eat with the others on the blanket."

"Come and sit next to me," said Eliza, patting the blanket. Nigel looked from Eliza to Jeremy and Sasha. Sasha looked down and continued eating, as did Jeremy.

"I have an idea, Gladys," said Rebecca. "Let's move the food over and we'll all sit at the table. Here, Nigel, you sit next to your dad and Eliza you sit next to him."

Gladys conceded, although caving into tantrums went against her grain. Rebecca noticed as the attention was deflected from Nigel, he began to eat and even responded to some of Eliza's attempts to engage him.

~

The meal was winding up. Jeremy and Sasha were back in the play area on the climbing structures. Nigel and Eliza were sitting on the picnic table, showing each other various methods of eating cream-filled cookies, twisting off the tops and rolling the filling into a ball.

The adults gathered the leftovers and were packing them up. Gladys took a couple of containers and went to the drinking fountain to rinse them out. Jeremy and Sasha called her over to watch them do their latest stunts on the monkey bars. Gladys watched several, clapped, and warned them to be careful.

"I have some more!" said Sasha eagerly. She hung with one hand gripping the bar, and then the other.

"Oh, that's nothing!" Jeremy exclaimed and went on to show a similar feat.

"OK, OK, real good." Gladys turned to walk back to the table. Rebecca and Ben sat at the picnic table across from each other, chatting and smiling. *So the bitch can be friendly when it suits her.* Ben passed Rebecca a slip of paper which Rebecca glanced at and then pocketed.

"He's a sensitive child," Rebecca was saying as Gladys came back to the table. "Seems tuned to nature."

Rebecca faced Eliza and Nigel who were now gathering little pebbles in the grass and around the trees, and making patterns with them on the blanket, oblivious to the adults at the table. Gladys sat next to Ben. He smiled at her, squeezed her shoulder, and continued on with the conversation.

"I've noticed the same thing. He'll be running around and then the apartment gets real quiet. I go to look for him and he is standing at the window, gazing at the sunset. Or he'll be out in the pouring rain, face turned up toward the sky, getting drenched."

The second example struck Gladys as more senseless than sensitive.

"What does he enjoy at school?" asked Rebecca.

"The hamster and the fish they have in the classroom," replied Ben. His tone turned more serious. "So often he seems lost."

Gladys looked at Ben and Rebecca as they continued their observations. Though welcomed, she felt like a spectator at some unknown sport, unable to participate in the exchange. *The bitch!*

~

Ben put his arm around Gladys's shoulders. "I think this was enough for the first encounter," giving a significant glance at Nigel. "We'd better be heading off." They kissed.

"Before you go . . ." The food was divided up, with Gladys generously supplying Ben, and Ben protesting. Gladys won.

Soon father and son were walking down the path together and Eliza ran into the play area.

Gladys watched them walk away.

"Nigel has Ben wrapped around his finger. If my kids tried any of his stunts, it would have been their first and only."

Rebecca munched on a pretzel as she put the last of the picnic items in the bags. Gladys looked at her. "What's with you?"

"Eliza got along with him just fine." She folded the plastic tablecloth. "He just needs some space."

"Oh, so now you're the great expert on kids." Gladys's voice grew hot.

Rebecca was surprised at her ire. "Kids are different, Gladys. You know that. Look at the differences in your own kids."

"He wants Ben's attention, that's all. And he got it."

"Maybe."

"How many kids do you have?" Gladys was clearly provoked. "Living alone in your apartment . . . and you know it all?"

Rebecca looked into Gladys's eyes. She could feel her heart pounding, her face blushing.

"You don't try to understand Nigel, Gladys, and I'll guarantee one thing: that kid will put a wedge between you and Ben."

Gladys stood up. "And maybe Nigel's getting a little help with that."

She grabbed the bags off the table, walked off toward the path, and bellowed toward the play area, "Come on, kids, time to go home."

CHAPTER 27

Gladys stepped off the elevator with a small group of co-workers and walked through the door into the second-floor office. Sally looked up and smiled but, staring straight ahead, Gladys didn't notice.

"Hey, Gladys."

Gladys turned her head.

"Hi," said Sally with a puzzled expression.

"Oh, hi," said Gladys distractedly as she passed.

Sally fought back her tears. Since her difficulties with Don began, she'd found some relief in Gladys's buoyancy. Her gregarious laugh lightened her mood. But Gladys's coolness this morning . . . She went over the past few days, trying to determine if inadvertently she had done something to offend Gladys. *You're being silly!* she chided herself. *You're becoming hypersensitive about everything.* Yet she could not ward off the heaviness and dread.

"Sally?" A claims agent was at the counter and Sally realized she was looking off in space.

"Oh, here's the file you were looking for."

~

Gladys clomped down the corridor. She passed Claudia's office. The door was closed with Rebecca and Claudia speaking inside.

Bitch, thought Gladys, but the nickname had none of its usual affection.

As she entered her own office, she noticed an envelope on the desk. She put down her purse and picked it up. It was addressed with her name and department and had Secure Star's return address. She opened it and pulled out a couple sheets of paper. The first was a cover letter explaining that Secure Star was exploring the possibility of offering a daycare/elder care subsidy to its employees and asked if the enclosed survey could be completed and returned within the month.

"Well, I'll be damned," Gladys whispered. The news was so unexpected that for the moment she forgot her previous irritation.

She put away her things and rapidly completed the survey, sealing it in a return envelope. According to the instructions, on each floor there was a box at the reception desk for completed surveys. She was on her way.

"Sally, can you believe this?" said Gladys, holding up her envelope.

Sally looked up, baffled at Gladys's change in demeanour. "Yes, I was rather surprised myself."

Gladys handed Sally her envelope.

"Is . . . ?" Sally looked up at Gladys. "Is everything . . . ? Did I do anything . . . ?"

"What's with you, girl?" Gladys was equally baffled.

"You were so . . . different this morning." Tears formed in her large eyes. "Is everything OK?"

Hell! thought Gladys. The possibility of daycare from Secure Star and, now, the realization of her thoughtlessness with Sally cooled her obsession with Rebecca's behaviour the day before.

"Oh, I just had my head up my ass," she said. "How are things with Don?"

Sally looked down. "I don't know."

"Why don't you guys come over? The kids have been asking about you. We never see you anymore."

Sally tensed. Gladys was a part of her life in which she did not want interference from Don. Bringing the two of them together . . . in the same place . . . for several hours . . . Sally cringed.

"You know what he's like. . . ."

"Yeah, I know what he's like." *A major, tight-assed fart.* "You think about coming over and get back to me." Gladys returned to her office.

⁓

There it was again. The fear of Don. What would he think? How would he react? What would he say? Always. Nothing could stop her growing awareness of how much these thoughts dominated her thinking and controlled her reactions and decisions. *It's always all about Don.* Her life was a charade.

"Denise," Sally said to the woman who replaced her for lunch, "could you watch the front for a bit? I have to take a break." Sally went out the door toward the bathrooms, but went down the stairs instead.

The cool spring breeze struck her cheeks as she crossed the street to the park and walked rapidly down a path.

Chagrined at her deference and compliance, Sally knew it had started way before Don. Different circumstances, different decisions, yet it had been the same with her friends throughout high school.

She hated herself. She hated her life. The thought of Don filled her with loathing. His smugness, his arrogance, his dominance.

And yet, she was the one who'd let it all happen, from the beginning, and day after day. She didn't know what to do. She felt trapped . . . and yet was she? She found herself walking faster down a path. And then her children came to mind.

She slowed down and leaned against a post-rail fence overlooking a stream making its way to the river. She was breathing heavily. The kids. For their sakes she could not just blow up and walk out on Don. And for their sakes she could not continue as she had.

When Sally returned to the office she picked up the phone and pressed Gladys's extension. "This Saturday, but at my house. Three o'clock."

~

"Hey." Rebecca stepped inside Gladys's door as she walked by from Claudia's office.

"Hey." Gladys continued with her work but her tone of voice had lost some of the antagonism of the previous day.

"So what was yesterday all about?"

Gladys looked up from the computer screen. "What was going on between you and Ben?"

"Between me and Ben?"

Gladys felt her irritation re-emerging. "Yeah, all that *Nigel talk.*"

The bewilderment left Rebecca's eyes. "Gladys, that was exactly what was going on—Nigel talk. . . . Ben's a nice guy and all—I'm happy for you—but Ben is all yours."

Gladys considered Rebecca closely. "Damn," she said at last.

"Gladys, come on. I'm not some sort of man snatcher. Give me a break."

"Sorry. Really I am." She shook her head and absently examined her fingernails.

"I used to be a teacher, Gladys. That's what the Nigel talk was all about."

"A schoolteacher?"

"Yeah."

"So what the hell are you doing *here*?" She gestured around.

"I'm not sure."

Gladys shook her head slowly. "You really are one screwed-up bitch."

Rebecca turned to leave but looked back, "And just so you know, I'll be talking with Ben to see if we can work out what's happening with Nigel."

Gladys sat straight in her chair. "What is going on? Is it serious?"

"I doubt it. But he's behind a bit in social skills. Ben needs to find out how he can help him."

"Why didn't he just tell me?"

"He probably didn't know what to tell. Ben's just beginning to accept that whatever is going on is not just a *phase* that Nigel will grow out of magically."

"I'm really sorry about yesterday, bitch."

"Yeah, let's just put it behind us."

CHAPTER 28

The kids were playing in their bedrooms. Sally was finishing up in the kitchen. Don stepped in from the garage and washed his hands after replenishing the washer fluid in the van.

"You have anything going on this Saturday?" Sally asked.

"No, not that I know of. Why?"

"I invited Gladys and her family over for dinner."

Don shifted his weight on one leg, gesturing with his hand. "You can't just go inviting people over without discussing it beforehand."

"You just said you had nothing going on, and besides, we've been encouraged at church to extend hospitality."

"Well, I would prefer a quiet afternoon with the family."

"That's what we pretty much have every Saturday," said Sally softly as she continued to wipe off the counters. Her heart was pounding but she was relentless.

"And who's going to pay for this?"

"That's ridiculous, Don. We're not that strapped for money. Besides, I work and bring in my share. Gladys is my friend. Her children are friends of our children."

"I barely know her . . . and never really cared for her."

"Well, maybe you'll like her better when you get to know her."

Don was baffled and irritated. He was not used to any resistance from Sally. "I am the head of the house," he said with anger.

Sally was prepared. "Well, the head looks out for the good of the whole body.

Gladys and I are friends, our children enjoy playing with each other. It's not just about you, Don. It's about us." Her voice was shaking toward the end. "We have nothing going on this Saturday. I've invited Gladys and her family."

"Then let them come," said Don impatiently as he walked out of the kitchen and flicked on the TV. He was still muttering to himself as the program came on.

Sally was trembling as she wrung out the cloth and spread it over the faucet to dry. She had done it. She had done it! She walked to the bedroom. "Come on, kids. It's time to get ready for bed."

~

"*Me*, with Don? Are you out of your mind?" Rebecca exclaimed.

"You've never even met him," Gladys replied.

"I've met enough of his type, believe me. Self-righteous, religious prudes."

"Come on, Rebecca, what in the hell am I supposed to do locked in with that guy for an afternoon. I'll lose it, I know I will."

"I'll second that."

"Shut up and help me out here."

They were silent for a while. "Why don't you invite Ben and Nigel," Rebecca suggested.

"Now you're out of your mind, girl. Why would I want to involve Ben with Don? And besides, we never know what Nigel's going to do from moment to moment."

"Look, Ben's an easy-going guy. And he's a man. Don and Ben can, you know, do guy-talk."

"Guy-talk?"

"Just tip him off about Don. Ben can handle it. If he is going to be part of your life, you might as well let him in on it. Then you and Sally stick together in the kitchen and I'll take care of the kids."

Gladys was beginning to relent. "It might work."

"Just avoid . . . ass, shit . . ."

"Hell, what a bastard that guy is."

"And hell, and bastard . . ."

"God, I was *insane* to suggest this."

"And God . . ."

Both began to laugh.

"I better just keep my mouth shut."

"I was hoping you would."

CHAPTER 29

They would arrive at Sally's together, that was the plan. Ben had a car, but not large enough for Gladys and her kids. Rebecca used a car so infrequently that it was cheaper to rent one when required. A bus stopped not far from Sally's home. They decided to meet at the stop and walk over together.

Sasha and Jeremy were in the lead, followed by Ben and Gladys. Eliza and Nigel were quite a ways back with Rebecca. She was teaching them how to walk "joined at the hip." They were getting the hang of it now and were giggling as they swung their legs together to the right and the left. Ben and Gladys turned around to see what was going on.

"Just what the hell are you doing back there?" Gladys hollered.

Rebecca had them run to catch up and they began their step again.

"Hey, Bitc—" Gladys caught herself. "Can't we speed things up a bit?"

"What for?" Rebecca replied as she and the two children continued with their fun.

Gladys turned her attention to Ben. "Just keep the conversation going with Don."

"I don't even know the guy. What's he interested in?"

"How am I supposed to know? Just do guy-talk."

"Guy-talk? What the hell is guy-talk?"

"You're a guy. You should know. Just talk to the man. It's for Sally."

Ben raised his eyebrows and shook his head. "This is going to be one hell of an afternoon."

They were soon standing in front of a modest home in a neighbourhood of bungalows built at least a generation past. The lawn, neatly clipped, was treeless. Some bushes and shrubs framed one side of the house; an attached garage, the other. They were walking toward the porch on a little pathway from the driveway when the door swung open and Sally's children spilled out, greeting Jeremy and Sasha. Eliza joined them. Nigel tightened his grip on Rebecca's hand and leaned against her. Sally came out to invite them in while Don stood at the door. Introductions were made as they entered the house. Nigel let go of Rebecca and began to cling to his father.

"It's a nice day," Sally said. "Why don't you children go out back and play?" Caleb led them to the back door and they ran out, all except Nigel. In the meantime, Ben and Gladys placed some containers of food on the kitchen counter. Then Ben, on cue, moved into the living room with Don, Nigel tagging along. Sitting on his father's knee, he watched the other children from the living room window.

Rebecca stood at the partition between the dining area and the living room. "Nigel, look what I brought." Nigel turned toward Rebecca. From her purse she pulled out a Slinky. Don was as surprised as Ben.

"Where did you find that?" Ben laughed.

"Oh, some of these toys are making a comeback: retro-toys."

Nigel slid off his father's lap and came for a closer look. Rebecca placed the toy in his hands and showed him by lifting one hand slightly higher than the other, how the Slinky would move back and forth, from hand to hand. Nigel giggled at the sensation.

"Here, I'll show you how you can make it go down the stairs."

Nigel followed Rebecca past the dining table and out the door to a small landing. He laughed as he watched the Slinky make its way down the steps leading to the backyard. He picked up the Slinky and returned to the top of the landing. Rebecca helped him get it in motion again. After a few attempts, Nigel succeeded on his own, much to his delight. Over and over he brought the toy to the top of the steps to watch its downward journey.

The other children were attracted to the swing set in the far corner of the backyard. Deborah and Sasha jumped on the two swings while the others tried out the slide. Eliza and Sarah began to explore the yard. Sarah pointed out the hole in the fence where she saw a rabbit hop through, and the bush that housed hundreds of ladybugs at its base: by lying on their stomachs they could watch them crawling up the budding branches. Eliza started teaching Sarah the "walk" that Rebecca had just taught Nigel and herself. Deborah and Sasha left the swings to join in. Caleb was showing Jeremy how he could position himself on the crossbeam of the fence and look into their neighbour's backyard. Rebecca leaned against the house, observing it all with a smile.

~

"Nice place you have here," said Ben, sipping the soda that Sally brought in.

"Bought the house a few years ago. How about you?" Don said. "You own your place?"

"No, living in an apartment on the other side of town. It's a little easier for now—just Nigel and myself."

"And your wife?"

"Oh, I'm divorced."

"You're raising your son alone?"

"Have been for several years. We're doing OK. . . . Nigel can be challenging at times but we're doing OK on the whole."

Don swivelled in his chair and looked over his shoulder into the backyard. The children were running about.

"They all seem to get along." Ben said.

Don couldn't locate Nigel and suddenly felt foolish for seeking him out. He turned back to Ben and took a sip from his soda. "What line of work are you in?"

"I'm with Robinson and McCrae, an electrical engineering firm. What about you?"

"I'm with Reliable Trucking . . . a forklift operator. Been there over twenty-five years now . . . one of their highest-paid forklift operators."

Don shifted and again felt foolish. He had been uncomfortable with this dinner party from the start. He didn't know these people, he didn't know their children. He liked his life the way it was.

Don went to work and did his job well. He was known to be dependable, hard-working, and conscientious. Assigned a task, it could be considered finished, correctly, to the last detail. He generally ate lunch with a couple of older men who shared his values, and avoided the young yahoos who passed in and out of the company with their tales of bars, booze, and babes. He scowled at the porn they taped to the locker room walls. Occasionally, Don would go to work early, clear the walls, then leave for a cup of coffee. When he returned later at his usual time, he would laugh to himself, hearing the complaints fly around the room. Outside of work, his time was spent between his family and church. He had known Rev. Martin most of his life, participating in all the youth programs growing up. He was held up as a model Christian husband and father. And now to have his house overrun . . .

~

"We're going to be toasting some French bread," said Gladys. "Do you men prefer garlic or just butter?"

"Either or," said Ben. "Whatever Don prefers would be fine with me."

"Just butter," said Don.

Who's surprised? thought Gladys as she returned to the kitchen.

"How's it going out there?" asked Sally.

"Looks OK to me."

~

All the while, Nigel had been busy with the Slinky. After he had mastered the steps, he tried the handrail but the Slinky fell off repeatedly. Looking around, he saw a board under the stairs. It was a one by four about a foot or so long. He placed this on the stairs near the bottom steps and got the Slinky to travel down the stairs and onto the slat. Happy with this success, he moved the slat to the top of the landing and lodged it in place with a few stones on a lower step. He was hoping to get the Slinky from the slat to the steps below. It didn't work. After several attempts, he gave up and coaxed the toy down the narrow cement walkway that led to the front gate.

~

"Well, would you look at that," said Ben.

Don turned rapidly in his chair and looked out into the backyard.

"Gladys, come here. You've got to see this!" Ben called.

Sally and Gladys moved into the living room and all four stared out the window at the antics in the backyard.

"Well, I'll be damned," said Gladys, smiling at Ben then Sally. The children were line dancing in a triangular formation with Sasha in the lead. Jeremy was in the back row with the older children, calling out the steps and totally into the rhythm—the obvious pro. Rebecca was off to the side singing and clapping. They were actually quite good. Don stiffened. Ben saw a deep blush rising from his neck to his face. Sally's smile dissolved into a look of apprehension. Don got up and walked to the back door.

Ben and Gladys looked at each other quizzically.

"I don't see Nigel," said Ben, "I wonder where he is." He followed Don out the back door.

Gladys turned toward Sally, "They are really—" The anxiety in Sally's eyes silenced her. "My God, don't tell me he has a problem with this." She gestured toward the dancing children.

Don opened the back door and proceeded with determined steps down the stairs, oblivious to Nigel's Slinky training track. His foot landed firmly on the top of the slat, which went flying with his leg into the air. He came down with a bang on the landing, his legs spread out in front of him on the stairs.

The dancing came to a halt. Nigel stared up from the walkway. All eyes were glued on Don.

"Are you all right?" said Ben, concerned and yet struck with the humour of it all. What he just witnessed was something out of the *Three Stooges* and Don on the landing, legs spread-eagled, did nothing to erase that impression. He didn't dare look at Gladys in the doorway behind him. He could just imagine her eyes sizing up the situation and would have lost it for sure.

Don pulled up his legs and Ben went to help him to his feet.

"I'm fine." Don waved off Ben's assistance.

The dancing was no longer an issue—it had ceased and now Don was the centre of attention. His deep blush intensified. Sally squeezed through the doorway to the landing as her husband began to rise.

"Don, did you hurt your back?"

"I'm OK!"

He turned and re-entered the house. The children began to stir. Sally walked across the lawn and exchanged a few words with Rebecca and then returned to the house.

"Caleb," Rebecca called, "do you have a ball?" Caleb ran to the garage and

Rebecca gathered the children to explain the game they were about to play. The only child who had not moved was Nigel. He remained squatting on the cement path, Slinky in hand, looking up at his father. Ben caught his gaze and surmised the rest. He walked down and knelt near his son.

"If you play on the steps, you have to clear them off when you're done. Did you see what happens when you leave things around?"

Nigel nodded, eyes wide and serious.

"So what do you have there?"

Nigel smiled and showed Ben some of his tricks with the Slinky.

In the meantime, Caleb had returned with a ball, and a game of dodge tag began. Ben picked the slat off the lawn, tossed it back under the stairs together with the remaining stones. Then he returned to his post in the living room. Shortly after, looking out the window, he noticed Rebecca engaging Nigel in the game and he was able to focus a little more easily on his assignment with Don.

～

In the kitchen, Gladys and Sally resumed their work of preparing dinner. Sally was sure Don was more rattled than hurt. Besides, the whole incident diverted a scene that could have been much worse. Gladys's children had stopped dancing out of curiosity. In the eyes of her own children she saw fear, something she was noticing more and more often.

"You think he's OK?" said Gladys, breaking the silence.

"He's fine, just a little shook up, that's all."

"He takes life pretty seriously, doesn't he?"

"Oh, yeah." Sally sighed.

"God, how do you live with it?"

"This is all new to him . . . and it wasn't his idea . . ." Yes, that's exactly it—it wasn't his idea.

"Gotta pull the chicken wings out of the oven," Gladys said. "These are good—hot and spicy."

～

"You follow sports?" Ben asked.

"A little baseball," Don replied.

"Which team?"

"Chicago Cubs."

"I'm a Yankee fan myself. . . . The Cubs had it tough last year."

The conversation sputtered on. Ben moved from subject to subject to see if he could find something that Don was likely to pursue. So far his batting average was very low. He looked out the window.

"You've got some good-looking kids."

Don looked over his shoulder to the backyard. "Yes, I'm blessed. I have wonderful kids."

At last! Prompting was still necessary, but Don shared willingly about each child.

~

"We're ready!" Gladys called out. Sally brought some old blankets to the backyard and spread them on the lawn. The children came bolting in through the back door and milled around the table, huffing from running, and pointing out their favourite foods on the platters that covered the dining table. They were sweaty, hungry, and pumped from their game of dodge tag.

"Go wash your hands, all of you," said Gladys, taking command of the energized band of children.

"Come on, Jeremy," said Caleb, running through the kitchen to the bathroom in the bedroom area. When Sasha followed, Jeremy closed the door in her face.

"This is the boys' bathroom, go somewhere else or wait."

"Mom!" yelled Sasha.

Sally directed Sarah and Emily to the small half bath near the garage entrance.

"Sasha, stop your bellowing," Gladys shouted from the kitchen, "There's another bathroom. Get your butt over here."

Ben lowered his head and scratched his forehead to shield a grin.

Toilets were flushing, water running, children laughing, talking, pushing. Nigel came in with the others and remained at the table looking at the food when the others ran off to wash up. Rebecca pulled up a chair to the kitchen sink and, at the same time, guided Nigel by the shoulder.

"Here's a sink just for you."

From the time the kids hit the back stairs, Don had ceased all conversation.

He was about to tell Caleb to settle down at one point, but with Gladys barking out orders, and Sally quietly directing the kids, he had been silenced to a furrowed brow. His children were active and playful but never had he experienced, or allowed, unruly behaviour in his house.

Jeremy and Caleb were back. Jeremy parked himself in front of the hot, spicy chicken wings and, holding on to the edge of the table, kicked up one leg and then the other. "My favourite," he said, looking at the wings.

Eliza and Sarah began to imitate him on the other side of table. Don started to rise from his chair.

"Knock that off, Jeremy, or you won't get even one," said Gladys.

Jeremy put both feet down and rocked from foot to foot, swinging his butt and snapping his fingers, still eyeing the wings. By this time, all the children were gathering around the table. Gladys was about to start passing out the paper plates when Rebecca made a slight motion to stop her.

Sally was at the partition to the living room. "We're all set. Don, do you want to lead us in prayer?"

Ben came in and, seeing the food prepared on the table, said, "Wow! This is some spread."

He stood behind Gladys, put his arm around her waist and kissed the back of her neck.

"Thanks, honey." Gladys smiled and kissed him back. He remained there with his hands resting on her hips. Deborah looked on, glanced at her parents and then back at Gladys and Ben. Jeremy continued to sway and snap. Gladys tapped his shoulder and glared. He looked up from the chicken wings to the quieting room and assumed a somewhat pious posture.

Don remained silent for a few moments. Rebecca caught Deborah's gaze which still rested on the affectionate couple. She speculated on the cause of Don's prolonged silence and then acknowledged she was being unfair. Perhaps he was just gathering his thoughts. With seven hungry children looking at a table of food, she wished he would round them up a little faster. The longer he paused, the less kindly she regarded his motives.

"Lord Jesus, we praise you, we always praise you, Son of God most high. You have redeemed us from our sins and nailed them to the cross. Praise God, praise his most blessed name. . . ."

Although Gladys kept Jeremy in check, Rebecca had always noted the similarities in their personalities. It became even more apparent at this moment, mother and son looking at Don with amazement as he went on and on, nonstop, praising Jesus. Rebecca had no doubt that the entire scene was, at this moment, being recorded to the slightest inflections to be mimicked by Jeremy at their next family meal. He was all ears.

"Eternal Father, provider of all good things, we thank you for this food; we bless you, we always bless you and praise you. . . ."

Eliza and Sasha now began their wide-eyed stare at Don.

"We praise you, Lord, we testify to your most holy name. . . ."

Nigel, growing weary, moved from beside Rebecca and walked around the table to his father and leaned against his leg. This seemed to trigger the need to conclude the prayer.

"We ask all this in Jesus's name. Amen."

Rebecca heard Sally let out a sigh as Gladys began to organize the children.

"OK, take a plate, get your food and juice box and move on outside."

The action began.

"Jeremy, don't you go filling your plate with chicken wings. Leave some for the others. . . . Put. Some. Back. NOW!"

Don watched, his brows burrowing. Jeremy let out a whine and grimaced as he scraped a small portion of his pile back onto the platter.

"More, Jeremy," said Gladys sternly.

"Ah, Mom."

Gladys took his plate, knocked off the majority and gave it back to Jeremy. Surprisingly, Jeremy took the plate without further complaint and Rebecca noticed a little glitter in his eyes. He had actually made off with more than expected.

As the children filled their plates, they made their way to the backyard and sat on the blankets that Sally had prepared. Then the adults served themselves. As Ben waited for Rebecca to spoon out her potato salad, he picked up a chicken wing from his plate and took a small bite.

"These are great, Gladys!" He leaned over to Gladys who was standing nearby and kissed her on the cheek.

Gladys put one arm around his waist and gave a brief hug, "I knew you would enjoy them."

Sally looked on. Her strained relationship contrasted sharply with the budding romance in front of her and Rebecca felt for her.

Rebecca took her plate and sat on the steps of the back porch. The children were sitting cross-legged on the blankets. Jeremy dug into his spicy chicken wings, hooted, waved his hands in front of his mouth and then took a bite of potato salad. Eliza and Sarah followed suit. While all this was almost a ritual with Jeremy, Sasha, and Eliza, hot wings were a new experience for Sarah. She was wide-eyed and panicky with the first bite and looked like she was ready to cry.

"Potato salad, Sarah, eat some potato salad and drink some juice," called out Rebecca, who was watching with amusement. This offered enough relief for Sarah to relax and join in the laughter of the others. Nigel smelt his one wing, gave it a small lick and returned it to his plate where it remained untouched. He was no fool.

Jeremy continued his antics until he was done with his wings. He was rising to go in for more.

"Jeremy, finish the rest of the food on your plate, then you can go in for more," said Rebecca.

He sat back down without a comment and continued his meal.

Eliza and Sarah looked over at Rebecca. They picked up their plates and came to sit with her on the steps. Nigel followed. So while the older children talked and laughed on the lawn, Eliza and Sarah chatted together, with Nigel occasionally joining in.

~

Inside the adults moved to the living room. "I've been meaning to ask you, Sally," said Gladys, "how did you respond to the daycare proposal?"

Sally spoke of the various options it opened for their family. Don nodded. Ben had not yet heard of the proposal, which led to further explanations and comments on daycare, company policies, and so forth. Don offered some comments now and then as well.

~

Jeremy finished his food, stood up, and approached the back steps. With a smirk, he held up his plate vertically in front of Rebecca and moved his hips back and forth. The younger children were peacefully settled on the steps, still eating their meal, blocking access to the back door. Rebecca hated to disturb them.

"Jeremy, why don't you go through the back gate over there to the front door. It's probably open. If not, just ring the doorbell."

Jeremy was off in a flash through the gate. He rounded the corner, passed the garage, and was heading up the little path to the front door when a car pulled up. Although Jeremy had his mind on chicken wings and his eye on the doorbell (he intended to ring it, door locked or not), this new development captured his attention.

"Is this Patster's home?" said the middle-aged man, a bit baffled, as he stepped out of the car.

"I guess so," said Jeremy with a shrug.

The man eyed the dark-skinned boy with the black, curly hair who was holding a soiled, empty paper plate. Jeremy likewise was taking in the pale, grey-haired, bespectacled man wearing a well-pressed, long-sleeved blue shirt, buttoned to his chin. His eyes fixed on the bucking bronco belt clasp that sunk into his thickened waist and cowboy boots that poked out from under the cuff of his slacks. He was holding a well-used book.

Jeremy hopped up the stairs, rang the doorbell and then tried the door. It was open. He entered just as Sally arrived.

"Hi, Mrs. Patster," Jeremy said as he turned into the kitchen and made his way to the table. Sally smiled and was about to turn back to the living room when she caught sight of the man and froze.

"Sally," the man said with a smile and extended his hand as he put one foot over the threshold.

Oh, my God, Sally thought. *Of all people to arrive at this time . . .*

CHAPTER 30

Sally regained her composure and shook hands with the visitor. "Chuck, this is a surprise." She didn't move to let him enter the house.

"Oh, I was just passing by and thought I would stop in." It was his typical line. However, from his dress, the Bible in his hands, and past experience, Sally knew their home was his predetermined target before he had gotten out of bed.

On hearing Chuck's voice, Don came to the door. "Chuck!" he said with much more enthusiasm than Sally. From his expression, Sally could tell Don was as surprised as herself but, unlike herself, very pleased. Don pushed by her to greet Chuck.

Chuck Blaston was a staunch member of the Centre City Christian Fellowship. He would pop over unannounced at various times, generally on the weekends. Don thoroughly enjoyed his visits. They would discuss issues from recent programs on the Christian cable channels they both watched. Chuck always had his Bible on hand for reference. Sally suspected these surprise visits were some personal mandate of Chuck's. She had heard from other members that he popped in at their homes as well.

Sally was uncomfortable with his visits, especially when they intruded on family activities. Over the past few months she had come to resent them. Don, on the other hand, always welcomed Chuck. They would talk for hours. Chuck's timing today could not have been worse.

"Come on in," Don said and patted him on the back.

As Chuck entered the living room, he noticed the other guests.

"Oh, I'm sorry. Am I interrupting? I didn't know you had guests," he said, smiling broadly and sitting easily in the chair Sally had vacated.

"Not a problem, not a problem," said Don, sounding relieved. "Make yourself at home. Would you like something to eat? We're having a little picnic here. Just help yourself." He was all ease and affability "Chuck, this is Ben and Gladys. They're friends," Sally said. Don again offered food, but Chuck refused. He had just eaten but would have something to drink. Out of the corner of her eye, Sally noticed Jeremy refilling on chicken wings. He was taking advantage of the distraction in the living room to break his quota and slip out the back door. Anxious though she was, Sally couldn't help but smile.

～

Knowing he wouldn't get past the kindergarten class with Rebecca in attendance, Jeremy sat on the top steps and feasted on his wings.

"Um, um. Are these good or what?"

"You could have gone back out the front door," said Rebecca. She enjoyed engaging Jeremy because she never knew what would come out of his mouth.

"Company arrived," he said between bites.

"Company?"

"Yeah, some old, spiffy dude." Jeremy never disappointed.

He wolfed down the wings, set his plate on the landing, climbed over the railing, jumped down to the little path below, and joined the older children.

The younger ones finished up and returned to their play in the yard. Rebecca picked up their plates and empty containers and went into the house. She was curious to see the newly arrived guest. As she entered the dining area, she was noticed and introduced to Chuck; however, when Rebecca moved into the kitchen to dispose of the garbage, the conversation returned to the circle of adults in the living room. This suited her fine, as she tuned in from the kitchen.

～

"So you attend South Side. They have quite the place. Are you longtime members or new to the church?" Chuck asked Ben.

"Both of us are relatively new. Gladys joined a couple of months ago."

"If I may ask, what attracted you to South Side?"

"After-school program and Gladys was into good-looking dudes," said Ben with a smile. He looked Chuck squarely in the eyes. For Sally's sake, he could humour Don, but Chuck was clearly a jerk.

"Where do you work?" he asked Chuck.

"Manager of a dry-cleaning business but, as I tell my wife, that just keeps food on the table. My real work is the Lord's."

"And what would that be?" Ben asked.

"Spreading the good news of our Lord, Jesus Christ. Our world is in a terrible state. Just have to click on the news to see that. The gates of hell are flooded. People have lost all sense of shame. Mankind is involved in every form of degradation."

Chuck opened his Bible. "Matthew, chapter 7, verses 13 and 14: '*Enter ye in at the strait gate: for wide is the gate, and broad is the way, that leadeth to destruction, and many there be which go in there at: Because strait is the gate, and narrow is the way, which leadeth unto life, and few there be that find it.*' Jesus needs missionaries, people who are unafraid to preach the need of repentance."

Chuck took a deep drink from his soda.

"I'm going for more chicken wings," Ben said.

When he arrived at the table, there were only three wings on the platter.

"Looks like someone else was here before me," he said softly to Rebecca who was leaning near the kitchen sink, nibbling on a piece of French bread.

"You have a lot of competition with Jeremy. With him 'you snooze you lose.'"

They both chuckled quietly and Ben joined her at the sink with his three wings.

"How's it going with Nigel?" asked Rebecca in a soft voice.

"Couple more tests and then we go for the results. Thanks for the references."

"He's a sweet child. Full of wonder."

Ben loved Nigel but was perplexed and unsettled with his behaviour. Rebecca saw beyond that. She gave him hope.

"Did you see him with the Slinky? He mastered a trick and moved on to another, trying different techniques."

"Yeah, one of which . . ." he turned his head in the direction of the living room.

"All's well that ends well."

"Well, I'm not sure it's going to end well with that arrogant bastard in there."

A comment like that from Gladys would have been typical. But from Ben . . .

"If it wasn't for Sally, I'd be out of here."

"How's Gladys taking it?"

"I'm sure we'll hear about it."

With that he returned to the living room.

~

Sally plastered a bland smile on her face and tried to stay focused on the conversation.

Chuck was holding forth. "Don, as I was saying, I happened to pick up Rev. Rodder last night on TV. What a program, what a program!" He turned to the others in the room. "Rev. Rodder is an outstanding preacher. Spirit-filled, *spirit-filled*. Wouldn't you say so, Don?"

"Oh, yes. He's one of my favourites."

Chuck turned back to the others. "He was commenting on the modern day confusion and how wolves in sheep's clothing are polluting the world with every form of error and deception. These wolves, disguised as Christian leaders, are watering down the message of our Lord, Jesus Christ." He continued to relate the highlights of the program—the contamination, the need to be watchful and protective of children in today's ungodly environment.

Sally began to say something, but Chuck interrupted and carried on.

"And yet he has confidence, such spirit-filled confidence, that the tide is changing." He cited the growing number of "godly men re-establishing their leadership in the family, mothers content to be keepers of the household, and the growing number of Christians home-schooling their children."

Only their financial situation constrained Don to keep Sally at work and their children in public schools, a concession Rev. Martin agreed was justified.

Chuck continued with Rodder's signs of hope: "Christian universities which refuse to cave in to secular values, the political clout of the Right. Spiritual warfare, spiritual warfare. The tide is changing!"

Sally glanced at Gladys and could tell by her scowl that she was fed up. Ben, she noticed, had dead skin to pick off his fingers or lint to sweep off his pants. Don was fixated on Chuck with obvious admiration. Sally looked back at Gladys who nodded toward the kitchen.

"Excuse me," Gladys said, interrupting Chuck. "Sally, don't you think it's about time we put out the desserts?"

"I'll give you a hand," said Ben and all three rose together and went to the kitchen where they found Rebecca leaning against the counter. Don and Chuck continued their conversation.

"What the . . . ?" mouthed Gladys as she raised her arms and gestured toward the living room.

Sally was washing her hands. "I'm so sorry," she whispered, taking up a towel. "I never expected Chuck to arrive, honestly. He's a friend of Don's."

"Who's blaming you?" Gladys gave Sally a squeeze. Keeping her voice down, "He's out of his mind. And so damn rude. Marching into your house unannounced and taking over the conversation with *your* guests. What an asshole!"

Sally saw Ben give Rebecca a look that seemed to say, "There, you have it."

Although still upset, Sally felt some relief in their understanding.

Four adults in the compact kitchen was overkill, but each tried to find something to do. Ben was about to clear off the remains of dinner from the table when he was stopped by Rebecca.

"Sally, what do you think? The kids are having so much fun outside, and desserts *can* be messy."

Sally saw where she was going. "Good idea. I'll serve Don and Chuck and then bring out desserts to the children."

"We'll *all* help you bring out desserts to the children," said Ben.

"I'm making coffee for Chuck and Don. Anyone else want coffee."

Nope. No. Not me. The fewer the cups, the faster they were out.

In no time, Sally had the coffee perking and the others were slicing cake and arranging cookies and bars on a platter. Sally brought out a generous sampling on a plate for both Don and Chuck and followed with the coffee.

"We're taking the desserts out to the children, Don." And with that, they all left out the back door into the yard.

The children grabbed a cookie or two but were intent on continuing their play. Rebecca got them started with the tag dodge ball they had enjoyed before lunch. The rules were simple and consistent, so Nigel joined in. Jeremy was beginning to make allowances for him, horsing around when Nigel trailed him with the ball instead of throwing it. Before long the adults were joining in as well. Sally felt some of her tension ease as laughter and yelling filled the backyard.

~

Chuck watched from the window as Sally and her guests entered the yard and children gathered around for their treats. Their lack of interest and mass exodus was not lost on the evangelist.

"Who are these people? I've never seen them here before."

"Sally knows them . . . from work," replied Don without expression. "Gladys invited Sally over to South Side when I was gone for my father. She was quite taken with it."

"High-octane entertainment."

"That's what I told Sally."

"So where do Ben and Gladys live?"

"They're not married, they're dating." Don shot Chuck a look. "Yeah, both are divorced. That little guy over there. He's Ben's son. And the other three belong to Gladys."

"What about that woman over there? She didn't bother joining our conversation."

"Don't know anything about her. She's been playing with the kids since they arrived."

Chuck looked at Don incredulously. "You know so little about these people and yet you allow them to come over to your home and interact with your children? Look at that cocky young boy."

Jeremy was finishing up a brownie to some bip-bop antics with Eliza and Sarah imitating.

"Sarah is mimicking everything he does," said Chuck with growing chagrin.

Don had noticed this earlier. He replied despondently, "They're friends of Sally's. I've just met them."

"You are the head of the household! Who do you want around your children, your wife? The devil is always lurking about just waiting for a chance to slip in."

Don's apprehension increased. He had never liked the plan. And Sally . . . she was different, but he could find no words to describe how. Not that he would confide any of this to Chuck. He didn't want to give him the impression he was weak. *He wasn't weak!*

Chuck didn't notice the lull in the conversation. He was busy flipping through his well worn Bible.

"Here it is! First Corinthians, chapter 11, verse 3: '*But I would have you know, that the head of every man is Christ; and the head of the woman is the man.'"*

Flipping rapidly again, he stopped at another page. "And again, Ephesians, chapter 5, verse 23: *'For the husband is the head of the wife as Christ is the head of the church.'* And again," Chuck moved on through his dog-eared pages. "Yes, here it is, Titus 2, verses 4 and 5: Young women are *'to be sober, to love their husbands, to love their children, to be discreet, chaste, keepers at home, good, obedient to their own husbands, that the word of God be not blasphemed.'"*

Chuck snapped the Bible closed and put his hand on Don's arm. "*You* are the head of this household with all the authority that comes from the word of God."

The game was in full swing and the two men turned toward the laughter coming from the yard.

"I'd better be on my way," said Chuck.

Don accompanied Chuck to the door. As Chuck stepped onto the porch, he turned and squeezed Don's shoulder. "*You* are the head of this household."

Don returned to the living room and looked out into the yard. Sally had the ball and took aim at Caleb. Although he swerved, Sally nailed him. Jeremy hooted, Sally was laughing, and Caleb took off after Sasha. Sarah and Nigel were jumping and cheering, more for the sake of jumping and whooping than in response to the game. Eliza split a brownie with Deborah then quickly moved into a position behind Caleb to avoid becoming his target. Ben shouted something to Gladys, causing her to laugh and nudge Rebecca. The scene filled Don with a sense of foreboding. Who were these people?

Don was totally devoted to his family. He enjoyed his work and was proud of his competence, but his real value came from the fact that he was the principal breadwinner of his family, husband, father, head of his household. Church and family—these were the anchors of his life, the pillars on which he was grounded. His guide for living was the Centre City Christian Fellowship . . . well, Jesus Christ, as taught consistently and faithfully by Rev. Martin at the Centre City Christian Fellowship. He had his principles to which they all complied and it had always gone so well.

But now? He didn't know these people: Gladys barking out her orders, Jeremy influencing the younger children, Nigel . . . what had Ben said? Challenging? What did that mean? Ben, he was nice enough but every chance he got he had his hands on Gladys. And he seemed to enjoy the company of women more than men. Bringing dessert to the kids when there were three women to do it? Sally was naïve.

She didn't know what she was bringing into the family. It had to be stopped.

The game was wrapping up. Some of the children were running to the plates of sweets, Gladys was hugging Sally . . . Don walked out the back door.

"We'd better be off," Ben said as he walked toward Don. They shook hands and joined the others in exchanging goodbyes. Gladys wanted to help clean up, but Sally would hear nothing of it. Soon Gladys, Ben, Rebecca, and the children were walking down the street.

Caleb, Deborah, and Sarah returned to the swing set, eating their latest selection of desserts. Sally transferred the remaining cookies and bars onto one dish and brought them into the house. Don followed behind her. She began to clear off the table and pack away the leftovers. Not a word was exchanged nor did Sally so much as glance in Don's direction.

"Sally, we need to talk about your friends."

"Talk, then," she said in a soft voice as she continued with her work.

"I wish you would stop what you're doing."

"I wish you would just say what you have to say." She carried on as before.

Don was in unknown waters. His authority had never been contested. He was determined. This was getting out of hand.

"Your friends are not a good influence on our family," he said in a firm voice.

"What!" Sally paused in surprise.

"You heard me."

Sally resumed her task. "You don't even know them." Her voice, low, now trembled.

"What I saw and heard today was enough."

"What you heard from Chuck?" Her pace quickened.

Don just managed to catch the muttered words and, irritated, said, "Stop what you're doing and listen to me!"

Sally reddened. She turned and looked directly at him. "I don't think *Chuck* is a good influence on our family." She went back to her work. Beads of perspiration rolled down her back.

Don was incensed. "Chuck is an outstanding member of the church and totally committed to the mission of Christ."

"Chuck is rude."

Don nearly shouted. "I'm the head of this household and I am telling you now: those people are never to come over again!"

The back door opened and Deborah and Sarah walked in. The taut silence brought them both to a halt. "We have to go to the bathroom."

Don walked out of the room. As he left, he could hear Sally forcing a bright tone into her voice.

"Well, you know where to go, right?"

That night Sally slept on the couch. It would become her regular bed.

CHAPTER 31

"Rebecca, I'd like to update you on the survey," Andrew said over the phone. "Are you able to come up to my office this afternoon for about a half-hour?"

~

"The response to the daycare survey has been amazing. Like I told you, 50 percent came back within a week and now at our month deadline, we have 82 percent!" Andrew smiled broadly.

"What's the overall thrust?" Rebecca asked.

"For the most part, positive. However," leaning back in his chair, "I think we've opened the floodgates."

"How so?"

"People added other issues to the survey." Andrew picked up a rough draft from the coffee table and flipped through a few pages. "There are requests to avoid early morning and late afternoon meetings because they interfere with drop-off and pickup schedules." Turning a page, "Concerns about emergency child care when the usual provider is down for sickness or some other reason. Or problems with school holidays or half days. Some employees think they could easily do their work from home on these occasions, and ask if they can log on through their personal computers."

"Would that be possible?" Rebecca got up and helped herself to a bottle of water from the credenza.

"Oh, it's very possible. But there are other considerations."

"Such as?"

"Such as accountability . . . although it is possible to monitor activity on a computer. My worry would be security, since so much of our data contains confidential information on our clients. And the recommendations go on and on." Andrew sipped some of his coffee. "We certainly hit a sensitive nerve."

Rebecca noticed Andrew's liberal use of *we*.

"Is there any chance that the proposal will be taken seriously by the board?"

"With the kind of response we received, they would be fools to dismiss it. Haverstock is going to push for an experimental period—couple of years in our division. We measure its effects on production and absenteeism and go on from there. He thinks we have a good chance of implementing some of the recommendations."

"Andrew . . ." Rebecca hesitated. "I admire you for moving ahead with this proposal . . . I do. But . . . you know, I'll be leaving . . . and soon enough."

Andrew knew. He had actually helped precipitate it. Rebecca didn't belong here. Yet he didn't want to lose her either.

"How soon?"

"A month, maybe two. I don't know."

"What will you do?"

"I haven't the slightest idea."

CHAPTER 32

Don stood his ground. Rebecca, Gladys and Ben, and their children never returned to the Patster's home. Sarah would occasionally ask about them but Deborah and Caleb were more perceptive regarding the chill between their parents and never brought up the subject.

Sally's resistance only increased Don's determination to exert his authority, not only over her friends but regarding other family decisions over which previously he had allowed more latitude. Chores, weekend activities, shopping—nothing was too insignificant for Don to demonstrate his God-given prerogative. Conversation with Sally trickled to the bare minimum. Don was adamant—Sally had to accept that he was the head of the house.

In one area, however, Sally was just as adamant—the couch. Throughout their married life, Don had enjoyed Sally's compliant lovemaking. That had come to a halt. It was just as well she moved to the couch. He had the bed.

⁓

Don opened the fridge and grabbed the bagged lunch Sally had prepared the evening before. He started work early and left before the children were up. Before he walked out, he glanced into the living room. Sally lay motionless on the couch, eyes closed. He turned to the garage, backed the van down the driveway, and travelled his customary route to work.

With problems at home, Don's work was a relief. He pulled into the parking lot as he had done for over twenty-five years. The locker, the time card, the hand-off with the night crew, firing up the forklift—a routine so familiar, so calming, so affirming.

As Don walked toward the dispatch office, he noticed that both the night and day crew were gathering outside. Don exchanged a few greetings and went through the door.

"What's up?" he asked pleasantly. Dorothy, the office manager, was typing on her keyboard. She had worked for Reliable Transport longer than Don and they always exchanged some small talk in the morning. She got up and walked quickly to the printer.

"We're having a general meeting in a couple of minutes. I have to bring these to Brad."

Brad? Brad never arrived before 9:00 a.m. And why was Dorothy so uptight? He walked out to join his older lunch buddies. "What's this all about?"

"Hell if I know," said one.

"Never seen anything like it," said the other, "Even the afternoon crew is arriving."

Don looked about. There was a hushed atmosphere, small groups of men talking softly to each other.

"Either this is going to be really good, or . . ." said the first man. "Damn, and I only had two more years to retirement."

Don's skin began to prickle with apprehension.

Brad walked out the door. "I'm sorry to have called you here this morning. The news I'm about to give is both good and bad. Let's get through the bad news first.

"Reliable Transport has been bought out by Ex-Fast Shipping. As you know, Ex-Fast has just built a new terminal right off the highway north of the city. This new warehouse will cut into our business because, using the Ex-Fast terminal, truckers don't have to deal with city traffic."

"I haven't noticed business slowing down, boss," called out one of the men.

"It will. It's only a matter of time. As of today, this warehouse is closed."

There was a murmuring of incredulity.

"Could everyone please keep it down," shouted Brad over the rumble of voices. "Since we have given you no notice, you will receive your pay for your hours up to today and an additional two weeks. We have also prepared your Record of Employment form so you can claim unemployment insurance while you hunt for a new job."

Brad rushed on. "Now, the good news: Ex-Fast is taking applications, so the sooner you apply there the better."

Don's head buzzed. Closing, applications, two weeks. Shock and denial befuddled his grasp of the situation. He looked around at the discontented men as they grumbled in small groups or yelled out their complaints. And then he saw them. Security guards. *Security guards!*

A middle-aged man from the group stepped forward and turned so he could face the group of men and Brad as well.

"Brad, I've been working for you a long time and always considered you a decent guy. But quite frankly, I consider your reason for selling out to Ex-Fast is nothing but Ex-Lax—a lot of shit spewing out damn fast."

Some of the men hooted and clapped their approval.

"What about our mortgage payments? What about our families, our food, our heating bills? We see the freight that still pours in here. And this is our last day?"

Then, raising his voice even louder, "What I want to know is: how much Ex-Fast paid you for the business? I don't think *you'll* be going on unemployment."

There was a rumble of consensus from the rest of the men.

"And I see you brought in the National Reserve," pointing to the security guards. "What do you take us for, Brad? Just give me my damn envelope. I'm out of here."

"I'm sorry for the inconvenience," said Brad, undaunted. "I strongly advise you to apply immediately to Ex-Fast. They assured me that they are looking for trained workers—"

"Cut the shit," someone shouted out. "With all of us pouring in for the same jobs, our wages will be slashed and you know it."

The discontented murmuring mounted.

Brad stopped. No one was listening anymore. He made a motion toward the office. Dorothy came out, passed a stack of envelopes to Brad, and quickly returned inside. A few security guards came over from the sides. One took the envelopes and began to call out names. Brad observed from behind.

Don stared at the men as they claimed their envelopes and walked away. This wasn't happening. One of his friends shook his shoulder.

"They called your name, Don."

He moved forward, took the envelope, and walked to the locker room. His jacket . . . Removing pictures . . . Security guards . . . His lunch—it seemed days since he opened his refrigerator and took it out . . . The van . . . The road . . . His home . . . He was in the living room and couldn't have told how he got there.

~

At 4:00 p.m. Sally received a call at work. It was Betty, a church member who lived across the street from the school and looked after the children for about a half-hour until Don picked them up. He had not arrived. Ordinarily, this would be no problem, Betty went on, but today she had another engagement and generally Don called when he would be late. Sally was as surprised as Betty. Just this once, Sally asked, could her children go along. The minivan would be packed, but it was possible, she was assured. Just an extra music lesson. They would be back home around 6:00 p.m.

Something must have come up. This was totally out of character. You could set your watch by Don's daily routine. If he had to remain longer at work, he always called both Sally and Betty. She picked up the phone and called Reliable Transport.

"I guess you haven't heard," said Dorothy.

"Heard what?"

"Reliable sold out. Today was Don's last day at work. He left with the others this morning and I haven't seen him since."

"Oh, my God!"

"Oh, my God is right."

"Can companies do this?"

"Apparently so. I wouldn't have believed Brad would stoop so low. The offer must have been mighty good."

Sally hung up and called home. The phone rang until the voice mail message came on. She hung up and dialled again. A dull, low voice answered, "Hello."

"Don, is that you?"

"Yes."

"Don, I heard the news. I'm coming home right now. Don't worry about picking up the kids. I've made other arrangements."

"What time is it?" said the expressionless voice.

"Don't worry about the time. I'll be there in less than an hour."

Within ten minutes she was on the bus.

~

"Don?" Although the days were getting longer, the house was dim. Not a light was on. Sally went from the front door into the kitchen. On the table she saw the bagged lunch she had prepared the evening before and, on a chair nearby, the contents from Don's locker. She walked into the living room. Don sat in his favourite chair, staring off into nowhere.

For weeks their communication had been merely what sufficed to keep the family functioning. They never touched. Sally could barely tolerate looking at Don. And now he sat before her, dazed. Gone were the furrowed brow, the determined step, the overbearing tone of voice. She looked into the face of a lost, bewildered man. Sally crossed the room, squatted on one side of the chair, and took his hand.

"Don, are you OK?"

"Sally." He squeezed her hand. "They shut down Reliable."

"Yes, I heard," she said softly.

"I've worked there all my life." His voice broke and he began to cry. If he had ever cried before, it wasn't in front of her.

"We'll get through this, Don."

He squeezed her hand tighter.

~

After putting the kids and Don to bed, Sally went through the things Don had brought home. Amidst the paraphernalia that had accumulated in his locker, Sally found the envelope he had been given in the morning, still sealed. She opened it. A cover letter announcing the sell-off, a letter of recommendation, a regular paycheque together with a check for two weeks' pay, and the Record of Employment form.

Sally had only been minimally involved in the family finances, never with Don's employment. *I can do this. I deal with forms and figures all day long. Calm down and read it through.*

The next day, Don arose to follow his usual routine . . . with nowhere to go. He arrived in the kitchen muddled and, having never been home for this part of their lives, only got in the way. Sally gave him a cup of coffee and sent him to the living room. With Don at home, the children really didn't need to go to Betty's before and after school; however, Sally decided that for the time being they would continue to follow the same routine. By 7:30 a.m. she and the kids were walking the few blocks to Betty's house.

"But, Mommy, the van is in the garage . . ." moaned Sarah.

"We can use the exercise."

Sally mulled over her plans as they trudged along. She could not leave Don alone today. She called in sick when she returned home.

~

Sally was still unclear about the details of Don's layoff and hoped he would share more today. They also had to assess their situation, come up with a plan, and draw up a budget. She bought a paper on her way home. Don needed a job, and not just to support the family—she had never seen him disoriented. She had to help him focus on new possibilities.

When Sally returned home, she cooked up Don's favourite omelette with pancakes and they had breakfast together. She could feel herself holding back, afraid at any moment the Don of old would re-emerge. And, at the same time, she was frightened of this new version. Don had always taken the lead. As much as she had grown to resent his domination, she had never had to assume full responsibility for herself or her family.

"What exactly happened yesterday?"

Don's description was sketchy and halting.

"I read the letter last night." She placed the envelope between them but Don did not reach for it.

After gathering up the dishes, Sally brought out a sheet she had worked on the night before. With her wages and his unemployment insurance, they could still make the mortgage payment and, if they were very careful, squeeze through their other expenses. So they would be OK while he looked for another job. They had some money saved, but they might not need to touch it.

"Where am I going to find a job?" His hands trembled.

Don had started at Reliable Transport as a teen on a recommendation from his father. The application form was a formality; he never had an interview. When his dad retired, his parents sold their house and moved south to be near their daughter. She was older than Don by several years and married with children. Don had been invited to come along but by that time he had his own apartment and was well established at Reliable Transport. His mom died shortly after. Sally never met her.

"You'll find a job, Don," said Sally. "You have so much experience, you're dependable, hard-working."

"Well, it won't be at Ex-Fast, not after what they pulled with Brad."

Sally didn't argue the point. She pulled over the classified section of the paper. "We can go through this together, Don. Just circle the jobs you find appealing."

And so passed the day. An employment agency had helped Sally write a resumé when she sought out her clerical job a couple of years earlier. So she drew out of Don the various positions he had held at Reliable Transport before and after she met him. She told him she had a friend at work who could whiz out a resumé. Don was too dazed to conjecture it might be one of the persons he had forbidden to enter their house.

~

Sally arrived home early Friday afternoon with an envelope of documents. Don now had multiple copies of a resumé with a cover letter produced by Rebecca. After a call from Gladys, Ben had supplied a couple of leads from reputable companies. Sally added these to the list that they had drawn up the day before. On Monday he would begin to drop off resumés.

"Why don't we walk over to the school and pick up the kids together?" she suggested.

The doorbell rang. This was unusual. Sally opened the door and came face-to-face with Chuck Blaston, the last person she wanted near Don.

On Wednesday, Don was so addled he didn't remember the mid-week service, and Sally certainly didn't remind him. She didn't want to see him break down under a barrage of questions from the well intentioned. On Sunday he could confide in Rev. Martin and receive blessings and prayers from the community for his job search. They would go to church with a plan in place.

Sally remained in the doorway, blocking Chuck's entrance.

"I hoped I'd find someone home. I read about the sell-out in the *Tribune*. Is Don here?"

"He hasn't been feeling well. He'll be at church on Sunday. Perhaps it would be better to speak with him then."

"This can't wait. I've got to speak with him now."

Don came over to see who was there.

"Don, Don, good to see you. Sorry to hear about the sell-out."

Sally could no longer prevent his entry. Chuck was in the living room; only this time, she wouldn't leave him alone with Don.

"Yes, yes, I read Ex-Fast is taking on all the men from Reliable Transport so you must be relieved."

Not waiting for a response from Don, Chuck leaned forward in his chair, elbows on his knees, tapping his fingertips together. He looked up at Don, then back at his hands as he tapped them together.

"Don, there have been some developments at church. It's going to hit the press and I want you to be informed before it does." Again he paused and looked up at Don.

"For a while now, I've been concerned about the church's financial reports. Some items just didn't add up. A group of us approached Rev. Martin and asked that the books be audited, and we didn't leave until the books were handed over. As it turns out, Rev. Martin has been dipping into the funds." He looked up to see the impact of his words.

"Dipping into the funds?"

"Stealing our money, Don."

Don gripped the arms of his chair. Rev. Martin was his mentor and model of Christian life. From his early teens, Don had been active in the church and throughout the years had been publicly recognized and honoured by Rev. Martin for his service. Don had such great deference toward Rev. Martin that their relationship never evolved into friendship as he grew older. A couple of times a year, the minister was invited for dinner, but Don was so formal that the conversation was little more than good-mannered pleasantries and religious truisms. Don would beam at Rev. Martin as he spoke, while Sally served, and his children, scrubbed and starched, watched in silence.

"This can't be true," gasped Don.

"We have proof, Don. It's very true."

Although surprised by the news, unlike Don, Sally's previous awe and admiration had been expunged in the past months. *The hypocrite . . . all the money we tithed!*

"Seems he invested in real estate, flipping houses at a profit. He got in over his head . . . Yes, he bought a deal that did not flip as fast as he expected . . . and got saddled with the mortgage. He swears he intended to pay it all back . . ."

After some moments of silence Don mumbled again, "This can't be true."

Chuck lowered his voice. "I want to tip you off, Don."

He tapped his fingers together and leaned in closer to Don.

"Because of your close involvement with Rev. Martin over the years, some parishioners are wondering . . . if perhaps . . . well, maybe you benefited . . ."

"What! And who's spreading these stories, Chuck?" said Sally, irate.

"Just when did you buy this house?" countered Chuck, his voice remaining calm.

Don looked dazed. "Our house?"

Sally was infuriated. Don might be controlling and domineering, but he was honest. He would never have suspected Rev. Martin of embezzling, let alone entered into a shady business deal.

"A forklift operator with three children can afford to buy a house?"

"Don has never taken a *penny* from the church. We tithed even when we could have used the money ourselves."

"You got a good deal on this house because Rev. Martin was trying to cut loose from a mortgage payment."

"If that's true, Don knew nothing about it," said Sally adamantly, but she felt a cold chill pass through her spine. She knew Rev. Martin had tipped Don off about this house.

"Maybe not, but—"

"It's time to go, Chuck."

"Sally . . ."

"Leave—now!"

～

Sally closed the door, walked into the kitchen, and watched Chuck drive away. For years she had endured his intrusive visits, his stilted conversations: the same scripture quotes pounded out with the same emphatic gestures, sitting on the edge of the seat, leaning forward, and sealing everything with his crystallized smile. A wave of rage surfaced with a force Sally had never experienced before.

Chuck Blaston using his well-worn Bible to climb to a position in an insignificant, aging church—the stinking, slinking bastard. Her rage soon enveloped all the well-meaning, smiling followers who now looked with suspicion on a man whose adulation had made him oblivious to Rev. Martin's faults.

She went to the living room. Don wasn't there.

"Don?" She glanced out the back window into the yard and then walked to their bedroom. Don was on the bed, his knees brought up close to his chest. Sally sat on the bed. "Don, we'll get through this."

Don did not respond.

"I have to go pick up the kids . . . I'll be back soon."

~

Don lay on the bed. He could feel his heart pounding, hear it in his ears. Rev. Martin was in trouble. What was it? He tried to recall what Chuck had said but all he could summon was a sense that Rev. Martin was in trouble. He needed Don.

Don sat up on the edge of the bed . . . dizziness . . . better now . . . out the door. The keys . . . not in my pocket . . . just walk . . . yeah, down the road here . . . Keep going . . . keep going . . . not far now . . . traffic sounds . . . very close . . . across the road. . . . Don looked up when he heard the screeching brakes of the truck; then everything went black.

~

On one point, Sally was adamant: there would be no church funeral. A simple service at a funeral parlour across town, cremation, no obituary, no eulogy, and family only other than her recent melange of friends. She sat there numb. Rebecca held her hand; Sarah was on her lap, Deborah and Caleb at her side. Nearby sat Gladys, her mother, Ben, and their children. Don's sister had driven in shortly before the service and, to Sally's relief, intended to return home the next day. Don and his sister had never been close and Don's intractable religious beliefs had seared what little feeling existed. A smattering of cousins and an uncle with his wife made up the rest of Don's family.

Sally hadn't even bothered to tell her own family. As a teen, her friends had been more important than her parents or sibling. And right when she was considering a move home, she met Don. Her "conversion" and marriage were met with shock to wide-eyed amazement. Trips to her family were few: Sally picked up their bemusement with Don, although all were polite in his presence. And Don was uncomfortable in so foreign an environment. When the children were born, her parents would come unannounced: *"We were driving through and thought we would stop."* But these were sporadic in the best of times and over the years had become more infrequent. Phone calls on Christmas and birthdays, and presents sent for the grandchildren were the principal staples of their languid union.

And Sally was in no state to see them. She realized now that she had never really loved Don. Admired him, been in awe of him, and initially flattered by his attention, yes; but loved him? Sadly, she had to admit, no. What she had experienced in these last months had dissipated the admiration and filled her with disgust for herself and for Don. In the past week she saw him for the frightened, fragile man he was. Now she was left with only pity for her husband and rage at the people who sought to undermine his sterling qualities that, in living them rigidly, had become his downfall—consistency and loyalty. She sat there staring at the copper urn. The service was over and she hadn't heard a word of it.

CHAPTER 33

The sun had set but the evening still held the warmth of the brilliant spring day. Ben and Gladys walked slowly down the street, holding hands. They had just finished eating out not far from Ben's apartment. Nigel was at the sitter's.

"Warm for this time of year," said Gladys. "Hope it stays for a few more days."

They strolled on quietly.

"You think Sally's going to be OK?" said Ben.

Gladys could really use a cigarette right now. The patch was a joke, but she felt she should give it a shot for the kids.

"Who knows? The story keeps getting worse."

Ben looked at her quizzically.

"I brought Sally a casserole that Mom made yesterday. Well, besides the pastor embezzling, that Chuck bastard . . ."

"The guy who crashed the party?"

"Yeah. He's insinuating that Don got some kind of cut under the table for their house. Sally says it's ludicrous. Seems Don flipped out when he heard the news."

"God . . . So what's going to happen with Sally?"

"We'll keep an eye on her. What a fucked-up church."

They walked on in silence.

"You're quiet tonight," said Gladys.

Ben swung her arm in an attempt to be playful, but then said, "Nigel has to go for more testing. To a specialist. A neurological exam."

"You tell Rebecca?"

"I will."

In a corner lot near Ben's apartment building was a small playground with several benches. It was empty and dimly lit by the street lights. Ben led Gladys over to one of the benches. They sat close together with his arm around her shoulder, Ben gently running his fingers through her hair.

"Remember when I told you about Nigel's mom . . . our divorce?"

Gladys met his eyes.

"Well, that's only part of it. . . . A few months after the divorce, she OD'd. Nigel was just two."

He took his arm from around Gladys and squeezed his fingers to his eyes.

"I don't know where she got the stuff . . . Is that Nigel's problem? Was she snorting when she was pregnant? Definitely after he was born. I couldn't trust her with him anymore."

He began to weep. "God, what did I do to make her so unhappy?"

"How do you know it had anything to do with you?"

"Maybe I should have stayed."

"She was snorting when you were there."

He shook his head and wiped his hand on his pant leg. They sat for some time. Ben, elbows on his knees, head resting in his hands. Gladys, gently stroking his neck.

"Sometimes I feel like such a screw-up."

"We're all a little screwed up, Ben."

Ben turned to face Gladys. They kissed and went upstairs to his apartment.

CHAPTER 34

"So where are we going?" Rebecca asked.

"A small town just off the interstate. There's a restaurant there with the best chicken I've ever tasted. Found it by accident when the highway was being repaired. We were detoured down a country road."

"How long does it take to get there?"

"Oh, about an hour, I'd say. We exit the interstate about twenty minutes out of town. And," he said with a grin, "we'll be able to take in some scenery we wouldn't see from the highway."

"Yes, I can just imagine. Closer views of the sprouting cornfields and intersections with dirt roads."

"We might even spot a pig farm."

"Tantalizing."

Rebecca gazed out the window as they made their way to the highway. The park that weaved its way along the river was in full bloom. She took in the trees with their unfurled leaves, the grass and shrubs, so green, so fresh. Flowers were blossoming in an array of colours and children were prancing around in their shorts and bright tops, free of their winter wear.

"What's on your mind?" said Andrew.

"Nothing in particular, just enjoying the scenery. I love spring."

"Looks like we're going to move right into summer today. Did you hear it may even reach ninety? And there's not a cloud in the sky."

They merged into the interstate and drove on for a while in silence.

"Are you into the oldies?"

"That's getting to be relative. What constitutes an oldie for you?"

"Sinatra, Cole, Martin . . . I have a mix."

"Sure."

Andrew put in the CD and was soon humming along, adding in words as he knew them. Rebecca leaned back into her seat.

Buildings and homes gradually thinned out until there was nothing but vast stretches of young cornfields.

This was their first outing without the intent (or pretence, as Andrew sometimes reproached himself) of discussing the daycare proposal. Personal appreciation is how he framed the invitation. He scored it as a date. Although there wasn't abundant conversation thus far, neither was the silence oppressive. More like calm togetherness. Yes, that sounded good—calm togetherness. In any case, she trusted him enough to go out of town . . . in his car. That was something.

Andrew exited off the interstate to a two-lane roadway. "The scenic route begins."

"What's the name of this town?" asked Rebecca.

"I can't really remember, but I'll know it when I see it."

"Oh."

On they drove for about an hour.

"Maybe the town relocated, Andrew." Rebecca looked at Andrew with raised eyebrows.

"Or maybe aliens sucked it up," Andrew quipped back. "No, really, it has to be coming up."

"You've been saying that for a while. Do you have a map?"

"Who needs a map in this state? There's nothing here."

"I'm getting that distinct impression."

"Try the glove compart—" Without warning, the car began to shake and veer to the right. Rebecca tensed and grabbed on to the door handle.

"Oh, shit!" said Andrew as he slowed to a stop. "I think we have a flat."

Both hopped out of the car. Sure enough, the back right tire was flattened right out. "Damn it."

Rebecca looked around. Cornfields as far as the eye could see.

"I have triple-A, let me give them a call." Andrew pulled out his cell phone and card and was soon talking to a representative.

"An hour and a half at the earliest? . . . OK, OK . . . that's right, going west . . ." He hung up. "All their drivers are out on calls."

"On a day like today, more like out fishing," replied Rebecca.

Andrew opened the trunk and began to fumble around.

"When was the last time you had a flat?" asked Rebecca.

"I've never had one," Andrew replied. "My brother did about fifteen years ago and I helped him a bit. How about you?"

"Well . . . during Driver's Ed in high school I saw a movie on how to change flats. *And* I watched my dad about ten years ago. So I actually have more experience."

"What a team." Andrew laughed. "So, we can put together our combined wisdom and change this thing, or wait an hour and a half."

The sun was high and hot, and not a car had passed. They looked at each other and said simultaneously, "Let's change it."

Both began rummaging in the trunk and uncovered the latch for a sunken compartment. They pulled out the tire, careful not to rub anything against their shirts and pants—they were still going out to eat. Then they discovered the various hideaways for the jack and wrench. They laid everything out near the lame tire.

"OK, we have to figure out how this jack works," said Andrew. "Where's the handle?" He went to look in the trunk. Rebecca was looking at the wrench and fiddled around with the jack.

"It's here," Rebecca called to him. "This end of the wrench fits into this hook contraption."

"Now, where does it go?" said Andrew. Both squatted near the deflated tire, bending to look under the car and at the same time avoiding the gravel and dust. "I think I see the spot." Andrew slid the jack underneath the side frame.

"Wait," said Rebecca. "Before you jack it up we have to wedge the front tires with something. Do you have the emergency brake on?"

"I told you we were a team!" Andrew continued adjusting the jack and cranking it up to the level of the frame while Rebecca hunted around for larger rocks. She pulled up the brake and soon was squatting next to Andrew again. The back tire began to rise off the ground.

"Are we good or what!" Andrew said, smiling at Rebecca. It took a few minutes, but the tire was soon off the ground. He put the wrench to a bolt, but it wouldn't budge. More pressure. Not a fraction of an inch.

"I should have loosened the bolts first. We'll have to lower the damn car." Andrew cranked down the jack until the tire was firmly on the road again.

Andrew set out again to loosen the bolts. He pulled up on the wrench; he pushed down, but the bolts remained intractable. "Who in the hell put on these bolts, Godzilla?" Beads of sweat were forming on his forehead and trickling down his cheeks.

"Here, I have an idea." Rebecca picked up a large rock from the side of the road and came back to the car. "Hold the wrench like so and I'll hammer." Andrew held the wrench on one side of the tire; Rebecca faced him on the other. She hit the wrench. Nothing.

"One more time," she said. Nothing.

"Tell you what," said Andrew, "*you* hold the wrench like so and *I'll* hammer." Both were kneeling in the dirt, facing each other. Rebecca held the wrench, Andrew gave a mighty whack. The wrench went flying, leaving bright silver glints on the bolts.

"Andrew, we're stripping the bolts!"

"God, did they weld on these damn bolts?" Sweat was running down their necks, soaking through their shirts. Their hands were covered with dust and grime. Any thought about staying clean was gone.

"Rebecca, we need better leverage. Let's try this. You come here." He positioned Rebecca in front of the tire. "You push into the wrench, holding it in place at the top of the handle and on the bolt." Rebecca settled into a cross-legged position. Andrew knelt behind, straddling her with his legs. He reached around her shoulder and held on to the edge of the car frame with his left hand. Then, with his right hand holding the rock, he stretched around Rebecca, attempting to hit the wrench.

"We're still too far away. Rebecca, can you move in a little more?" Rebecca scooted in and Andrew moved in from behind.

"Here we go." He resumed his position, reached around Rebecca, and gave a bang on the wrench. The bolt gave way. Both cheered and hooted. Andrew took hold of Rebecca's shoulder and gave it a shake. "On to the next!"

Rebecca repositioned the wrench on the next bolt and Andrew leaned in. Rebecca's back was tight against his chest as she pushed against the wrench and he held onto the frame of the car. His arms encircled her shoulders and his cheek was resting against her forehead. He could smell her fading shampoo mixed with their fresh sweat. Rebecca Holden was in his arms . . . maybe not in the most romantic manner, but in his arms nonetheless. Whack!

One by one the bolts gave way. After they congratulated each other on their mechanical astuteness, Rebecca got up and pulled out the water bottles they had packed for the trip.

"Time to celebrate with a drink! If I wasn't so thirsty, I'd pour this over the both of us." They were soaked through with perspiration; blotched with dust, grease, and grime, their hair matted and wet.

"Aren't you glad we didn't wait for the AAA?" Andrew smiled. An hour had almost passed.

"It's a toss-up." Rebecca grinned. "I hope they have a hose when they finally show up."

They cranked up the car and removed the wheel. Down the road they could hear the noise of an oncoming vehicle—the first one they'd heard on this deserted rural route since their flat.

"Don't tell me it's the tow truck," said Andrew.

Both straightened up and looked down the road. A forty-foot livestock transporter was barrelling toward them. The road was a simple two-laner with no shoulder, and the driver showed no sign of slowing down.

"Rebecca!" exclaimed Andrew. He grabbed her arm and they ran off the road toward the cornfields. The truck passed with a gush of wind.

"Oh, my God," whispered Rebecca. The car was jacked up, the wheel off, and the bare axle exposed. The force of the air rocked the car toward the right. Both held their breaths. The car rocked back toward the left, then again to the right, and gradually stabilized.

"Oh, my God," Rebecca repeated as they both began to breathe again. The truck had disappeared in the distance. "Where in the hell did that come from?"

"Let's get that tire on before his brother comes by."

They hoisted up the tire and replaced the bolts.

"When this is done, we're going to party!" said Andrew. "Do we have anything in the car that hasn't melted or wilted!"

"I wish we had brought a shower!"

Andrew cranked down the jack and tightened the bolts.

"Are we good or what!" Both were in high spirits as they packed up the flat tire and tools, and kicked out the rocks that had wedged the front tires. Rebecca bent down to pick up an empty water bottle near the newly installed tire. She stopped, stared, and straightened up.

"Andrew, come here." He walked next to her and she pointed to the tire. Although not flat yet, the tire had definitely lost air since it first hit the ground.

"You have got to be kidding!"

The absurdity was beyond both. They laughed, Andrew with his arm around Rebecca's shoulder and hers around his waist.

"I cannot believe this!" Rebecca laughed, gesturing to the tire. She looked up at Andrew. It was so spontaneous, Andrew was barely aware of what he was doing. He pulled Rebecca in and kissed her gently on the lips.

Rebecca paused and looked at Andrew with a mixture of surprise and wonderment. Andrew kissed her again. Rebecca shifted, put her arms around his neck and kissed him back. She stayed in his arms and then began to weep on his shoulder.

"My God, Rebecca, what happened to you?" he whispered.

PART TWO

CHAPTER 35

The pipe organ intoned the opening chords; then the flutes and violins crescendoed in concert. Over a hundred nuns and dozens of young sisters-in-training stood in unison and began to sing. She closed her eyes, transported by the music and the harmonic commingling of their voices. A co-novice standing in line behind her tapped her back. Sr. Rebecca Marise looked up and noticed that the procession had begun to the front of the convent chapel.

The Feast of the Presentation of Jesus in the Temple: the day dedicated to Consecrated Life. It was a celebration of religious life, a life committed solely to Christ and his Church. Chosen to represent the entire community, the novices followed the solemn cross bearer flanked by two candle bearers. With a candle held aloft in their right hands, their left arms straight at their sides, and their heads slightly bowed, the novices proceeded in measured pace, two by two up the centre aisle. Their flowing garb and the glow from their flickering candle flames formed nebulous shadows on the burnished marble floors. The instruments and voices rose and swelled in the arches above. As they reached the front aisle, the novices bowed solemnly, genuflected, then concurrently turned in opposite directions and entered the gleaming pews from the sides. Sr. Rebecca Marise continued to sing in her pew, her voice blending and melding in symphony with the voices that enveloped her. The celebrant who had followed the novices up the aisle now gently swung a thurible as he walked around the altar, issuing clouds of incense, reverencing the sacred space. The chapel, the music, the singing, the movements, the incense, the flowers, the myriad of nuns in their long, graceful habits—everything synchronized, brilliant . . . ethereal.

"In the name of the Father, and of the Son, and of the Holy Spirit," proclaimed the priest.

Sr. Rebecca Marise discreetly wiped her welling tears.

~

It was unusually mild weather for March, so after cleaning the kitchen and washing the dishes from the noon meal, the sixteen second-year novices trooped down the wide, well-travelled path to the lake that bordered the property of the Sisters of Christ the Redeemer. Their novice mistress, the nun responsible for their training during their two-year novitiate, generally came along for their hikes but today had some other matters to attend to.

As they approached the shoreline, Sr. Patrick Marian brought up their escapade from the previous summer. "Admit it, Sr. Clement, you pushed me in."

"Pushed you in?? You were jumping from stone to stone with those old sandals of yours. You didn't need a push."

"That's exactly right," said Sr. Maura Fede. "You wanted to fall in."

Sr. Patrick Marian laughed and refuted the statement as preposterous, but her laughter and bright eyes showed Sr. Maura Fede was on the mark.

That day last summer had been so hot. The novices preferred to be inside their air-conditioned community room or at least under a tree reading a book. But the novice mistress felt they could all use some exercise, so suppressing their displeasure, they set out on their mandatory march and tried to make the best of it. Some of the novices reached the lakeside before the others who were walking at a more leisurely pace with the novice mistress. Waiting for the rest to catch up, these novices began to walk on the large stones that extended into the lake. Shrieks and screams brought the slower group running, only to find seven novices in the lake in full habit with one standing by the shoreline. Sr. Patrick Marian had fallen and the rest went "to assist her." The water only came to their waist when standing but Sr. Patrick Marian and a couple of others managed to slip and slide until they were soaked from veil to shoe. That brought the hike to an abrupt end—to the silent contentment of all the novices.

"And only Sr. Rebecca Marise could not have cared less whether I drowned. She just stood there and watched from the shoreline," said Sr. Patrick Marian, still laughing.

"I wasn't going to spend the rest of the afternoon washing my habit," said Sr. Rebecca Marise.

"Well, it's a little too cool for a fall today, so let's stay off the rocks," said another novice.

They followed the lakeshore until they reached a natural clearing that had been improved with benches and a barbeque pit. The novices sat in a semicircle around the empty pit. Beneath their light-hearted chatter, smoldered a mutual unspoken apprehension. Their letters requesting permission to make first profession and, with that, formal admittance into the congregation of the Sisters of Christ the Redeemer, had been submitted to Mother General, but they had no idea when they would receive her letter of acceptance.

If there was a problem or impediment, surely the individual would already know . . . you would think. . . . But this was a subject they were not to discuss except with their novice mistress or their designated priest confessor. Of course, in doing chores with one or the other, the subject could be broached without notice. Inevitably, though, the novice mistress would come to find out. And disobedience and morbid curiosity weren't traits to support one's continuance in religious life.

Their taut frame of mind eventually squelched the small talk and the novices found themselves sitting on the benches, pushing pebbles with the toes of their shoes, stirring the ashes with a branch, or gazing out into the lake to the housing development on the other side.

In an attempt to break the silence, one novice said, "What did you think of Sr. Petrina's class?" Sr. Petrina was a general councillor and taught the novices her purported specialty, the history of the SCRs.

～

Sr. Petrina's presentation had begun with a series of images projected on a screen in the darkened room, pictures of religious orders from the fifties and early sixties. Newly professed sisters, all in starched, fresh habits, stood several rows deep on stairs leading to their basilica-sized chapels—thirty, fifty, even a hundred new sisters per year. Aerial views captured sprawling convent grounds that encompassed the schools, hospitals, and colleges run by the sisters as well as the extensive residences and classrooms for their sisters and numerous recruits.

Maps showed the expansions of religious orders throughout the US and in mission countries.

In stark contrast were current photos of the same religious orders. Diminished bands of elderly sisters posed in gardens or sat in some undistinguished room, dressed in blouses, skirts, slacks, a few with veils, most without. Convent complexes, once vibrant with young sisters and apostolic activity, were now decaying retreat centres or had been renovated and renamed by the organizations who had purchased them.

The before-and-after sequence was followed by statistics: in 1965, 180,000 sisters in the US; currently only 70,000, with a vast percentage over retirement age.

Sr. Petrina lifted a window shade in the back of the room, illuminating the classroom enough to see the faces of the novices. Returning to the front of the room, she pointed to the image of the aging, weary sisters she had left on the screen.

"How could this have happened?" Without waiting for a response, she proceeded to answer her own question. "The misinterpretation of Vatican II. A discontinuity with the traditions of the Church."

For these young sisters Vatican II was not a distant memory. It was ancient history, much like the Civil War, the Great Depression, or World War II. Before their entrance to religious life, most had never studied the Vatican Council, which, well over thirty years before, was alleged to have opened the windows of an anachronistic Church to the realities and needs of the modern world. Throughout their years of training—formation, as the nuns called it—the new SCR recruits were brought up to speed.

Vatican II, they learned, had been misinterpreted and the experimentation that followed it in religious communities, ill-advised. The effects of this "reform" had been drastic—at least in the Western world. Within congregations of religious life, communal prayer lessened to little or nil. The habit was abandoned. Indiscriminate reading and viewing of TV programs and films, the novices were taught, opened convents to confusion and worldliness. Sisters left their schools and hospitals to develop other apostolic endeavours that they considered more suited to the times. "Personal" missions replaced the united, corporate apostolic works of the past, leaving these "renewed" congregations without focus and direction. Educated in universities that opened Church teaching to discussion and revision, these sisters grew to disrespect the Pope and the hierarchy. Radical feminism infiltrated their communities and some sisters demanded that women be ordained. As a result thousands of sisters defected and few entered to replace them. The novices were astounded by the blindness and audacity of these religious orders.

The young candidates of the Sisters of Christ the Redeemer were told that not all religious orders capitulated to this interpretation of Vatican II. Some courageous religious women stood firm in their resolve to preserve religious life in all its fullness. The Sisters of Christ the Redeemer, the SCRs, had been blessed with Sr. Mary Ambrosia, God rest her soul, and Mother Mary Thomas who, though young at the time, stood faithfully beside her.

~

The SCRs had been almost invisible among the burgeoning institutions in the fifties. Founded at the turn of the twentieth century and bound within a relatively isolated diocese of sprawling farmland and limited industry, their members hovered around eighty nuns for decades.

They reviewed their constitutions and customs as required by the Council; however, Sr. Mary Ambrosia had the astuteness to see through the ambiguities of the time and held fast to the traditions of their founder. Their sacred habit was slightly modified to a more simple design and sewn with a fabric easier to launder, as were their numerous undergarments. But to anyone outside the community, the alterations were imperceptible except for the veil. It now lay across the head with the hairline slightly visible rather than elevated on a boxed headpiece that had framed their faces and pinched their foreheads. Some phrases from the documents of Vatican II were integrated within their constitutions but, by and large, the SCRs continued as staunchly as before.

And now the foresight and fidelity of Sr. Mary Ambrosia, and those who followed her, had been rewarded. The documents—*Essential Elements of Religious Life* and, later, *Vita Consecrata*—confirmed all they believed in. Unlike the majority of religious congregations who were diminishing with age, they, and several like-minded religious orders, were receiving growing numbers of new recruits.

Mother Mary Thomas often reminded the novices, "We have forged a foundation rooted in fidelity to Christ and his Church. On this foundation an edifice of religious life is soaring upward through the grace of God." A conviction that was underscored by her arm bolting heavenward, stopped only by a jolt from her shoulder. "As St. Paul exhorted the Ephesians, we are called to attain the fullness of Christ. We are not children tossed to and fro (she moved her hand in a dismissive motion from side to side) and carried about with every wind of doctrine coming from the mouths of the proud and deceitful. And what preserves us from being tossed about? Fidelity to the Pope and the teachings of the Church."

~

One of the novices jabbed her branch into the pit, breaking a disintegrating piece of charcoal.

"I just don't get it. The SCRs follow the teachings of the Church and look how many vocations we have. Don't the other orders notice that? It seems rather obvious to me."

"It must have been great to live in the fifties when Catholics were strong in the faith and there were so many sisters and priests," said another. "Here we are in the culture of death."

There were many aspects of religious life that energized Sr. Rebecca Marise: singing and prayer, camaraderie with young women sharing the same ideals, working with children in SCR schools, the joy on the faces of people when they saw young sisters . . . and in full habit! Yet when conversations centred on the woes and evils in the Church and the world, Sr. Rebecca Marise was filled with a sense of foreboding, like she was on a sinking ship in polluted water.

Sr. Petrina's class had left her numb. "Remember," she had cautioned, "the decline of great religious orders begins with the little things: neglecting time of prayer, giving into distractions, fretting about your appearance, wanting eyeglass frames, shoes and sweaters other than those prescribed. . . . I hope you're writing this down!"

The novices jotted down her words with greater intensity.

"Neglecting the little things"—Sr. Petrina walked back and forth in front of the desks, closely observing the novices—"laxity in following the schedule, dissipating your spirit during the days with your families by watching worldly films and TV programs and reading worldly novels . . ." She paused. "What we read—this is very important. We endanger our vocation, indeed, our immortal souls, by reading materials that are contrary to the teachings of the Church. Follow the recommended list given by the superiors. The devil is sly."

Sr. Petrina then began to walk up and down the rows. "You may think these things are all rather insignificant." Sr. Rebecca Marise tensed as she passed and wrote feverishly in her notebook. "A slight neglect here, a little disregard there. But look at the other orders"—she pointed to the picture still projected on the screen: the dwindling group of older nuns. "It all begins with the little things and this is the result!"

Sr. Petrina was again at the front, looking directly at each of them.

"Follow the traditions of the Sisters of Christ the Redeemer as they are laid out in our constitutions and taught by our superiors or," her voice surging, "our end will be no different. Our constitutions have been approved by the Church—*by the Pope*—and therefore are a guaranteed path to sanctity. Always adhere to the words of the Pope. St. Catherine of Siena called him 'the sweet Christ on earth.' This is the surety left us by Christ. Fidelity to the Holy Father and the hierarchy in union with him. This is our rock in these times of darkness. Is this not what we profess in the Act of Faith? Let us recite it now."

The novices bowed their heads and recited the prayer they knew by heart: "O my God, I firmly believe that you are one God in three Divine Persons . . . I believe your Divine Son became man, and died for our sins . . . I believe . . . all the truths the Holy Catholic Church teaches because You have revealed them, who can neither deceive nor be deceived."

Sr. Petrina picked up her Bible from the desk and opened it.

"I conclude our class with a reading from Galatians, chapter one. May these words of the apostle Paul never be applied to any of you:

"I am astonished that you are so quickly deserting the one who called you in the grace of Christ and are turning to a different gospel— not that there is another gospel, but there are some who are confusing you and want to pervert the gospel of Christ. (Sr. Petrina raised her voice.) But even if we or an angel from heaven should proclaim to you a gospel contrary to what we proclaimed to you, let that one be accursed! As we have said before, so now I repeat, if anyone proclaims to you a gospel contrary to what you received, let that one be accursed!"

With that, Sr. Petrina left the room. Sr. Rebecca Marise, still holding her pen, blanched.

~

The crunch of gravel underfoot turned their heads to the path near the shoreline. They expected the novice mistress but instead saw Sr. Miriam Pistós.

"The novice mistress told me I would find you here," she said as she approached the semicircle.

The novices greeted her and made room on one of the benches. When the novice mistress was busy, Sr. Pistós was generally sent to "be" with them. She was one of the few professed allowed to converse with the novices, and only when replacing the novice mistress. She took out her handkerchief and wiped the bench, then turned and arranged her pleats so that, as she sat, they fell in line. Sr. Rebecca Marise felt some resentment at her coming—the novices were rarely left alone. No sooner had this feeling surfaced than Sr. Rebecca Marise, ashamed, dismissed it as wilfulness and pride.

The conversation stopped at the arrival of Sr. Pistós and was slow to resume. "So what have you been talking about?"

One of the novices told Sr. Pistós about Sr. Petrina's class and their perplexity over the stance of other religious communities who were aging and shrinking while the SCRs were thriving.

"They thought they had all the answers after Vatican II but even as they see their communities declining, they're too proud to rescind. Like adolescents who never grow up," Sr. Pistós elucidated.

Sr. Miriam Pistós was different than most of the younger sisters. Sr. Rebecca Marise had attended SCR schools from elementary to college and had always been enamoured by their life and work. After a year in their college, she joined their order. Outside of a few vacations, her life had been spent in the state. Sr. Patrick Marian met the sisters for the first time at a pro-life rally. She called it "love at first sight" and entered within months. There were some novices from other parts of the US, with varied experiences, but very few entered with an MA and a previous career as Sr. Pistós had. She came from outside the state and had attended a progressive Catholic high school yet managed to preserve her faith within a lay movement of committed Catholic teens. Many stories from this period of her life were known by the novices because Sr. Pistós was often asked to share her vocation story with the groups of young women discerning their vocation. After high school Sr. Pistós went up north to a university known for its fidelity to the Church. She obtained a teaching degree and an MA in theology, then taught for a few years before discerning her vocation to religious life. She came to the SCRs with "experience" and was fast-tracked through the formation process: the period of temporary profession was shortened to the requisite minimum due to her maturity and her solid Catholic education. She had made her perpetual profession—committed herself permanently to the SCRs—the previous summer.

Sr. Pistós continued, "I went to an ordination of a friend up north, and outside the cathedral there was a group—with nuns among them—who were protesting, demanding ordination for women. It was so disrespectful . . . so disruptive for the families and friends who were there to celebrate with the newly ordained."

"How immature. The Pope has spoken so clearly. Women aren't meant to be priests."

"They just want power," added another novice. "If Christ had wanted women ordained, he would have included the Blessed Mother among the apostles."

"There are so many things we can do as nuns and women," said another. "Why get so hung up on the priesthood?"

"It's the radical feminists—everything a man does, women have to do," continued Sr. Pistós. She sat upright with her hands folded on her lap, just as they were taught to do. "Women have particular gifts and men, their own. The Pope has clearly delineated this in his teachings. Equal in dignity, complementary in roles. Mary supported the apostles, she wasn't one. And she didn't demand to be one."

"It's such a pity, looking at the pictures of some religious communities and seeing what they have become," said Sr. Maura Fede.

"You cut yourself off from the Vicar of Christ and the teachings of the Church and you drift," said Sr. Pistós. "Vocations are a sign of God's blessing." Then, looking at her watch, "We'd better head back."

∽

Sr. Rebecca Marise went to the chapel a few minutes before community prayers were due to begin. This was her favourite time—silent, quiet, alone before the

Blessed Sacrament. The anxiety of waiting for her acceptance letter and talk of the darkness of the times left her restless and depressed. But here in the silence, here in the presence of Christ, she could settle. Her relationship with Jesus was simple, had always been.

Although the sisters were discouraged from talking about their families and their pasts, they could share their "vocation stories"—the journey that brought them to the SCRs. Some of the sisters recounted their "reversions" to Christ and the Church—their "coming back" to the faith or taking it more seriously. Others recounted their resistance to Christ's call before finally yielding to his grace (although Sr. Rebecca Marise had to hold back a smile when one nineteen-year-old postulant said she struggled with God for seventeen years before accepting his call). But neither reversion nor resistance had been the case for Sr. Rebecca Marise. She came from a devote Catholic family, had been raised in the teachings of the Church, and believed them. She loved Jesus. It wasn't an exuberant, *stand-up-and-shout* kind of love. It just was. She wanted to please Christ and easily turned to him for help throughout the day. Above all, she wanted to do God's will in her life. She felt increasingly drawn to spend her life totally for Christ among the SCRs and entered the order.

Sr. Rebecca Marise cherished these quiet moments alone. She didn't have to worry about the future, she told herself. Jesus would be with her. Jesus would be with his Church and his Vicar, the Pope. All she had to do was trust and be faithful.

The next day as the novices sat in their desks going over their notes and adding citations from their prescribed reading, they were interrupted by the entrance of their novice mistress and Mother Mary Thomas. They rose to their feet as one. This could only mean one thing, couldn't it? Though not really knowing what to expect, the room was charged with anticipation of the news of their acceptance.

"You may be seated," said the general superior. Down they went Mother Mary Thomas sat behind the desk while the novice mistress pulled up a chair and sat off to the side.

"I have some news I believe you have been waiting for."

Some of the novices let out a muffled, jittery laugh.

"All of you have been accepted and will make your first profession among the Sisters of Christ the Redeemer."

A cheer went up among the novices, and the novice mistress smiled broadly at their joy and relief. She and Mother Mary Thomas exchanged glances of contentment. After a few moments, Mother Mary Thomas tapped on the desk to bring them to order.

"You may have noticed that Sr. Maura Fede is no longer among you. It was discerned that God is calling her elsewhere and she left the community this morning. She wishes you all well. Let us keep her in our prayers as she continues her search for God's will in her life."

Sr. Maura Fede? thought Sr. Rebecca Marise. She was at breakfast.

Today their normally scheduled class had been replaced with spring yardwork, and with all of them divided among different chores, Sr. Rebecca Marise hadn't missed Sr. Maura Fede. She could usually tell when someone was slated to leave the SCRs, but Sr. Maura Fede had slipped under her radar. *Not accepted to make her first profession? What could have prompted her dismissal?* Not that they were especially close—closeness was not encouraged and Sr. Maura Fede was quite reserved—but she seemed committed and content. Just once, shortly after both entered the convent, had they shared a confidence. Sr. Maura Fede's parents were refugees and read little English, yet all correspondence had to be written in English because their letters were reviewed by the postulant mistress. Sr. Rebecca Marise had found Sr. Maura Fede crying in the bathroom because she could not write directly to her parents—a relative or friend had to translate. She rallied when, during one of their first classes, their postulant mistress said that their families would be blessed through their obedience. Sr. Rebecca Marise never mentioned the incident to anyone and Sr. Maura Fede never brought it up again.

Sr. Maura Fede . . . gone! Sr. Rebecca Marise had to put it out of her mind. The superiors knew more, knew best. As with other departures, there would be no further mention of Sr. Maura Fede in community or among the novices. With the ebb and flow of class, prayer, community chores, and immediate preparation for first profession, memory of her gradually dissipated.

CHAPTER 36

St. Patrick's Elementary School. All practicums for the sisters' teaching degrees took place in schools a stone's throw from the motherhouse. The SCRs had a college in Slandail close to the motherhouse where their nuns were educated and trained. Sr. Rebecca Marise had always longed to be a teacher. Three years after the first profession of her vows, her degree was just around the corner.

At St. Patrick's, Sr. Rebecca Marise was assigned to the fifth grade class of Sr. Roberto Mary. Jerome caught her attention immediately. He rarely smiled, responded only when pressed, and struggled in every area except art. In addition to teaching religion and language arts, Sr. Roberto Mary assigned Sr. Rebecca Marise to students who needed coaching in various subjects. Jerome was an unusual case—he needed assistance in everything.

"Hard to believe he's from the same family as Angela," said Sr. Roberto Mary one day after class.

"Angela?"

"His sister. I had her a few years ago. Stellar."

St. Patrick's was one of the SCR's private schools with high standards for admission. After a couple of weeks with Jerome, Sr. Rebecca Marise was amazed that he had been admitted. From his records, she could see that he barely managed to maintain their minimum prerequisites and often slipped under.

"He also has a younger brother in third grade—Joseph, I believe. The parents didn't want Jerome to go to any other school and promised to supplement with private tutoring." She lowered her voice a bit. "They're also big donors."

One day during recess, Sr. Rebecca Marise saw Jerome sitting on the steps of a side entrance, drawing in his sketch pad. She joked with a few students and kicked a couple of stray balls as she gradually made her way to Jerome.

"You really like to draw," she said as she got closer.

Jerome continued without responding or looking up.

"May I see what you are drawing?"

He shrugged his shoulder slightly. Sr. Rebecca Marise sat down next to him and peered over his shoulder. A motorcycle. The detail and precision amazed her. Not wanting to push her tenuous success, she sat quietly and observed Jerome as he continued his drawing.

That afternoon, the fifth grade students filed out of their classroom to the gym for PE. At noon, Sr. Roberto Mary had gone to the motherhouse for a meeting, so Sr. Rebecca Marise had the classroom to herself. She went to Jerome's desk and pulled out his sketch pad. Bikes, motorcycles, cars. Mostly motorcycles. Sr. Rebecca Marise didn't know the difference between one motorcycle or another but she could tell Jerome did. Each bike was different from the others, with its logo carefully replicated. At the back of the pad were several pictures of motorcycles torn from newspapers. Sr. Rebecca Marise closed the pad and returned it to the desk. She knew Jerome was bright. She worked one-on-one with him every day and as he began to relax with her, his answers expanded from the monosyllabic responses of the first week. He struggled with comprehension and retention, but once he grasped a concept, he had it. Three weeks into her practicum, she saw him smile for the first time when he was able to explain the difference between a country and a continent.

Sr. Rebecca Marise walked to the teacher's desk and began marking papers but, before long, she was looking out the window and thinking of the sketch pad. She got up and went to the school library.

The librarian looked up at Sr. Rebecca Marise over her reading glasses. "Motorcycles?"

"Anything on motorcycles. Stories about motorcycles . . . how motorcycles are made . . . famous people and motorcycles . . . Jesus and motorcycles!"

"I see where we are going. Unfortunately, the pickings are slim."

They managed to find a pictorial history of motor vehicles, which included motorcycles, a junior novel with a young man on the cover sitting on a motorcycle, and articles in the encyclopedia.

"I think this is it," said the librarian. "We would have done much better if you had asked for dinosaurs."

That evening in her room, Sr. Rebecca Marise poured over her treasures and reviewed her curriculum outline for LA.

The next day Sr. Roberto Mary listened as Sr. Rebecca Mary laid out her plan. Substituting in some cases, supplementing in others, she incorporated motorcycles into Jerome's study plan.

"Well, it certainly won't hurt him and just might help. Give it a try."

Sr. Rebecca Marise never mentioned her plan to Jerome. Casually, she opened the history of motor vehicles in one of their sessions together.

"I found this book in the library. I wondered if you might like it." Jerome turned the pages with a regard that bordered on reverence. "There's a section over here on motorcycles. You can look it over while I help Amy with her LA assignment."

As Sr. Rebecca Marise circulated throughout the room, she kept an eye on Jerome. She never saw him so engrossed in a book. After school she wrote a quick letter to her brother, Rob, who lived with his young family in California.

By the end of the week, even Sr. Roberto Mary acknowledged Jerome's engrossment in "the book" and allowed Sr. Rebecca Marise to meet with Jerome's mother. Mrs. Padia was delighted with her suggestions for his private tutoring.

Every afternoon when Sr. Rebecca Marise returned to the convent after school, she glanced expectantly at a side table in the refectory, the convent dining room, on which the community newsletters and the personal mail for the sisters was placed. One afternoon on her way to perform this little ritual, the local superior called out from her office door, "Sr. Rebecca Marise?"

"Yes," said Sr. Rebecca Marise as she walked back a couple of steps to the door.

"Have a seat."

Perplexed, Sr. Rebecca Marise stepped into the office and sat in a chair, conscious all the while of being observed closely by the superior, her hands resting on an oversized envelope in the centre of her desk.

"A packet arrived for you today. It was a little out of the ordinary, so I opened it."

Sr. Rebecca Marise reddened. Reading personal mail, both incoming and outgoing, was the norm throughout the initial years of formation. After two years of temporary vows, the practice was sporadic, reserved for particular cases. Rebecca had nothing to hide, she had done nothing wrong, yet the mere hint of distrust filled her with guilt.

"Motorcycle magazines?" the superior asked with a touch of sarcasm, holding up a periodical.

"They're for a pupil . . . a special project. Sr. Roberto Mary knows about it . . . has approved."

"And," pulling out a short, handwritten note, "who is Rob?"

"My older brother . . . in California. He often sends teaching supplies. He likes to—"

"Oh . . ." She laughed, leaning back in her chair. "It was all so odd. I thought you were getting ready to speed off into the wild blue yonder."

Sr. Rebecca Marise laughed on cue like a squeeze doll, but she wasn't amused. The suspicion and implications were so unexpected and nocuous. Although the clarification was swift and amusing to the superior, for Sr. Rebecca Marise it was hardly a relief in comparison to the gravity of the insinuation. Her hands were clammy and wet as she took the large envelope from the superior and left the office.

Rebecca, how could you be so stupid? she berated herself as she walked down the hall. *You should have told the superior the magazines were coming in—the whole scene could have been avoided.* It just never occurred to her. Sr. Roberto Mary had approved of her plans. *Had the superior already spoken to Mother Mary Thomas? They were so vigilant of the "young ones."* Another wave of distress washed over her. She opened the door to her cell, grateful for the private room that came with the profession of vows. She sat on the wooden chair near her desk— the bed was only used for sleeping. Accusing, debasing thoughts tumbled one over the other, exacerbated by the fear of being reported. From past experience, she knew this brooding would only lead to a spiral of intensifying anxiety.

Rebecca, stop it. Stop. It. Now, she told herself. *There was nothing wrong with what you did. God knows. What others make of it is their problem. God knows the truth,* she coaxed herself. *Let it be.*

Gradually, her mind calmed. Her hands still trembled as she lifted the open envelope and shook out its contents onto her desk. A little note dropped out with them, falling to the floor. Sr. Rebecca Marise picked it up and shook her head as she read,

Rebecca,

Any time.

Rob

Lest it be misunderstood again, she tore the note into small pieces, turned on the faucet in the small corner sink and removed the drain stopper. One by one she dropped the fragments into the swirling water and watched them disappear down the drain.

~

Jerome sucked his breath back in astonishment when Sr. Rebecca Marise slid the shiny, new *Cycle Planet* across his desk. His reaction more than made up for the angst it had created the previous afternoon. She had decided to dispense the magazines as incentives. However, she underestimated Jerome's enthusiasm. He was spellbound with the issue and a few days later told her that his parents had purchased the same copy *and* gotten him a subscription. He pulled out a glossy motorcycle picture from his own edition—a mechanical centrefold.

Sr. Rebecca Marise went full throttle. Visits to the library and conversations with the maintenance men and a science teacher expanded her meagre knowledge of cars, motors, and mechanics. Math concepts and problems were converted into combustion, horsepower, and mileage. Reading assignments were enriched with large doses from the magazines and other vehicle-related material. She even found a biography of a missionary who did all his travelling by motorcycle. Unfortunately, the author did not think it important to note the model and year, a real disappointment for Jerome. He could only speculate from some fuzzy snapshots in the book.

Jerome still struggled with his school work, but his enthusiasm and attention grew and his outlook brightened. He came to school with snippets of information regarding the latest models, and a couple of boys began to share his affection for motorcycles. In time, he allowed the other students to see the pictures in his sketchbook and some wanted Jerome to draw them riding one of the bikes. His grades moved up and he even managed to squeak out a B in an LA assignment. Mrs. Padia was elated. She never passed Sr. Rebecca Marise without giving her a hug. The highlight was Jerome's class presentation: "Motorcycles through the Ages." If some students found motorcycles dull, they enjoyed trying to identify the various classmates Jerome attempted to sketch in some of his pictures.

Jerome's story would have remained in the fifth grade classroom if it were not for comments made by Mrs. Padia to the superior and the teachers of her other children. However, little was said among the sisters regarding Sr. Rebecca

Marise's techniques or her success with Jerome—pride was always lurking around the corner. Besides, Jerome was a special case not frequently encountered at the school.

Sr. Rebecca Marise was oblivious to their prudence. Modest regarding her achievements, she instinctively refrained from ever speaking about Jerome or the other students, but in her heart she never stopped thanking God. At the conclusion of her practicum, she was given a positive evaluation from Sr. Roberto Mary and had an even greater desire to be in the classroom.

The student sisters returning from their practicum experiences were welcomed back to their residence on the SCRs' college campus with a special supper. Sr. Henrietta, a general councillor, came from the motherhouse and gave the opening remarks on behalf of Mother Mary Thomas. The customary spiritual reading was dispensed and replaced with lively conversation. As the young sisters were leaving the refectory, Sr. Henrietta came up from behind and tapped Sr. Rebecca Marise's shoulder.

"Motorcycles," she whispered with a smile, "well done," and walked on.

Sr. Rebecca Marise glowed.

~

Sr. Henrietta was relatively new to the general council. For twenty years she served as a mistress of the young women entering their community. Personally, Sr. Henrietta preferred the title, Formator or Director, but the use of Mistress was so ensconced within SCR practice and tradition that the incongruity of its use within religious life, given the prevalent connotation of *mistress* in society, eluded the mother general and those who surrounded her. The title, Mistress, remained despite a few gentle suggestions by Sr. Henrietta to reconsider it.

Her first several years as mistress were spent with the postulants—those new arrivals just crossing the threshold of religious life from the secular world. It was a period of instruction, adaptation, and selection before the secluded, incisive period of novitiate.

However, the majority of her years as mistress, and those she enjoyed the most, were among the student sisters completing their studies following novitiate. Sisters at this stage were called temporarily professed, student sisters, junior sisters, or, more commonly, just "the juniors." Beginning with their first profession at the end of novitiate, the sisters in this five-year period, renewed their vows annually, finished the education requisite to become teachers, took up teaching positions within the congregation's schools, and, in the final six months, prepared to make a lifelong commitment to the SCRs—perpetual profession or final vows.

Sr. Rebecca Marise had just entered postulancy when Sr. Henrietta was elected to the council. As general councillor, Sr. Henrietta was responsible for overseeing the programs of formation and studies. Since the formation of young sisters was considered the heart and pulse of the SCRs, Mother Mary Thomas was involved in every detail and every decision as well. Yet, due to her past experience, Sr. Henrietta was more attuned to the individual sisters as they progressed through the ranks.

Amidst the large number of women joining the community, Sr. Rebecca Marise drew no particular attention. She had entered at nineteen with some college education—typical of many—and went through the formation process in stride with the rest. She was neither tall nor short, fat nor thin, gorgeous nor homely, blending in with her hazel eyes and brown hair. Her reports were consistently positive: faithful to prayer, collaborative, thoughtful of others, dedicated to her studies and assignments, committed to the spirit and mission of the SCRs, yet in no way remarkable in comparison to the others.

As councillor of formation, Sr. Henrietta had access to the reports of the temporary professed sisters and she reviewed them all. And so it was that she read the practicum evaluation of Sr. Roberto Mary. It was the first time Sr. Rebecca Marise blipped above the median. From the evaluation, Sr. Henrietta sensed that Sr. Rebecca Marise did not just love teaching, she was passionate. She had connected and adapted in order to draw out the abilities of the children. The superior's evaluation, on the other hand, was similar to previous reports. Sr. Rebecca Marise was observant and prayerful, generous in community, devoted to the Church and its teachings. These qualities were mere check marks without comment, at par with the expected.

Not that Sr. Henrietta considered this a fault.

During the turbulent years following Vatican II, the SCRs clung together and braved the battle as a small, local congregation. They had few but steady numbers of vocations. Staunchly clinging to the traditions of the past and insisting on absolute loyalty to the Pope and to Church teaching, they were tolerated or ignored among the more prominent and progressive religious orders. The SCRs lost some members who questioned the wisdom and authority of Mother Mary Ambrosia, but being a small congregation these had been few. In time, John Paul II was elected Pope and the dust began to settle. As the mainstream congregations haemorrhaged hundreds of members and gained few, the number of vocations to the SCRs slowly increased. During the past decade, their growth had been unprecedented and they garnered the notice and support of high-ranking members of the hierarchy. Mother Mary Thomas was honoured among the leaders of like-minded religious orders, several of whom were also growing prodigiously. It was amazing to witness.

At the same time, a stance, difficult to name and even harder to address, was also surfacing. Sr. Henrietta noted among the superiors and many of the sisters a . . . a . . . It was so nebulous, she found it hard to even articulate. It was a . . . particular flourish when expressing their gratitude to God for the blessing of their numerous vocations—always linked to their fidelity to the Pope and religious habit. In her later years as mistress, and now as councillor, she perceived a certain zeal, . . . surety, . . . even hauteur, among some of the younger sisters. They were thoroughly convinced of their vocation, resolute in their allegiance—jubilant, really. Wasn't that right, wasn't that to be lauded? And wasn't their distain justified on occasion, given the trends prevalent in society and among certain sectors in the Church? So what was it that made her uncomfortable?

In this regard, Sr. Rebecca Marise was inconspicuous. Had Sr. Henrietta known her better, it would not have been surprising. Sr. Rebecca Marise had no experience of religious life outside the SCRs. Her education and extracurricular activities revolved around the sisters and organizations that shared their perspective, or her mother's, which was one and the same with the SCRs. Regarding the deviations, virtues, or dissipations of other religious orders and the dismal condition of humanity, she accepted what she was taught. She had heard plenty throughout her childhood—and continued to hear plenty—from her mother. It was all reinforced by what she learned in class, gleaned from sermons, and read in the periodicals recommended by the superiors—the world was on a fast track toward impending doom. The sisters, instead, were buoyant and so zealous to have new members share their life. When among them, Sr. Rebecca Marise felt lifted up, banded together with sisters under the guidance of superiors who supported them on their journey toward eternal life. Together they brought Christ's light to the darkness surrounding them.

When Sr. Rebecca Marise dwelt on the dire prognosis of the world, desolation seeped through her pores and enveloped her spirit, strangling hope and suffocating her initiative. Avoidance of this despondency filtered her spiritual reading. She focused on the passages that inspired her, and threw herself into the mission that gave her meaning and joy: serving Christ in the children she taught.

CHAPTER 37

The bus wound its way through the foothills toward the mountains, leaving behind the flatlands and its meandering lakes, headed toward Whitewaters. Sr. Rebecca Marise looked out the bus window at the rolling hills. Her mother found the mountains confining, so their family vacations took place in a rented cottage on the lake. Driving into the mountains was unknown and mysterious.

Whitewaters, on the western rim of the state, was several hours from Slandail; however, it was so inconsequential it could have been on the moon. Toward the end of the nineteenth century, talk of an extensive ore deposit attracted speculators and brought in itinerant labourers hungering for work and a new life. But the deposit proved to be smaller and less accessible than alleged, diverting the fortune seekers to a flourishing site further south. Without knowing its early history, the town would appear to be a dead end: a group of settlers, wending their way through the tortuous contours of the Appalachians, unable to skirt the precipitous ravines or see into their misty depths, set up camp and never left.

Whitewaters remained on the map due to its modest furniture industry, a rail line that the speculators had pushed through, and, surprisingly, its location. Whitewaters butted into mountain country with its scattered hamlets and family plots where the inhabitants had sought to eke out a livelihood from the rough terrain. To the north, a few subordinate coal mines had burrowed into isolated hollows, following veins of ore until it was no longer profitable. Like the streams and tributaries that flowed into the narrow Whitewaters River, the inhabitants of these small rural communities made their way to Whitewaters to sell what they could and stock up on staples. Early on, an affluent and judicious Whitewaters family began a modest teachers' college in order to provide educators for the rural communities. Eventually, a community college developed and a regional hospital was established. In time, the reasons for trekking down to Whitewaters expanded beyond shopping to truck repairs, doctors' appointments, minor operations, entrance exams, community theatre, and blockbuster movies. Tourists passed through on their way to the national park or larger cities to the south.

Although predominantly white and Protestant, the Whitewaters region was also home to a smattering of minorities, and a token representation of the native American tribe that once inhabited the region.

~

For the SCRs, establishing a school in a locale such as Whitewaters was unprecedented—the Catholic population was less than 5 percent. And truth be told, the decision would never have been made without the strong encouragement from the bishop at the time.

In the mid-seventies, some local priests drew up a statement indicating the diocese's negligible presence among the poor in the sparsely populated, marginally Catholic mountain region. This small group of clergy drew heavily from the Council document, *Gaudium et Spes*, which emphasized Christ's solidarity with those who suffer, and they challenged the local church to do the same.

The statement, signed by the members of the group, concluded with a proposal for a diocesan outreach project in Whitewaters and it was presented to the bishop. Local support was pledged by a few wealthy Catholics in the mountain community. A national Catholic outreach organization also promised financial assistance, reducing to a minimum the financial commitment from the diocese. So, in a flush of concern and a desire to minister to the less fortunate, St. Martin de Porres parish was established in the heart of Appalachia. The SCRs were invited by the bishop to join this missionary venture and staff an elementary school. The school would be subsidized with promised funds from the outreach organization in order to offer a Catholic education to those who would not otherwise be able to afford it. The SCRs accepted, considering it their "missionary territory."

In the beginning, the new foundation generated much interest and esprit de corps among the SCRs. The seven "missionary" sisters mailed in anecdotes and progress reports. The community was often featured in the congregation's internal newsletter. At the end of the school year, the sisters returned to the motherhouse amid much fanfare for annual retreat, vacation, and professional development. They departed with similar pomp in August.

Over time, the novelty waned and other apostolic initiatives took precedence. Due to greater needs in larger centres, the Whitewaters community was reduced to four sisters approaching retirement age, not that any sister actually retired. While Whitewaters always maintained the distinction of *the missionary project* (which kept it in existence), the tiny community drifted into the shadows of the congregation's attention, and its current inhabitants sought to keep it that way.

Unfortunately, a couple of weeks before school began, one of the four, Sr. Anita, had a heart attack, sending Mother General and her councillors into a flurry. Sr. Anita was brought by ambulance to a hospital near the motherhouse to have her condition assessed. A replacement was imperative. But whom to send? All the sisters slated to teach were in their local communities gearing up for the first day of classes, now only a week away. In addition, the diocese's anniversary celebrations were set to launch within the year and the SCRs held key positions on the coordinating team. As the preparations progressed, a select group of sisters were designated to fill out committees for various events. These sisters had been assigned teaching positions close to the motherhouse specifically for this reason, further reducing an already limited selection.

Mother Mary Thomas sat behind her desk and scanned the list of sisters once again. Sr. Henrietta, called in to assist her, sat in front of the desk with her own copy, marking a few possibilities with an asterisk and putting a line through the names of those definitely out of consideration. For a while they carried out their task in silence.

"Have you thought of Sr. Rebecca Marise?" Sr. Henrietta asked.

"She just made final vows," Mother Mary Thomas said without looking up. "She's too young."

Mother had reduced her search to middle-aged and senior sisters—the *seasoned* sisters, as they were called. However, the majority of their sisters currently teaching were in their early thirties or younger. The seasoned sisters that Mother would even consider already occupied a position of authority or held a non-teaching assignment for which it would be difficult to find a replacement, such as the head cook at the motherhouse. And the remaining seasoned sisters were marked "definitely out of consideration" by Sr. Henrietta due to disposition or health. Truth be told, Whitewaters was no longer among the preferred assignments and a mere allusion to the possibility of living there was enough to provoke a host of ailments among the disinclined.

After another unsuccessful search through the list, Mother's curiosity was piqued. "Why would you want to send Sr. Rebecca Marise all the way to Whitewaters?"

"I was thinking of a temporary placement. After all, she only transferred to St. Stephen's a couple of weeks ago—Sr. Mary Catherine taught there for years. We could reassign her to St. Stephen's *temporarily.*"

Mother Mary Thomas set down her list and leaned back in her chair. "You know as well as I do that Sr. Mary Catherine has been, let's say, waning for the last five years."

"Five years is being kind," said Sr. Henrietta. Waning was even kinder. Backsliding would be more accurate.

"Nothing would make her happier than a lounge chair and a stack of books," said Mother. "And I'm not talking about spiritual reading either."

"As I said, *temporary* replacement."

Sr. Mary Catherine's reputation as a minimalist began long ago. She operated on *energy-saving mode* both in the classroom and in the community. A mystery novel, covered in plain paper and smuggled in by her sister during their periodic "visiting Sundays," was stashed amid her pulpous folds under her multilayered habit. In whatever snippet of time she could find, the novel was pulled out of hiding, making her bathroom breaks extended affairs. She was even caught in chapel during meditation. If the novel was confiscated, another would appear. No amount of encouragement, persuasion, or admonishment had any effect on her lackadaisical attitude. Sr. Mary Catherine had been recently transferred to the motherhouse to assist in the infirmary for their senior sisters, much to the relief of the sisters at St. Stephen's. Her replacement had been Sr. Rebecca Marise.

"Sr. Mary Catherine won't want to go out to Whitewaters," Sr. Henrietta said. "For all her talk of wanting to come here to work with the older nuns, we know that the big pull is her sister's home a few blocks away."

Mother nodded sadly.

"So if Sr. Rebecca Marise goes *temporarily* to Whitewaters while Sr. Anita recovers, Sr. Mary Catherine can go back to St. Stephen's, *temporarily*, and resume her position until we can better assess the situation and make the necessary changes."

If Mother Mary Thomas insisted, Sr. Mary Catherine *would* go to Whitewaters but her unspoken discontent would translate into even more languid conduct until she was brought back again. Why bother? Sr. Rebecca Marise would go willingly and tackle her assignment enthusiastically. Mother's hesitation, however, did not stem from the young sister.

"Your solution is tempting—it would cause the least upset in the communities. . . . I just have some reservations. . . . Sr. Rebecca Marise's rather young for Whitewaters, don't you think?" Mother Mary Thomas gave a significant glance to Sr. Henrietta.

"She's steady and solid. And it's only temporary. We're most likely looking at one semester."

At another time, in other circumstances, Mother Mary Thomas would have deliberated longer over the list of sisters and perhaps would have found a more satisfactory solution. However, the need was urgent, the anniversary preparations pressing, and this solution was the least disruptive to their schools.

"And Sr. Henrietta, we needn't mention to Sr. Rebecca Marise or the sisters at Whitewaters that the placement is likely to be only one semester. I don't want this transfer to be taken . . . lightly. . . ."

Sr. Henrietta doubted that Sr. Rebecca Marise or the sisters in Whitewaters would have such an inclination, but it was Mother Mary Thomas's usual stance, so she didn't argue the point.

CHAPTER 38

Within twenty-four hours, Sr. Rebecca Marise gathered up her materials in St. Stephen's second grade classroom, packed her clothes, said goodbye to her community of two weeks, and was on the bus to Whitewaters.

A car could have made the journey in several hours but the bus, with its numerous stops and a connection, took over fourteen. Sr. Rebecca Marise didn't care. It gave her a chance to pull her thoughts together and orient herself to her new assignment. So much had happened, so much had changed in so little time. Her perpetual profession was just two months ago, but seemed like years.

~

Eleven sisters to make final vows! This was one of the largest cohorts to persevere until final vows—since first profession the group had only decreased by four. The motherhouse chapel, larger and more ornate than most churches in the diocese, was filled to overflowing.

Bishop Hubert Patterson was elated. With him in the sanctuary were fourteen concelebrating priests, a visiting bishop, and five seminarians who were the altar servers. From the pulpit the bishop looked over the hundreds of people in attendance. Family, relatives, friends of the SCRs. And the nuns, the nuns! Old and young . . . young, so many young sisters; all in full habit. In the front pews sat the superiors and the sisters making their final vows, followed by family and guests, and then pew after pew of sisters. Postulants and novices packed the choir loft. A few sisters in aprons peered from the vestibule, catching a few minutes of the liturgy before returning to the kitchen and reporting to the head cook how far along the ceremony had progressed. As the bishop stood looking at the expectant faces, he was moved by the beauty of the ambient, the singing, the music, the devotion and faith, and above all, by the number of young women willing to give their lives totally to Christ. It was an overwhelming experience. Although ordinarily known for his reserve, some tears briefly moistened his eyes.

Standing erect, he closed the leather folder containing his prepared sermon and gripped either side of the podium with his hands.

"We are living in dark, difficult times. The world lacks faith and denigrates anyone who professes it. The media, with every form of enticement, strives to bring down the morality of our youth. Daily we witness the blatant disregard for human life and the widespread assault on Christian marriage. Attendance at Mass is dwindling. Lines outside the confessionals have diminished—in some cases, vanished. Long-established Catholic institutions have lost their identity. These are dark times indeed."

The bishop paused and looked gravely at the faces below him that mirrored his concern.

"And yet there is hope. A remnant has stood fast against the tide. We have devout young people who refuse to be caught up in the trends, the immorality, the godless music, films, and fashions." With an almost jovial tone, "They are affectionately called the JPII generation." Smiles broke out on the faces and someone began to applaud. Soon the entire congregation was clapping enthusiastically.

Smiling widely now, the bishop continued, "These young people have taken up the challenge of John Paul II: faithfully united in married love, committed to raising truly Christian families, *and*"—pointing to the women about to make perpetual profession—"what we are witnessing today: young women who are willing to make the ultimate sacrifice, giving themselves totally to Christ in religious life."

Applause filled the church once again. Buoyed by the enthusiasm, the bishop continued, gesturing to the young men in the sanctuary.

"And let's not forget the seminarians here, studying for the priesthood."

Another wave of applause thundered through the congregation and reverberated in the arches overhead.

Raising his voice, "We have here today young people who exemplify to their peers—to all of us—what it means to live in faith, or as the contemporary saying goes, 'walk the talk.' We have surrounding us," he said, gesturing empathically to the sisters in the congregation, "those who refuse to buy into the prevailing culture, who are unafraid to bear witness to Christ, continually wearing with dignity and honour their religious habit. They are willing to follow Christ no matter the cost, spending their lives to educate our children, standing firm in the teachings of the Church, faithful to Christ's Vicar on earth, the Pope."

The bishop was interrupted again by another burst of applause. When the congregation quieted, he continued by congratulating those about to make their final vows and thanking their parents for nurturing them in Christian living. In conclusion, he praised the Sisters of Christ the Redeemer and, in particular, Mother Mary Thomas, on her outstanding leadership and unfailing loyalty to the Pope and the magisterium of the Church.

"And I can tell you that during my recent *Ad Limina* visit in Rome I had a private conference with the Holy Father. I brought to the attention of His Holiness the piety, the dedication, and the service of the Sisters of Christ the Redeemer in my diocese. He told me that I was a very fortunate bishop and he extended his apostolic blessing to all of you."

Applause resounded throughout the chapel as the bishop returned to his seat of honour in the sanctuary and the rite of religious profession continued.

During the celebratory meal that followed the ceremony, the bishop continued his praise of the SCRs and Mother Mary Thomas with those who sat at the head table.

Mother Mary Thomas, seated next to him, looked down at her plate. "Well, now, thank you, Your Excellency."

It was a modesty easily assumed as he only voiced what was felt by the general councillors, the local superior, the visiting bishop and the chaplain who surrounded her at the table. They added their compliments and continued with a discussion on the current state of religious life.

The novices were assigned to serve the general assembly—the new perpetually professed, their families and guests—while a select group of professed sisters watched over the head table. They made sure the bishop's glass was filled with wine, "an Episcopal privilege," Mother Mary Thomas joked . . . and a privilege all at the head table shared by association.

It was a perk not lost on Sr. Rebecca Marise's father who, nodding toward the nun filling the bishop's glass, winked at his son, Rob, and said, "We're sitting at the wrong table." The rest of the assembly served themselves fruit punch or water from the pitchers on their tables.

Amongst the sisters and their guests, the meal proceeded blithely: the newly perpetually professed caught up on family news, and relatives of the eleven honoured sisters met or renewed their acquaintance with another. Children made new friends, skipped together between families, and grabbed a few sweets or strawberries each time they passed the dessert table. As the meal ended, people ambled into the spacious convent grounds outside the refectory, the dining area of the sisters. Sr. Rebecca Marise's mother, Margaret, took her daughter by the arm.

"I must have a word with Mother General and some pictures."

"Mother!" Sr. Rebecca Marise looked imploringly at her father.

"Margaret, it looks like Mother Mary Thomas is occupied with other matters."

"Robert," Margaret said curtly, "Mother is here to enjoy this wonderful event with all of us."

He raised his eyebrows to Sr. Rebecca Marise as if to say, *I tried*. With a firm hold on Sr. Rebecca Marise, Margaret steered her toward Mother Mary Thomas, who was saying goodbye to the bishop. Her father, instead, turned and walked toward the door leading to the convent grounds with her brother, his expectant wife, and their three children.

Margaret was always more pious than her husband and grew increasingly so through the years. However, her piety intensified after Sr. Rebecca Marise entered the convent. If she had lived in the same city as the motherhouse, Margaret would have attended Mass every morning at the convent. Distance, instead, kept Margaret faithfully present in her parish church and very active with the local community of SCRs.

Margaret was so intent on catching up with Mother Mary Thomas, she didn't notice that the rest of the family had failed to follow until they were out the door. Repressing her irritation and with her captive in tow, she graciously approached the two personages. The bishop recognized Sr. Rebecca Marise as one of the new perpetually professed and, still exultant from celebration and the generous servings of wine, jovially motioned them over.

"Well, who have we here?" he asked.

188

Seeing his ease and pleasure, Mother Mary Thomas smiled at his side.

"Your Excellency, I'm Mrs. Margaret Holden." She genuflected and kissed his ring. "This is my daughter, Sr. Rebecca Marise." Sr. Rebecca Marise paid the same respects.

"Such a joy, such a joy," gushed her mother, "and your words were so inspiring . . . could not be truer."

Sr. Rebecca Marise was mortified into silence and smiled weakly.

"Mother Mary Thomas, you know my great esteem for you and the manner that you have preserved religious life."

"Thank you, Mrs. Holden, you are always so appreciative."

"I tell my daughter often"—she smiled at Sr. Rebecca Marise—"that could I live my life over, I would become a Sister of Christ the Redeemer."

"Well, you've given the Church a wonderful young woman and that must be a consolation," replied the bishop.

"This has been the happiest day of my life!"

"Maybe some of your other daughters will follow . . ." He looked at Sr. Rebecca Marise, unable to recall her name.

"Had I been so blessed," said her mother, diffident. "Although I would have welcomed many more, I only had two children, Sr. Rebecca Marise and her married brother."

"Well, there are always grandchildren."

Mother Mary Thomas straightened her habit and twisted her watch. "The bishop must be off. It's been a pleasure speaking with you." And with that, both departed, much to Sr. Rebecca Marise's relief.

"I've never spoken with the bishop for so long. How obliging!"

Not until she was outside with the rest of the family and the elation of the moment had abated, did she realize she had forgotten to ask for a picture. And as she complained about this lapse to her daughter-in-law, Sr. Rebecca Marise's father flashed a grin toward his daughter.

At the established time, friends and family departed amid tears and hugs. Within a few hours, the chapel and refectory were restored to their customary order, the leftovers organized in the walk-in fridge, the kitchen prepped for breakfast, and silence resumed. In accord with the *horarium*, their established schedule, the sisters filed into the chapel for night prayer and sat once again in their assigned places.

Sr. Rebecca Marise looked over at Sr. Patrick Marian in the next pew. They had met at a vocation retreat and entered the convent the same day. Although different in many ways, they shared an affinity throughout their journey in religious life. Sr. Patrick Marian had been utterly blissful all through the ceremony and effervescent during the feast. While Sr. Rebecca Marise experienced the beauty of the moment—the music enthralling—she had none of the raptures described by the saints when they became forever the "brides of Christ," sentiments echoed by Sr. Patrick Marian. Though she wondered at this, it didn't worry her. She rarely felt exhilarated, especially when the occasion seemed to demand it. Confronted with high religious emotions of others, her own went underground. It was in solitary moments, when she was alone at prayer, on a walk in their grounds, or with the children, that she experienced a quiet peace before God about her calling.

~

The bus jolted as the driver shifted down. After leaving Slandail, the bus exited to a secondary road with a stop every couple of hours at some roadway diner or convenience store with, if they were lucky, enlarged bathroom facilities.

"Fifteen minutes. The bus leaves in fifteen minutes," the driver hollered from the front of the bus. Sr. Rebecca Marise and a couple of other sleeping passengers remained on board as the rest straggled off at the rest stop. Sr. Rebecca Marise leaned her head against the window. From the looks of it, she would have some grease spots to remove on her veil as a result. With several hours of travel remaining, she was ready to move on. Hopefully, the seat next to her would remain empty. Her religious habit seemed to be either a magnet or a repellent. As they moved closer to the mountains, repellent seemed to predominate. At the onset, an admiring, middle-aged woman hastily filled the adjoining seat and through two stops, confided her family troubles and asked for prayers. When she left an older man took her place.

"Tell me, why would a good-looking woman like you hide away in a convent?" he had said with a smirk.

Sr. Rebecca Marise had pulled out her rosary beads and lowered her eyes. Eventually, the man fell asleep, with his head, thankfully, lolling toward the aisle. He departed at the next stop and the seat had remained empty ever since.

The bus driver slid into position and revved up the motor. After a few seconds he honked the horn as a warning to those who leaned against the outside wall of the diner, sipping their sodas or drawing deeply on what remained of their cigarettes. The doors slammed shut and the bus lurched forward with Sr. Rebecca Marise content in the company of her unclaimed seat.

~

Whitewaters. The possibility of being stationed in Whitewaters had never entered her mind—ever. In order to augment their teaching skills, or to experience religious life in various settings before their commitment, novices and young sisters were sent for brief periods of time to smaller branch communities. Whitewaters was never among them. The little Sr. Rebecca Marise knew about the community, she had heard during novitiate when they studied their congregation's history: it was remote and considered missionary territory. However, the sisters' activities there did not seem to differ from the other SCR school communities dotting the state.

Sr. Rebecca Marise's impressions were mixed. On the one hand, Whitewaters intimated the unknown: unique, challenging, missionary. On the other hand, she had, over the years, picked up a few inadvertent comments from veteran members: "What would you expect from *Whitewaters*? She was almost sent to *Whitewaters*. . . . We should *close down* Whitewaters." The comments were muttered with sidelong glances in a knowing tone of voice, and they ended when Sr. Rebecca Marise was noticed.

If Whitewaters was the last place Sr. Rebecca Marise thought she would ever be stationed, the reaction of Sr. Patrick Marian confirmed it was the last place anyone expected her to go.

"Whitewaters??? That's . . . that's another country . . . another planet." She laughed.

Sr. Patrick Marian was the only co-novice to remain at the motherhouse after perpetual profession. She was part of the preparatory team for the anniversary of the diocese and would teach at a school nearby. Sr. Rebecca Marise had been summoned to the motherhouse by Sr. Henrietta for a morning meeting and was still reeling from the news of her transfer when she bumped into Sr. Patrick Marian in the corridor. Sr. Patrick Marian always seemed to be in the right place at the right time. She walked with Sr. Rebecca Marise through the large compound to the parking area.

"Whitewaters? You know they only send the *seasoned* nuns out there," drawing out the word *seasoned*. She looked at Sr. Rebecca Marise, her eyes wide, holding back a laugh. "There's no one there under fifty!"

"Mother General must be desperate," said Sr. Rebecca Marise.

"You know it's too far away to come to the motherhouse during the school year. Whitewaters is never here for the big celebrations. They barely make it for Christmas."

While all the other communities were situated toward the motherhouse like spokes on a wheel, Whitewaters was in a different orbit—missionary territory.

Sr. Rebecca Marise hadn't considered this. "I'll miss the singing."

When they reached the car, Sr. Patrick Marian gave her a hug.

"You write . . . you write down everything so when we get together you won't forget a thing."

~

Her head rattled hard against the window as the driver sped over a series of potholes. It was night. Lights flickered in the windows of the houses scattered along the roadway. The full moon flitted in and out of view as they swerved around the mountains and wound through the hollows. *Why was I chosen? Of all the nuns, certainly there had to be "seasoned" nuns willing to venture into missionary territory.*

CHAPTER 39

The engine automatically shifted to a lower gear as the van climbed the side of a steep embankment. The narrow road turned sharply and the van swung into a gravel drive and stopped in front of a church, its façade barely perceptible in the ring of light from the door lamp.

"Here we are," said Sr. Maureen, the local superior of St. Martin de Porres convent. "We'll just take your suitcase for now. Tomorrow we can unload the boxes."

By the time Sr. Rebecca Marise pulled out her backpack from the side door, Sr. Maureen had unloaded her suitcase from the back and was extending the handle.

"I'll take that!" said Sr. Rebecca Marise with solicitude.

"Oh, don't give it a thought," said Sr. Maureen, pulling the suitcase behind her. "We're a hardy bunch out here."

Sr. Rebecca Marise already liked Sr. Maureen. In her mid-sixties she was down-to-earth and kind without any affectation. There was something else as well, something which Sr. Rebecca Marise could not immediately identify.

During the ride to the convent, Sr. Maureen asked about Sr. Anita and the sisters at the motherhouse, then shifted abruptly: "It must have been quite a jolt, being transferred so quickly. When did you find out?"

"Yesterday morning."

Sr. Maureen let out a hoot. "Yesterday! And you packed yourself up by this morning?"

"It wasn't that bad."

"It wasn't that easy either," said Sr. Maureen, giving her a glance. "Thanks for your willingness to come and help us out."

It had never occurred to Sr. Rebecca Marise to say no. And to be thanked for saying yes . . .

~

Sr. Rebecca Marise followed Sr. Maureen along the side of the church, the wheels of the suitcase hopping and popping over the uneven seams of the narrow concrete slabs. Then it came to her. At the motherhouse, many of the senior sisters, thrilled at the presence of younger members, called them "dear ones." Like affectionate grandmothers they squeezed their arms, even patted their cheeks. Superiors and middle-aged nuns, depending on their temperament, mood, or position, oscillated between vigilant supervisors and wise guardians. They imparted instruction, advice, and admonition, taking every opportunity to correct and prevent infractions of the rules, and to infuse in "the young ones" the traditions of the order and the wisdom of the saints. There was none of this in Sr. Maureen.

They passed a hedge and came to a small, wire gate. As Sr. Maureen opened the latch, she said, "I want you to have a front door entrance at least once. We'll find out if the hinges still work!"

The suitcase clattered along the same cement slabs as the nuns made their way along the side of the convent. A light on the back corner of the church, not more than ten feet to the right, lit their way. Sr. Rebecca Marise noticed there were no windows on this side of the convent or on the back of the church.

Sr. Maureen rang the front bell and opened the door. "We're home," she called to the sisters inside as she walked over the threshold. They entered a small reception area with a closed door to the left. Sr. Rebecca Marise had no time to even wonder where it led because Sr. Maureen continued through a door directly in front. Over her shoulder, Sr. Rebecca Marise could see a dining area and beyond, a door that opened to a kitchen. Sr. Maureen turned immediately to the right, which led to the community room. By the time they'd both entered the room, the two sisters who had been waiting were out of their chairs and approaching Sr. Rebecca Marise.

"Rebecca, this is Candida," said Sr. Maureen.

Sr. Candida, short and plump, smiled broadly and embraced her affectionately. Sr. Rebecca Marise felt like she was receding into a marshmallow.

"So happy to have you here," she said as she continued to hold her shoulders.

Sr. Candida appeared to be about the same age as Sr. Maureen. Her round, jovial face was bespectacled with frameless lens, and a few unruly hairs sprouted from her double chin.

"So happy to have you here," she repeated and embraced her again.

"And this is Jeanne," said Sr. Maureen as the other nun walked toward her.

Sr. Patrick Marian had been right about Whitewaters and seasoned nuns— *where did she get her information?* Sr. Jeanne was probably mid- to late fifties, wiry, and of average height.

"So this is Rebecca," she said with a quick, light hug. "Welcome." Her eyes were intelligent and penetrating and when their gaze met, Sr. Rebecca Marise sensed both curiosity and reticence.

"Would you like some tea?" she asked. "You've had quite a journey."

~

Sr. Rebecca Marise woke with a start. She threw her legs over the side of the bed and sat for a moment, trying to register where she was. *Whitewaters.* She looked at her watch: 4:40. Everyone would be up in twenty minutes. She might as well get a head start.

On her way to the door, she stumbled over her backpack. Quietly she turned the knob, eased open the door, and peered down the hallway. From what she observed the night before, the convent was U-shaped. Bedrooms lined this side of the complex: four on each side and, at the end of the hall, a common bathroom with a couple of toilets and bathtubs. Sr. Rebecca Marise tiptoed down the hallway.

Moments later, she slipped back into her room, quietly closed the door, and flicked on the light. Rather than assigning her room, Sr. Maureen had, surprisingly, given her a choice of those available. All the cells were the same. Along one wall was a small square sink wedged in the corner near the door. Next was a built-in closet with a section for hanging her garb and a row of shelves for folded underclothes, followed by a similarly built-in desk with bookshelves above and a wooden chair tucked under. A twin bed, covered with a white cotton spread used in all the SCR convents, ran along the opposite wall. A crucifix hung over the head of the bed and a picture of the Blessed Mother was on the side wall. Centred on the back wall was a small window with beige Venetian blinds.

It took Sr. Rebecca Marise longer than usual to get herself readied as she rummaged through her suitcase and backpack for her toiletries, articles of clothing, and prayer books. By the time she was dressed, she could hear the others moving about. Oddly, she hadn't heard the community wake-up bell. She flicked off the light and slipped again into the hallway, headed for the chapel.

Sr. Rebecca Marise had no idea where the chapel was. The night before she almost fell asleep drinking tea and eating toast, so Sr. Maureen deferred her tour and orientation and Sr. Rebecca Marise went directly to bed. She figured the chapel was behind the closed door in the reception area.

The bedroom corridor opened to a small foyer, dimly illuminated by tiny shafts of lights from an outside lamp stealing through the slats of the Venetian blinds. A storage closet was to her left. On one door was a faded label, handwritten in perfect penmanship, *Linens*. The closet extended in an L-shape to the adjacent wall. On this side, the door bore a label, *Community Supplies*, in the same careful script. She reached out and pulled on the knob. Although the door had a lock like all the others, it opened easily with a long squeak. Feeling like a prowler, Sr. Rebecca Marise shut the door without looking at the contents. The closet ended with the door that led to the community room. On the opposite side of the foyer, between the front wall and the first bedroom, was a door with a metal plaque—OFFICE.

Sr. Rebecca Marise entered the community room, closed the door behind her, and turned on the light. She glanced at the bookcase to her left and the windows that extended the length of the back wall. Sr. Rebecca Marise passed the rectangular wooden table with its four straight-backed wooden chairs. In the middle of the front wall was one large window. Its beige Venetian blinds, oddly, were open to the darkness outside. Sr. Rebecca Marise found herself staring at her own image. With no mirrors permitted in the convent, she couldn't resist the urge to take in her appearance and straightened her veil. On either side of the window were framed photos seen in every SCR facility: two on one side were from a previous century, black and white enlargements, slightly unfocused, preserving the dour countenances of the SCRs founding bishop and mother superior. On the other side, were photos of their current bishop and the Pope.

A few steps ahead were three chairs and a recliner arranged in a semicircle so that persons sitting in them could see the TV and each other as well. The recliner was faded maroon, partially covered by a brown throw. The chairs had armrests and a flattened, warped layer of foam covered by worn, brown fabric. Near the four chairs were sturdy wooden TV trays acting as end tables. They held a couple of lamps, a book or two, a mug, and other such items.

The room would have been quite tired and colourless except for the vivid painting above the TV and the flowering plants spilling out of their pots, which were placed around the room on the same wooden TV trays.

The most unusual feature was an easel with a canvas stretched on a frame, only the back of which Sr. Rebecca Marise could see. She was tempted to view the work in progress but, restrained by the self-consciousness of a guest, she continued through the door ahead of her.

To her left was the dining area followed by the kitchen: she had been there for her tea and toast. To her right was the front entrance with its small reception area. Sr. Rebecca Marise opened the door she had passed the night before and groped the wall until she found the light switch. Instead of a chapel, she was standing in a small parlour area. Of course—every SCR convent had at least one parlour where visitors were received. In the motherhouse, there were several and a wing of guest rooms as well. The sisters' quarters were reserved solely for their nuns.

From the looks of the room, Whitewaters didn't receive many visitors. One striking feature caught Sr. Rebecca Marise's attention as the lights came on. On the wall in front of the door was a large, impressionistic painting—a sunrise in the mountains. It was stunning. Underneath was a small couch with undersized end tables on either side—one held a lamp, the other, a statue of the Blessed Mother. In front of the couch were two chairs identical to the ones in the community room, faded but not as worn. A window with beige Venetian blinds filled the front wall. In the back of the room were two doors. Sr. Rebecca Marise succumbed to her curiosity and opened one door—a small closet; behind the other was a compact half bath. She surmised that the couch would be a pullout bed. Hearing footsteps, she stiffened, turned and saw Sr. Maureen in the doorway.

"I was looking . . ."

"Oh, here you are! Wonderful painting of Jeanne's, don't you think?"

"Why . . . yes . . . it's amazing."

"You might want to bring a sweater or jacket. It's a little cool outside this hour of the morning."

"Outside?"

"Yes, the walk to the church . . ." Seeing her confusion, she added, "We pray in the parish church. It's right next door."

On their brisk walk over, Sr. Rebecca Marise asked why they had no private chapel.

"The Catholic community here could barely afford to build a church, let alone a school and convent," said Sr. Maureen as she continued toward the church. "To cut costs, adjustments were made in the original design. There's only so much room on this ridge and expanding on stilts . . . it's expensive."

"On stilts?"

Sr. Maureen stopped under the church door light and gave Sr. Rebecca Marise a quizzical look, then smiled.

"You haven't seen Whitewaters in the light of day, have you? In any case"—Sr. Maureen searched through a ring of keys—"being that the church was next door to the convent, the bishop at the time reasoned that the sisters could use the church for community prayer. Considering Whitewaters our 'missionary outpost,' Mother Ambrosia agreed, provided that an area designated for a bedroom be converted to a small oratory with the Blessed Sacrament. It's fine for periods of personal prayer but much too small for all of us at one time. We'll give you a complete tour of the convent and school today. . . . Last night you were exhausted."

Sr. Maureen unlocked the side door of the church. "I have a full set of keys for you as well."

While Sr. Rebecca Marise waited near the door, Sr. Maureen went into the sacristy where the ministers and altar servers vested for Mass. In a few moments the lights flashed on in the sanctuary and over the front pews. Sr. Maureen walked through the sanctuary, genuflected before the tabernacle, and entered the first pew. Sr. Rebecca Marise walked up the carpeted aisle toward the pew and felt a crunch beneath her shoe. She had reduced a bit of cracker or cookie to flour. As she made her way down the pew toward Sr. Maureen, she noticed scuff marks on the kneeler and inconspicuously leaned forward as she knelt so that the front of her habit went over the kneeler. Her stockings were much easier to launder. She placed her prayer books in the hymnal holder and, without thinking, straightened the collection envelopes into one stack, putting those crumpled and scribbled upon at the back.

Sr. Rebecca Marise tried to recollect herself before the Blessed Sacrament but her focus was drawn to her new surroundings. The spartan sanctuary was embellished with a rustic altar, crucifix, and tabernacle. On either side of the sanctuary were quilted wall hangings, the cloth pieces cut out in stained-glass fashion, one depicting the Blessed Mother and the other, St. Martin de Porres. The walls weren't much higher than her convent room and running down their length along the top was a row of narrow, clear-glass windows with cords hanging down to open and close them. A rustle at the door interrupted Sr. Rebecca Marise's perusal and Sr. Candida scurried up the aisle. Sr. Jeanne followed then paused to open a couple of windows, wreathing the sisters in cool, fresh air. They began, as in the motherhouse, with their ritual of prayers, but with just four sisters the empty church swallowed their voices.

During their meditation, morning prayer, and Mass, Sr. Rebecca Marise could not help but notice the breaking dawn soften the dark sky to a pinkish hue. When she exited the side door, she was facing a rocky embankment, not ten feet away studded with grasses and stunted shrubs. About ten or more feet up, she could see a fence and the side wall of what must be the school.

"Rebecca, come with me," said Sr. Maureen, "I want to show you something."

Sr. Candida and Sr. Jeanne entered the back door of the convent while Sr. Rebecca Marise followed Sr. Maureen down the same cement path as the night before, toward the front of the convent. The path remained flat while the earth graded incrementally until, by the front of the house, the sisters were on a small landing about five feet above the ground below.

"Oh . . . my . . . goodness . . ." Sr. Rebecca Marise walked transfixed to the railing that bordered the landing. Before her was a panorama of exquisite beauty. The sun was just breaking over the crest of a mountain. Its tentative rays illuminated the mountains and ridges that rose up in every direction and flowed into the shadows still lingering at the bottom of the steep ravines. Mist wafted around the sides of the mountains, while above the blue-grey clouds increasingly glowed pink, rose, and orange-yellow. The initial glints of sun grew and glistened in the dew that dripped from grass and leaves around the nuns. Just beyond the landing, the ridge dropped to a sharp escarpment, slanting down about a hundred feet. A narrow road hugged its side as it wended down toward the town.

Whitewaters still remained in the shadow of the mountains. Constrained by the jagged contours of the ravines, its inhabitants settled in whatever flatland could be carved out of the narrow vale and, like the sisters, had begun to climb the sides. Throughout the vale, up the ravines to the very tops of the mountains, trees, bushes, grasses, and wild flowers anchored in whatever soil was offered, enveloping the terrain in every imaginable shade of green.

"After all these years, I am still amazed," said Sr. Maureen.

"This is Sr. Jeanne's picture," whispered Sr. Rebecca Marise still gazing at the view.

"Yes, from the front window."

"I hope we never close the blinds," Sr. Rebecca Marise said softly to herself.

"They're always open."

~

Sr. Maureen and Sr. Rebecca Marise retraced their steps and entered through the back door. As they hung up their sweaters in the small mud room, they heard the toilet flush from behind a door near the hooks.

"If you need the bathroom after Mass, wait until after Candida or go to the dorm area," said Sr. Maureen quietly. "It's part of her routine."

"What a wonderful morning," said Sr. Maureen as they entered the kitchen. "Rebecca and I were just admiring the view."

Sr. Jeanne responded and a conversation regarding the weather ensued.

At the motherhouse, the sisters would still be under "the grand silence." This practice began with night prayer the evening before and was not lifted until after breakfast. During the day, conversation was limited to matters related to their mission, except for an hour of recreation in the evening. However, during the grand silence, no one was to speak unless there was an urgent need. Sr. Rebecca Marise assumed her arrival was considered a "festive exemption." She washed her hands at the kitchen sink and looked out the window into a little courtyard. It was framed on one side by the kitchen and dining room, on the other side by the bedroom wing, and horizontally by the community room. The back of the courtyard was closed in by a thick, tall hedge like the hedge that closed the gap between the convent and the back of the church.

Sr. Rebecca Marise shook the dripping water from her hands into the sink and glanced around.

"There's a hand towel on the rack at the end of the counter," coached Sr. Maureen.

As she dried her hands she walked to the entrance of the dining room and saw the door leading to a patio. From the dining room window she could see that the patio extended the width of the courtyard and had a round cedar table with four chairs and a couple of large flower pots filled and overflowing with annuals of bright red, orange, and yellow.

"Who has the green thumb?"

"That would be me," said Sr. Candida as she walked into the kitchen.

"The flower pots are lovely."

"You should take a look at her vegetable garden," said Sr. Maureen.

"There's a vegetable garden? Where?"

"In front of the kitchen window."

Sr. Rebecca Marise opened the dining room door and took in the rest of the courtyard. Beyond the patio was all lawn except for a flourishing vegetable garden about three feet wide, stretching along the side of the house under the kitchen window. When she returned to the kitchen, the other sisters were moving around, putting bread into the toaster, filling a small pot with water and putting it on the stove, removing a bowl from the cupboard.

"Rebecca, make yourself at home," said Sr. Maureen. "There's cereal, eggs, bread, cheese, fruit . . . just help yourself."

For a moment Sr. Rebecca Marise did not move. "We each make our own breakfast?"

"No one else is going to do it for us," said Sr. Jeanne with a smile. "Maureen, I'm making a scrambled egg, do you want me to add one for you?"

"No, just having cereal today."

"How about you, Rebecca?" Sr. Jeanne asked.

Sr. Rebecca Marise already felt disoriented, not knowing where anything was in the house, let alone in the kitchen cabinets. But this breakfast . . .

Since the day she entered the convent, no meal was ever . . . *just help yourself.* Every meal was prepared and portions meted out.

She couldn't think of what she wanted for breakfast. *What she wanted?* She had grown so used to just eating whatever was put before her . . . in whatever fashion . . . that she had ceased to even care.

"I think I'll just have some cereal," she replied and began to follow Sr. Maureen around the kitchen.

One by one, they made their way to the dining room.

"Since this is Rebecca's first day, we'll dispense with the silence as we have some things to discuss."

Sr. Maureen briefly recapped the situation: About a week after the sisters returned to Whitewaters, Sr. Anita had her heart attack. She taught the third grade and Sr. Rebecca Marise was prepared for second grade at St. Stephen's. This meant new lesson plans as well as classroom prep for Sr. Rebecca Marise.

Sr. Maureen turned to Sr. Rebecca Marise. "I have a few interviews this morning, so Jeanne will give you a tour of the school and show you your classroom. Get your bearings and we'll size up the situation this afternoon. If you would like help with the classroom prep, there are a couple of girls, past students, who would be happy to give you a hand.

"Candida, what did you have planned for this morning?" And on it went as the day's tasks were laid out.

CHAPTER 40

Sr. Jeanne and Sr. Rebecca Marise left by the back door. An overhang spanned the short distance from the door to a covered stairway. The sides were open with rails on either side, and the roof was made of corrugated plastic. Over the years, the colour had faded and the grooves had become studded with grit and leaves that even the rain and melting snow could not dislodge. This created jagged stripes in the green hue that the roof cast on the steep wooden stairs. The roof could not have been much more than six feet high—even Sr. Rebecca Marise, though clearing it easily, felt like ducking.

"A little awkward, but in the pouring rain or a snowfall, a definite benefit," said Sr. Jeanne as they climbed up.

As the sisters walked out onto the ledge above, Sr. Rebecca Marise was at last able to take in the whole complex. Before exploring the school, the sisters walked along the fence that bordered the top of the embankment.

"What's that little house over there?"

Across the road from the church was a small house nestled in a nook of the ridge.

"The rectory. Doug will be over soon enough, I'm sure. He often celebrates Mass in smaller communities during the week—had to leave early today."

Sr. Rebecca Marise looked down on the church and the convent, and much further on, the town below.

"This is incredible."

Sr. Jeanne glanced at Sr. Rebecca Marise. "Incredible, indeed. It wasn't always considered so."

"Why wouldn't anyone love this place?"

"Decades ago, this location was very inconvenient and the property was considered of little value. As you can see, it's a split landing on a ragged ridge with soil difficult to farm. At the time, the boundaries of Whitewaters didn't extend to the edges of the holler as it does today, so a person would have to travel down some ruts beyond the town, then up a rough path switching along this ridge. What with the snow in the winter, the mud in the spring . . . Those with means had homes in town."

"What's a holler?"

"A hollow, a valley. . . . In time, you'll have a handle on the 'localisms.'"

"So how did we get the property?"

"Strictly speaking, 'we' didn't. The diocese did. Years ago an immigrant worker scraped up enough money to buy the plot. His son did well for himself—became a dentist and bought a house near his office in town. He and a few other influential Catholics in the area were continually badgering the bishop for a church. So when the missionary project unfolded, he offered the diocese this land. By that time, the hospital and community college were expanding and vying for the limited property in town. This plot was considered a blessing.

"Now, with the influx of wealthy retirees looking for summer homes . . . with this view . . ." Sr. Jeanne tapped the fence. "The diocese would make a lot of money if they decided to sell the property."

"Oh, there's no chance of that."

"We'd better move on with our tour before it's time for lunch."

The school was a two-storey building built on the larger upper landing of the ridge. After coming up the covered stairway, the sisters had only to cross a gravel drive to the side entrance. Sr. Jeanne unlocked the door and both entered. A fresh coat of wax glimmered on the linoleum floor and filled the building with the aroma of a school about to open.

"Hard to believe that in a week these quiet halls will be bustling with children again," said Sr. Rebecca Marise.

"Must be hard for you to believe you're even here."

Sr. Rebecca Marise chuckled. "It did take me a while to figure out where I was this morning."

"You have quite a week ahead of you . . ." Sr. Jeanne walked forward a few paces and paused. "This is called the primary floor. First through fourth grade have their classrooms here." Pointing to the right, "This is your third grade classroom. But before we go in, why don't we do a quick walk-through of the building."

"Sure."

The sisters climbed the staircase and began walking down the corridor. Sr. Jeanne pointed to the doors on the right and left: "Eighth, seventh, fifth, sixth . . ."

By this time the sisters were halfway down the corridor.

"And we come to . . ." Sr. Jeanne opened the door.

"An art room!" said Sr. Rebecca Marise.

"Art and music room."

"I'm assuming you're the art teacher."

"Yes, for grades four to eight. And across the hall . . ." Sr. Jeanne opened the door.

"The library."

Unlike the classrooms she had peered into, the windows were high up on the wall above the bookshelves. Sr. Jeanne flicked on the lights.

"We're early . . . the teachers and staff will be arriving shortly."

The sisters walked to the end of the hall, down the back stairway and out to the far end of the first-floor corridor. Sr. Jeanne pushed open the exit door. Only several feet from the door, the wooded ridge began its ascent up the mountain.

"An emergency exit. The children use the door near your room for recess."

She closed the door and turned around. "Staff room on the right, and staff bathroom to the left"—moving down the hall—"followed by the boys' bathroom. Right across we have Sr. Maureen's office."

Through the window in the door the sisters could see Sr. Maureen on the phone. She waved as they passed.

"And next to Sr. Maureen, the school office across from the girls' bathroom."

At this point they reached the school "foyer," which was merely the intersection of hallways.

"The main entrance, as you can see, is to your right but we are going to take a left."

Sr. Jeanne walked to the double doors at the end of the corridor and Sr. Rebecca Marise stepped into a large hall.

"Our gym, theatre, cafeteria, church hall—you name it. Our bathrooms have doors opening to the gym as well as to the school. For church functions, we lock the doors leading to the school and during school hours, we lock the doors leading to the gym."

"That was well-planned."

"And now, to your classroom. Feel free to come back through and explore all the nooks and crannies. I don't want to overload your circuits this morning."

Although adequate and well maintained, the school was devoid of any architectural flair. Inside and out, its style was stamped with pragmatism and economy. The interior, though, was energized by murals and borders that covered the walls; scenes depicting the life of Christ in the everyday life of the children, all in brilliant colours. On their way back to the third grade classroom, Sr. Rebecca Marise stopped to admire them.

"Did you do all these murals?"

"Yes, 'with a little bit of help from my friends.'"

"They're wonderful."

"And here we are," said Sr. Jeanne.

Sr. Rebecca Marise surveyed the third grade classroom. It was smaller than any she had ever taught in. Sr. Anita had been in the process of taking down the June décor and putting up September's, but she had not gotten far.

Sr. Rebecca Marise walked up to the front of the room. "There's only twelve desks."

"Rebecca, sit down a moment."

Sr. Rebecca Marise pulled out the chair from behind the teacher's desk while Sr. Jeanne brought over a stool from the side of the room.

"You're going to find this school . . . different from any of our other schools."

"How so?"

"What exactly do you know about Whitewaters?"

Eyeing Sr. Jeanne, she decided to omit *seasoned nuns only*. "It's missionary."

"Well, that's comprehensive."

Sr. Rebecca Marise grinned. "Seriously, I don't know much, other than there are not many Catholics."

"The Catholic population is very small: around 5 percent. The whole endeavour—the church, the school, the convent—was, as you said, part of a missionary project."

"To convert people to Catholicism?"

"I'm sure that was one of the hopes, but also to provide support for the small Catholic population . . . and as much as possible for non-Catholics, as well. In any case, the conversions didn't happen. How many years have you been teaching?"

"Full-time, for two years."

"Were you ever part of the admission process?"

"No."

"However, you are aware of the waiting lists for admission?"

"Certainly. Our schools are known for their high level of education and solid Catholic values."

"Yes . . . ," said Sr. Jeanne cautiously. "The waiting lists are also due to the growing Catholic population in the eastern part of the state—Northerners are moving south and Latin Americans are moving north. Rebecca, with greater numbers applying, the admission standards have also risen. Poor-performers don't get in . . . And that contributes greatly to the overall high test scores."

Sr. Rebecca Marise began to feel uneasy. "The kids receive a good education."

"Of course, they do, Rebecca. I'm just saying that when the initial launch pad is increasingly higher, so are the chances of greater academic success. In any of your classes, did you have anyone who was consistently under a C?"

"Just one."

"Honestly? Slipped under the wire?"

Rebecca hands, folded one over the other, tightened.

"He had siblings, his parents promised extra tutoring . . . and they were donors."

Sr. Jeanne raised an eyebrow. "That always helps." She moved off the stool and leaned against one of the desks.

"Rebecca, we also aim to maintain a high standard of education. However, we do not have the same prerequisites for admission."

"Because there are limited numbers applying?"

"In part, yes. However, even if we had the numbers, our application process would remain."

"So what's different about it?" said Sr. Rebecca Marise, twisting a bead on the rosary dangling at her side.

"The child's capacity to learn is not gauged solely, or mainly, on standardized test scores. We use other tools of assessment as well. Kids learn in different ways."

"Like Jerome . . . the student I mentioned," said Sr. Rebecca Marise, somehow feeling the need to defend the other SCR schools.

"What happened?"

Sr. Rebecca Marise related the story of Jerome, the approaches she used, and how he responded. Sr. Jeanne listened intently.

"Did the school accept more students like Jerome as a result?"

"I don't know . . . I was only there for a practicum." But Sr. Rebecca Marise knew it was very unlikely.

"If a child has a desire to learn, but is struggling . . . why not give the child a chance?"

"So we accept children here with disabilities?"

"To a certain extent. We are not equipped . . . or trained . . . for children with severe disabilities or children with severe emotional and behavioural problems. But there's a range that we can work with very well . . . and these are the children that generally fall through the cracks."

"What do you mean?"

"Well . . . like Jerome, the boy you were just talking about. The difficulties of these children are subtler, so they don't always get the help they need. They may appear sullen, restless, disinterested, but other issues are at play. They could struggle because of some 'short-circuits' in their brain that need to be identified . . . or they just learn differently . . . or there are problems at home."

Sr. Rebecca Marise's interest intensified despite her ambivalence with Sr. Jeanne.

"So, who does the testing? How do you determine . . . ?"

Sr. Jeanne looked steadily at Sr. Rebecca Marise.

"I've been doing my own reading," said the younger sister. "It's a personal interest . . ."

"Well, well." Sr. Jeanne continued to observe Sr. Rebecca Marise. Growing self-conscious, Sr. Rebecca Marise looked down at her lap and began to brush a few motes from her habit.

"In town we have a centre for children with special needs. Every month a team from the East comes in for testing and follow-up. Occasionally, there's a seminar offered for educators and—"

"Do we ever go?" cut in Sr. Rebecca Marise intently.

Sr. Jeanne laughed. "Yes, Rebecca, I'm sure you'll be able to attend." Then becoming serious, "Regarding your class, the lesson planning, the students—Maureen and I are here to help and you'll meet others on staff who are quite perceptive regarding the students. Anita was brilliant with the children."

Sr. Rebecca Marise brushed off her sleeve. "You haven't mentioned Sr. Candida."

"Candida is a dear person and very kind. Perception in this area is not her gift but she's open to input on the children."

Sr. Jeanne stood up. "This abrupt transfer has got to be difficult for you. Your lesson plans for the second grade at St. Stephen's must have been well on their way."

"Yes, they were."

In fact, they were complete. When she was told in June of her assignment at St. Stephen's, she was relieved—she had taught grade two before and had all her unit and lesson plans ready—she just had to hone them. This enabled her to complete her course work and finish off her thesis for an MEd degree over the summer. Her greatest concern regarding the transfer was how she would ever be prepared to teach in a week. She tried to face it with faith—this was God's will. He would help her—yet her anxiety increased.

"Rebecca, in one way, it's almost better you weren't placed here in the second grade. It's going to be tough in the beginning, but you'll adapt the class to your students. I've put the third grade curriculum here on your desk . . . as well as a personal laptop."

"A *personal* laptop???" Very few sisters had personal laptops at the motherhouse.

"It's much more economical for us here. We have no desktop computers in the convent. Everyone brings their laptop back and forth . . . Well, almost everyone. Candida isn't into computers."

Moving to a two-drawer file in the room, Sr. Jeanne said, "Anita's plans and notes are over here."

Sr. Jeanne took out a key from her pocket, opened it, and handed the key to Sr. Rebecca Marise. "Go ahead, open the file. See what Anita left behind. If you need anything—just ask."

Sr. Jeanne left the room. Sr. Rebecca Marise was immensely relieved to discover that Sr. Anita was so organized that she had her lesson plans filed. She brought the stool to the file and opened the top drawer. Her relief waned as she went through the files. Sr. Anita had been teaching for almost forty years and the files had been developed by herself, for herself, over the decades. Sr. Rebecca Marise couldn't make out the logic behind the system.

There! A binder. She opened it on her lap. Course outlines, unit and lesson plans! She flipped through the pages. Unfortunately, the content was so familiar to Sr. Anita that she merely scrawled a few lines, sometimes just a phrase, to jog her memory. Sr. Rebecca Marise set down the binder, randomly pulled out several file folders and looked through their contents. They were filled with project descriptions, activities, stories, newspaper and magazine clippings. Others contained articles and research notes. If she went through the whole file cabinet, Sr. Rebecca Marise was sure she would garner a lot of background information, but with only a week to prepare . . .

She went back to the desk and opened the third grade curriculum. There was no easy fix.

CHAPTER 41

"Since this is Rebecca's first supper, I thought we would dispense with the spiritual reading, so she could let us know what is happening at the motherhouse," said Sr. Maureen. "You said you spoke with Anita?"

"Yes, as you know, Sr. Anita is home from the hospital. I went to visit her in the infirmary after my meeting with Sr. Henrietta. She said she's doing better and really misses you."

"I bet she does," said Sr. Jeanne, half to herself.

"Let's see . . ." Sr. Rebecca Marise's mind was so filled with the novelty and the urgencies at Whitewaters that the motherhouse and its concerns seemed distant and faded. "There's lots of planning going on for Celebrating Faith and Life."

"What exactly is that all about?" said Sr. Jeanne. Sr. Candida smiled from across the table.

Sr. Rebecca Marise looked at Sr. Jeanne, puzzled. Planning the year-long diocesan anniversary celebration dominated their congregational communiqués. A diocesan coordinating team heavy with SCR representation was formed a year ago. Their religion curricula were being tweaked to incorporate the anniversary celebration's themes and events. How could Sr. Jeanne be unaware?

"You know, the diocese's anniversary celebration." Then recalling with relish, "And the Pope is coming next year. What an opening to the celebration!"

"The Pope is coming to the state?" said Sr. Jeanne with surprise.

"No, no. To New York, Washington, and Baltimore."

"Oh, yes, heard about that."

Sr. Rebecca Marise continued on. "Delegates from the diocese will be travelling by bus—three buses altogether including a group of our sisters."

"Really? Who would they be?" said Sr. Jeanne. Sr. Maureen gave her a pleading glance that was lost on Sr. Rebecca Marise.

"The general council for sure. I imagine others more involved in the planning. *However*," said Sr. Rebecca Marise with ardour, "if a sister would really like to go, she can submit her name. You haven't heard of this?"

"It was in the summer newsletter, Jeanne," said Sr. Maureen.

"I must have missed it."

"And mentioned at our summer meetings," Sr. Maureen chided. "Someone's been sleeping."

Sr. Jeanne laughed and turned to Sr. Rebecca Marise. "So are you submitting your name?"

"I already have. This is an opportunity of a lifetime. Who knows if I'll ever have a chance to see the Pope again."

"How old are you?"

"Twenty-seven."

"I'd wager your chances are pretty high."

"I might die young, like St. Thérèse of Lisieux," Sr. Rebecca Marise teased.

"Great, then we can tell people of your sanctity, get special seats at your canonization, and tour Italy while we're at it. How does that sound, Maureen?"

"I'm in. Candida, start taking notes so we can have her application ready as soon as she dies."

~

The sisters finished up the dishes and Sr. Rebecca Marise and Sr. Maureen remained to wipe down the counters.

"Do you have an alarm clock?" asked Sr. Maureen.

"I've never needed one."

"You will here."

"Don't you ring the bell in the morning?"

"It's a bit jarring. And if a sister is not feeling well and needs to sleep in, there is no need to wake her. A number of years ago, the flu hit our community and we found alarm clocks work just as well. I'll give you one when we finish up here."

~

After the evening community hour, Sr. Rebecca Marise went to her room to finish unpacking. Although Sr. Maureen had given her a free slate during the day, Sr. Rebecca Marise had remained in her classroom working at her lesson plans. Just before nine o'clock she left her cell for the community room. On her way, she stopped at the tiny oratory. The reredos, or altarpiece, in which the tabernacle was placed was beautiful but oversized for the limited space and allowed for only two kneelers with chairs. Just the same, she was grateful to have the Blessed Sacrament within the convent and so close to her cell. As she walked into the community room, Sr. Maureen looked up, a file opened on her lap.

"Hello, Rebecca. We were just talking about you."

Sr. Candida put down the book she was reading; Sr. Jeanne continued to paint.

"Are we going to say the Angelus and Compline?" asked Sr. Rebecca Marise.

Throughout the congregation, in every community, all the sisters gathered in chapel one last time at 9:00 p.m. to recite these prayers before going to their rooms under the grand silence. By 9:30 the lights were out in the dorms of the postulants and novices. But with their individual cells, the professed sisters could read, study, or pray as long as they liked, provided it was alone and in silence—and they were ready to start their day at 5:00 a.m.

"Why don't you lead the prayer tonight, Rebecca?" said Sr. Maureen. None of the sisters showed any sign of preparing to go to the church.

"Here?" asked Rebecca.

The others looked up surprised.

"Rebecca," said Sr. Maureen, "the time it takes to unlock doors, light up the church, bundle up when it's cold . . . Umbrellas in the rain, boots in the snow . . . For a few minutes of prayer?"

Sr. Rebecca Marise knew she was right. It was just . . . different.

"Didn't Jesus say, 'Where two or three are gathered in my name, there I am'?" continued Sr. Maureen. "A few copies of the *Liturgy of the Hours* are in the bookcase."

Sr. Rebecca Marise moved hesitantly over to the bookcase, then passed out the prayer books to the other sisters and sat in the empty chair. Sr. Jeanne put down her brush.

Still feeling uncomfortable, Sr. Rebecca Marise bowed her head. "The angel of the Lord declared unto Mary."

The others responded, "And she conceived of the Holy Spirit."

"Hail Mary, full of grace . . ."

~

The next morning, Sr. Rebecca Marise sat behind her desk, already feeling more at home. The day before, she found the text, workbook, and manual for every subject she would teach and stacked them neatly on the window ledge. She had opened every drawer in the desk, discarded the junk, organized what she retained, and put the undecided in Sr. Anita's filing cabinet. Then she removed the June decorations and left only the classroom organizers she intended to use. She would work on the bulletin boards at the end of each day. Her goal was to outline one unit and prepare at least one week of lessons for every subject before school began.

"Maureen told me I would find you here."

"Why, Fr. Doug," said Sr. Rebecca Marise flustered. She rose and extended her hand over the desk to the priest who approached her.

"So, Rebecca, you've come to join us here at Whitewaters," he said as he sat on the top of a student's desk and put his feet on the seat of the desk in front. Sr. Rebecca Marise hoped this wouldn't happen in front of the children. She sat back down in her chair.

"I understand you had quite a sudden transfer."

"Yes . . . it's part of our life. Sr. Anita's illness was a shock to us all."

Fr. Doug was what—fifties, early sixties? Unlike the priests she knew, who wore black clericals from neck to toe, Fr. Doug wore sandals, khaki pants, and a maroon shirt—clean but "ironed" only by being pulled warm out of the dryer.

"Are you familiar with these parts?"

"No, no, I was raised closer to the motherhouse, about an hour out of Slandail."

"Any brothers or sisters?"

"A brother."

Sr. Rebecca Marise picked up a pen and began to twist and click it until, conscious of what she was doing, put it back down on her desk.

"Have you ever been to this part of the state?"

"No, first time."

Although respectful and kind, Fr. Doug unnerved Sr. Rebecca Marise. She had never been so casually addressed by a priest. In the past, all business with the pastor was handled by the superior. Sr. Rebecca Marise's conversations with parish priests had been brief, strictly related to the apostolic work and, for the most part, cordial greetings exchanged in passing. Classroom visitations were exactly that, visits with a classroom full of students.

"You have a great group of sisters here. You're fortunate."

"Thanks," said Sr. Rebecca Marise and immediately felt foolish.

"So I understand from Maureen that you'll be preparing the children for First Communion and First Reconciliation . . . or confession as they still call it here."

"As they still call it everywhere," said Sr. Rebecca Marise with a grin.

Fr. Doug smiled and stood up. "I know you're busy, so I won't keep you. However, I would like to chat with you before too long on how you intend to prepare the children."

"Sure . . . ," taken off guard, "maybe in a couple of weeks."

"Good. I'll be back." And Fr. Doug walked out the door.

Sr. Rebecca Marise put her elbows on the desk, rested her forehead on her fists, and let out a sigh. What a place! Everything was . . . OK, sort of . . . always just a little . . . off balance. This was Whitewaters. Things were bound to be a little different. She got out of her chair and walked to the windows. The clouds had lifted. There were the mountains, traces of mist still hovering near the tops. So beautiful and yet so haunting; calming and unsettling. The day was warming up, so she opened all the windows to freshen the room. There were lessons to prepare—every other consideration would have to wait.

~

Sr. Jeanne brought out the bubbling macaroni and cheese and placed it on a hot plate in the centre of the table.

"It's very hot. You should all be able to reach it from here," said Sr. Jeanne. She took off the oven mitts, leaned around the kitchen door and tossed them on the counter.

After grace, Sr. Maureen said, "I have a new CD."

"Can we wait until the community gathering?" said Sr. Jeanne. "Some of the recordings from the gen—"

"This is something else," cut in Sr. Maureen. "*The Lord of the Rings*. A great classic, Catholic author. I thought we could listen to it for spiritual reading, refresh our memories. Might be useful in class."

Sr. Rebecca Marise was amazed. *A novel*, for *spiritual reading?*

After about ten minutes Sr. Maureen clicked off the recording. "We have some matters to discuss so we'll shorten the spiritual reading."

"I'm sure whatever you have to say will be just as edifying," said Sr. Jeanne.

"The macaroni is wonderful," said Sr. Candida.

"Very good macaroni . . . as usual," said Sr. Maureen. "Which brings us to the topic at hand. Rebecca, do you cook?"

"I *have* cooked in my life but not much."

"Well, that's about to change."

"You're kidding!" said Sr. Rebecca Marise.

This was more alarming than her class preparation. During her eight years of religious life, she had never prepared a meal, ever. Assisted, yes. But responsible for a meal, no.

Thus far, Sr. Rebecca Marise had lived most of her religious life at the motherhouse where a few sisters prepared all the meals with help from the postulants and novices. In the branch houses where she had been stationed, a senior sister generally did all the cooking and was quite possessive of the task.

At home she had managed the basics—like scrambled eggs and toast. Her mother, a gourmet, was finicky about meal preparation. When Sr. Rebecca Marise tried to help, her mother became ruffled and after a few minutes would send her out to study or play.

To make matters worse, Sr. Rebecca Marise had stopped thinking about food. The gospel maxim "Eat what is put before you" was a religious principle in the convent; gluttony, to be avoided at all costs.

When she first entered the convent, meals were difficult. The dishes were prepared so differently from home and the portions were allotted. If you didn't care for something, there was no getting around the full serving. Food donations were common and periodically they would have a "food rush"—a couple of weeks when morning, noon, and night they would have yogurt under some guise, or aging pastries for their mid-afternoon snack (although she noticed a few sisters who would drop into their pockets a couple of extra donuts wrapped in paper napkins). Leftovers were recycled until they ended their days unrecognizable in a miscellany soup.

Whatever and however the food was prepared, for better or for worse, the sisters were to eat it without comment, without complaint. Food was a means to an end—sustenance. The cooks did their best and feast days were always exceptional; just the same, food was to be enjoyed with discretion. Quoting the saints, the sisters were urged to make at least one mortification of the palate each meal.

Gradually, Sr. Rebecca Marise became utterly indifferent. If she had been asked in the evening what she ate for breakfast or lunch, she would not have been able to answer. She had zero confidence when it came to cooking and, at this point, zero inclination.

"*You* want me *to cook*?"

"We all cook here, Rebecca."

"Honestly, I have no experience. I don't know where to begin," said Sr. Rebecca Marise with growing anxiety. "I can clean. . . .That's it! I'll clean for you and you cook for me!"

"My goodness!" laughed Sr. Jeanne. "We could take advantage of this situation!"

Blindsided by the prospect of cooking, her words spilt out without reflection. Now she recoiled. Never had she offered objections to a request from a superior.

Sensing real angst, Sr. Maureen offered, "Tell you what we can do." She looked at Sr. Candida and Sr. Jeanne. "Why don't we alternate every three weeks? In the first round, Rebecca, you can cook with me. In the second, with Candida; the third with Jeanne until you get your confidence up. How does that sound to everyone?"

"I don't mind cooking two weeks each month . . . I'd rather enjoy it," said Sr. Candida.

It was agreed and Sr. Rebecca Marise continued her meal very grateful and much relieved.

~

That evening during community hour, Sr. Jeanne was at her painting and Sr. Maureen was again reviewing the files of some students. Sr. Candida had been snipping and watering the many plants in the room, then moved to her stash in other parts of the convent. This didn't seem to bother Sr. Maureen but Sr. Rebecca

Marise knew Sr. Candida would have been called on it in other communities. Sr. Rebecca Marise had bulletin board materials laid out on the table. She walked over to a chair near the other two sisters with a few pieces of construction paper and began to cut out her designs. From the time she arrived, something bothered her . . . but she had just arrived. Should she even bring it up?

"Can I . . . ?" she started hesitantly.

Sr. Maureen glanced up, looking over the top of her glasses. The room was silent. "Can you . . . what?"

Just ask, Sr. Rebecca Marise told herself. Softly she said, "Why don't you call each other 'Sister'?"

Sr. Jeanne looked at Sr. Rebecca, then continued to paint. After a moment she asked, "Is using 'Sister' important to you?"

"Yes."

"Why is that?"

"It reminds us of our consecration, that we belong to God."

"You tend to forget that?"

"No."

"Neither do we."

Sr. Maureen set down her files. "Rebecca, if using 'Sister' is important to you, use it. It's fine."

Sr. Rebecca Marise worked her scissors, faltering. "Mother Mary Thomas . . . she wants us to use 'Sister' when speaking to each other . . . all of the superiors do."

"As I said, if using 'Sister' is important to you, do it. There is no rule here that you can't."

"Well," Sr. Rebecca Marise asked softly, "why don't *you* use 'Sister'?"

"Rebecca," said Sr. Maureen with a sigh, "Jeanne, Candida, I, and until recently, Anita, have been living together for years . . . like family. Do you call your father Mr. Holden? If your brother was a bishop, would you call him "Your Excellency" when he came home to visit? In the classroom we use our titles as all the teachers do. But among ourselves . . ."

Sr. Rebecca Marise kept her eyes down.

"We're sisters here, Rebecca."

Sr. Jeanne tapped her brush in the palette and gently added highlights to parts of her painting. "And, Rebecca," she said, "all people belong to God."

~

Lying in bed that night, Sr. Rebecca Marise tried to sort through the disparate thoughts and feelings that competed for attention. *It begins with the little things*, a maxim drummed in from her earliest days of formation. All the aging, disintegrating congregations had begun their demise by neglecting the little things.

Sr. Henrietta—how long ago was their conversation? Three days, four? *Life will be different in Whitewaters—missionary territory.* Then looking at her intently, *If you need anything, anything at all, just write or call me.*

In all that was obligatory, Sr. Rebecca Marise consulted her formators and superiors. However, going to them for minor concerns was not in her character. She spent her youth evading her "helicopter mom." She didn't want to involve the superiors if she didn't have to nor engage in *reporting*, the practice of informing the superiors of infractions to the rules. And these sisters at Whitewaters were so welcoming, so down-to-earth.

And yet . . . not using *Sister*. And *The Lord of the Rings* for spiritual reading? That was a stretch. Yet as she lay there, she had to be honest with herself: the spiritual reading they did at the motherhouse went in one ear and out the other. The texts of the Pope, theologians, and the saints were fine for study but, for Sr. Rebecca Marise, they required too much concentration at a meal. During novitiate, she felt guilty for her lack of attention, and made an effort to listen. But as the years went by, she reasoned that there was a limit to what she could absorb. Spiritual reading at meals was a background hum for her private reflections. But a story! And *The Lord of the Rings*! Yes, it was stretching spiritual reading to the limit. . . . However, Tolkien *was* a devote Catholic. . . .

Then her pressing anxiety surfaced and wiped out all others—how many more days before school began? Her class preparation had become a scramble. She had no idea what to expect from her students. As she lay in bed, her forehead dampened with sweat and she could feel her heart pounding.

"Hail Mary, full of grace . . ." She squeezed the rosary in her hand. Slowly, calmly she repeated the prayer she had learned before memory: "Hail Mary, full of grace . . ." and eventually drifted off to sleep.

CHAPTER 42

Sr. Rebecca Marise stood by her desk and looked at the children before her, polished for the first day of school—clean uniforms, fresh haircuts, new school supplies. And the students looked at her—the *new* sister, the *young* sister. And *their* teacher. She had twelve children: five girls, seven boys—eight Catholics.

About half the class were Hispanic and Black, the other half, Caucasian. The racial mix did not match the region's demographics—in Whitewaters over 90 percent of the population was white. Yet the third grade ratio was no different than every other grade in the school.

Four of her students were new to the school: a Hispanic brother and sister, a child from the deep hollers and one of the three children of a new hotel manager.

~

From the children's perspective, their first two days of school were play days—games and activities from beginning to end. They were fun for the kids and essential for Sr. Rebecca Marise. The children were mixed and matched in some games, for others they could choose their teammates. The games called for various skills—drawing, writing, role playing, singing, team building, computing, motor skills. She alternated between outdoor games with those done in the classroom. Through these activities she was able to get an idea of their strengths, their interests, their weaknesses; who tended to lead, to follow; who were friends, who lagged behind; how the newcomers integrated with the others, how the others included the newcomers. With the games, she also taught them her classroom rules and got them acquainted with their texts and workbooks. And with the results of some activities, she was able to finish off her bulletin boards.

The idea of the "game days" came to her as she finished her unit outlines and began the lesson planning. Who were her children? Sr. Jeanne, and later Sr. Maureen, had both emphasized that her class would be more diverse than any she had ever taught. She had used games before to come to know her students, but she wanted to expand and diversify them so that she could observe and assess the children better. She broached the idea during one of their community hours.

"How enticing," said Sr. Maureen. "What have you planned?"

Sr. Rebecca Marise described some of the games she had done before and some new ones she wanted to try. But there were still some skills for which she was trying to find suitable games.

"What about the math games Anita used?" asked Sr. Maureen.

"Yes, you should try her 'Jumping Chips,'" said Sr. Jeanne.

"'Jumping Chips'?" Sr. Rebecca Marise asked.

"I'm sure they're in her filing cabinet," said Sr. Jeanne.

"There are *lots* of things in her filing cabinet. I haven't had a chance to sort through them all."

"We can improvise." Sr. Jeanne took a sheet of paper and painted long, parallel lines and then divided them with short, vertical lines until there were seven squares lined up like a railroad track. As this dried, she cut out six round circles, dabbed three with red, mixed her brush in blue, and dabbed the other three in purple. The three red circles were lined up in the squares at one end and the three purple at the other with an empty square between them.

"Now," said Sr. Maureen, "You want the red chips where the purple chips are and vice versa. You can only move the chips forward. You can slide a chip forward or jump a chip forward—but only over one chip each move and only a chip of another colour.

Sr. Rebecca Marise began. Both Sr. Jeanne and Sr. Maureen watched her progress.

"No, no, no! No moving backwards," chided Sr. Maureen.

It looked relatively easy, yet Sr. Rebecca Marise was still stumped after a couple of tries. Sr. Jeanne went back to her painting. Sr. Rebecca Marise continued but was growing increasingly sceptical and frustrated. She had other plans for the evening and felt she was just wasting time. However, she managed to maintain a calm demeanour.

After several attempts she asked, "This is possible?"

"Oh, yes, Anita played this game with the kindergarten class," said Sr. Maureen.

"You've got to be kidding!"

"No, I'm not . . . and they were quicker than you!" said Sr. Maureen with a smile. "If I hadn't seen it, I wouldn't have believed it myself."

Not to be outwitted by five-year-olds, Sr. Rebecca Marise set out again. It took a few more tries, but Sr. Rebecca Marise finally managed. "Well, I'll be."

"Oh, you're not finished yet!" said Maureen. "Do it again and count how many moves it took."

Coached by Sr. Maureen, Sr. Rebecca Marise played the game with four chips and then with two, always noting the number of moves. Looking over her figures, she saw a pattern and was able to predict the moves needed for eight chips.

"That's kind of neat," said Sr. Rebecca Marise, leaning back in her chair, "but what does it really teach the children about math?"

"It's the basis for a formula in algebra."

"And third grade students will understand this?" she replied, dubious.

"No, not the formula . . . not yet, Rebecca. But it teaches the children to observe, to see patterns and relationships. Mathematical formulas don't come from abstract principles. They're rooted in reality. Someone observed them. And there are others, still unnoticed, still undiscovered. It seems like a game, Rebecca, but it's teaching the children to think outside the box . . . even when it comes to math. To be open to new patterns, new ways of looking at things."

Sr. Jeanne put down her brush. "In the past, before I even brought up the concept of pi to students, we hunted around the school for anything circular— pipes, tubes, buckets, bongo drums—you name it. Then the kids measured the circumference and divided it by the diameter. Lo and behold, they discovered the result was always something a little over three. Then we talked about pi."

"What a great idea!"

"You know when the ancients discovered pi they were so awed by this universal constant that they believed they had found the key to the divine."

"I didn't know that."

"Pi was discovered," Sr. Jeanne continued, "because someone was aware, observant, and open. That's even more important than the math."

Various games and techniques were brought up and discussed well beyond the time apportioned for their community hour. Even Sr. Candida joined in after she finished her gardening. Sr. Rebecca Marise went to bed buoyed by their support and full of ideas.

~

Sr. Rebecca Marise had developed a chart for each child, listing the skills that she was observing. During the game days she jotted down notes at the breaks or discreetly during an activity. At the end of the school day, she filled in the charts and completed her notes on her laptop.

One activity was a gold mine: "The Mind Reader." Each child had a sheet of paper with their name on the top and the words, *My Favourite*. Then listed down the page, Sr. Rebecca Marise had typed,

My Favourite Food,

My Favourite Animal,

My Favourite Movie,

My Favourite Book,

My Favourite Time, and so on.

The children went through the categories one at a time. After they filled in a category, Sr. Rebecca Marise selected a couple of children who were waving their hands to be chosen. Then she asked the class, "What is Heather's favourite food?" The children had three chances to guess with clues given by Heather. By the end of the exercise, the children knew each other better and Sr. Rebecca Marise had a list of their interests, a sample of their handwriting and spelling, as well as some idea of their ability to communicate, be attentive to others, and stand up before the class. Knowing from Jerome how important interests were to learning, Sr. Rebecca Marise was desirous to discover all she could about her children.

~

"How did your games go?" said Sr. Maureen as she paused in the third grade classroom at the end of the second day.

Sr. Rebecca Marise was typing on her laptop. "I have so much to tell you," she said as she continued to type. "Just trying to get it all down before I forget."

"When you're ready, I'd be very interested to hear the results," she said then left Sr. Rebecca Marise to her work.

~

"Here they are." Sr. Rebecca Marise held up the drafts of her reports as she walked into the community room the following Sunday.

"Bring a chair over here," said Sr. Maureen as she began to look over the reports. Sr. Jeanne and Sr. Candida had not yet arrived.

Sr. Rebecca Marise pulled up a chair next to Sr. Maureen. "They need more work, but most of the information is there."

Some moments passed.

"This is extraordinary, Rebecca. Where did you learn this?"

"I've been doing reading, trying to keep up with the research."

"Would you like to learn more about assessments?"

In her astonishment and delight, Sr. Rebecca Marise took Sr. Maureen by the arm and shook her. "Absolutely!"

The papers slipped from Sr. Maureen's hands, sliding around the floor.

"Oh my God—I mean, my goodness, I'm so sorry." Her effusiveness flipped to shame over her spontaneous outburst—she hadn't done something like that for years. But her embarrassment eased when she saw Sr. Maureen laughing and heard, "Good God, girl!" from Sr. Jeanne who had just entered the room.

"Maureen, keep this one at an arm's distance!"

Sr. Rebecca Marise laughed with the others, though still a bit flustered.

"Jeanne and I will pick up the reports, Rebecca. In the kitchen there's a bag of cookies a mother made for us. Put them on a plate and bring them for community hour. We'll celebrate."

As the two older nuns picked up and sorted the reports, Sr. Maureen said softly, "This girl's a natural, Jeanne. Look at these reports! With some training . . . and she's so keen."

"Yes, I picked that up."

"Do you suppose this is part of their preparation now?"

"As I understand from Rebecca, a couple of years ago, a colleague of one of her professors was visiting who specialized in learning theories and she gave an impromptu lecture on the subject. Rebecca was enthralled, spoke with the visiting professor after the lecture, and received a bibliography. She's been doing her own personal research since then."

"Where is she getting the books?"

"Our college library is now linked with the other colleges and universities in the region—an open exchange system."

"My, how the horizons have opened."

"Not exactly. As I understand, bibliographies used by our sisters are inspected and approved by Mother Mary Thomas or one of her delegates. Whether Rebecca's aware of it or not, she went out on a limb here—she received the bibliography in an approved class, took the ball, and ran with it."

"Well, certainly there would be nothing objectionable in the literature."

"Who's doubting that? But, as you well know, without the general's sanction, the suggested readings would be considered a waste of time, 'inordinate curiosity.'"

Sr. Candida arrived, followed by Sr. Rebecca Marise with the cookies. Sr. Maureen picked up a cookie from the plate and toasted, "To a blessed beginning of the school year."

CHAPTER 43

Sr. Rebecca Marise may have gone out on a limb—of sorts—but she was no rebel. Through most of her childhood, she had dreamed of becoming a sister. By the sixth grade, she and a few other classmates were gathering around their favourite nuns during recess. In time, they were assisting the sisters with the Saturday catechism lessons, and attending the SCRs monthly retreats. Her desire to enter the convent took a downward dip during a period in her teen years when a couple of guys caught her attention. However, love for the SCRs and their way of life won over.

This is not to say all her experiences with the sisters were pleasant. Her father was outspoken when he thought the SCRs were narrow minded, especially regarding several incidents involving her brother. However, her deep admiration all but obliterated these negative moments. By her senior year in high school she was fairly certain she would join.

Her father respected her desire; however, since she wanted to be a teacher and would need a bachelor of education to do so, he advised her to finish college first. That made sense to Rebecca. She registered in the SCR college and threw herself into campus life. She continued to volunteer for the sisters and attended the seasonal retreats offered by the SCRs for young women discerning their vocation.

The February retreat that year was well attended with many women Rebecca's age and younger fervently exploring a religious vocation. Jennifer—later to be Sr. Patrick Marian—was particularly enthusiastic. Although this was her first retreat with the SCRs, she was altogether enamoured and circulated among the attendees, tallying up those who were planning to ask for their application forms and encouraging those who were timid. The vocation directress took time, as she always did, to speak to each participant, but she devoted particular attention to those who seemed both promising and captivated with their life. Unbeknown to her, Rebecca was among the young women identified with this distinguished status.

"Sister, I have a question about something you said during your talk," said Rebecca meekly after a few moments of polite exchanges.

The vocation directress sat across from Rebecca, her hands folded in her lap.

"You said that religious life is superior to married life," continued Rebecca. "I've had discussions with my dad and he disagrees with that."

"Well, I didn't mean that married people aren't called to holiness—there are very holy married couples, I'm sure. And the most important thing is to follow the vocation to which God calls us. However, the Pope himself says that religious life is a superior way of life. It is the life that Jesus chose for himself. That's why religious life is called *the state of perfection* and our vows are *the way of perfection*. If a sister is faithful to the rules of her congregation, they will lead her to holiness and eternal life with Christ. Just look at all the canonized saints who are religious men and women! Through our witness we make the love of Christ present in the world. Through our lives we show how to live the Gospel in this world with our hearts fixed on the world to come.

"No one is worthy of such a call, Rebecca. But isn't it true that God chooses those who are weak to confound the strong? As Mother Mary Thomas often says, blessed are the women chosen for this complete gift of self, this ultimate sacrifice of self for God and souls."

"It's all so beautiful," said Rebecca. "But at times it seems beyond me, you know, to be like Christ on earth. Sometimes I'm worried . . ."

"If God is calling you to be one of our sisters, he will give you the strength to be faithful. When you walk through the doors, his grace will already be waiting for you."

"I'm pretty certain this is what God is asking of me," replied Rebecca tentatively.

"You *are* eligible to apply now. You know that?"

"Yes, yes, I know. But I'll have to complete my BEd to be a teacher even if I enter, so I thought I would give myself a little more time with my family . . . a little more time to reflect . . ."

"God is calling you, Rebecca. Didn't you just say that?" the vocation directress said with a smile.

"Yes."

"Why keep him waiting?"

Rebecca flushed.

"God loves you so much. He is inviting you to be his spouse, to dedicate your life totally to him. He has given you a heart for him alone. God can take care of your family better than you can."

Suddenly her reasons seemed so narrow, so selfish. Of course, if God is calling, why would she hesitate? Why would she put up impediments to her Creator and Redeemer who loved her so?"

"And you wouldn't want to risk losing such a precious vocation by stalling. The devil can be so crafty in the doubts he sows. He knows the power of a life fully dedicated to God."

Rebecca left with her application forms and in the spring she received her letter inviting her to join the incoming postulants in August.

Her mother was overjoyed; her father, resigned. Rebecca knew this would not have been his preference, but he respected his daughter. In only one instance did he interfere.

He had named her Rebecca and cringed at the thought that within a year after her entrance she would acquire something like Dolorosa, Bonaventure, or, as in their parish, Sr. John Chrysostom. When he heard the name, Sr. Pistós, he wrote an appeal to Mother Mary Thomas asking that Rebecca's baptismal name be retained. He pointed out the biblical roots of *Rebecca*, how significant the naming of his daughter had been to him, and assured her that neither Rebecca nor her mother knew about his request. Although the mother general was not one to capitulate, a request such as this—from a father no less—was singular and his manner so endearing and unassuming. Some of the sisters *had* maintained their baptismal name and added another. And she could laud the Blessed Mother in the second name with a variation she had recently heard.

During the ceremony of her entrance to novitiate, "Sr. Rebecca Marise" was pronounced, much to her father's delight and Rebecca's unspoken relief. Had she known about his intercession, she would have been horrified at his audacity. Only years later did he tell her.

Sr. Rebecca Marise plunged into her life with the SCRs, desiring to live it to the full—chastity, poverty, and obedience, lived in community with others who shared the same calling. Obedience was the kingpin. Christ came to do the Father's will: "Obedient until death, even death on a cross." He held nothing back—a complete surrender of himself in love. This was the ideal to which Sr. Rebecca Marise and the sisters aspired in religious life. But how to know the will of the Father?

In his mercy, they were taught, Christ founded the Church to communicate his truth and grace, perpetuating his message and life throughout the ages. He appointed Peter as head of the apostles: "You are Peter and on this rock I will build my Church." Down through the ages his successors, the popes, were duly elected, and retained the leadership and primacy given to Peter, a leadership shared by the bishops in communion with him.

Local bishops and Vatican prelates review and sanction religious congregations with the authority of the Pope. Therefore, superiors of religious communities are invested with authority that derives from Christ himself. Superiors stand in the place of God—what they ask is God's will. Not, of course, if the command is something sinful or contrary to their rules, but this certainly would be a rarity if ever a reality, they were taught.

During their years in formation, Sr. Rebecca Marise and the other aspiring members were exhorted to ignore the human qualities of the superiors, their weaknesses and strengths, their qualifications, competence, or lack thereof, and focus on solely on God who inspired their commands.

If a directive was not to their liking, the sisters were instructed to cheerfully adapt and adjust their attitude; after all, Christ, "who though he was in the form of God, ...emptied himself, taking the form of a slave . . . and became obedient to the point of death."

The sisters' customs and practices, their schedule with its rhythm of prayer, work, and rest, preserved a lifestyle that led to union with God, the gradual transformation of the person in Christ, and the salvation of souls through their prayer and apostolic work. The sisters had this surety because their constitutions were examined and approved by the Church and blessed by the Pope, the Vicar of Christ. For the SCRs, this approval was continually affirmed by the approbation of their bishop as well as other visiting prelates and clergy.

Sr. Rebecca Marise embraced these principles fully. She entered the convent to give her life to Christ, without compromise, serving his Church.

From her experiences in the branch houses, Sr. Rebecca Marise realized that not everything could be done exactly as it was in the motherhouse. Evening events at the school, the parish Mass schedule, smaller numbers of sisters—these all factored into minor adjustments of the schedule. However, all modifications were subject to the approval of Mother Mary Thomas.

At times the modifications made sense; in other cases, less so. While assisting in the kitchen as a novice, Sr. Rebecca Marise noticed that the sisters gave particular care to the platters that were brought to the general superior and her council. No "miscellany" soup was ever served on their table. They were the superiors after all, and had a heavy burden to carry. The extra attention to their food was an expression of the sisters' gratitude, some way to make a return. This expression of gratitude extended to the extra polish and prep of their table, the care of their laundry, and the marked deference and respect whenever they were present. But, then, everyone was happy to do so: they were the superiors, they represented Christ and deserved the reverence.

During their evening community hour, all conversation abruptly halted the moment the recreation period was scheduled to end. The superior or directress clapped her hands or rang a bell and not another comment was allowed. If Mother Mary Thomas happened to be with them for the evening and was giving an exhortation, this period could extend indefinitely; after all, she was the general superior. Generally, Sr. Rebecca Marise didn't care, but when this extension cut into her already limited study time and an essay was due, she prayed that Mother would wind up her thoughts quickly. Then, remorseful, she would tell herself that if she listened respectfully, God would help her finish her school work in less time.

Sr. Rebecca Marise didn't linger with these observations, or allow herself to arrive at any judgment—she loved Christ and wanted to please him in all things. That was all the mattered. She was in awe of Mother Mary Thomas and admired her from a distance. The SCRs were truly fortunate to have such a leader. This was affirmed by the bishop and superiors of other religious orders who occasionally came for meetings.

There was one area, however, that Sr. Rebecca Marise had unconsciously cordoned, and to which her creativity was funnelled—her classroom. To be sure, unit and lesson plans were evaluated and classroom visitations carried out, but how she conducted her class and regarded her pupils was largely her realm. Sr. Rebecca Marise loved her students and wanted to see each of them grow in confidence, to discover the excitement of learning. Her experience with Jerome only made her more ardent. So while she listened to and respected all they were taught regarding the education of children, she was always in search of new insights, better methods. She was low-key about her ongoing study—humility: it was just a humble little pursuit for the sake of the children.

CHAPTER 44

The bell disrupted the babble and play, and the children quieted down and stood next to their desks.

Through the intercom, a young boy led them in the Our Father and the pledge of allegiance. Then Sr. Maureen came on: "Good morning, children. Today Cheryl will read our story."

Cheryl cleared her throat in the microphone: "Jamie held his brother's hand, half-walking, half-running, to keep up with Michael's long legs. Jamie did not complain—he wouldn't think of it. He loved Michael. Jamie loved every minute he could spend with his older brother, even these five-minute walks to and from school. Michael, instead, had his mind busy with other concerns and barely noticed his little brother trotting at his side. Jamie was one of his chores: take Jamie to school, bring Jamie safely home. Michael wasn't mean to Jamie, he just didn't see him. How different each day would have been if Michael spent those few minutes coming to know Jamie's world and letting Jamie know his."

A whine, a click, and the intercom was off.

"Let's all sit down, close our eyes for a moment, and think about the story," said Sr. Rebecca Marise.

In those few moments, she looked over the students and took attendance. Most of the children wore navy tops. Unlike the other SCR schools, there were no plaid jumpers, no white blouses and shirts, no sweaters with embroidered school emblems. The children at St. Martin's wore navy-blue or white polo shirts, the same colours for sweat shirts and sweaters, and navy-blue or black pants. Period.

Parents could buy the clothing wherever they liked, although a local store kept a stock of the polo shirts.

"Before we talk about the story, let's act it out. Who wants to be the older brother or older sister?" Hands shot up. "Remember, this part will have to be someone who is taller." A few hands went down. A girl was chosen as the older sibling and for the little brother, a boy. Sr. Rebecca Marise had them walking back and forth in front of the class, but not before massive giggling about holding hands. A compromise was reached: the "older sister" held onto the "little brother's" sleeve. The older sister did a superb job of ignoring her little brother.

"How do you suppose Jamie felt when he was ignored by his sister?"

"Sad." "Not good." "Lonely." "Sad."

"What about school? Can something like this happen in school?"

"You can feel lonely."

"When can you feel lonely at school?"

A number of hands waved.

"When no one will play with you."

"When people won't help you."

Sr. Rebecca Marise drew out a few more examples then asked, "So what can we do to make sure everyone feels welcome?"

"Play with them at recess." "Talk to people at lunch."

"If people give the wrong answer, should we laugh at them?"

"Nooo," came the group response. A hand waved.

"Sometimes mistakes *are* funny."

"You're right, Jacob." And so began a discussion on laughing at people, laughing at oneself, and respect.

"Since we were just going to start English class, let take out our workbooks and write a story on respecting others. You can write about something at school or home, it can be real or pretend."

Some students set out immediately, a number appeared to be thinking of a story, and others looked lost.

Three children needed immediate assistance. Alessandro and Mariarosa were brother and sister. Alessandro was two-grades behind his peers and Mariarosa, one. What made matters more complicated, Mariarosa appeared to be the more eager learner. Their parents had been migrant workers, following the crops, house painting, and doing other odd jobs. A cousin of their father had come to Whitewaters to be part of a construction crew when the community college was expanding. On completion he became one of its janitors and was now a junior foreman in the maintenance department. With a position opened, he encouraged his cousin and family to move to Whitewaters, offering a place in his home until they were on their feet. Both parents could manage in English but preferred Spanish. With the moves from school to school and English as a second language, the children lagged behind. Sr. Rebecca Marise could tell Alessandro was self-conscious among the younger children, but Sr. Maureen's options were limited. Outside of private tutoring, which both the school and the parents could not afford, Alessandro would have to be placed in the third grade in order to catch up.

The third child in need of special attention was Cody. His roots lay deep in the hollers of Appalachia. Children from the remote mountain communities were rare in Whitewaters and even more so at St. Martin's. He was the son of a single mother who was sufficiently un-churched and anxious enough about her child's well-being to lay aside her lingering misgivings regarding Catholics. Insecure and fearful, Cody Watson was a loner and a target for bullying. His mother, Holly, was born in a small, mountain holler and at sixteen became pregnant. She never revealed the father of the baby and, as a result, was ostracised by her family and looked down upon by the neighbours.

Holly ran away to the larger town of Birchbark where she kept to herself and survived through waitressing and social assistance. A women's outreach organization came to know of Holly, offered her counselling, and helped her finish high school. Through this organization, Holly was able to connect with another agency and move to Whitewaters where she had more opportunities for education, work, and assistance for her son.

Cody had not done well in Birchbark and declined even further in Whitewaters. Already shy, he was teased for his *hillbilly* colloquialisms that stymied his speech even further. Small for his age and easily intimidated, Cody did not retaliate when shoved in the playground or the corridors. He was friendless and withdrawn.

Holly had heard about St. Martin's through the learning centre and visited the school last spring. For Holly, more off-putting than the Catholicism was the high percentage of blacks and Hispanics, but when Holly saw the small class size and the children playing together during recess, she knew this was the school for her son.

For Sr. Rebecca Marise, the problem was dividing herself among the children. She decided on the butterfly approach: encourage and help each to get started and then begin the rounds again.

Alessandro and Mariarosa had enough English comprehension to understand the instructions but lacked the skills and confidence to begin the task. Sr. Rebecca Marise managed to pull out some ideas for stories from Mariarosa and encouraged them both to write without worrying about spelling or grammar—she would help them later with this. She then moved on to Cody who gazed out the window. From him she could elicit not a syllable. Fleeting eye contact she chalked up as a victory.

"Maybe you could draw your story with stick people."

She drew a few samples on his paper and left him to his contemplation. Hopefully, he would pick up his pencil.

Leah was another case altogether. She excelled in all things verbal. Fortunately, this information had been passed on and Sr. Rebecca Marise had called her mother to discuss ways to entice her in the classroom. Coached by Sr. Maureen and assisted by the librarian, she had begun a reading plan that would take Leah through a series of novels with a number of projects. Leah, she was told, was close to a grade six reading level, but Sr. Rebecca Marise wanted to ascertain how much she understood and could relate to her life. Leah was finishing up the writing assignment so Sr. Rebecca Marise set out the first novel and her new "novel journal."

Glancing at the work of the students in various stages of completion, Sr. Rebecca Marise moved back to Alessandro and Mariarosa. Mariarosa was making an attempt at her story but Alessandro was slumped back in his chair, staring at the desk. Sr. Rebecca Marise squatted near him. "So, how are you doing?"

Alessandro made no response.

"Have you thought of a story?"

"*Para bebé*," muttered Alessandro, staring at his desk.

"He thinks it's for babies," Mariarosa translated.

"We'll talk more about this later."

Sr. Rebecca Marise went to the front of the class. "Everyone, write your name on the top of the page and hand in your assignment. It's OK if you didn't finish. Just hand in what you have." And she went on with her plan for the day.

In the afternoon, when the rest of the class was completing a task in their workbooks, Sr. Rebecca Marise took Alessandro aside. Her attempts to engage him were futile until she asked, "Would you rather be with the older children?"

Alessandro said nothing but she could see tears in his eyes before he looked down. Sr. Maureen hoped that Alessandro, being older, would catch on quickly and she would be able to move him up swiftly to his class level. Sr. Rebecca Marise could see that this would be unlikely with Alessandro. He was too cognizant of his age difference and being with a younger sibling only added to the humiliation—she had witnessed this throughout the games.

It was only the third day of school, reasoned Sr. Rebecca Marise. Alessandro may just need some time to adjust his attitude and move on. She had no experience with a situation such as this. With their school transcripts, neither brother nor sister would have been admitted to a standard SCR school. Sr. Rebecca Marise hoped to make the best of the situation. *Surely, God will give me the grace if I obey.* Yet, her instincts were throwing up red flags. She feared Alessandro's negative attitude toward school would only become more entrenched the longer he remained in the current setup.

Sr. Rebecca Marise approached Sr. Maureen's office after school, torn between her understanding of the situation and her misgivings in differing with the decision of a superior. When she arrived, there was a furor of activity regarding a pickup, a delay, a child left behind . . . Sr. Rebecca Marise was about to turn around and leave when Sr. Maureen noticed her.

"Give me a half-hour, Rebecca. I'll meet you in your classroom."

Sr. Rebecca Marise was correcting assignments when Sr. Maureen walked in and leaned against the windowsill.

"So what's up?"

"It's about Alessandro and Mariarosa." Then, haltingly, she continued, "I know we thought . . . We don't have many options . . ."

"Rebecca, to the point."

"I don't think Alessandro will succeed if we go ahead as planned."

"It's only the third day of school."

"He's ashamed."

Sr. Maureen glanced down then said, "I'll be back."

To Sr. Rebecca Marise's surprise, Sr. Maureen returned several minutes later with Ms. Meagan Turner, the fifth grade teacher, Ms. Cheryl Weston, the fourth grade teacher, and Sr. Jeanne.

Sr. Rebecca Marise related what she had observed in the past three days. "I'm afraid the longer we let this continue, the more set Alessandro will become. He's ashamed to be with the younger children."

"And if we move him to the fifth grade?" said Sr. Maureen, turning to Meagan.

"He will be overwhelmed with the work and be just as humiliated being so far behind the others."

"I think the same would happen in the fourth grade," said Cheryl.

"Riverview Elementary has a remedial program," said Sr. Jeanne.

Silence.

"So we split up the family?" said Sr. Maureen.

"Or we can send both," said Meagan.

"I think Mariarosa will do fine here," said Sr. Rebecca Marise.

Silence.

"Alessandro may profit with the remedial program, but he's also Hispanic," said Sr. Maureen.

"What does that have to do with it?" asked Sr. Rebecca Marise.

"The other schools in Whitewaters, with larger enrolments than ours, might have one black child and a couple of Hispanics—max—among *all* their students," said Cheryl.

"And delayed as he is . . . Alessandro will stick out like a sore thumb," said Sr. Maureen.

"You're right. And to make matters worse, some people in the area feel that Hispanics steal jobs from the locals and should be shipped back across the border," added Sr. Jeanne.

"So let's say Alessandro stays here, what can we do?" said Sr. Maureen.

"He needs a lot of one-on-one to bring him to the fifth grade level," said Sr. Rebecca Marise. "I believe he has the capability, I just can't give him the time . . . and being in the third grade with his sister is insulting to him."

"Are there other children his age who could also use some remedial attention?" asked Sr. Maureen.

"In the fifth grade, Clayton and Jessica for English; Tanner for math," said Meagan.

Cheryl mentioned a few children from the fourth grade

Through the discussion a conceivable plan developed. A retired teacher in the parish would be consulted as well as a couple of mothers who had already shown skills as teacher assistants. The librarian might also be able to give a hand. If the volunteers could be rounded up, Alessandro would join the fifth grade and participate in all non-academic subjects, receiving tutoring for the academic. Meagan would prepare the children to welcome and accept him. Alessandro and Mariarosa would be recommended for subsidized tutoring at the learning centre downtown if their parents could provide the transportation. Sr. Rebecca Marise would talk to Alessandro the next day and Sr. Maureen would try to arrange a meeting with one of the parents.

~

As Sr. Rebecca Marise walked down the wooden stairs from the school to the convent that afternoon, she became acutely aware of the nagging discomfort she had felt for the past few hours. *That stocking again!* She went to her room to assess the damage. Darned and re-darned, there was no hope of repairing the stocking this time. And because she had run around in it all day, a blister had formed where her big toe had pushed through. *I should have come down and changed during lunch break.* Sr. Rebecca Marise changed her stockings, washed the worn-out pair, wrung them out in her towel, hung them on her chair in front of her opened window, then dashed off for prayers.

That evening at the beginning of community hour, Sr. Rebecca Marise went to her room and returned with her battle-scarred stockings. She sat next to Sr. Maureen and, extending the stockings, said, "I've mended these stocking for a while now and I think I need a new pair. Holes are popping out on the soles."

Maureen barely glanced at the stockings, continuing with the project she had brought for community hour. "You know where the community supplies are, Rebecca. If you need something, help yourself."

Sr. Rebecca Marise looked puzzled. "You don't want me to ask you for anything? Soap and shampoo and—?"

"Rebecca, you're managing an entire classroom. You've come up with a very creative approach to teach your children, and, I might add, in a very limited period of time. I believe," said Sr. Maureen with a touch of humour, "I can safely say that you have the judiciary powers to decide when you need a bar of soap."

"But . . . but I thought we asked . . . you know, to grow in humility."

Sr. Maureen set down her work. "Rebecca, humility is not condescending to ask your superior for soap, Q-tips, and bobby pins. Humility is being at peace with who you are: loved by God, grateful for the talents and gifts you have . . . not pretending to have more, not feigning to have less . . . and grateful for the gift of others and the world that surrounds us. Now, go and get the stockings you need." Sr. Maureen returned to her work but Sr. Rebecca Marise remained sitting next to her. Sr. Maureen looked back at her, "What?"

"I need . . . need some Band-Aids and peroxide, too. I got a blister."

"Let me see those stockings." She took the still-damp pair of stocking from Sr. Rebecca Marise. "Rebecca! What is this?" The toes and heels were nothing but a bundle of criss-crossed darning upon darning. "This is crazy. You must have calluses all over your feet!"

In fact, she did.

"Rebecca, to repair a small hole here and there, OK. But to walk around on these . . . knots? And the time you're taking to sew and re-sew?"

Sr. Maureen handed the stockings back to Rebecca. "Throw out any stockings you've darned, replace them with new sets and make an appointment with the podiatrist—Candida sees one."

"And . . . and the peroxide . . . is it in the closet, too?"

"Rebecca, all the supplies are in the closet: aspirin, Band-Aids, et cetera, et cetera. Take what you need and let me know if you notice anything is running low or you need something else."

From the day Rebecca entered the convent, she had never had access to the supply closet. Through their consecration, she had learned, the sisters surrendered themselves to Christ. They owned nothing. Never did they say "my shoes" or "my notebook" but "the shoes of my use" or "the notebook of my use." Clothing, toiletries, and common medications were always locked in a room or cabinet. Everything was requested from and distributed by the superior or mistress in order to enable sisters to grow in humility and to manifest their complete dependence on God. It was belittling at times, especially when the line was long and others could hear more personal requests. However, by offering up this sacrifice to God, graces were obtained for the needy on earth and in purgatory. And here she was, standing before the open supply closet, timidly picking out a couple pairs of stocking and about to arrange an appointment with the podiatrist. Relieved and reticent. *Whitewaters* . . .

~

Several days later, Alessandro was placed in the fifth grade. There were some adjustments to the initial plan, but the volunteers came through. Although still diffident, Alessandro appeared more relaxed and less sullen within the small circle of children who came in and out of the newly formed remedial program. From his parents, Sr. Maureen discovered he loved soccer and bought a couple more balls. It wasn't long before Alessandro and a few boys were kicking them around during recess.

CHAPTER 45

L ife zipped by for Sr. Rebecca Marise. With the prep, presentation, and assignment correction, she had little time to consider much else than her teaching. One afternoon, toward the end of September, Fr. Doug was again at the door of her classroom.

"I hear you are doing great work here with the children."

Sr. Rebecca Marise rose. "Thank you."

Fr. Doug made himself comfortable on the desks as he had previously.

"I understand you will be handling the First Communion and Reconciliation prep with the second grade."

"Yes, that's correct."

"So, what's your plan."

Her plan? Of all the course prep for which she was responsible, First Communion and Reconciliation were the least of her worries. In her teens, she had assisted with catechism classes, most often with children receiving First Communion. She had been teaching second grade for the past two years. For Sr. Rebecca Marise, teaching First Communion and First Reconciliation was practically memorized.

Together with other like-minded religious congregations, the SCRs had developed a religious education curriculum based on the *Universal Catechism*. The content for each lesson was detailed and expected to be followed. Such strictures in other subjects would have been asphyxiating for Sr. Rebecca Marise, but regarding the teachings of the Church she understood the need for such vigilance. The current state of the world and confusion among the members of the Church pointed to the need for strong leadership and clear teachings. It was a sacred duty to pass on the message of Christ as taught and safeguarded by the Church for two thousand years.

"Father," said Sr. Rebecca Marise as she moved to the bookcase, "here is the text and the workbook."

"No need to bring over the books. I have them."

So, what's the point of asking? Sr. Rebecca Marise sat back down. "Well, that's the curriculum I follow for First Communion and First Reconciliation."

"And that's what I came to chat about."

Fr. Doug was nice enough, very personable with the parishioners and students but some of his comments in his sermons made her sceptical. She picked up a pencil and began to turn it between her finger and thumb.

"I assume you will begin with First Reconciliation," said Fr. Doug.

"Yes, and the children should be prepared by the beginning of December. We start with First Communion preparation after Christmas."

"How do you handle the topic of sin."

"As the Church teaches, Father, sin is an offence against God." *What was this all about?* "Father, I follow the text—everything I'll be teaching is there." She tried to control the edge she felt growing in the tone of her voice.

Fr. Doug moved from his chair and looked out the window. "The clouds are low today. It's amazing. On a cloudy day, you could believe we were living in the plains." He turned around and leaned against the windowsill.

"In the textbook, Rebecca, sin is personified in animals. I gather you intend to follow this pedagogical line?"

Sr. Rebecca Marise shifted in her chair and fingered a paperclip.

"Well, I don't find the animal approach helpful or sound. In fact, when young children come to confession and tell me they are pigs, clams, and donkeys, I find it disturbing."

"I believe it's only meant to be an allegory, Father, to help them understand."

"It's categorizing children with uncomplimentary personality traits that have little or nothing to do with sin. 'I'm a pig because I didn't clean up my room?' 'I didn't talk to my classmate when I got mad—I'm a clam'? Rebecca, I'm not making this up. One child even confessed he was a turtle—he did his work slowly. What allegory are we talking about here, what is it you want them to understand?"

Sr. Rebecca Marise cheeks burned. In another school, she had heard children saying, "You're just a stubborn donkey" or "a puffed-up old peacock": characterizations they had heard in religion class, meant for self-reflection but used as put-downs. Sr. Rebecca Marise had dismissed it then, but the memory now made her uncomfortable. At the same time, she found herself defending the text.

Fr. Doug continued, "Anita and I had a long chat about this. When she began teaching all First Communion and Reconciliation classes, the zoo was eliminated."

He pulled a folded booklet from his back pocket and handed it to Sr. Rebecca Marise. "This is what Anita used, with her superior's approval, I might add. Talk it over with Maureen. I do not want the animals trotting back into the confessional."

"I'm sure the intent of the lesson is only to convey the teachings of the Christ in a way the children can understand."

"The teachings of the Christ? What makes you so sure?"

"Christ founded the Church, appointed Peter as the head, and Popes have been appointed in succession ever since. We can be sure we are following Christ if we follow the teachings of the Church. And these religion texts are based on the *Universal Catechism*."

"Rebecca, are we having a conversation or is this a catechism lesson?"

Sr. Rebecca Marise bristled.

"The Popes haven't always been right. What about those wealthy pontiffs who fathered children and manoeuvred their relatives into high places?"

"They never taught anything officially contrary to the gospel. The Church survived even with its human weakness. It shows the power of the Holy Spirit and God's beneficence and protection toward his Church."

"So the people of that time had to listen to the Pope and observe his actions and then discern what, if anything he said or did, was according to the Gospel?"

Sr. Rebecca Marise wasn't sure if this was what she intended. "We're blessed with saintly men today."

"Saintly men. . . . So we have no worries. We just have to trust and obey."

Sr. Rebecca Marise said nothing.

"Is that really following Christ? Did *he* obey the Pope?"

"He was God."

"And also man, Rebecca. He was born a Jew in a Jewish culture and assumed the customs, the beliefs, the laws of his people. But he did not feel bound by them if the situation called for some other response: gathering grain from the fields to eat on the Sabbath, interacting with the "unclean" prostitutes, sinners, tax collectors, lepers, and haemorrhaging women. He had to discern."

What began as irritation was mounting to anger and getting harder for Sr. Rebecca Marise to suppress. Her voice trembled in her effort to maintain control.

"We can spend our lives questioning everything, rationalizing everything, or we can radically follow Christ—that's what religious life is all about. And the Pope represents Christ." Never had she been so aggravated.

"Christ discerned the Father's will. And it wasn't always easy," said the priest. "He sweat blood and went ahead with his decision even though he was misunderstood and condemned by the religious leaders of his time . . . and all the while feeling that he was abandoned by God. Are you willing to radically follow that?" Fr. Doug stood up. "Obedience can also be a cop-out from taking responsibility for our lives." And he left the room.

Sr. Rebecca Marise tried to go back to the work on her desk, but could not focus. Her anger led to confusion, confusion to anger. Who did he think he was?

A half-hour before prayer. Sr. Rebecca Marise gathered her things, but rather than drop them off in the convent, she walked directly to the church. It was empty. The red sanctuary lamp flickered near the tabernacle. Sr. Rebecca Marise knelt in their customary pew and mentally began to say the perfunctory prayer they always recited after entering a church.

O, my Jesus, I adore you present here in the Blessed Sacrament. You are all good, I praise you . . .

But her simmering emotion broke through and she could not continue. She hated Fr. Doug and yet she could not account for her own conflicted emotions. As he spoke, she recalled the image of the schoolchildren referring to each other . . . she had to admit it, calling each other names, using the animal litany of sins. That was exactly what they were doing and deep down she had always known it. But, she hastily reminded herself, that wasn't the intent of the lessons. They had been carefully planned and approved by her superiors. Anything could be twisted. . . . And why hadn't Sr. Maureen told her about "the zoo"? Why did she have to be informed—or confronted—by Fr. Doug? In this instance, however, Sr. Rebecca Marise, knew she was being unreasonable. With all that was going on in the school in the past month, and the sudden transfer, Sr. Maureen wouldn't remember an adjustment made years ago to the Reconciliation program. Well then, Fr. Doug should have gone to Sr. Maureen. She didn't want to deal with him. And she resented his feet on the children's chairs, the slob . . . the pig. So there!

She sat down in the pew and put her feet on *his* kneeler . . . they were dirty anyway. With her elbows on her knees, she rested her head in her hands. At the motherhouse, she would have been called down for this, but right now, she could not have cared less. Upset, tense, confused, she silently repeated over and over, "Jesus, help me, Jesus, help me. . . ."

Gradually, she relaxed. She could not dismiss, however, the insight that came to her while Fr. Doug spoke of his concerns. She realized then that she had never felt comfortable with "the zoo." Her superiors had the children's good at heart. They wanted to pass on the teachings of the Church, but perhaps this detail had been missed. But why had she never acknowledged it before?

As this question came up, another thought took over—the booklet prepared by Anita. She flipped through the stack of material she had brought from school, found the creased booklet and looked it over. Love of God and love of others— the two essential commandments of Christ. Anita's examination of conscience for the children could be summarized by respect, consideration, acceptance, and compassion. At first her defences were stroked again—this is what they were teaching using the animals. But she knew Fr. Doug was right—the animals branded children with negative traits, which she herself had heard them flinging at each other. Anita's approach encouraged respect and empathy, directly and simply. Sr. Maureen had already approved . . . it was a better presentation.

The question still remained, like a burr in her brain: Why had she never given weight to her own misgivings? *Obedience can be a cop-out.* She really did not like Fr. Doug. The pew jostled. Sr. Rebecca Marise looked up to see Sr. Candida smiling sweetly at her as she made her way down the pew for evening prayer.

CHAPTER 46

Confession. The SCRs went every week, following the practice set by the old *Code of Canon Law* and continued in their rules. Reconciliation at the parish was scheduled on Friday afternoon, before Mass, or one could make an appointment. In all other SCR communities, the sisters went to confession on the same day during an established time. At Whitewaters, the sisters were free to choose their own time. Sr. Rebecca Marise kept to the regularly scheduled Friday hours.

She didn't have a problem with confession, per se, but weekly had always been a chore for her. Sure, she made mistakes, sure, she had her failings, but deliberately, consciously, intending to hurt another person and offend God? Long before, she had decided not to split hairs: just say failings, forget about whether she really intended it or became aware afterwards. Otherwise she tied herself into a moral knot. Confession with Fr. Doug only made matters worse . . . and there were no other options. Anonymous? Even with the screen, Fr. Doug knew her by voice and referred to her by name.

Just get in there and out, she told herself as she walked into the church. She had made up her mind that it was going to be a standard, "Lack of charity." That about covered everything. After her three-word confession, a long pause ensued from the other side of the screen.

"Rebecca, I'd like to say something about our conversation the other day."

Sr. Rebecca Marise stiffened.

"I have great admiration for what the SCRs are doing in Whitewaters. As

I've mentioned before, you are living with phenomenal sisters here."

Sr. Rebecca Marise said nothing.

"Following Christ does not mean to live without doubts, that we never ask questions. There was a time when popes and bishops owned slaves. Even the great Thomas Aquinas justified slavery. So, were the people who dared to question the practice of slavery unfaithful to Christ?"

Again Sr. Rebecca Marise said nothing.

"What we treasure, what we allow to govern our lives, we should be free to question and examine. If it is of God, our questioning will only lead us closer to God."

Sr. Rebecca Marise stared straight ahead at nothing and clung to her silence.

"Before you go, Rebecca, I do want to say that you are doing wonderful work with the children. They love you and their parents are pleased—I hear about you often."

Rebecca blinked back tears in the darkness of the confessional.

"For your penance, continue what you are doing with the children. We're fortunate to have you here. And I absolve you from your sins, in the name of the Father, and the Son, and the Holy Spirit. Amen."

As resistant as Sr. Rebecca Marise was to making any reply, she had to be honest with Fr. Doug.

"Father, you were right about the zoo. Sr. Anita's approach is better."

Then she got up and left before the conversation could be continued. At the front of the church she knelt in the pew, more confused than ever.

~

Fr. Doug was relieved. He had no intention of being confrontational regarding the Reconciliation preparation. Over the past twelve years, he and the local sisters had come to know each other well and collaborated continually in parish-school events. A few times a year, he invited the sisters over for dinner. He had grown so accustomed to openly discussing issues and opinions with the four veterans that he had forgotten just how unique they were among the SCRs. Rebecca was so concerned about the development of each student, so open toward the teaching approach used at Whitewaters; all of which he heard from the parents, the sisters, and other teachers. He had not been prepared for her reaction regarding the animal categorization nor how quickly an issue of methodology became entangled with fidelity to the Pope. He had no intention of disrespecting her beliefs and yet, as she spoke, he felt he needed to question her blind adherence to an authority structure that, being human, was also fallible. Knowing her regularity in confession, he had hoped he could soften what he felt he expressed too harshly. He never expected Rebecca to reciprocate and he was grateful. He, indeed, had an unusual group of SCRs in his midst.

~

Not everyone in the diocese—Fr. Doug included—was pleased with Bishop Patterson's conventional orthodoxy and the manner with which he conveyed it in his sermons and letters, and in the distribution of diocesan funds to various programs and organizations. A marginal group of priests questioned his close alliance with the SCRs and referred to them as the bishop's harem. In a position to observe the machinations of the diocese, they were astonished at his blatant favouritism.

The SCRs taught at a host of Catholic schools in the diocese and administered a substantial number. One matronly SCR served as the bishop's secretary. She lived in a wing of his residence together with two other sisters who were in charge of the practical aspects of running his household. For Christmas, Easter, and his birthday, the bishop was wined, dined, and entertained at the SCR motherhouse. The SCRs were found in many diocesan committees and were involved in the planning of every significant event in the diocese. Their attentiveness and unswerving loyalty could not but gratify the bishop, who was already inclined to be favourably disposed in their regard. Once a crusty, old priest, seeking funds for his rural parish, arrived for his appointment with a plate of homemade brownies for the bishop. But the raillery was lost on His Excellency who had the sisters bring in coffee and their chocolate chip cookies as well.

There were a few other religious orders in the diocese. Among these sisters, one held a key administration post at the hospital once operated by her congregation, another was a professor at the university, and a handful were hired by social agencies. For the most part, however, members of these religious orders were elderly, ministering to the sick in parishes and hospitals. They could be easily overlooked and dismissed, perhaps in the same way the SCRs had been years ago. None of these religious orders attracted the young women as did the

SCRs, in fact, most hadn't received a recruit for several years. They could not but wonder, observe, speculate and, in a few cases, even envy the SCRs and their confident leader, Mother Mary Thomas.

Fr. Doug watched the Church he loved move from the openness and social responsibility following Vatican II to its current fixation on doctrinal and sexual purity. It was incongruous to hear these themes repeated over and over at every level of the Church when, among the clergy and hierarchy, sexual and financial scandals emerged. A little humility would go a long way, he thought, and perhaps crack open the window to see Christ in the very world they were condemning.

He volunteered for Whitewaters when its aging pastor went into retirement. He had covered for the old priest during his vacations and enjoyed the beauty and simplicity of the remote mountain communities. Mission churches in the back hills brought him face-to-face with the hidden poverty of Appalachia, and the illness, substance abuse, and domestic violence that compounded it. Together with other concerned leaders in the community, he and the sisters did what they could to raise awareness and address the issues that plagued the mountain people. At Whitewaters, Fr. Doug could distance himself from the rhetoric and the politics of the diocesan hierarchy and focus on the values and needs of the people.

And now Rebecca was part of the scene, aspiring and reluctant. He hung his stole on a hook in the confessional and walked toward the front of the church to vest for Mass. A small group of people had already gathered, praying the Liturgy of the Hours with the sisters. He should have the sisters over for one of his spaghetti dinners. . . .

CHAPTER 47

The weekend schedule among the SCRs varied from the weekdays. At the motherhouse, the community rose a half-hour later. Following their prayers, Mass, and breakfast, sufficient time was given for a thorough cleaning of the premises—a duty divided largely among postulants and novices, although the professed sisters had their private quarters to tend to as well. After lunch, a speaker addressed the professed community on some aspect of spirituality, church teaching, philosophy, or an issue of the day. These lectures were commonly done as a series with one topic continuing over a few weeks. More often than not, they were prepared by members of the SCRs, many by Mother Mary Thomas who read from an article or book and added her commentary. If the superiors were fortunate, a distinguished Catholic leader, generally a member of the hierarchy or clergy, could be coaxed into a side trip to address the sisters. If not, recordings of their presentations, delivered in more prominent settings, were used. In any case, all presentations were either dutifully recorded or purchased and then sent throughout the branch communities for their Saturday "ongoing formation" sessions. The rest of Saturday afternoon was left for personal cleaning and study. In the evening, as always, the sisters gathered after supper for community time, prayer, then silence.

In the branch houses, the schedule followed that of the motherhouse, although local adjustments were made if the sisters had other ministries to carry out. In Whitewaters, these adjustments were liberal. After supper, when typically all the sisters of a branch community pitched in for dishes, at Whitewaters, one of the sisters cleaned the community room. The following evening another member saw to the parlour-reception area, and so forth. By the time the dishes were done, an area of the convent was in order as well. As for the ongoing formation recordings, they were heard one evening a week during a community hour while Jeanne painted, Maureen ironed, and Candida "rested her eyes," although a sudden jerk of her neck now and then indicated more than her eyes were resting. Rebecca continued to take notes as they were all encouraged to do at the motherhouse.

So, outside the communal prayer and their gathering after supper, Saturdays and Sundays were freed up. Sr. Rebecca Marise had never experienced such a length of time wholly at her disposal. She looked forward to it as an oasis to catch up and prepare for the upcoming week. In the weeks ahead, she would also be responsible for periodic retreats for young women and collaborate occasionally with parish initiatives, but for the moment, keeping abreast of her responsibilities at school consumed her on the weekends.

~

Sr. Jeanne's Saturday apostolic service lay elsewhere. Right after Mass, she was picked up by Pam, an outreach team member, and together they drove into rural Appalachia.

Sr. Rebecca Marise was intrigued by Sr. Jeanne's mission ever since she eluded to it one morning as they washed the breakfast dishes.

"You go into the mountains? What is it like? What do you do?"

"I help out in the Women's Centre in Birchbark."

"What type of work does the centre do?"

Sr. Jeanne was not forthcoming."

"What do you do?" Sr. Rebecca Marise urged again.

"My God, Rebecca!"

Rebecca blushed, flustered at her own intensity.

"She's just interested, Jeanne," said Sr. Maureen.

"I'm sorry. I've got some things to prepare before class." And she left the room.

Sr. Rebecca Marise's embarrassment turned to guilt. "I'm so sorry. I didn't mean . . ."

"Don't worry about it, Rebecca. You're passionate—that's good. With Jeanne, you just have to learn . . . at times . . . to be a little more . . . subtle."

"Subtle? She's not exactly subtle herself," said Sr. Rebecca Marise in a low tone.

"In some areas she's more reserved. Be careful not to barge in."

"I'm that intimidating?" She wiped away a tear.

"No, she's frightened."

At supper, Sr. Rebecca Marise sat next to Sr. Jeanne so she wouldn't have to look at her during the meal. One thing about a community of four, you couldn't avoid sisters as easily as in the motherhouse. Fortunately, Sr. Maureen put on *The Lord of the Rings.*

Later at the community gathering, Sr. Jeanne was painting and Sr. Rebecca Marise was cutting out shapes and forms in various colours for a class activity. Sr. Candida settled into the easy chair that, Sr. Rebecca Marise noticed, was always left for her. Whatever task she brought would soon be resting on her lap, her chin gently bobbing toward her chest. Sr. Maureen rummaged through the supply closet in the foyer near the community room. "I'll be there in a minute."

Sr. Jeanne dipped her brush in her palette and began to stroke the canvas. "The Women's Centre was set up around 1980."

Sr. Rebecca Marise stopped cutting. *Just shut up and listen*, she told herself. She began again to work her scissors.

"It's one of several spread throughout a number of counties." There was a long pause. "So what happened to the eager beaver of this afternoon?"

Sr. Rebecca Marise looked at Sr. Jeanne, genuinely perplexed. "I don't get it," she began hesitantly. "I asked you questions . . . and hurt you somehow . . . but now . . . ?"

Sr. Jeanne gently stroked the canvas.

"Sometimes I'm a little strange." She held her brush up, tilted her head back, and gazed at her picture. Then, resuming her previous position, she lightly touched the canvas.

"A couple of sisters, Judy and Bev, came from New York in the late seventies and joined a network that sought to help the people of Appalachia. They were instrumental in setting up the Birchbark centre. But they weren't the only sisters to come to Appalachia. Nuns from other congregations became part of the network and other centres opened. Over the years, the leadership and expertise of the Birchbark staff developed to the point that Judy and Bev were able to move on and assist at another centre. However, Bev comes occasionally to present seminars for the staff as well as for the women coming to the centre. She'll be dropping by Whitewaters in a few weeks. You can find out all you want to know about the Birchbark centre from her."

CHAPTER 48

F r. Doug's conversations and the other novelties of Whitewaters would have troubled Sr. Rebecca Marise longer and much more deeply had her school work been less demanding and she less absorbed with her students. Her interest prompted many conversations with the sisters, other teachers, and parents, sparking ideas and initiatives.

Cody continued to perplex her. His trust in her was obviously growing. On the one hand, this was encouraging and, if she was honest, flattering. On the other, she worried about the direction it was taking.

"He won't begin an assignment unless I go over to help him get started," she explained one day to Sr. Jeanne. "When we are outside for recess or lunch break, he comes near me and holds my hand, watching the other children."

"And how do the kids react to that?"

"Wide-eyed stares . . . smirks. It's only through some heart-to-heart chats with the other students that he is accepted. Honestly, the children seem at a loss. They don't interact with him. His behaviour resembles a shy three- or four-year-old—and he's almost nine."

"So what are you doing?"

"I don't want to stop the individual help in class, because he is improving and moving ahead with the lessons. He's actually quite bright. If I stop, I'm afraid he'll backslide. On the other hand, I don't want him to become dependent on me. So, for now I just make sure I don't go to him first all the time."

"Good."

"At recess, when I join in on the games Cody is more likely to participate, although he still remains on the fringes. The point is he has not made one friend. He doesn't interact with the other children."

Both were silent for a moment.

"I have no idea what he enjoys . . . really. Do you know what's going on with his mother?" asked Sr. Rebecca Marise.

"She's very young herself and anxious about Cody's welfare," replied Sr. Jeanne.

"I've picked that up. That's why I haven't told her about his lack of participation with the other children. I'm afraid she'll only make it worse."

"For all that girl has been through, it's amazing she is doing as well as she is. Cody is all that she has. She doesn't want him to get hurt . . . and, at the same time, she's thwarting him. . . . I know the agency that's helping her in Whitewaters."

"Can we work with them?"

"I'll see what we can do."

~

Two days later an eighth grade student knocked on the classroom door during a morning lesson and passed Sr. Rebecca Marise a note from Sr. Jeanne.

"Meeting arranged with agency we discussed—rep available this morning. Librarian willing to watch over your class. Meet me at my classroom in a half-hour."

~

Sr. Rebecca Marise slipped into the eighth grade classroom. Sr. Jeanne signalled to give her just a few more moments, so Sr. Rebecca Marise sat in an empty desk in the rear. Faint notes of music grew in volume and filled the room. The students began to put away the assignment they had been working on and pulled out the text for the next subject. Not a word was said by Sr. Jeanne who continued to go through some notes at her desk. When the sound of clanking desks tops and rustling papers had subsided. Sr. Jeanne looked up, smiled at the class and put on another melody, more energetic. The children got up, stretched, chatted, and went over to gaze out the window. A few of the students remained sitting.

"Daniel, Kristy, Leslie, let's see some stretches." They groaned, stood up, and made a half-hearted effort to move about. The music changed again and the students went back to their desks as their science teacher entered.

"Sorry for the short notice, Rebecca," said Sr. Jeanne as they walked down the stairs. "Just found out the rep working with Cody's mother was able to come for a meeting this morning. A new girl, her name is Debra. We're meeting in Maureen's office."

The three nuns had just gathered together in the office when the receptionist announced Debra's arrival and ushered her in. Debra halted as she entered the office. Self-conscious, she seemed to have trouble taking in the names of the nuns as they introduced themselves. Perhaps she's never had such a concentrated dose of Catholicism in her life, Sr. Rebecca Maris thought with an inner smile. Sr. Jeanne tried to ease her discomfort with some exchange on the agency's work in Whitewaters and her own involvement in the Birchbark Women's Centre. Debra's fixed smile began to relax and she stopped smoothing out her V-neck top in an attempt to cover her cleavage.

"We certainly appreciate your coming at such short notice," said Sr. Maureen. "We understand that you work with Holly and hope that we can find a strategy that will help both Holly and her son."

Sr. Rebecca Marise explained Cody's behaviour, with Sr. Jeanne adding input concerning the mother's possible overprotection. Moving fully into her professional role, Debra's discomposure faded away.

"I can tell you, Holly speaks highly of your school and is pleased with Cody's progress. The fact that the bullying has stopped is an immense relief."

"So what do you suggest to help Cody connect more with others?" asked Sr. Jeanne.

"Patience. For you, no bullying may be a matter of course, but for them, it's huge. Both have been ostracised. Both are insecure. Holly is a part-time office clerk and student and doing well enough. And now Cody is coming home happy. I think the safer they feel, the more they will come on board. It's going to take time. And," she said, looking at Sr. Rebecca Marise, "you were right not to tell Holly about Cody's lack of interaction with the other children. Let's go slow and see how it goes. Whatever you are doing seems to be working." She gave them each her card and told them to keep in touch.

Debra declined a tour of the school and an offer of snacks. As her heels clicked out the main entrance, Sr. Jeanne said, "I think she's ready for a beer."

Her companions chuckled.

"That was encouraging, but where do we go from here?" Sr. Rebecca Marise asked.

"Go slow, like Debra said, and follow your intuition. It's directed you well this far," said Sr. Maureen. "Keep Jeanne and me abreast of what's going on. We'll just take one step at a time."

"I think Holly needs a 'school buddy' as much as Cody," said Sr. Jeanne.

Sr. Jeanne was about to turn toward her classroom when Sr. Rebecca Marise said, "What were you doing with the music?"

"What music?"

"When I came to your classroom."

"Oh, we're back there. Hard to keep up with you sometimes, Rebecca," she said with a laugh. "It's transitional. The kids know what the tunes indicate and move into their next activity. It keeps me from barking out orders—they get enough of that. Sets a tone. Works for me."

"You pick out the music?"

"I'm open to their suggestions." Sr. Jeanne turned to go back to her classroom and stopped. "Start slow . . . just one transition at a time until they get the hang of it."

~

That afternoon, Sr. Rebecca Marise returned to the convent after school. She generally remained in the classroom until evening prayer, correcting papers and mapping out the upcoming day. But today she wanted to avoid interruptions in order to reassess the special needs of the students, in particular, Cody and his mother.

Holly was younger than herself, yet had an eight-year-old son. What different worlds they came from. Sr. Rebecca Marise wanted to reach out to her without having her in the same classroom as Cody. But how?

Sr. Rebecca Marise entered her bedroom, opened her laptop and, while it was booting up, walked into the group bathroom at the end of the hall. Sr. Jeanne was sitting on a chair and Sr. Maureen was cutting her hair—not at all uncommon. All the sisters cut each other's hair. But instead of having her ponytail trimmed at the nape of her neck, she was getting a trim . . . a real haircut . . . a styled haircut. Sr. Maureen had a styled cut as well. Sr. Rebecca Marise had never noticed before.

When their veils were off, they all wore coifs, a cap-like covering. According to her novice mistress, all their sisters wore their hair the same: pulled back at the nape of the neck with a rubber band and cut a couple of inches below in order to avoid vanity and to maintain simplicity and uniformity. Haircuts were a waste of time and bred self-admiration. "The demise of religious orders begins with the little things."

Sr. Rebecca Marise remained at the entrance of the bathroom, her hand on the door. She didn't realize she was staring.

"Well, hello to you too," said Sr. Jeanne. "Do you want a trim while the salon is open? Maureen does a great job."

"You're not so bad yourself," said Sr. Maureen as she continued to trim.

"Aren't we supposed to wear our hair in ponytails?"

"Are we? Why?" asked Sr. Jeanne.

"We shouldn't be concerned about worldly things, like the way we wear our hair."

"I wasn't concerned at all," said Sr. Jeanne. "My hair is getting long; Maureen is cutting it. You're the one who is anxious about it." Sr. Maureen continued to snip.

"Why do we need our hair styled? Isn't it vanity?"

"Rebecca," said Sr. Maureen, "there is nothing wrong with looking one's age, even if it's under a veil. Resembling orphans from the 1900s doesn't protect one from vanity."

She took the half sheet from around Sr. Jeanne's shoulder and shook out the hair.

"Vanity is a condition of the heart and has a lot of guises, from finely tailored habits to those that look like potato sacks . . . to the expectation of deference from others. The desire for penance can also be loaded with vanity. As the saying goes, 'not all is what it seems.'"

Sr. Rebecca Marise went to her room and leaned against the door. There was always something off in this convent, just a little off . . . always. It made her uneasy. *You can call me anytime*, Sr. Henrietta had said.

Sr. Rebecca Marise slipped into the front parlour and closed the door. This was the most isolated and least used area of the convent. In order to cut the draft that whirled into the dining area, the door from the front entrance reception area always remained closed. Sr. Rebecca Marise sat near the phone and picked up the receiver. The dial tone was loud even a few inches away from her ear. From memory, she slowly punched in the number of the motherhouse.

A sister answered. "Convent of the Sisters of Christ the Redeemer ... Hello? ... Can I help you?"

The room was dim, the air closed and stale. Sr. Rebecca Marise could hardly breathe. She returned the receiver to its cradle and cut the connection. Then she pulled open the blinds and opened the window. The cool autumn air swept past her face as she gazed down the mountain hollow, the leaves shifting into their fall array.

Srs. Jeanne and Maureen were the most down-to-earth and committed sisters she had ever met. And there was truth in what they had said: had she not walked into their "salon," she would have never known their hair wasn't according to code. They showed none of the primping she had been warned against as a novice. And today's meeting regarding Cody's mother, the transitional music in Sr. Jeanne's class ... that only pointed to a total dedication to the students and families. She had only been in Whitewaters, what was it? Just weeks ... yet it seemed like months. And she had learned so much, had received so much encouragement.

Sr. Rebecca Marise didn't try to figure it out. If they wanted to cut their hair, let them. She didn't have to. And besides, she had a lot of work to do this evening. She shut the window but could not bring herself to close the blinds—why should she deprive this neglected little room of such beauty?

CHAPTER 49

Sr. Rebecca Marise rushed from the school to the church. The other sisters had already gathered in their pew for afternoon prayer. As soon as she had genuflected and knelt, Sr. Maureen began. A smattering of laity knelt throughout the small church and participated in the liturgy of the hours and rosary with the sisters. After a period of silence, the Mass began. Due to Fr. Doug's commitments in outlying missions, the Mass was scheduled at 5:00 p.m. a couple times a week. During the Sign of Peace, Sr. Rebecca Marise noticed an older woman standing beside Sr. Jeanne. This was unusual. Generally no one sat in the front pew used by the sisters. Sr. Jeanne was the cook for the week and left immediately after the final blessing, a general practice if some prep was still needed for the meal. The woman left with her.

When the three remaining sisters entered the back door of the convent, Sr. Jeanne said, "Great, we're all set."

Sr. Rebecca Marise hung up her jacket in the mudroom and walked into the kitchen. Standing off to the side was the woman she had seen during Mass!

"Bev, this is Rebecca who replaced Anita. Rebecca, Bev is one of the sisters who began the Birchbark Women's Centre."

She was a nun?! They exchanged civilities while they tactfully took each other in. Bev was about the same age as Sr. Maureen, maybe a little older. Her hair was a short trim, parted casually to the side. She was plump, yet her floral-print blouse and deep blue sweater hanging comfortably over the top of her dark blue pants had a slimming effect. Her face was round and frank and conveyed both warmth and acumen. Given her mission in Appalachia, Sr. Rebecca Marise took an interest in Bev, but at the same time, felt wary of this "secular" nun.

Sitting down to their macaroni and cheese—a regular Sr. Jeanne dish—Bev turned to Sr. Rebecca Marise. "Jeanne tells me you'd liked to hear about our work in Appalachia."

"Very much so." The novelty of having a visitor share a meal, let alone a nun in secular garb, threw her. She couldn't think of a single thing to say.

Sr. Jeanne laughed. "Rebecca, you are a study!"

Sr. Rebecca Marise laughed in spite of herself.

"Bev, start at the beginning. Tell us how you came to Appalachia," said Sr. Jeanne.

Bev and Judy belonged to an order in New York. Moved by the plight of the people in Appalachia, they had requested and received permission in the seventies to minister among the people there. They were not the first. A small group of priests and religious had already been organized and were carrying out various forms of service. Bev and Judy joined their ranks. Bev was appalled by the destitution she witnessed.

"Why? Why are they so poor?" Sr. Rebecca Marise asked.

"It's complex. But briefly, we are dealing with fiercely independent people who for many years had lived in isolated hollers throughout the mountains trying to scrape out a living from the difficult terrain. The forests that surrounded them were filled with stands of ancient hardwood, but given the nearly impassable landscape, the people and their resources were largely ignored. As inroads were made through waterways, trains, and roads, speculators began purchasing large tracts of land. Some people, unaware of the value of their property and the resources on them—or under them—sold for mere pennies an acre. Others were swindled—many of the people were illiterate and only an X was needed to close the deal."

"Yes," said Sr. Jeanne, "and who can contest an X?—even when it's discovered later that some contracts signed by an X were owned by people who could read and write!"

"So," continued Bev, "the forests were razed for the lumber, and major floods came as a result. Coal was discovered and another wave of speculators swept through. Questionable deals were made between elite local middlemen, partisan county governments, and the speculators. Privately owned land shrank as corporations and companies procured more and more property. In an attempt to preserve some of the forests that were rapidly disappearing, the federal government bought out even more land for national parks."

"Even so, the corporations and companies still hung on to the mineral rights underneath a good chunk of it," interjected Sr. Jeanne.

All of this was news to Sr. Rebecca Marise. Her head turned back and forth from Bev to Sr. Jeanne, bewildered how such a massive exchange of land ownership could take place.

"Why did they sell their land?" she asked.

"Rebecca, remember, many of the people were from very isolated communities with limited possibilities for education," said Bev.

"And little or no experience with speculation and investment," added Sr. Jeanne. "Many did not know how to read or write. At the time the coal speculators swept through Appalachia, there were people who did not want to sell their land. They were told that they could sell the mineral rights under the surface and continue to live off the land as they were accustomed. What was not explained was the fine print—the coal company had the right to build roads, or do whatever was deemed necessary, to access the coal. Often the land was destroyed and the water polluted, making the property uninhabitable."

"It was a travesty of justice, Rebecca," said Sr. Maureen.

"And it gets worse," said Bev. "The profits from the lumber and coal weren't reinvested in the people. The locals worked for the companies as labourers, but for a pittance. The big money was lining the pockets of investors and owners who, by and large, lived outside these parts. The profits didn't find their way back to the education of the local people who did back-breaking work to extract the coal. Nor were the profits reinvested to build up local communities or local leaders. When the markets dropped, production stopped. The people were left without work, often in squalid conditions."

"Yes, amid the rubble of slag-polluted valleys and streams and denuded, eroding mountainsides," said Sr. Jeanne.

"Rebecca," said Sr. Maureen, "the ancient forests of Appalachia didn't just contain immense tracts of hardwood trees. The lower growth was filled with a vast array of bushes, plants, and herbs not found elsewhere. All of it was decimated as the forests were razed for the lumber and coal—the locals were left in the quagmire, not the investors. Their bank accounts were full and most of them lived elsewhere."

"Even now over 70 percent of the surface land and 80 percent of the mineral rights are owned by absentee land owners, largely corporations. Some of these corporations still own mineral rights under the national parks!" said Bev.

"This is unbelievable." Sr. Rebecca Marise shook her head.

"Oh, you haven't heard the half of it," said Bev. "When the coal companies got under way, you had an impoverished population looking for work. But they were insufficient. Labourers were brought in from other parts of the US and immigrants were recruited as they were cleared from Ellis Island.

"All those who came to work, outsiders and Appalachians alike, required gear and a place to live. No problem, it was all given to them on credit. The hastily constructed homes, at times not much more than shacks, were rented from the company. Food and supplies were purchased on credit from the company store. With no competition the company could set its own price for rent and goods."

"There were no other stores?" Sr. Rebecca Marise asked.

"Many of these coal towns were located in isolated hollers," said Sr. Jeanne. "And remember, whatever they owed the mining company was deducted from their wages, leaving them with little or nothing when payday rolled around."

"Rebecca, we're talking about complete dependency on the company," continued Bev. "The owners and managers wanted a band of labourers. Many schools were substandard, especially in the smaller communities. And if you were from a small community and wanted to continue high school you would need train fare to a larger town, which families often could not afford."

"Besides," said Sr. Jeanne, "the immediate needs of families were so urgent that frequently sons went to work when they were quite young. Children were paid to be 'bone-pickers,' cracking off rock from the ore with hammers. Education gave way under the weight of survival. You learned to be docile to survive—you got the boot if you didn't, and if you had a family to support . . ."

"Then add alcohol and gambling to the mix," said Bev.

"When miners did object and wanted to form unions, families were ousted from their homes. There was a lot of violence and bloodshed when people protested. We're just scratching the surface here. If you want to delve deeper, there are a number of books in the teachers' resource library on the issues of Appalachia," offered Sr. Maureen.

"Rebecca," said Bev, "there were some coal companies who provided better facilities than others; remember, however, the owners were always in control of everything. Maintaining docile labourers was the goal—dependency was fostered."

"And when profits were down, production stopped. Period. None of the profits were directed to retrain the miners. Very few of the closed, unused facilities were made available for community use or were allowed to be purchased!" exclaimed Sr. Jeanne.

"Even today, the corporations pay so little taxes, that some coal-rich counties, owned largely by these corporations, have impoverished roads, sewage systems, schools. . . . The profits are not reinvested in education or infrastructure."

"It makes you wonder," said Sr. Jeanne, "if some 'higher-uppers' would prefer, as in the past, a dependent population—dependent on welfare, rather than an educated, skilled population that may challenge the status quo."

The conversation paused for some moments as the sisters reflected on the enormity of the problems that the people of Appalachia faced.

~

Rebecca's stomach tightened—it was all so unfair and yet seemed impossible to reverse.

"So what did you and Judy do?" she finally asked Bev.

"Before establishing anything in a new location, members of our network would go to the community and try to get to know the people, develop some level of trust. Then, together with the locals, they would discuss the needs, what the people wanted, and come up with a program together. Now right about the time Judy and I came on board, some women from Birchbark, who had heard about the network, asked if a couple of members would help get something going in their area. I had a background in teaching, Judy in nursing, so away we went.

"There was a myriad of issues to be addressed but women's issues were central. The local women thought if they began with medical care, which was sorely lacking, the women in the region would come to know and trust the centre, and other programs could follow. As a location, Birchbark was ideal, because there was nothing for women developed in the area and several smaller communities nearby would also benefit."

"So the clinic took off right away?" asked Rebecca.

"Well, yes and no. The clinic needed supplies, a place to operate—property, a house, something . . . At first we had only weekend hours using the front rooms of the home of one of the local women!

"Believe me, property is not so easy to acquire in the communities where corporations still own most of the land. An older widow in town was willing to sell her house but there was no money to buy it. So the local women organized quilt raffles, bake and craft sales, and the like. In the end, the majority of the funds came from our congregation and from grants our sisters in New York applied for on behalf of the clinic.

"Having the support of the local women was key and there was also an enormous need. The first to venture in were expectant women or mothers concerned about their children. As trust developed, these visits opened doors to early childhood education and tutoring for the mothers . . . and we could address the cause of the bruises we saw on some of the women.

"Now we have a full-time counsellor and female nurse practitioner. A couple of doctors and a psychologist from Whitewaters volunteer a few hours every month and a mobile dentist clinic is scheduled periodically."

"Aren't there any doctors in Birchbark?"

"It's hard to get doctors to come to these small communities—and even harder to retain them. Most of their families are used to the larger schools and amenities of the city. Besides, the people who come to the clinic can't afford a doctor or a hospital. We have a minimal fee but if people can't afford it, it's waived. If the people require more expertise than the clinic can offer, we refer them to the hospital and help them access social assistance that might be available. But still, getting to Whitewaters is a problem, especially in the winter with all the snow. And there are no buses, no form of public transportation, that go there."

～

As Bev and Jeanne spoke, Maureen placidly cleared the dishes, leaving them to soak in the sink. Rebecca rose to help with the tea and cake but Maureen had her sit back down. "You learn all you can while Bev is here."

Rebecca's initial block had dissolved. She was both enthralled and disturbed by all she heard.

"You mentioned bruises . . . What about the bruises?" she asked.

"Put together the poverty and feelings of helplessness to ever get out of it.

Add anger at whatever is perceived to be the cause . . ." said Bev.

"And maybe being abused or seeing abuse growing up," Jeanne interjected.

"Combine this with alcohol or drugs and you've got a keg of dynamite ready to blow," said Bev. "Men are considered the head of the family. If nowhere else, in the home they have complete dominion. And the women and children bear the brunt of their power and control—really, it's the brunt of their insecurity. In any case, domestic violence happens and it's heartbreaking to see the aftermath."

"Good God," gasped Rebecca.

"Rebecca, it's not all the men, remember that," said Bev. "However, the rate of domestic violence and abuse is higher in Appalachian communities."

"Why do the women put up with it?" asked Rebecca, "Why don't they just leave?"

"Or better," said Jeanne, her voice on edge, "why do the men abuse? Why are our communities so slow to face the problem and address it?"

Bev put her hand on Jeanne's arm, "And go where, Rebecca? Put yourself in their position. You are in an isolated holler . . . maybe in an isolated farm in one of these hollers. There's no public transportation and your husband controls the truck. The life you see is all you know. You might be beat, but so was your mom, and so were you. In your mind it's the way things are. And even if you weren't beat before, you're stuck with it now. The man is the head of the house, what he says goes. And your responsibility is to make it work. Your pastor says so as well, so now God's favour and eternal salvation are part of the package. If you're beat, well, what are *you* doing wrong? You'll be the one accused of destroying the family if you leave."

"Rebecca," said Jeanne, "when one of the first shelters for battered women opened up on the other side of these mountains, a right-wing group picketed outside, chanting that the centre was breaking up families. That was, when? Twenty years ago?"

"If women were attacked by a stranger it was a crime, but within her own home?" Bev raised her eyebrows. "Only in the last decade or two have there been any laws recognizing family violence as a crime.

"Besides, Rebecca, even if a woman dreamed of leaving her abusive husband, where would she go? Imagine yourself: these are your hills, you're surrounded by extended family. Who do you know outside your immediate neighbours? On the rare occasion when you might go to a larger city, people give a second glance at your clothes and a smirk at your manner of speaking.

"And where are you going to get the money to leave? Your family is barely getting by and you don't control the money. You may not have even finished high school. Never had a job. You feel inferior, you feel you don't fit in. You're beaten by your husband, perhaps ridiculed by his friends. You look in the mirror and feel so ashamed. You're suspicious of outsiders, of getting enmeshed in the 'system.' How can you trust them? In fact, you may not even realize there are organizations to help you. Do you see their dilemma?"

"Don't they have TV?"

Jeanne laughed out loud. "And this coming from nuns who occasionally watch the news and *TV Catholic*."

"Some perceptions can change when another reality is presented. But just remember its competing with all the other baggage we just talked about. And with years of reinforcement," said Bev.

"It's hard to imagine," said Rebecca.

"It can happen anywhere, Rebecca. Take religious life, for example. Say a young woman enters. She's in a congregation which limits contact with her family, perhaps she has little or no family. Years go by. All the people significant to her are in the community. She begins to feel unsettled, discontent, but she continues because she does not want to question God's will or be unfaithful. The very thought of leaving fills her with fear—what would she do if she left? Will people look down on her for leaving?

"Do you see how her decision is compromised? And this with much more education, more contact with a greater number of people. . . . Life can be more complex than it seems."

Rebecca veered from this detour in the conversation. "So did you open a shelter in Birchbark?"

"No, we didn't have enough funding for that—we offered counselling, referrals . . . transportation to shelters if the situation demanded it. There were other problems that called for our attention . . ."

"Such as?"

"Alcoholism was huge at the time; now prescription drug abuse is rampant."

"Prescription drugs?"

"OxyContin, for one."

"I've never heard of it."

"It's a painkiller that's been overprescribed and is highly addictive."

"You know," said Jeanne, "I've read that more money is made on its illegal sales in Appalachia than in major US cities."

"So the centre deals with drug abuse?"

"Little by little we developed programs that go beyond immediate medical needs. Some deal with parenting, domestic violence, addictions, job training—a lot of issues overlap. And from the beginning, early childhood education."

And so the conversation continued. Candida excused herself at a certain point—Rebecca barely noticed. The tea was replenished several times as the discussion continued. Education, pollution from coal blasting, nutrition, rotten teeth . . . one topic flowed from the other and back.

At a certain point, there was a pause as they reflected and sipped their tea.

"Ahem," said Maureen as she looked up at the clock. It was after ten o'clock. They had been at the dinner table for four hours! Rebecca couldn't believe it. It was an hour after they generally said night prayer and the grand silence began.

"This calls for abbreviated night prayer, "said Maureen.

Maureen folded her hands, elbows resting on the table, and bowed her head. She thanked God for the presence of Bev in their community, all that they had shared regarding Appalachia, the ministry to which Bev and Judy dedicated their lives and which Jeanne also shared every Saturday, and, in particular, for the people of Appalachia. She raised her head. "Good night." And with that, they left for their rooms. As they entered the community room on the way to the bedrooms, Maureen stood at the entrance and shook her head. Candida was asleep in her chair.

"Why don't you just leave her? She's out like a light," said Jeanne.

"Yeah, and you can deal with her sore back for the next month," said Maureen as she walked over and shook Candida's arm.

~

In her room, Rebecca lay gazing at the ceiling. So stimulated by all she had heard, it would be a while before she could sleep. She would love to go with Jeanne to Appalachia on Saturday, but it was impossible for the time being.

Her mind drifted over the extended conversation: disturbing and inspiring, and, as she reflected, most unusual. In the motherhouse, and likewise in the branch houses, meals had specific time limits: breakfast, twenty minutes; lunch and dinner, a half-hour. Other than feasts, meals were eaten in silence or with spiritual reading. And festive or otherwise, when the bell rang at the designated time, the community rose simultaneously for the prayer after meals.

At Whitewaters, a similar pattern existed for breakfast and lunch, due mainly to necessity. However, the evening meal did not have the hustle of the other two. As Rebecca discovered with time, books such as *The Lord of the Rings* were not unusual spiritual reading material. And the "festive occasions" that permitted speaking during the meal were common. No conversation ended mid-sentence. Rebecca reasoned things were different in a community of four. Besides, she had to admit, she enjoyed it.

And Bev. This was the first time Rebecca had spent any length of time with a sister from another religious community, let alone with a sister not in religious habit.

Generally, visitors to the SCRs were served in a separate parlour. There were exceptions, of course. Young women coming for retreats ate with the postulants. On occasion, a visiting prelate, a notable priest, or superiors of other religious orders were invited to dine with the sisters, but always at the head table with Mother Mary Thomas and her council. And anyone spending the night slept in quarters strictly separated from the sisters: the clergy in a guesthouse, women and nuns from other orders in a sequestered wing. Laymen stayed in local hotels.

And Bev, with such naturalness, followed the sisters to their bedroom area and went into one of the unused rooms. It appeared to be a common practice. The visitors' parlour that could be transformed into a bedroom remained unused . . . But it would have been cramped and stuffy. This was mission territory. Things had to be different in Whitewaters.

~

The next day was Saturday. Rebecca had hoped there would be some time to resume the conversation from the previous evening, but it was impossible. Bev, who had given a workshop at the Birchbark women's centre the day before, would return with Jeanne today and then, after lunch, set off to another centre.

"I hope you'll be coming back soon. I really enjoyed your visit."

"After the snow."

"Stay longer the next time."

"Bev knows she is always welcome," said Maureen. They waved as the car with the two sisters drove off.

CHAPTER 50

The term was flying by, and back at the motherhouse, plans for the diocesan anniversary celebration began to solidify. By November, the bishop announced he would visit every parish in the diocese during the year of commemoration. Annual confirmations and the anniversary celebration at the parish would take place during his visit.

Due to its distance and unpredictable fall and winter mountain weather, Whitewaters was slated for mid-July, one of a few outlying parishes scheduled during the summer before the principal celebration at the cathedral in late September. Henrietta called Maureen with the news.

"So what does this mean for the summer? We usually close down."

"Yes, yes, we discussed this. For this year, you'll remain for an extra couple of weeks and return after the celebrations."

"How long is the bishop staying?"

"He arrives on Friday evening and leaves Monday morning."

Maureen smiled to herself, knowing how much Doug would enjoy the companionship of the bishop in his tight quarters.

"Sr. Maureen, are you there?"

"Oh, yes, right here."

"Mother Mary Thomas and Sr. Petrina will be travelling with him."

Maureen almost gasped. She should have seen this coming.

"Bishop Patterson thinks that since the SCRs have had so much to do with the development of the Whitewaters' missionary outpost, Mother Mary Thomas

LINDA ANNE SMITH

should be there. Sr. Petrina is coming with her."

"Petrina!? Why Petrina?"

"As you may recall, Sr. Petrina was one of the first sisters in Whitewaters."

"What I remember is that she was only here for a couple of months before . . . before . . ." Maureen raked her memory for the circumstance that recalled the pioneer back to the motherhouse.

"She was appointed secretary to the general council," filled in Henrietta. "Just the same, Sr. Petrina was at Whitewaters at the start. And there's also the issue of propriety. The bishop will be travelling with the sisters by plane to 'the Crossroad.'" The Crossroad was a nickname in the state for a city to the south, about an hour and a half drive from Whitewaters.

"Henrietta, what possible impropriety could happen in a plane between the bishop and Mother?"

Henrietta ignored the remark. "Fr. Doug will pick them up. Mother and Sr. Petrina will also take advantage of this trip to carry out your annual visitation."

Maureen shook her head. *This keeps getting better and better.*

"You know that when the general makes the visitation, another councillor assists and writes up the report."

"I could write up the report for her. I mean, really, does it take two superiors to carry out a visitation in a community with only four sisters? Besides, you generally visit Whitewaters. Wouldn't it be more appropriate for you to accompany the general?"

According to their constitutions, the general superior or one of her delegates was to visit each branch community annually. For the past five years, Henrietta had been the delegate assigned to Whitewaters. Mother Mary Thomas hadn't been there for years. Not that Mother neglected the community. Every summer she gathered all the sisters from Whitewaters for a spiritual exhortation and to glean the highlights of their year. And to each individually, she allowed an extra day after their retreat for rest and spiritual enrichment. Mother did care for them in her way. And Maureen appreciated it—from a distance.

"Henrietta, why aren't you coming?"

"As I already told you, Sr. Petrina was part of the initial community. Besides, I'm not going to be a general councillor forever. It was thought that a change would be good for the community."

"'It was thought . . . ,'" repeated Maureen. "Henrietta, I have a hunch Petrina

272

wouldn't be the least interested in coming to Whitewaters if the bishop and Mother were not in the party. And so what if your term will end. You could be re-elected for another term and after that rotated into an assistant or secretary position until you're re-elected as councillor for another few terms . . . ad infinitum. Petrina has been in the general government for what? Over twenty-five years now?"

"She's been elected by the sisters."

After the general's desires were circulated. Henrietta, you know this! thought Maureen. In fact, Henrietta would not be part of the general government if she had not had Mother's implicit consent before the election. There was a pause.

"How's Sr. Rebecca Marise doing?"

"Great," said Maureen, feeling winded. "She's adapted so well. Always looking for ways to improve, to reach out to the students. . . ." Then with alarm, "She *is* staying, right? She's in the middle of the school year . . . doing so well . . . and with diocesan anniversary celebrations to prepare . . . You're not planning . . . ?"

"Sr. Maureen, calm down . . . To tell you the truth, I think everyone on the council has forgotten she is even there. You can't begin to imagine how busy we are."

In fact, she could. The council, occupied with meetings and formulating plans, often overlooked the impact of their decisions on the sisters in the branch communities who were already fully occupied running their schools.

"I wasn't planning on bringing up Sr. Rebecca Marise to the council if she is . . . is OK."

"From what I can see, she is fully immersed in the apostolate and seems comfortable in community."

"What about prayer?"

"Oh, prayer . . . Well, you know how it is, Henrietta. We sleep in until we hear the school bell ring."

Sr. Henrietta laughed. "Just checking . . ." Then, cautiously, "How does Sr. Jeanne relate to Sr. Rebecca Marise?"

"Just fine. I think she actually likes Rebecca."

"Everything's OK?" she asked softly.

"You know Jeanne. She loves the mission. So does Rebecca. They're fine."

CHAPTER 51

"W hat!" exclaimed Jeanne, "—the general *and* Petrina?"

"It's only for the weekend," replied Maureen.

"This is great, just great!" Jeanne said, gesticulating with her hands.

In the fading beauty of late autumn, the lingering leaves on the trees took on an air of resignation. Winter was, indeed, just around the corner. Maureen buttoned her jacket and wrapped her scarf more tightly around her neck against the brisk, cool wind. She had suggested a walk up the narrow path into the mountain behind the school in order to break the news of the upcoming festivities to Jeanne first—in private and out of earshot. They continued on in silence for some time.

"Just the thought of them coming with their self-assured rectitude . . ." said Jeanne, subdued. "When we're miles away, all the 'who's more faithful than who,' all the pandering for approval from the hierarchy, is nothing but static, background noise. Up here, who really cares?"

Jeanne kicked a rock, caught up with it several feet later, and kicked it again. "If you were thirty years younger, Maureen, would you make the same choice?"

"I'm not thirty years younger."

"So you would."

"I would be a different person if I were thirty years younger," said Maureen. They walked on again in silence.

"I'm beyond 'what if?' Jeanne. Life is what it is."

"How philosophical. You get irate, I know you do."

"Am I angry at times? Yes. Am I dismayed at the retrenchment in the Church? Absolutely!"

"And our community is totally behind the movement."

"So what can we really do about it?" Maureen stooped to pick up a branch and used it as a walking stick. "I can either simmer with resentment and regret, or make the best of the situation where I am. And you know that we are making a difference in this community—which, ironically," giving Jeanne a sideways glance, "would be impossible without the backing of our superiors."

"And if this changes, will you stay?"

"I don't know."

The two walked on.

"How far do you bend?—that's what I struggle with," said Jeanne.

"We're not spring chickens, either. God, I'm in my sixties."

"I'm not far behind."

For a while they walked in silence.

"Do you think God really wants us to continue . . ." said Jeanne tentatively, "you know, to be complicit in furthering some idealized image of religious life that plasters up the cracks and flaws?"

"I don't feel we're plastering up anything at Whitewaters."

"So we're absolved from what goes on in the rest of the congregation?"

"You think too much."

Jeanne raised her voice, "But how do you—?"

Maureen cut her off, taking her by the shoulders, "Jeanne, Jeanne, we tried." Then she let her hands drop and turned back down the path toward the school. Jeanne caught up and for a while neither said anything as they trudged downhill.

"God has brought me along this far, Jeanne. Whitewaters has been his greatest gift. Whatever happens in the future happens. God's love will be there to catch me."

CHAPTER 52

Doug's dinner invitation to the sisters came around the same time as the news from the motherhouse. Rebecca's relationship with Doug had evened out over the past several weeks. She no longer went out of her way to avoid an encounter; they were both cordial when they met, but she warded off a conversation of any depth or length. A meal with the community was safe— nothing personal.

After the Friday evening Mass, the sisters walked with Doug out the front door of the church, through the parking area, and across the narrow road to the parish office.

"You've never been to the office or the rectory?" asked Maureen.

"Never had a reason to," replied Rebecca.

"Well, it's time for a tour," said Doug.

He unlocked the door and led Rebecca and Maureen into the tiny foyer while Candida and Jeanne waited outside. To the right was a cramped office area and a bathroom. On the other side, enclosed, was Doug's office.

Since there was no interior connection to the rectory, Doug and the sisters followed a small stone path to the entrance of the rectory, which faced the wooded ridge behind. Rebecca walked into an open room with the kitchen and a dining table on one side and on the other, a living room with a desk in the back corner.

"Well, this is it," said Doug. "There's a bedroom with bath behind the door near the computer, the next door is a bathroom, and there's a guest room beyond that.

The table was set and the smell of spaghetti sauce filled the room.

"I just have to boil up the pasta and we are all set," said Doug as he pulled the salad from the refrigerator.

The sisters offered to help but Doug shooed them into the living room area and offered them some wine. Candida, however, would not be deterred. She could never get used to the idea of a priest cooking for himself. When preparing meals for the sisters, she often made up an extra portion and ran it over to the rectory. Ignoring Doug's urgings to sit down and relax, Candida remained in the kitchen and assumed her position in front of the stove.

The rectory's furnishings had more character than the convent's. Over time, Doug had accumulated pieces from local craftsmen in mountain communities as well as pieces of art.

"I see Fr. Doug has a couple of your paintings," Rebecca said to Jeanne.

"Yes, the waterfall he bought at a school fundraiser and the sunset he commissioned."

When they were seated and the serving bowls were being passed around the table, Doug remarked, "So I hear we'll be having some visitors this summer."

"Rebecca, would you pass the salad, please," said Jeanne.

"Father, here, more sauce," said Candida, spooning out the sauce over his plate. "Your pasta is much too dry."

Doug began to pass the toasted garlic bread. "Do we have a problem with the big celebration?"

"We're so busy getting ready for Thanksgiving and Christmas," offered Rebecca in an attempt to account for her own unspoken disquiet over the impending visit. Although Rebecca revered her superiors, she was intimidated by Petrina and in awe of the bishop and Mother Mary Thomas to the point of discomfort when too close to them. She preferred to admire them within the anonymity of a large group.

"Do you have something in mind, Doug?" said Maureen.

"Not really. Just thought we might want to throw around a few ideas. I'll be presenting the bishop's visit and celebration to the parish council next week."

"It's going to be tricky from the school's standpoint," said Maureen.

"Why is that?" asked Rebecca.

"Because the school year will be over and nearly half of our students are non-Catholic, so they most likely will not get to participate in the parish activities."

"And yet a major element of St. Martin de Porres's outreach is precisely the school," said Jeanne.

"So we have to do something to bring the students back to school during the summer," said Rebecca, thinking out loud.

Candida got up to replenish the spaghetti sauce.

"What is likely to bring them back?" started Doug.

"Sports," said Rebecca.

"Art," said Jeanne.

"Music . . . not only the students but their families as well," said Maureen.

"Are you thinking of a competition?" asked Doug.

"More of . . . an open mic? Just a possibility."

"Maybe some kind of summer camp . . . It could culminate with the celebration," said Jeanne.

"We could have a community barbeque with games and a few sports events," said Doug. "The parish could look after this. We usually have a summer festival anyway."

"Make sure you add a soccer game," said Rebecca.

"The music and barbeque potluck could follow the games," suggested Maureen.

"I have to write this down," said Doug as he got up for a pencil and some paper.

"I'll type up a summary," offered Rebecca.

Somehow focusing on the people, the students, and a summer camp changed the mood of the Whitewaters veterans as the honoured guests took the sidelines. This could work. . . .

CHAPTER 53

No sooner had the summer festivities been briefly discussed with Doug than they dropped into the background of the sisters' considerations. Rebecca was still operating hand-to-mouth with her class preparations, Thanksgiving was coming up fast, and Christmas was just six weeks away.

Rebecca and her band of third graders had settled into a comfortable rhythm. At this point, about one-third of her class transitions were done through music, and from what she could tell, the children enjoyed it. Another technique Jeanne taught Rebecca was "changing the recess channel." When her students returned from the playground, huffing and sweating, Rebecca had them rest their foreheads on their desks in the nook of one arm and close their eyes. She then hit a gong and the children were told to raise their hand at the moment when they could no longer hear the vibrations. Children took turns ringing the gong and, at times, Rebecca would bring in a cymbal. Closing their eyes and focusing on the sound of the gong for a few moments helped the children move from vivacity to calm and to put aside the playground dramas.

Rebecca also became increasingly cognizant of a passion among her students—dogs. Although an affection for dogs appeared in her initial games, only as the weeks went by did she grasp its intensity within a little gang of boys. Jacob was its most ardent member. With his kinky black hair cropped close to his scalp, his hands gesturing emphatically, and his conversation seasoned liberally with "doggone," Jacob never ceased to sing the praises of his beloved pet, Spiky.

"Spiky?" Rebecca had repeated the first time she heard the name.

"That's right," Jacob confidently replied, "Spiky. And he's the doggone best hound in this school."

With a general interest continually fanned into flames by the aficionados, dogs appeared in art projects, writing assignments, and book reports. When the class studied different cultures, Rebecca always brought in the role of dogs . . . although, she didn't think it was necessary to tell third graders that in some countries, their treasured hounds could wind up on the dinner table.

At times their pets became a source of contention. The boys who were most enamoured of their dogs would vie over their accomplishments. And since these feats were verbal accounts, authenticated only by the owner, they would be hotly contended if an unacceptable level of exaggeration was suspected. Jacob was often accused of such a felony. After breaking up a particularly hot argument during recess one day, Rebecca had to administer four successive gong "treatments" at the beginning of the class in order to relax the disgruntled looks of the contenders. But other than these occasional spats, dogs provided entertaining discussion matter.

Cody was becoming more relaxed . . . not that he spontaneously joined in group activities, but Rebecca noticed him watching the others with attentiveness rather than scrutinizing them under hooded eyelids with his chin cocked down. Cody was especially observant of Leah who enjoyed helping around the classroom after she finished her work. When the class was divided for team activities, Rebecca began to match Leah with Cody. Occasionally, Cody would leave Rebecca's side during recess and stand near Leah if Rebecca remained with the group of playing children.

Rebecca observed the development expectantly yet found it painful to witness Cody's minute, timorous moves in forming just a simple affiliation. Rebecca could only imagine the anxiety that soddened his desires, restrained his attempts, and threatened an all-out retreat from any gains he'd made. She could understand Holly's solicitude to shield Cody from anything and anyone that might hurt him, understand how Holly was blind to the fact that her overprotection was, itself, damaging.

CHAPTER 54

One afternoon a few days after their meal with Doug, Maureen stepped into Rebecca's classroom. "I have some news you may find welcome."

Rebecca looked up from her desk.

"We may be able to put on a production of *A Christmas Carol* with a professional theatre group, rather than the pageant."

Rebecca put down her pen. "What is this all about?"

"Meagan Turner has a brother who teaches down in the Crossroad. His school had scheduled a troupe that travels around the state performing in elementary schools. They include all the children in the production. I'm not sure what happened, but their scheduled date now conflicts with another event at their school. It's too late to cancel with a refund, so through the negotiations of Meagan's brother, we may be able to have the troupe come to Whitewaters for a reduced price. Seems the school is willing to absorb part of the loss if we can come up with the remainder—and Meagan thinks a couple of theatre buffs she knows may provide some, if not all, of the funds."

"The group doesn't mind travelling to Whitewaters?"

"The production is scheduled for the second week of December—the last one for the term. So they're willing to make the hour-plus drive since they so rarely come this far west."

"This is wonderful!" exclaimed Rebecca.

Due to their limited resources, theatrical programs were sorely lacking at St. Martin de Porres School. Their salute to drama consisted of a Christmas pageant and a school-end concert.

"How does it work? I mean, how do they get all the children involved?" asked Rebecca.

"From what I understand, the troupe has the preparation down to a science. Everything is done within a week. So the school day would be a half day of lessons and half day of practice. Tomorrow I've scheduled an impromptu staff meeting to discuss the possibility—we need to give an answer in two days."

"Well, you can count me in."

"Good, because I'd like you to take on playground supervision during tomorrow's lunch break while we have our meeting." Maureen smiled and left.

As it turned out, it didn't take long to decide. Meagan walked out to the playground well before the bell rang. "It's most definitely a go!"

~

Rebecca wanted all her students to participate in the play, in particular, those who did not excel in other areas. Cody was a case in point, but she was realistic enough to know that unless he was hiding behind her robes, he was very unlikely to get on the stage. But his mother . . . this might be the perfect project to draw her in, to help her come to know the other parents.

Rebecca gave Cody's mother a call. Holly had never been in a play but Rebecca discovered that she loved music and storytelling. When she was young, she had started to learn the fiddle from an aunt, but never continued. With some encouragement from Rebecca, she recited part of a ballad from memory.

"We are going to need help with this production, especially on the last day. You know, getting the children organized back stage, costumes, makeup . . . Would you like to give a hand?"

"I'm not sure . . . with work and classes. . . . Let me look at my calendar."

Her classes would be over by the second week of December . . . She could possibly help out for the last two afternoons and the final production on Friday evening.

"Someday, I would love to have you come to my class to recite your ballad."

Holly gave out a timorous laugh, but didn't say no.

CHAPTER 55

The Thanksgiving meal was served late afternoon. With the dishes done and the leftovers packed away in the refrigerator, the sisters gathered in the community room, each busy about their various projects.

"I was thinking," said Maureen, "Do you suppose we could pull off a production during the summer like *A Christmas Carol*?"

"No," said Jeanne emphatically as she continued to paint.

"Why not?"

"Because I doubt the theatrical troupe would travel all the way to Whitewaters for one group. And besides, they probably need the summer to prepare a new program for the fall."

Rebecca listened, astonished.

"Why do we need the troupe? If they can pull it off in one week, why can't we?"

"Are you feeling well?" asked Jeanne humorously. "They come with all the backdrops, the costumes, the music, the principal parts rehearsed, the choreography down to a science—just to mention what immediately comes to mind."

Maureen and Rebecca laughed.

"Keep laughing," Jeanne said as she painted.

"She's right. We'd better stick with the music, art, and some sports—that's plenty for a summer camp," said Rebecca.

Candida was tending her plants—however, not with her regular complacent disposition. She snipped her withering leaves at a rapid gunshot pace. Candida chafed at the idea of remaining at Whitewaters a few extra weeks for a superfluous program that they now had to plan, prepare, and carry out. Her leisurely summer days of tending the garden at the motherhouse were not only stymied but additional responsibilities had been thrown on as well.

"Why do we even have to have a summer camp?" said Candida, her voice pitchy.

The others turned to her in surprise.

"Do you have something else in mind?" asked Maureen.

"All we need to prepare is a weekend event. None of the superiors said anything about a summer camp."

"Don't you think the summer camp will help the children and their families become part of the celebration?" asked Jeanne.

This jogged Rebecca's memory. "Did I tell you that Cody's mom, Holly, recites ballads? She might perform for the celebration."

"I just think we are making a whole lot of unnecessary work for ourselves," Candida returned, "We're busy enough as it is."

The two seasoned nuns knew the Candida would have preferred to transfer her gardening skills to the motherhouse as soon as the school term ended, but they had no idea that planning the summer camp had irritated her to such an extent.

"It won't be a full day, not like school. And it's only art, music, and games," said Rebecca perplexed.

Candida didn't reply, but her silence was neither agreement nor resignation.

"Candida, you and I can discuss this another time. I think we'll be able to work it out," said Maureen.

Of all the sisters, Candida was the sweetest. She smiled warmly at everyone and was generous with her gentle squeezes to the shoulder. Her mood rarely varied. She went through her days and weeks contented and unperturbed.

She had been teaching for almost forty years and would teach, she said, until she died. A veteran of Whitewaters almost from the beginning, she preceded both Maureen and Jeanne at the missionary post. Years ago a previous superior had astutely shifted Candida's assignment from being a teacher of a primary class to being the religion teacher of grade four and the art instructor for grades one, two, and three—a shift Candida welcomed but had never requested.

Candida's system of teaching and testing rarely varied. No curriculum change was implemented unless it was mandatory. Change itself was not the problem. Nor was the novel deterred because it challenged any values. Candida resisted alterations when they were inconvenient. If something unexpected came up that demanded a little more time or effort on her part, she developed a sudden headache, indigestion, muscle pain—you name it—and all with a pleasant smile. When people were speaking about their work or concerns, Candida smiled sweetly and nodded but anyone observant could see that after several minutes, unless she had an invested interest, Candida was up, up, and away.

~

"What!"

Rebecca had been baffled by Candida's reaction to the proposed summer camp the week before. Now, while she and Maureen remained to finish up the dishes after a Saturday lunch, Maureen informed her that during summer camp and the visitation weekend, Candida would prepare supper. Other than that, she would contribute to the community by tending her flowers and vegetable garden.

"So she is not going to do a blooming thing?" Rebecca said, irritated.

"Where do you come up with things like that?" said Maureen.

"Like what?" said Rebecca, taken off guard.

"*Blooming thing*," said Maureen, imitating Rebecca.

Rebecca laughed in spite of her irritation and continued drying a plate. With less anger she continued. "Why does she only do the minimum?"

"Candida does more than the minimum. You haven't lived with a minimalist if you think she's one. Have you noticed the flowers?"

Catching her eye, Maureen continued, "When you reach a certain age, you can't always maintain high gear . . . especially when living at that momentum has been generated by someone else. Do you understand?"

"Well, look at you and Jeanne. You're about the same age and you're not—"

"Comparing us old folks, are you?" cut in Maureen, amused.

"Well, it's true."

"My, my," Maureen said with a smile, "you *are* speaking your mind today. Why do you suppose Jeanne puts in the extra effort to finish her school work during the week so she can go to Appalachia on Saturday?"

Rebecca thought for a moment or two. "Because she loves the people there." She dried a couple of glasses, then gathered up her courage. "And since you brought it up . . . May I go with her some day?"

Maureen looked over at Rebecca. "I like your enthusiasm, but weren't we discussing another topic?"

"You made your point."

"Which was?"

"We're not all the same. Some attitudes I don't understand. . . . I need to be more compassionate."

"Hmmm . . . Not as thick as I thought . . ."

"I have to give you what you're looking for if I ever want to get to Birchbark," she returned with a smirk.

Maureen laughed and, in a rare gesture, gave her a sideways hug, her hand wet with dish water. "You *are* something. We'll see about Birchbark. Right now I think you have plenty to keep you occupied."

CHAPTER 56

The troupe arrived promptly Monday morning in the second week of December. With Christmas just three weeks away and the drama production about to begin, the school pulsated with anticipation. The lead roles were performed by the theatre company and auditions for the minor roles began immediately. Since information on the process had been sent in advance, children who wanted specific roles shifted about in their seats waiting for their turn to audition.

Alessandro and his partners in the tutoring program had been offered the privilege of being technical assistants throughout the week. This also served as an incentive for completing their assignments. Together with their retired teacher and the librarian, who would be the permanent staff members for the production, the children were the first to be introduced to the troupe. The technical director explained the aspects of the play he looked after, such as lighting, sound, backdrops, sets, props. Alessandro took a liking to the technical director and wanted to help with the sets and props. Soon he and another student joined "the tech," as he was called, in opening storage containers and dividing the materials.

Monday afternoon, practice began in earnest. Each grade took turns coming to the school gym to learn a dance routine, a song with percussion instruments, or both. Day by day the hall took on the aura of a theatre. The dusty stage with its tired curtains revived with the bustle and elation of the students. The children became increasingly confident in their songs and dances, and those with individual roles ran to the gym at their designated times to be coached by actors.

Cody observed all the activity like a turtle peeping out its head in unfamiliar circumstances. The third grade did a song and dance routine and joined all the students in the grand finale chorus. During their practices, Cody sat on the sidelines holding a wooden frog and beater, quietly testing the sounds it made. However, when the singing and dancing was in full swing, his eyes were fixed on the action.

On Thursday, the children were brought to the gym class by class to receive their costumes and go through their routines. The third grade was scheduled for the afternoon, and as they stood waiting to be fitted, Holly arrived as promised. Seeing his mother, Cody appeared consoled, mystified and, at first, torn between Rebecca and his classmates, and his mom. To Rebecca's dismay he regressed, running to his mother and latching on to her leg.

"Doggggggone," said Jacob with wide-eyed amazement, voicing the unspoken sentiments of the rest of the class as they looked on.

"OK, we need to line up according to height," said Rebecca, distracting the students. "Mariarosa, can you help with this?" A year older than the others, Mariarosa had shown herself to be quite the organizer during the past months and set to work as the children determined who was taller than who.

Rebecca then greeted Holly and explained what was going on with the play.

"So, Cody, this must be your mother," said Kim, gently ruffling his hair.

"Holly, this is Kim, one of our teachers' assistants who has been helping out with the play all week," said Rebecca. Kim had raised her family and found tutoring rewarding. She knew Cody well.

Rebecca, Kim, and Holly, with Cody hanging off her arm, walked over to the tables where the costumes had been piled and began to distribute them among the children. The costumes were roomy and made to be worn over their shirts and slacks. In no time, the children were dressed, pointing at each other and performing dance steps and kicks they'd seen on TV. With a call to order they went through their routine with the troupe instructor. All the while, Cody maintained some form of physical contact with his mother: her sleeve, leg, pants pocket. She tried to encourage him several times to join in with the other children, but without effect. Watching the other students interacting and skipping about, Holly became increasingly subdued. Kim approached her and put her arm around her shoulder on the opposite side of Cody.

"Don't worry about it, Holly," she whispered in her ear, "One of my sons tended to be like your Cody. Stuck to me like glue. You'll see, he'll come out of it in his time."

Back in the classroom, Rebecca had the children stack their costumes neatly on the windowsill. Cody now securely in his desk, Kim motioned for both Rebecca and Holly to come to the back of the room.

"I have an idea. Holly, why don't you get dressed in a costume? You can stand near the side of the stage, clap to the music, be part of the scene, and maybe Cody will come and stand next to you. At least he'll be on stage with the others," said Kim.

"Are you in for it, Holly?" asked Rebecca, "Kim can talk it over with the troupe, but I don't think it will be a problem."

Although shy herself, Holly enjoyed watching the children and Rebecca could tell that she suffered when her own child did not join in. "Won't I stand out?"

"Oh, I can come and stand with you," said Kim. "If there aren't any costumes our size, I have a few things at home that I've used for heritage day. They'll do fine. Besides everyone will be looking at the kids—they won't give us a second glance."

The next afternoon was a complete dress rehearsal and, better, the first performance. Family and friends unable to come in the evening were welcome to attend. Chairs were neatly arranged in the hall and the children sat by class in their costumes. At the appropriate time, they were lined up backstage for their entrance.

Rebecca noticed Alessandro sitting off to the side next to the tech. A mixer and light board were set up before them on a small table and Alessandro watched the tech's every move. Occasionally, the tech would signal Alessandro and he would fade out a particular light or bring it on and then smile broadly at his mentor.

Kim and Holly had pulled together their costumes and the troupe leader was happy to accommodate the slight variation. Holly told Cody she was going to be in the play and, if he wanted, he could join her. Both Rebecca and Kim told her to say nothing further. If he came out from the side wing, fine. If not, well at least they got him that far. Seeing his mother in costume, he dressed up like the other children. During their scene, he stood near his mother and at the appropriate time struck his frog with the beater.

That evening, the school was vibrating with energy and activity. All the children were to be in their classrooms an hour before show time. Some parents wanted to help with their child's costume and makeup, only adding to the hoopla. Rebecca kindly but firmly encouraged them to go to the hall to find a good seat. In the first-floor corridor, women from the school council set up tables with refreshments for the reception following the play. They were as busy setting out plates with cookies and bars as they were keeping little hands off the snacks.

Every available space in the gym was filled with folding chairs, and ten minutes before the play, all of them were filled. Relatives and friends began to line the back of the hall. Nothing like this had ever happened before at St. Martin de Porres—their children were in a real theatrical performance.

Maureen stood near the front of the hall, ready to make the opening remarks. Doug arrived and stood next to her. "This is amazing."

Black, White, Hispanic, Catholic, and non-Catholic were packed together and chatting with one another.

"If many more arrive . . . ," mused Doug.

"Try to get any of them to leave and we'll have a riot on our hands," replied Maureen as she left for the stage.

With the troupe's experience in organizing school productions and the children's enthusiasm, the production of *A Christmas Carol* was proceeding without a hitch—or none that the audience couldn't enjoy. The grand finale was approaching and the children, lined up by grade, were walking down the corridor to the gym. Rebecca and Holly, with Cody in tow, led the third graders and Kim brought up the rear. When they reached the side of the stage, Rebecca and Holly stepped back for the students who climbed the stairs to assume their positions. Kim and Holly planned to slip to the side of the stage with Cody after all the students were in place. Cody watched his classmates pass in front of him. Leah looked at him as she neared. Just as she went by, he let go of his mother's hand and joined Leah as she walked up the steps and onto the stage. Rebecca, Kim, and Holly looked on, astonished. Rebecca had never heard Cody emit a note, yet, there he was, his mouth moving in sync with the others. Whether he was actually singing, Rebecca couldn't tell, but he certainly knew all the words and the gestures.

Back in the classroom, the buoyant children leaped out of their costumes so they could feast on the refreshments they had been ogling on their treks back and forth to the gym. Rebecca, along with any adult who appeared to be connected with the play, was hugged, thanked, and complimented by the parents.

Rebecca was both overjoyed and relieved. She wanted to congratulate the troupe, who remained in the gym; however, the school entrance and corridors were packed with people snacking and chatting. To get to the gym she went back to her classroom, put on her coat, and walked out the side door. The moon was high and bright. She turned into the play area behind the school—now a parking lot—and began to walk toward the gym entrance. Children hopped and ran to their cars. Their parents, some carrying sleepy toddlers, trailed behind them, lingering a minute here and there to wind up a conversation with a relative or friend. Under the light of the gym entrance Rebecca noticed Kim introducing Holly and Cody to some friends; then they walked on together to Kim's car.

How blessed, how very blessed she was.

CHAPTER 57

The first blizzard pummelled the Appalachian community right before Christmas, dropping over a foot of snow on Whitewaters in one night. In the foothills, the roads were covered with several inches of snow then iced with freezing rain. Driving conditions were treacherous. Secondary routes were put on hold while road crews fought to keep the major highways open.

Packed and ready to depart for Christmas at the motherhouse, the sisters in Whitewaters watched the weather forecasts while Maureen made numerous phone calls to Mother. With the current conditions and another blizzard predicted within days, Mother decided it would be best if the sisters remained in Whitewaters for the entire holiday.

Rebecca was disappointed. She had looked forward to gathering with all the sisters at the motherhouse, joining in the music and song during their festive liturgical celebrations—something she sorely missed at Whitewaters. Even more disheartened were Rebecca's parents. Her mother had prepared dozens of Christmas cookies that she intended to bring over to the motherhouse the Sunday after Christmas when families were permitted to visit for a few hours.

"Now I'll have to repack everything and try to mail it. Rob told me the cookies I sent him arrived just fine, but I have my doubts, you know how delicate the shortbread is. . . . Oh, and the nutty nuggets . . . and getting them up into those mountains . . . Oh, they'll be nothing but cracked and crumbled."

"Mother," said Rebecca on the phone, shaking her head, "you'll be happy to know that truck deliveries have begun here at Whitewaters. The mules are only used for emergencies."

Her father chuckled on the extension but her mother was too upset over the cancelled visit to be humoured. With the exception of her novitiate, when no visits were allowed, Rebecca's mom and dad had come faithfully for every quarterly "visiting Sunday." With the Christmas visit off, they would have to wait until June to see their daughter again.

To ease Margaret's chagrin, Maureen encouraged Rebecca to call her mother a couple of times over the Christmas holidays.

~

Stubborn snowdrifts were still melting when Bev was unexpectedly asked to fill in as a speaker for the annual convention at the Whitewaters learning centre. This year's theme, "Behind the Eyes of Our Students," would focus on factors outside the school that impact learning, from nutrition and exercise to family violence, to the environment. Given her years of expertise, Bev was asked by a colleague to step in for domestic violence. So toward the end of March, Bev was again with the sisters at St. Martin de Porres.

The convention took place on a Thursday and Friday, and Maureen wanted all the teachers at the school to attend. Substitutes were arranged and everyone registered for two sessions, either in the morning or afternoon. Since Rebecca was new and keen, her length of time at Whitewaters unknown, Maureen offered her the full two days. Rebecca pored over the program and carefully made her selections.

~

Bev arrived travel worn late Wednesday evening and the SCRs saw little of her on Thursday due to a supper and evening session for the presenters. Candida and Maureen attended sessions on Thursday and Jeanne planned to attend a couple on Friday morning. Since Rebecca was to remain for the entire day, she drove with Bev to the convention.

When the sessions finished that afternoon, Bev walked with Rebecca to the car, "Let's go for a coffee or tea. Do you know of a good place?"

"Not really."

"Well, it shouldn't be too difficult to find a coffee shop."

She headed for the centre of town, and before long they were walking into Mountain Biscuits Cafe. With the lunch hour rush finished, less than a dozen people were scattered among the tables. A few people looked quizzically at Rebecca when she entered and lowered their heads when their eyes met.

A waitress came to take their order.

"Just water for me," said Rebecca.

"Rebecca . . . ," said Bev menacingly.

"I don't have any money, Bev." Rebecca sighed. The convention had included lunch and breaks. She hadn't anticipated the need to ask for money.

"I didn't expect you to pay. Now don't be silly and order something."

In the end, they both chose pie and tea.

During her seminar, Bev spoke on the prevalence of domestic violence and explored some theories on its underlying causes. The main segment of her presentation dealt with the effects of family violence on children's capacity to learn. Rebecca shared with Bev how much discussion her talk provoked during the lunch break.

"Typically, we don't consider that children in our classrooms could be exposed to domestic abuse in some form or other."

"During your talk I was imagining each of their faces and wondering . . . It's more complicated and pervasive than I ever imagined. Where to start, what programs to use . . ."

"The worse thing we can do is to ignore it, pretend it doesn't exist," said Bev. "I've had teachers tell me that they're in the classroom for academics only. They say they don't want to know and don't want to get implicated in family matters. Well, whether we like it or not, whether we want to face it or not, when a child walks into the classroom he's bringing in his family with him. If a child is dealing with trauma and we don't address it, then we are not helping that child academically either. And when the child's trauma leads to disruptive behaviour in the classroom, then we aren't helping our other students academically as well."

"One teacher at our table said she was upset with all the talk on domestic violence," said Rebecca. "She said she wasn't trained to be a psychologist."

"In some respects, she's right. What do you do when cases emerge and your town doesn't have resources to provide follow-up? Unfortunately, we are willing to spend billions on prisons 'getting tough on crime' and at the same time we neglect early intervention programs, after-school programs, family-support programs, which would cut down the need for prison expansion." She shook her head. "It's exasperating at times. . . . So what do we do, just give up and say, 'It's not my problem, I'm not a psychologist'? We have to have the courage to begin and hope that with a growing awareness the funds will be diverted to prevention."

Bev took a sip of tea. Rebecca was keen about the issue and Bev seemed to have such a wealth of experience and knowledge. But something else was on her mind.

"Bev," she began slowly, "you're the first nun I've ever spoken to who didn't wear a habit."

"What an honour."

Rebecca laughed. "Why don't you?"

"Do I need to?"

Rebecca began to toy with her paper napkin, "You don't mind if I ask you these things do you?"

"Not at all. Go ahead, Rebecca."

"The Pope has asked us to . . . the Pope wants us to wear the habit."

"Does Christ?"

"It's the same thing."

Bev raised an eyebrow.

"The Pope says the habit is a witness," continued Rebecca. "It puts Christ on the streets."

"Rebecca, I respect where you are coming from, I do. But think a moment. Is there any indication in the Gospels that Christ went out of his way to dress differently than the rest of the population? John the Baptist did . . . but in his case—if you go by artists' renditions," Bev said with a grin, "he didn't add clothing; he stripped down to the bare minimum.

"But Jesus didn't follow the lifestyle of John. And from what I gather, he dressed in common garb. He lived among the people of his time and willingly engaged with everyone: those who supported him and those who were cynical. From the Gospels, it appears people were attracted to Jesus because of his integrity, his hope, his forgiveness . . . the way he treated other people—his goodness . . . his respect."

Rebecca was nervous to even bring up the subject and it wasn't getting any easier as the conversation continued. However, her desire to understand pushed her on. Bev did not fit her image of an aging, habit-less nun.

"But the habit also reminds us of our consecration, it helps us live in poverty."

Glancing down at her outfit, Bev laughed. "This ain't exactly in the designer league. And—since we are being honest here—based on my experience, it took me a whole lot less time and money to pull this outfit together than your garb . . . and under-garb, I might add."

Putting her elbows on the table, Bev continued, "Rebecca, you're talking to an old bird who's seen it all. I wore a habit for years. I lived with sisters, in habit, who exemplified self-giving, concern for others, and certainly brought Christ's spirit to the streets. A-n-n-n-d I lived with sisters, in habit, who were petty, self-seeking, and condescending. And they were a witness to the entitlement and privilege that they felt they deserved because of their 'calling' or the position they held in our community . . . or simply a witness to their frustration and resentment.

"And I can tell you, those who were self-giving in the habit are just as self-giving in a skirt and blouse . . . and those who were arrogant and self-centred, still are. Rebecca, whether you, or any religious sister, wear a habit or not is immaterial to me. Trust me on this point, however: it's our attitude, our concern for others that is in any measure 'our witness to Christ.' It comes from within, not from what we wear.

"I took off the habit not because I was afraid of being known as a religious but so I could interact with people without an antiquated garb from the 1700s that, I believed, was irrelevant and, at times, got in the way. I wanted to relate one person to another. I believe to the core of my being that I am loved by God. If somehow through my respect and care, others come to know that love, if it gives them insight to their worth and dignity, if through that love they can rise above some of the pain in their past, that's enough for me. I really don't care if I'm 'identified' or not, if I get credit or not. It's not about me. It's about the value of the other."

Rebecca sipped her tea. She tried to process what Bev was sharing but was becoming increasingly defensive.

"Bev, I really don't mean to be . . . offensive, honestly. I'm just trying to understand. . . . So why doesn't your congregation have vocations? Why does it seem that only religious orders wearing the habit still have young women joining them?"

"I don't know . . . I don't." Bev leaned back in her chair. "I could tell you some theories floating around, but they may smack of sour grapes, so I won't. What I can tell you is this: I entered the convent when many of my friends did, right out of high school. The enthusiasm, the energy, the idealism was contagious. We revelled in our apostolic endeavours and the difficulties we endured for Jesus's sake. We moved on together toward first profession and rejoiced together at our final vows. Then, over the course of . . . what?—two years, three, five years?—the initial enthusiasm petered out, and for some, that's all they had. We weren't permitted to talk about ourselves with each other. We all marched to the same daily schedule, we all wore the same thing but we were living very different realities and, for the most part, we had no idea what was going on within a sister sitting next to us in chapel."

"How many sisters were in your novitiate group?" asked Rebecca.

"Twenty-three."

"Wow!"

"Don't think that with our large numbers, it was all roses, Rebecca. Like I said, I have happy memories of the time. Just the same, there was a good deal of suffering as well. 'Testing one's virtue' and 'the chapter of faults'—which I'm sure you're familiar with." She looked straight at Rebecca who lowered her eyes. "Yes . . . they can be motivated by more than wanting a person to grow in virtue. Let's face it, sisters are human and personal dislikes can develop. Nuns can be put down and disregarded by their sisters and superiors because of their personalities, their gifts, and their weaknesses. And they were . . . and may still be. Not everything in religious life is done 'all for the love of Jesus.'"

Rebecca made no reply, poking her fork at the crumbs of pie crust on her plate, occasionally looking up at Bev.

"And remember, Rebecca, people can enter religious life for a whole slew of reasons. I look back at our huge novitiate groups . . .What might initially have seemed like a calling could very well have been a flight from . . . domestic abuse, to name one; or not wanting to get married; or just wanting to teach or nurse."

Bev brushed some crumbs off her blouse. "Rebecca, Rebecca . . . As the saying goes, 'Time will tell where wisdom lies.' In the end, it's not the numbers who enter, but those who remain for the long haul . . . and *why* they stay for the long haul."

Bev picked up her cup. "How are your paren—"

"So why did so many leave after Vatican II?"

"You're relentless."

The waitress brought a refill of hot water and fresh tea bags.

"Rebecca, you can't look at Vatican II in isolation. Take the divorce rate: Did divorce increase after the fifties because, within a decade, people were less happy with their marriages than before? Maybe people had remained in relationships, even harmful relationships, to avoid being socially ostracized. But when divorce became more socially acceptable, they weren't so inhibited. Maybe with greater education women were in a better financial position to be independent of their husbands and leave a difficult relationship.

"You could leave the convent today, Rebecca, get a job as a teacher—or whatever—and go on with your life as a single woman. Some people might not be happy with your decision, but it wouldn't be considered scandalous. Before long, your time in the convent would be considered just another chapter in your life."

Bev paused to take a bite of her pie. "It wasn't always that way. In Catholic populations, leaving the convent, leaving the priesthood, getting a divorce—they carried a stigma. To do so was a disgrace to the family.

"I know a priest who submitted his request for laicization the day after his mother's funeral—he was in his fifties. He realized years before that he had become a priest just to please his mother but didn't have the courage to leave and disappoint her while she lived. Let's just say, in the sixties and thereafter, it became easier to leave and begin a new life."

Bev finished off her tea. "If you really want to understand why so many religious left the convent after Vatican II, read up on the Church and religious life before Vatican II, read up on the social changes of the time, what went on in the Council. From my experience, I can tell you, the motives for the massive departures were far more complex than the revisions made to the rules and custom books . . . and much more complex than wearing or not wearing the religious habit.

"You're bright, Rebecca." Bev reached for her coat. "Do some research."

Bev's answers did not bring the clarity Rebecca had hoped for. They only raised more questions and anxiety. She had grown to admire Bev during their first encounter last fall and from what she had since learned about her from Jeanne and Maureen. Hearing her presentation today and watching her interact with the participants, Rebecca experienced the depth of her insight, her compassion, and respect. Yet, Rebecca's growing admiration was at odds with her own understanding of religious life. She wanted to ask more but couldn't articulate the ambiguity and ambivalence she felt.

"Thanks, Bev," said Rebecca subdued.

"Really?" said Bev with a raised eyebrow. She put on her coat and picked up her purse. As they were about to leave the table, she took Rebecca by the shoulders, "You're a bright young woman, Rebecca. Do some reading. I can still see your wheels churning."

That night, after the grand silence, Rebecca slipped into their tiny chapel. She always experienced an inexplicable sense of Christ's presence before the Blessed Sacrament and tonight she longed for his calming peace. Knowing she would be alone with Bev, Rebecca had resolved to bring up the questions that percolated whenever she reflected on Bev's style of religious life and mission. And now with Bev's answers, Rebecca was left in a greater muddle and a certain defensiveness. She admired Bev, but the SCRs were family. They had been part of her life for as long as she could remember and with them she had committed her life. She looked at the tabernacle: Was there room for both points of view . . . somehow? Her mind went over and over their conversation until, weary of the effort, she pulled out her rosary and slowly repeated, "Hail Mary, full of grace . . ."

~

The next morning Bev drove with Jeanne into the mountains and Rebecca corrected papers and planned for the upcoming week. She also had to finish a draft of the summer camp program for a meeting next Wednesday with the parish planning committee. Generally, with the urgency of her work, the incongruences she struggled with subsided into the background. But this time, Rebecca's questions and restlessness were intruding as she prepared her lesson plans. She had to continually force herself to refocus. With the evening's announcement, however, her broodings would be shot right out of her mind.

~

"Well, it looks like we have a lottery winner," said Maureen after answering the telephone. The other sisters looked up from the projects they had brought for community hour.

"Rebecca, you are one of the chosen to see the Pope!"

Rebecca was stunned. "You've got to be kidding!"

Maureen sat down in her customary chair. "Henrietta would have spoken to you personally but she has a number of other calls to make tonight."

Candida reached over from her chair and squeezed Rebecca's arm. "Congratulations!"

Jeanne continued to paint.

See the Pope! "When?" said Rebecca, stupefied. "And I'm here in Whitewaters!"

"Henrietta will fill you in with the details, but from what I understand, there's a group of younger sisters going to Baltimore. The Pope will have an audience there with religious and priests and those in formation. It seems the organizers would like to have as many young sisters and priests and as many novices and seminarians as possible."

"Oh. So what about Boston and New York?" asked Jeanne, "Didn't we hear something about busloads going from the diocese?"

"That's still on. But Rebecca will be going with a smaller group and just to Baltimore."

"I wonder who won the all-inclusive jackpot?" Jeanne said.

Rebecca didn't even hear Jeanne's comments. She was beyond herself. Although she had submitted her name, she was sure that most of the sisters had done so as well. She never dreamt she would be chosen, especially since she was way out in Whitewaters. Through their internal newsletters, she followed the SCRs' preparation for the Pope's visit, but as a distant observer. It seemed so remote from Whitewaters. And now, to be made part of it all, to actually be going to see the Pope! It was overwhelming.

"So how will I get there? What's happening?"

"It was a very short phone call. . . . Sounds like a whirlwind trip. . . . When is the Pope in Baltimore?"

"May," said Candida.

"Yes, that's it, at the beginning of May. If I understood correctly, you leave here on a Friday, will be in Baltimore Saturday and Sunday, and return to Whitewaters on Monday. Tomorrow give Henrietta a call. She'll tell you all the details."

Rebecca was still dazed. The Pope! And what . . . in just over a month!

CHAPTER 58

Rebecca stood in the parking area of the motherhouse, her backpack hanging from her shoulder. It was early, dark, and chilly. She and her fellow pilgrims were leaving before the community's regularly scheduled 5:00 a.m. rising and planned to arrive in Baltimore around noon. Sr. Mary Augustine, local superior of the motherhouse, and the driver and leader of the trip pulled up in a minivan. It had barely stopped when her stocky figure hopped out, veil tucked into her cincture. She rubbed her hands together, walking briskly to the back of the van.

"Where are the others? We need to get moving," she said as she opened the rear hatch. Her ruddy cheeks glowed even brighter after her run to the garage. Rebecca picked up the large thermos of coffee at her side and went to the tailgate.

"They were right behind me, getting the cooler out of the refrigerator."

Muffled laughter came from the back of the convent compound.

"Here they are," said Sr. Mary Augustine. "I'll take your bag and you can put the thermos near the driver's seat. I'll be needing it."

"If you need a break I'd be happy to drive."

"No, no, I'll be fine."

"Do you need help with the map?"

"Sr. Amata Christi is going to sit in the front."

"Amata Christi?"

"One of the novices."

Two novices arrived carrying a cooler between them. A couple of temporary professed sisters followed, laden with other supplies for the trip. Sr. Mary Augustine continued directing and loading. Rebecca felt a tap on her shoulder.

"Look who's coming!"

Rebecca swung around. "Patrick Marian!" Rebecca gave her a hug. "This is wonderful. I had no idea."

"When did you get in?" Patrick Marian asked.

"After ten. The bus ran a little late."

"Come on, let's get in the back and we can catch up on the news."

This particular detachment of the SCRs included two representatives from the novices, temporary professed, and newly perpetual professed.

"The Pope arrives this afternoon and drives from the airport to the cathedral for an ecumenical service. They estimate that there will be thousands there to welcome him. For part of his journey from the airport, the Pope will travel in the Pope-mobile. We'll be staying in a convent a few blocks from the route. If everything goes as planned, we'll be on the route to greet the Pope as he passes by."

"Who are the sisters we'll be staying with?"

"I forget the name. . . . From what I heard, there are a few older sisters living in an empty convent, you know, the typical."

"It is *kind* of them to be offering us hospitality."

"Who's denying that?" said Patrick Marian puzzled. "Anyway, the next morning the Pope will meet with religious and priests at the university auditorium."

"After which we head home, I understand."

"Yes, unfortunately. We don't have tickets for the *huge* concluding Mass in the afternoon so we return to the motherhouse." Patrick Marian sighed. "I would love to go to that Mass. The Pope leaves for Rome afterwards."

"What about the sisters in the buses?"

"Oh, they are actually only in one of the buses. They've been following the Pope since his arrival in Boston with the other pilgrims from the diocese. Three busloads in all. I hear they have tickets to some of the events and were going to visit a few shrines and see some attractions in the cities as time permitted."

"The bishop is travelling with them?"

"Not really. He and his vicar general and Mother Mary Thomas and a couple of the councillors flew to Boston. They're attending many of the events. But they planned to join the other pilgrims as much as they could."

"So, are our sisters going to be staying with us in the same convent?"

"No, they have their own accommodations but we'll be meeting up with them tomorrow morning."

How Patrick Marian garnered her information was beyond Rebecca, but she always knew the whole scoop, even in their novitiate days.

The novices and temporary professed climbed into the van. Rebecca and Patrick Marian squeezed together to make room in the back seat for Kathryn Michael, who had just made first profession in June. Rebecca had seen her during the summer retreat but had never spoken with her. Rebecca exchanged introductions with Kathryn Michael and the other travellers. Patrick Marian already knew them all.

"In the name of the Father, and of the Son, and of the Holy Spirit," interrupted Mary Augustine as she fastened her seat belt and started the car. They drove out of the convent compound and down the quiet streets, reciting a series of prayers for a safe trip.

Spiritual reading, the rosary, hymns. When they weren't praying, silence would have generally been the norm, but today chatter and laughter filled the van. The excitement was tangible. Rebecca nudged Patrick Marian when Amata Christi squealed and they quietly laughed together. Even Mary Augustine's "no-nonsense" tone mellowed as the trip progressed.

Arriving in Baltimore on schedule, they were warmly greeted by a small group of elderly nuns who gave them a brief tour of their convent, showed them their rooms, fed them lunch, and pointed them in the direction of the papal route. The last detail was unnecessary. Mary Augustine had everything mapped out and briskly led the way with a novice on either side and the two temporary professed close behind. Rebecca and Patrick Marian brought up the rear but they could still hear Amata Christi's high-pitched giggle at various comments made by Mary Augustine.

Patrick Marian laughed. "That one's tightly wound."

The convent was about twelve blocks from the papal route and the sidewalks began to fill with a festive crowd the closer they drew to their destination. Many approached the SCRs and asked who they were, where they were from, and expressed their delight in seeing young sisters.

"Oh, this is just a few of our sisters," said Mary Augustine, gesturing toward the young people who surrounded her. "We have eighteen postulants and twenty five novices."

"Isn't that wonderful," was the typical response.

"Yes, the average age of our sisters is thirty-five," Mary Augustine would add, leaving the well-wishers commenting among themselves as she and her band sped forward.

One couple who stopped the small band were equally amazed at the numbers Mary Augustine relayed. But before Mary Augustine could move on, the husband turned directly to Kathryn Michael and asked why she entered the convent.

"My heart was made for God alone. I couldn't give my love to just one man, to just one family. My heart was made to embrace an infinite number of spiritual children from the whole world."

The couple looked quizzically at each other but this was lost on Mary Augustine who wished them well and forged ahead with her troop. Bringing up the rear, Rebecca heard the wife say to her husband, "I guess you can be grateful for my pint-sized heart."

~

The street the sisters travelled on opened to a wide boulevard with broad sidewalks. People were already pressed against the barricades that lined the route. However, by walking a few blocks down, and with some tenacity, Mary Augustine managed to usher them just three-people deep from the barricade. Although it would be another two hours before the Pope passed, the expectancy pulsed through them like an electric current. Some people nearby had brought a boom box, and turned the volume up high so all those around could follow the progress of the Pope on the radio. When the reporter announced the Pope had stepped out of the airplane, a roar of cheers arose from their group.

Then Rebecca felt the first drops. The heavy, grey clouds, gathering since they arrived in Baltimore and menacing as they walked to the papal route, would hold off no longer. The sisters were prepared with jackets and umbrellas, as were most on the street. In no time, the sides of the avenue were hooded with umbrellas. As the drizzle turned into a steady rainfall, Rebecca began to understand the impracticality of umbrellas in such a crowd. Patrick Marian stood slightly ahead of her, the edge of her umbrella tilted near the front of Rebecca's neck. The edges of the umbrellas held by people surrounding her were just above her shoulders. To cover her head, Rebecca was forced to hold her own umbrella over theirs.

When the rain increased, she could feel the water from all the umbrellas pouring over the front, the sides, the back of her jacket, down her veil and habit. With the constant jostling of the crowd, the edges of the umbrellas would come closer to her neck, and then the water poured over the collar of her jacket and down her underclothes. She was contributing to the problem as all the rain she kept off her head with her own umbrella, hit the tops of the others and made its way all over her. At first Rebecca cringed as she felt the cool water trickling down her body and puddling in her bra—but what could she do? She couldn't move, no one could. The absurdity of the situation was growing, then the downpour hit and she was drenched inside and out. The throbbing crowd sang, chanted, and rooted. Rebecca laughed to herself. Nothing could chill out this moment.

Thundering cheers were heard further up the street. He was coming, the Pope was coming!!! The crowd surged with emotion. As if on cue, umbrellas closed as all strained forward for a better view.

Here he is! The Pope! The Pope! The Pope waving, the people thrusting their hands forward; the Pope blessing, the people crying; the Pope passing, the people chanting, "John Paul II, we love you, John Paul II, we love you!" and "Viva la Papa!" It was exhilarating! Within seconds he was gone, cheers following him as he went, growing more and more distant.

Despite the rain, high cheer prevailed as the people turned and disbanded, wiping away tears and reopening their umbrellas. Within seconds, Mary Augustine was away from the barricade and leading her charges back to the convent. She and the novices had actually manoeuvred to the front—the earlier arrivals eventually giving way to the persistent nun. Rebecca had never been so wet, in so many clothes, in her entire life. Layers of long, cold, water-logged undergarments tangled with her habit, inhibiting every step. It didn't matter: she was filled with bliss, pure bliss.

"What a moment, *what* a moment!" exclaimed Mary Augustine, picking up her pace as they cleared the crowd and walked back through the side streets. The novices were again at her side, all effusively exchanging their impressions. Patrick Marian was laughing and chatting with the temporary professed sisters.

Rebecca had no words. She walked back in silence, treasuring the presence of the Pope and the enthusiasm of the crowd. The faith *was* alive and vibrant in the US!

CHAPTER 59

The next morning Mary Augustine and the young sisters were among the first to line up for security. The event began at 9:30 a.m.; the entrance opened at six. Mary Augustine didn't want to hunt around for parking so she had them all at the university auditorium with a brown bag breakfast at 4:30 a.m. Another late night and very early rising.

When the sisters returned from greeting the Pope, they were in no condition to go to evening Mass as planned. Instead the washing machine and dryer handled load after load of undergarments and habits while they took turns in the shower and at the ironing board.

Clean, dry, and pressed, the sisters now stood waiting in the cool, dark morning. Rebecca was grateful that it wasn't raining and that soon enough, she hoped, they would be sitting in a warm room. Her shoes were still damp from the day before. As the crowd swelled, so did her expectations and she all but forgot her discomfort.

Security opened and the crowd inched forward. Reaching one of the entrance doors, the sisters entered a large vestibule, passed through metal detectors, and moved into the auditorium. Tickets in hand, Mary Augustine marched them to their seats.

Priests, religious sisters, religious brothers. So many! It was incredible.

"Can you believe this!" said Rebecca to Patrick Marian.

She and Patrick Marian sat together in the centre of their row. Mary Augustine set up camp in an aisle seat, determined to shake the Pope's hand if by miracle he decided to descend the stage. Her faithful novice companions were close at hand. The sisters travelling by bus would fill the rest of the empty seats reserved for the SCRs. Rebecca was mesmerized by the sheer number of priests and religious, seminarians and young people preparing for religious life. So many in habits and what a variety!

"Here they come!" exclaimed a novice, standing and waving to an advancing group of SCRs.

Mother Mary Thomas, stout, upright, and confident, walked in the midst of her sisters. There was something in her manner. . . . Mary Augustine bustled down the aisle to greet them. Watching Mother approach, surrounded by her many sisters, Rebecca felt on edge but it didn't last long. The arriving SCR sisters began to fill the empty seats and greetings abounded. Patrick Marian went to sit next to Pistós who accompanied a contingent from their college—young women discerning their vocation to religious life.

Rebecca didn't know if she should leave her place to greet Mother Mary Thomas and the other general councillors—a tacit practice when they arrived at the motherhouse from the branch houses. There was so much commotion within the whole auditorium and among the SCRs as they settled into their seats, that for a while she was caught up in the hugs and greetings being exchanged among them. When Rebecca looked over next, Mother Mary Thomas was standing in the aisle speaking with Mary Augustine and a few other SCRs. At that point, a couple of sisters, perhaps in their sixties, approached Mother. They were from another order, wore no habit other than identical medallions, and appeared to be introducing themselves. They seemed interested in the jubilant delegation of SCRs. Rebecca watched Mother Mary Thomas turn to regard them. Although civil, Rebecca, even at a distance, could pick up her dismissive attitude. The sisters went their way and Mary Augustine offered Mother Mary Thomas her aisle seat. Mother declined and, waving to her sisters, walked to the front of the auditorium accompanied by Petrina. As Rebecca would find out later, there was special seating for major superiors close to the stage. Mother Mary Thomas had been placed in the front row.

Rebecca turned to see Patrick Marian laughing with Pistós. This was surprising—Patrick Marian used to mimic Pistós' ramrod posture with her hands folded primly on her lap or the way she held her back pleats before she sat to keep them from wrinkling.

But these were fleeting observations, mere mental photographs, amidst the high-spirited greetings she exchanged with the sisters around her who were happy to have someone with whom they could share the highlights of their pilgrimage with the Pope.

The music started. The Pope would not arrive for another couple of hours, but in the meantime a program of Scripture and music was gearing up.

A bishop led the multitude in prayer, assisted by a choir for the singing. Words were projected onto jumbo monitors. Morning prayer from the Liturgy of the Hours: traditional hymns and psalms they all knew and sang with fervour. Tears trickled down Rebecca's cheeks.

When the prayers were finished, the choir filed off the stage and guitars, drums, and keyboards took their place. Amid the cheers of the audience, musicians and singers from a religious community of men walked on stage and picked up their instruments. The praise and worship segment of the program began with an explosion of music—Christian pop/rock. The melodies were simple and catchy, so the uninitiated easily picked them up. For the fledging religious and priests—and the young people contemplating religious life and the priesthood—these songs were the mainstay of their Christian youth groups, summer camps, and conventions. Thousands of participants began singing, clapping and, at times, standing and swaying to the music. The atmosphere was literally electrifying.

Then the Pope arrived! When he came on stage, unbridled ardour and devotion let loose. Cheers, applause, tears streaming down faces. Some stood up on their chairs—even Amata Christi until Mary Augustine yanked at her habit to call her down. Banners were lifted, flags waved, and the unending mantra shouted together: "John Paul II, we love you; John Paul II, we love you." Weariness vanished, time dissolved into now. All was subsumed in a massive expression of belief, triumph, and jubilation.

Though not generally one for public displays of emotion, Rebecca was too tired to contain her tears and sobbed. She loved the Church and from her childhood her mother had instilled the greatest respect for Christ's Vicar, the Pope. And now that faith throbbed and overflowed with the thousands who chanted, "John Paul II, we love you."

It took some time before the audience settled down enough for the Pope to begin his speech. Rebecca was hard-pressed to follow all that was said. Aside from the pedantic reading, the speech was frequently interrupted with applause and standing ovations. Some phrases, however, stood out: "set apart," "life of self-oblation through obedience," "sign of contradiction amidst secularism," "fidelity to Christ through the Church." More than what he said, it was the experience: all of them there, together, united with the Pope in the Church they all loved; revitalized, affirmed, charged. Rebecca had never experienced anything like it—yesterday dimmed in comparison. She was euphoric.

The Pope concluded and gave his apostolic blessing. The massive assembly again erupted into applause, cheers, and tears. Banners once again lifted high. After multiple gestures of blessings to the exuberant crowd, the Pope moved off the stage and out of sight, surrounded by his entourage.

Praise and worship music played over the loud speakers as the rapturous participants picked up their belongings and attempted to leave. Amata Christi was one continual squeal. Rebecca wiped the tears from her eyes and was embraced by one of her sisters who went on to embrace every SCR she could get close to. Patrick Marian laughed with the young women from the college. One of the students continued to exclaim, "What a *God high*! What a major *God high*!"

Rebecca slowly made her way down the aisle, basking in the experience. As the crowd erupted into the broad expanse in front of the auditorium, Rebecca was pushed away from her companions and found herself in the midst of a small group of middle-aged sisters. When they introduced themselves, Rebecca discovered that two of the sisters were from the same community as Bev and Judy.

"I know one of your sisters," she exclaimed. "Bev!"

This sparked an animated conversation on Appalachia and the work of Bev and Judy.

～

Seated in the front, Mother Mary Thomas was among the last of the SCRs to leave the auditorium. She was flanked by her companion, Petrina, and Pistós, who had lingered inside in order to accompany Mother Mary Thomas out.

"What a grace, what a blessing," said Petrina, smiling broadly.

"The Pope has such charisma. What an effect he had on all of us! Truly a man of God," added Mother.

"You should have *seen* the young women from the college," said Pistós. "They *love* the Pope! One kept squeezing my arm saying over and over, 'the Vicar of Christ, can you believe it, Jesus Christ on earth!' Another one"—Pistós laughed at the thought of it—"another one called him the 'Daddy of the Church.'"

Mother smiled and shook her head. "Our young people."

"Who says the Church is out of touch with youth . . . they should be here to witness this!" said Pistós.

The three SCRs exited the auditorium and stopped near the entrance, gazing out over the expanse, which was slightly elevated from the roadway and walkways that led to other parts of the campus.

Getting her bearings, Pistós said, "We're meeting in a small park just this way," indicating to the right. But something else caught Mother's attention. Off to the left, in the middle of the broad sweep leading to the auditorium entrance stood a young SCR speaking intently and happily with a group of sisters in secular garb.

"Who is that sister?" asked Mother Mary Thomas in a tone decidedly different from their previous comments.

Petrina and Pistós tried to follow her gaze. "Where?"

Mother's eyes never left the scene. "There," giving a slight nod.

Pistós shaded her eyes with her hand. "It's Sr. Rebecca Marise."

"I thought you said all the sisters were instructed to meet in a designated area in a park."

"That's right," replied Pistós.

"So why is she keeping everyone waiting, chattering away. Sr. Petrina, would you please go remind her of where she should be."

Petrina moved toward the lively group.

~

Rebecca startled when she noticed Petrina at her side. She was the last person Rebecca expected to see. "Sr. Rebecca Marise, weren't you told about the gathering point?" Although politely spoken, her manner and tone immediately chilled the atmosphere.

"I was just greeting . . . I know—"

"All the sisters are waiting for you," cut in Petrina with a tight smile. "You should be getting on." The other sisters watched this exchange with wonderment.

As Rebecca turned to go, she saw Mother Mary Thomas and Pistós gazing down at her from the distance. *Oh my God!*

Petrina remained a while longer with the sisters, gathering information for her report to Mother. Rebecca hurried off to the designated area, her euphoria diminishing rapidly. The exchange with Petrina became more confusing as she saw many other SCRs still making their way to the park. The sisters were certainly not waiting on her. Why had Petrina been sent to fetch her? And with Mother and Pistós watching on! What had she done wrong? She had been talking about the missionary outreach in Appalachia for goodness' sake!

By the time she arrived at the park site, the elated spirits of the other sisters were at odds with her bewilderment and her growing anxiety. She could see Mother and her entourage approaching and merged into a group of sisters near the rear. *This is stupid, Rebecca*, she berated herself. *You have done* nothing *wrong.* She resolved not to cower behind the others. As Mother came into the enthusiastic group of sisters and they fanned out around her. Rebecca, although in the rear, remained in view.

"What a blessing! What a manifestation of faith!" Mother beamed.

The enthusiastic response of the sisters and young people assured her they felt the same.

"We are called to be at the heart of the Church," Mother said, raising her voice to let the joyous group know she had a reflection to share, "and we are at the centre of this beating heart when united with the Vicar of Christ. We were founded to spread the truth, and we are never so secure in that proclamation than when we are teaching the Gospel with and in the Church, guided by our Holy Father."

Rebecca noticed Petrina gazing at her, but turned her attention to Mother.

"Not all agree with this. Their pride leads them to trust their own opinions, their own judgments over the teachings of the Church. Religious orders who have taken this route, abandoning community life, abandoning prayer, abandoning their habits, are dying!" Mother looked squarely at Rebecca. "It is obedience that sets us free! Dying to ourselves, dying to our way of thinking, and submitting to the teachings of the Church. This leads to true freedom and joy! Our peace, our surety, the very reason for our existence lie within the heart of the Church. Sisters, let us be faithful above all else! Our love of Christ is manifested in our love for the Church, united to the Pope."

Mother often gave these spirited "sermonettes"; however, the intensity in her voice and the exuberance already within the group led the sisters to burst into cheers and applause. Mother was immediately surrounded by a smaller group of sisters. They waved to the others and left with Mother Mary Thomas—off to lunch, then to the Papal Mass with tickets for the VIP section. Mary Augustine called together her group. They would return to the motherhouse. The rest of the sisters were going to the final Papal Mass as well, but in less prestigious seating.

Rebecca felt a nudge at her side. "You're never going to believe this!" said Patrick Marian, euphoric. "I get to go to the Papal Mass!"

Rebecca turned, surprised. "Sr. Pistós told me that Sr. Maria Scholastica isn't feeling well. She left for the motherhouse this morning with some benefactors who had to be home today. So there's an extra ticket! An extra seat on the bus! And an extra bed for tonight! And *I* get to take her place! Sr. Pistós arranged everything!"

Rebecca smiled and congratulated Patrick Marian but could not match her ebullience. Patrick Marian didn't notice. She gave Rebecca a quick hug. "It was great seeing you again." And she was off, running ahead with Mary Augustine so she could transfer her overnight bag from the van to the bus. Rebecca suddenly felt very, very tired.

~

Three more hours and they would be at the motherhouse. Rebecca rolled up her sweater and used it as a pillow against the window. She closed her eyes and tried to block out the high-pitched squeals of Amata Christi. They were no longer amusing.

The departure from Baltimore had been delayed—major. Mary Augustine felt it was her responsibility to personally walk Patrick Marian from the van to the SCR bus, which was in a entirely different parking area. When she returned, she inched the van out of the parking lot and wormed her way through the traffic. They had finished off the last of the food from their bagged breakfasts and all the drive-through restaurants near the university were crammed. Mary Augustine had to go out of their way to find one. Through it all high spirits prevailed. Kathryn Michael leaned over the seat in front of her, laughing and sharing her experiences. Rebecca smiled and nodded when the conversation was directed at her, but after eating, she leaned back in her seat and closed her eyes. By the time the band of pilgrims reached the highway, Mary Augustine's carefully timed schedule was off by hours. They would not arrive at the motherhouse before ten that night. It was just as well. Rebecca would not have to appear with the ecstatic novices and temporary professed as they relayed the wonderful events of the past couple of days. That would happen tomorrow after breakfast and she would already be on a bus to Whitewaters.

CHAPTER 60

"Well, you're a bundle of news and jubilation," said Maureen, driving home from the bus depot.

"I'm exhausted." Other than greeting Maureen, Rebecca had barely said a word.

Maureen glanced at Rebecca gazing out the side window into the growing dusk. "What happened?"

"Nothing happened," said Rebecca, exasperated. "I'm just tired." Her voice cracked and she knew if she said one more word, she would break down.

Maureen had never heard Rebecca snap with impatience. She let her be and they drove on in silence.

The car stopped in the driveway. "I'll go ahead and tell Candida and Jeanne that you're not feeling well and just want to go to bed. Tomorrow you sleep in. Do you want me to bring you some toast and tea?"

"Thanks, Maureen, that would be great."

~

"The dead has risen," said Jeanne as she walked into the kitchen after their morning prayers.

"You feeling better?" asked Maureen.

"Oh, yes," Rebecca reassured Maureen. It was true that a solid and extended night's rest had been of great benefit, and she hoped that by getting back to the ordinary rhythm of her life the deflated feeling that still plagued her would dissipate.

"So what was it like to see the Pope?" asked Candida gleefully as they gathered in the dining room to eat their breakfast.

"It was great," she said. She related a few details about greeting the Pope on the boulevard and several more about the Pope's audience with the religious and priests. But as much as she tried to replicate the events for the sisters, she could not generate any degree of enthusiasm, let alone the exhilaration she had felt the day before. She found herself relaying facts and forcing her smile and emotion.

"And what about you?" Rebecca said to ward off any more questions, "What's been going on in Whitewaters since I've been away?"

"Not a whole lot. It's been, what? Just a weekend since you left," said Maureen with a smile. "Your students will be happy to have you back."

"And I'll be very glad to be back with them."

This was the one thing that Rebecca looked forward to and had gotten her out of bed that morning. She finished off her breakfast in haste. "Maureen, do you mind if I leave a bit earlier? I want to read the notes of the substitute and get my mind wrapped around the lesson plans for the day."

As usual, Rebecca scurried up the stairs to the school building and walked at a brisk clip to her classroom. She stopped at her door and hung on to the knob. Her head was spinning. She walked inside, closed the door, sat in the nearest desk, and put her head down. *You're exhausted, Rebecca. Slow down.* Her head cleared. She remained sitting for a few minutes more, gazing out at the mountains circled with their hazy, mysterious mist. *Whitewaters.* She dared not reflect on the past few days.

Rebecca got up slowly and walked to the staff room. She prepared a pot of coffee, poured herself a large mug, and brought it to her desk. The weekend experience had taken a toll far beyond what Rebecca could have foreseen.

~

It was Maureen's week to cook. Rebecca had yet to assume a week on her own. Instead her responsibilities in the kitchen had evolved to preparing certain dishes on an "as-needed basis" with one or the other of the three sisters. And if the seasoned sisters were OK with that, Rebecca certainly wasn't going to lobby for more culinary arts time.

"Rebecca, want to give me a hand with a salad this afternoon?" said Maureen as she past Rebecca's classroom at the end of the school day.

Rebecca looked up. *Not really.* She smiled, "Sure, I'll be right there."

A few minutes later Rebecca was in the kitchen putting on her apron. Maureen had the vegetables on the counter ready to slice.

"You haven't been yourself since you came back, Rebecca," said Maureen as she mixed her ingredients in a bowl.

Rebecca pulled out a cutting board and began searching for a knife.

"What happened?"

"Nothing much."

"But enough."

Rebecca began to slice the cucumbers. "The more I think about it, the more I think I'm making a mountain out of a molehill."

This is what she had been telling herself for the past few days, but she couldn't shake the sinking feeling that hovered over her every time she was quiet—at prayer, before sleeping, or just walking from the school to the convent.

"What molehill are you talking about?"

She was giving Rebecca a searching look. "Come on, Rebecca, you've always been honest with me. Tell me what's dimming your spark. The molehill?" she gently prompted.

Rebecca washed a pepper and began to remove its seedy core. "Petrina."

"What's she been up to?" asked Maureen cautiously.

"After the Pope's audience"—Rebecca sighed—"I left the auditorium and met a couple of sisters from Bev's community—imagine the chances in that crowd. We were just greeting each other . . . talking about Appalachia. Then Petrina appears at my side, telling me to get back with the group, like I was holding them up or something. I turned to go and there was Mother and Pistós watching a little further off. . . . As I walked toward the group I realized no one was waiting. . . . It was kind of embarrassing. . . . Then Mother gave us a sermon about fidelity. . . . It was all . . . just so different . . ." Her voice trailed off.

"Different from what?"

Rebecca hadn't really thought about it before, but her answer came immediately.

"From here."

∼

Saturday after lunch Rebecca went to the tiny convent chapel for some quiet time of prayer; however, Candida was already there, loudly whispering the prayers of the rosary. From past experience, Rebecca knew that she would soon be snoring. She quietly closed the door and walked over to the church. The insight that glinted yesterday with Maureen continued to nag her. She wanted to clear her thoughts. When she had first come to Whitewaters there was a quality about Maureen, really, about all the sisters, that eluded her. She had a partial answer now: they treated her like an adult. Mary Augustine herding them around like schoolchildren; Petrina interrupting a conversation and sending her on her way; the pilgrimage sisters gathering around Mother Mary Thomas, gleefully clapping and cheering . . . It was all so foreign to her experience of the past several months. And why had she never noticed it before?

Sisters in secular garb, living without a structured common life, were presented as progressives at odds with the teachings of the Church or as cop-outs seeking worldly compensations. But Rebecca didn't find either in Bev. She was committed to her ministry in Appalachia, knowledgeable about the people and their traditions. She was unassuming regarding her accomplishments and those of the organization she helped direct. Everything about her spoke of simplicity, of love for Christ and the people she served.

Do your own research. You're a bright young woman, Bev had said. Why did these words unsettled her? She was constantly reading up on all matters regarding the education of children. She had a master's in education, for God's sake. So why was research on Vatican II so off-putting?

Throughout their formation, the sisters had been warned over and over about the danger of reading material outside that recommended by the superiors. The devil is sly in sowing seeds of doubt, they were told. Studying sources that question the position of the Pope would only lead to confusion and disbelief. Their vocation, their very faith, was at stake. That's why only professors, clergy, and religious known for their steadfast adhesion to the doctrine of the Church were ever permitted to teach, preach, or discuss issues with the sisters. And after reading their critiques of "questionable" theologians, Rebecca was wary of confronting their original writings.

Rebecca had an MEd, this was true. However, the degree was determined, the specialty selected, and the courses chosen by her superiors. Rebecca obtained her degree through a distance learning program and through courses taught at the motherhouse, both under the auspices of St. Gabriel's, a university known for its conformity to the Church. The proviso for on-campus courses had been waived due to the number of sisters enrolled in the program and the SCRs willingness to maintain the standards and the specifications of SGU in all the MEd courses. During the summer, sisters chosen for the degree attended classes at the motherhouse. The professors selected were known for their competency and fidelity to the Church—all of them were cleared by Mother and authorized by SGU. For their theses, the sisters could propose a topic to their superiors, but often the subject was assigned by the superiors and then submitted for the university's authorization. A list of books, articles, and websites authorized for research was provided. Permission was required for anything further. The community server recorded the websites hit by all the computers in their compound and printed reports.

Some SCRs went on for specialized studies in theology, philosophy, canon law, and the like. These sisters actually attended courses on the SGU campus and lodged together in a house close by. Their presence on campus was also considered a means of recruitment—the sisters were active in the campus ministry office. Even in these cases, however, the courses and professors were determined and scrutinized just as meticulously as those teaching at the motherhouse.

As Rebecca sat in the dim light of the church, a thought surfaced that she had dismissed for some time. She could give herself leeway to study educational theories, yet why did she doubt her ability to discern the truth when it came to matters of faith? Who was actually discerning this truth on her behalf, on her community's behalf? How was it that these people could read, research, and remain unscathed by "questionable" authors but she could not?

Up to now, Rebecca had accepted what she had been taught: discernment of truth concerning the faith called for advanced studies in theology and philosophy, much experience, unswerving allegiance to the Church, a fervent prayer life, and a deep relationship with Christ. The arguments used by opponents were clever. Pride and curiosity were ever lurking to bring about one's downfall. So Rebecca had cringed from pursuing Bev's advice. It was like eating forbidden fruit in the garden of Eden.

The red tabernacle light flickered before her. Rebecca closed her eyes, laid her hands open on her lap and repeated a verse drawn from the scriptures that was becoming the mantra of her life, *Give me light, and show me your way; Give me light, and show me your way.* Suspending thought and judgment, she repeated the phrase and lost track of time.

The side door slammed. Rebecca startled and turned to see Doug.

"I'm sorry, Rebecca," he said in a hushed voice. "There's generally no one here at this hour. I didn't mean to . . ."

"It's OK."

He sat in the pew in front of her and turned to face her. "So how's the Pope?"

Over time Rebecca had grown to respect Doug. One thing was certain—she could trust him to be honest with her, whether she agreed or not.

"What happened at Vatican II?" Rebecca asked.

"Where did that come from?" he said with surprise.

"Why did it take place at all? Why did so many religious leave afterwards?"

Rebecca never ceased to amaze him. "A conversation won't cover it, Rebecca. If you really want to pursue this topic, I have plenty of books I could lend you. You can read whatever you like and then, if you need to, or want to, we can discuss it."

Rebecca tensed. She felt she was entering a field of land mines. "I don't know."

"Look, I have a few biographies on John XXIII. They should shed some light on why Vatican II took place. Wouldn't take me long to get them for you."

Biographies . . . and of a Pope? That seemed harmless. "Would you mind?"

∼

Maureen was in the kitchen when Rebecca returned from the church. "So how was your prayer?"

"Youth choir rehearsal drove me out."

Maureen laughed, "Another reason we scheduled our Saturday community prayer in the morning."

Rebecca put a stack of books on the counter, got a glass of water, and nibbled on a cookie. "Doug came in while I was praying. He lent me some books on John XXIII."

Maureen dried her hands on a dishcloth and picked up the books Rebecca had placed on the counter.

"You'll enjoy these," she said, pulling out one. "This is my favourite."

Night after night, Rebecca read.

~

Angelo Roncalli, who later became John XXIII, was the son of a peasant farmer in northern Italy—simple and hard working. His seminary training and initial years as a priest took place in a progressive region of Italy. Counteracting the rising tide of communism, church leaders in the region were active in supporting the rights and spiritual development of the urban working class and farming communities. Catholic credit and trade unions sprung up throughout the district as well as the organization of circulating libraries. Spiritual gatherings and retreats were arranged for the factory workers.

Although these initiatives were supported and encouraged by the social teachings of Pope Leo XIII, there were still many within the Vatican bureaucracy who were uncomfortable with the progressive stance of the bishops, clergy, and laity in northern Italy. Vatican authorities received numerous complaints when Bishop Radini-Tedeschi of Bergamo, a mentor of Roncalli, gave a sizable donation to the bread fund for the strikers in Ranica. Both Radini and Roncalli travelled to Rome in order to prevent the censure of Niccolò Rezzara. He had raised the ire of Vatican authorities when he sent a memorandum to the head of the Italian Catholic Electoral Union, stating that Catholics should be permitted to vote for candidates who not only had solid religious principles but who were also sensitive to the social problems of the time—a memorandum that Roncalli had signed. At this point in history, Catholics in Italy were still under the partial constraints of *non expedit*. The *non expedit*, issued by an embittered Pope Pius IX in 1868 after the papal states were taken over and a unified Italian government was forming, forbade Catholics to vote or assume office under the threat of excommunication. It was mitigated in 1905 by Pius X who, in particular instances, allowed voting and holding office by Catholics after the bishop of the area requested and received permission.

In time, Roncalli was made bishop and was stationed almost twenty years in assignments where the Church was on the fringes of the prevailing social and religious environment: Bulgaria, Turkey, and Greece. This was followed by nine years in France as the *nuncio*, a diplomatic representative of the Pope. France at the time was one of the most progressive centres of Catholic thought. When Roncalli was later appointed the archbishop of Venice he thought it would be his last assignment. Then, at seventy-seven years, he was elected Pope John XXIII.

Perhaps his early years with an intelligent, perceptive, and innovative bishop; perhaps his many years outside a Catholic cultural milieu observing and, at times, butting against the machinations of the Vatican; perhaps his warm, approachable, humble demeanour, which allowed people to communicate freely with him: perhaps with all these attributes and experiences, together with a spirituality rooted in the love of Christ, Roncalli could catapult a pastoral renewal within the Church that fissured centuries of defensiveness; of calcified, antiquated practices; of strata of entrenched bureaucracy, so the Church could listen with respect and without fear to the human family of which it is a part.

Rebecca was amazed when she read that in the morning on the day following his election in 1958, John XXIII called the official Vatican newspaper, the *L'Osservatore Romano*. Among other goals, *L'Osservatore Romano* was founded to inspire and promote the reverence of the Pope who was often designated as the august sovereign and pontiff. John XXIII had called to request that all ostentatious expressions referring to the papacy cease immediately. Rebecca couldn't believe that the practice of genuflecting three times when coming into the presence of the Pope could have possibly existed in the twentieth century. She laughed when she read that Pope John considered it a victory when he finally convinced the household staff to limit the practice to one genuflection per day. Within three months of his election Pope John called the Council of Vatican II in order to "open the windows of the Church so that we can see out and the people can see in." Rebecca's amusement ceased as she entered this final chapter of John XXIII's life: the preparation for and opening session of Vatican II.

The preparation of the initial Council documents had been dominated, for the most part, by Vatican cardinals and bishops of the *integralist* tradition. For these prelates, the Catholic faith was absolute, eternal, above history. Change of formulation and structure was resisted. Immersed in their occupations within the Vatican milieu, these prelates had limited contact with the work-a-day Italians, let alone the millions living throughout the five continents with their diverse cultures and histories. Yet these multitudes were the very people the *integralists* alleged to teach and keep free of errors. From the *integralist* perspective, the Church, the perfect society, was open to all people—that is, open for people willing to conform to the Church. The Church itself did not move. At stake was preserving the purity of Church doctrine, morals, and liturgy from the rising tide of evil in the world.

John XXIII challenged the prophets of doom for whom the modern world was nothing but sin and ruination. He recognized the good in the present age and looked toward the future with hope. Pope John cautioned the participants of the Council not to fearfully guard the treasure of faith, obsessed with the past, but to make a leap forward in doctrinal insight, to study the teachings of the Church using research methods and the language of modern thought. He distinguished between the substance of the faith and manner in which it is expressed. Some of the key phrases in this opening address were deleted or modified in the official Latin records of the Council. However, Pope John continued to quote from his original version in subsequent speeches.

Rebecca had no idea of the politics and manoeuvring that occurred within the Vatican and was disconcerted as she continued with her research. Early in the Council proceedings, she read, bishops and cardinals from around the world rejected all but one of the prepared documents. New articulations of the faith were proposed. Prelates of differing theological positions hotly debated the issues at hand. The documents were revised and revised again. To her surprise, theologians who had formerly been censured by Vatican authorities, were invited by Pope John to the Council, and many of their previously condemned formulations were accepted and incorporated into the final documents.

She had always believed that encyclicals and other church documents were inspired entirely by the Holy Spirit and free of any internal dissent. In her mind, these documents rolled out seamlessly from the pen of the Pope, or Vatican prelates with the approval of the Pope. They were official proclamations bearing the weight of infallibility at times and submission always. Now her perception of Church teaching, ever faithful to Christ, cutting through the errors of the times, began to falter. And as her conceptions were challenged, her anxiety mounted.

Rebecca had been taught that the Church was currently reforming the renewal of Vatican II. The Council documents had been misinterpreted and misapplied, launching a misguided renewal. Presently scholars in harmony with the bishops and the Pope were interpreting the teachings of the Council in continuance with Church doctrine throughout the centuries, ushering in a reform of the abuses.

Rebecca now questioned, was this true? What about the theologians who were silenced and censured before Vatican II, then invited to the Council as theological experts? Who was right? The Vatican authorities who silenced the theologians or Pope John who allowed formulations drawn from their banned works to be incorporated in the final documents? From what she had read, Pope John *himself* had been under suspicion of Vatican authorities. Who should she follow? Who was infallible? To whom was her submission due?

What about the Vatican prelates, those bishops and cardinals who opposed John XXIII *while* he was Pope? Didn't they owe the Pope the submission of their minds and wills just as she did?

CHAPTER 61

Maureen, Jeanne, Rebecca, and the parishioners who were organizing the summer program walked about the grassy play area behind the school. Rebecca carried a pad of paper and made a rough map of the sections they were designating for the various activities.

"That's about it," said one of the parishioners. "Any more issues or concerns we need to bring up?"

"I think we've covered all we can for now," said another.

"Good. We'll meet again next week at the same time," said the parish leader.

"I'll type up the notes and make a proper diagram," offered Rebecca. "You'll have them tomorrow."

And the group disbanded.

Maureen and Jeanne remained on the grass and watched Rebecca go back toward the school with the others.

"What's with Rebecca?" asked Jeanne. "She hasn't been the same since she came back."

"What have you noticed?"

"She's always been generous. But now . . . it's like she can't find enough to do . . . running around. And at the same time she seems withdrawn."

"Withdrawn?"

"I don't know. . . . Maybe preoccupied is a better word. You haven't noticed?"

"Yes, I have."

They walked to a picnic table under a leafy tree in the corner of the schoolyard and sat down. It was a perfect late spring day with a gentle breeze blowing through the leaves.

"Guess what she has brought up again," said Maureen.

Jeanne looked over at her.

"Birchbark."

"God, she is like a dog with a bone."

Maureen chuckled. "After the First Communion service last Saturday, during the pancake breakfast in the hall—"

"Great sausages, by the way."

"Rebecca finally gets a plate of pancakes and comes to stand next to me. She says, 'The First Communion classes are finished and I have all my lesson plans completed to the end of the school year. May I go to Birchbark next week with Jeanne?'"

"What a nun."

They both remained silent for some time.

"So what do you think?" asked Maureen.

"You know what it means if she doesn't understand. . . ."

"She understands."

The leaves rustled above them and young birds chirped for their mother.

"Do you think they'll pull us out?" asked Jeanne.

"Who knows? Henrietta says Mother has requests from bishops outside the state who want the SCRs to run schools in their diocese."

"The SCRs have become the cat's meow. How things have changed. . . ."

A couple of squirrels chased each other in the grass before them and then dashed up the tree, sending the swallows flying.

In a sombre voice Jeanne asked, "What will you do if we have to leave Whitewaters?"

"I have no idea." Maureen turned to face Jeanne. "What about you?"

Jeanne just shook her head.

After some moments, Jeanne said, "So Rebecca . . . She really wants to come?"

"Apparently."

"Let her come."

~

Thursday afternoon, Jeanne knocked on the door frame of Rebecca's classroom on her way back to the convent.

"Come on in. Just give me a couple of seconds to finish off this note."

Jeanne leaned against the windowsill with the mountains as her background. "So Maureen tells me you want to come to Birchbark."

Rebecca dropped everything and gave Jeanne her full attention.

"You want to come this Saturday?"

Rebecca ran to Jeanne and gave her a hug and then squeezed her shoulders. "Thank you, thank you, *thank you.*"

It was the return of Rebecca-past and Jeanne rejoiced to see it.

"OK, OK. Rebecca, bring over one of your chairs."

Rebecca could hardly sit.

"I'm going to be really honest with you," said Jeanne slowly. "The ministry we do in the hollers is quite different from here."

"Sure, I understand that."

"Catholics are scarce in Whitewaters and they're even more rare in Birchbark."

"Yes, I've heard that."

"And among the population there is still suspicion and mistrust of the 'papists.'"

"OK."

Jeanne paused a moment. "So when we minister in the back country, we don't wear—" Jeanne lifted up the front pleat of her habit. "We wear what is more suitable for the people."

"Oh."

~

Rebecca had not seen this coming. Yes, this was Whitewaters, and as she knew from experience, things were different in Whitewaters, but this was *very* different. The habit was the symbol of her total consecration to Christ, a reminder of her vows of poverty, chastity, and obedience. The habit, she had been told, was a protection against all that could distract her from her commitment to Christ. By taking off the habit weren't they endangering their vocation? She hadn't worn secular garb since the day she crossed the threshold of the SCRs eight years ago.

My God, the sisters hiked, cooked, gardened, mowed lawns, played basketball—all in the habit.

In a subdued voice she asked, "Do you think it would matter much if I wore my habit there just once?"

"If you wore your habit what do you think would happen?"

Rebecca chewed her lip, perplexed.

"Rebecca, *you* become the centre of attention . . . like . . . like a new attraction at the zoo. Don't think that everyone who sees this habit is reminded of the love of Christ. Most of the people will wonder why you're bundled up in so much clothing in June." Then in a softer tone, "We're not going for ourselves, but for the people."

"What about our witness?"

"Jesus said, 'People will know that you are my disciples by your love for one another.' That is all the witness necessary. That's the heart of it all."

"Why are we hiding the fact that we're sisters?"

"Oh, the people know we're religious sisters. They call us 'the Catholic ladies.'"

"And . . . and the superiors?"

"What about them?"

"Like . . . do they . . . know?"

"Henrietta knows I help out on Saturdays. It's been cleared with Mother."

"And the habit?"

"They've never asked."

Neither nun moved or said a word. Rebecca's long rosary, attached to her cincture, slid off her lap and clattered on the floor. She lifted it, lay it again across her lap and then began to turn one of the beads around and around. Birchbark. Deep, rural Appalachia. After all these months, within reach, and now bittersweet.

"The habit keeps Christ on the streets. This is what the Pope teaches." As she spoke, Rebecca felt she was reciting a script.

"You may have noticed that the Pope didn't choose Whitewaters or the hinterlands of Appalachia for his visit. When the Pope puts on a pair of jeans, a flannel shirt, and a ball cap . . . when he slips out unattended and shares a cup of coffee with the locals . . . just to talk to them . . . just to listen to them and learn about their struggles, their pains, and hopes . . . then, perhaps, he may be in a better position to talk about what puts Christ on the streets."

Rebecca said nothing. Jeanne straightened up.

"If you're not comfortable, that's OK, Rebecca. I understand. You don't have to come." She began to move toward the door.

"I'm coming."

Jeanne looked over with a glance Rebecca could not decipher—warmth, pain? Certainly trust. "OK, then."

CHAPTER 62

Jeanne generally drove out to Birchbark with another team member, Pam Duncan, and changed into her Appalachian apparel at her home. Pam's husband died years before, leaving her with two young daughters. Both were now grown and settled in larger cities in the State. Pam dedicated her time to the people in the back country of Appalachia.

"Well, look who we have here," Pam said warmly as she welcomed Rebecca on her porch and gave her a hug. "I hear you've been itching to help out at the centre."

"Relentless," said Jeanne.

Jeanne wandered into the kitchen as Pam lead Rebecca to a bedroom, "You can change in here and hang your clothes in the closet."

Pam walked back into the hallway, calling out, "Jeanne, just use my room." Munching on a cookie, Jeanne walked into the room Rebecca was using, took out a stack of clothes from the dresser, and crossed the hall into Pam's room.

So this was the routine, so familiar and comfortable for both Pam and Jeanne. Rebecca closed the door. She set her bag of clothes on the end of one of the twin-size beds and turned to see her reflection in the full-length mirror on the back of the bedroom door. Sr. Rebecca Marise. She walked closer to the reflection. Who was this nun staring back at her?

Rebecca heard the door open across the hall. "Pam, where are the . . ." Jeanne's voice trailed off as she walked down the hall.

She's changed! Already! Rebecca snapped into action. Where to put all her parts and pieces. She opened a drawer of the dresser—largely empty. She put what contents remained into a lower drawer. Cincture, rosary, crucifix, in the drawer. She took off her veil—her hands were shaking. Coif, veil on top. Piece by piece—it took so much longer here. In her own room the process would have been automatic and swift. Now, every movement seemed out of place, awkward.

Her bag of clothes sat waiting at the end of the bed. Rebecca pulled up the jeans and buttoned her blouse. A young woman appeared in the mirror, one she hadn't seen for years. Rebecca felt self-conscious, like she was in front of someone she had lost touch with and who had unexpectedly reappeared. The image had a figure; she had forgotten that and blushed. Her hair . . . Maureen had trimmed it the evening before but now it was matted down from the coif and veil. On the top of the dresser was a comb and brush. Rebecca sat on the bed, bent her head and began to brush her hair down and out. Thank God, she had inherited her father's natural wave. Combing it back in place, her hair didn't look so bad. . . . Rebecca Holden. She opened the door and, after some hesitation, walked into the hall and toward the voices coming from the front room.

"We thought you had passed out," said the woman across from Pam.

Rebecca glanced sheepishly at Jeanne without her habit.

"Don't you look nice," said Pam. "Come on over and have a bite before you go."

"I'm OK."

"We'll be on the road for about an hour," said Jeanne. She passed Rebecca a glass of juice. "You look fine."

"I was just telling Jeanne that I won't be coming today as we had planned. My daughter called last night and is driving up with her little girls for the weekend. Since you were going with Jeanne today, I felt it would be OK to stay home and have an extra day with them."

Jeanne got up. "When do you expect them?"

"Around noon." Pam raised her voice a notch as Jeanne walked into the kitchen. "The lunches are prepared—they're on the table. Keys in the regular place."

Rebecca finished her juice and pocketed an apple as Jeanne appeared again with a small cooler.

"We'd better be off, Pam. See you this evening."

"Enjoy your day, Rebecca."

"Thanks." Rebecca picked up a backpack near the door that Jeanne had brought in and the two sisters, incognito, walked out to the Jeep parked in front of the house.

~

Rebecca sat in the passenger seat, acutely aware of the fresh denim against her legs, the smell of her crisp, new blouse, and the familiar voice issuing from the unfamiliar woman next to her. She opened her window and experienced a sensation she hadn't felt for years: the wind blowing through her hair. As they journeyed deeper into the hollers, Rebecca was mesmerized by the beauty surrounding her. The initial roadway was two lanes with narrow shoulders. But when they forked off toward Birchbark the lanes tapered in and the shoulders disappeared altogether. Trees and undergrowth drew closer to the road, sometimes forming a canopy with sunlight glistening through the leaves.

"I've never seen anything like this," said Rebecca.

"I prayed we'd have a beautiful day so you could enjoy it."

The road curved sharply, hugged a mountain closely on one side, and opened a panorama on the passenger side.

"Oh . . . my . . . God . . . ," whispered Rebecca.

Down the steep incline toward the river, with a mountain as a backdrop, was a meadow alive with brilliant colours of the wildflowers.

Jeanne smiled. "After all these years, it still surprises me."

~

They drove on in silence for some time, both nuns held by the beauty surrounding them. In the background, instrumental music played on Pam's sound system. Rebecca had forgotten about her jeans until Jeanne spoke up and Rebecca turned toward her. *How weird!*

"When we arrive, there won't be much time for an explanation. In fact," glancing at her watch, "we'll be pulling in just in time for the art session. So here's the rundown. Pam generally works in child care with Kate and another volunteer. Kate will be OK for a while. You can come with me, help set up the room,, and stay a bit; get a feel for what we're doing."

"How did you get involved in the first place, Jeanne?"

"Long story. Someday we'll get to that. For now let me tell you about Birchbark. The art program is designed to help women and children who are coming from some form of abuse, to help with the healing."

"How does art heal?"

"People can voice pain that they may not be able to put into words. Art also gives them the opportunity to envision a different, more hopeful world and create something of beauty."

"So do the women just drop in?"

"Some come here in conjunction with counselling. Others come with a friend or relative. For many, it's the first time they are touching the emotions and fears connected with the abuse. They might move on to counselling, they may not. However, friendships are made, advice is bantered back and forth, networks of support grow. . . ."

"Why is there so much violence in the families here?"

"You think it's particular to the hinterlands in Appalachia?"

"Sure seems that way. Bev speaks about it. You just brought it up as the reason for your art program."

"Don't think domestic violence is limited to these backwoods. It's a lot closer to you than you may imagine . . . in our classrooms . . . and I'm not just talking about Whitewaters . . . in *all* our classrooms. . . ." More tentatively, Jeanne added, "And in our convents. . . ."

Rebecca continued to look out the window, saying nothing.

"So what's up, Rebecca?"

"It all seems so big. You know, the question that kept coming up during Bev's seminar this March was: How can we ever address these problems in the classroom and still teach?"

"And the rebuttal: Can we teach if these issues are being neglected? Can children learn when they're being traumatized?"

"What do you think?"

"Can we bring up issues in the classroom that we're afraid to address personally?"

"What do you mean?"

"Has it ever crossed your mind that some of our sisters might have suffered domestic violence?"

"I don't know . . . really. I've never heard anyone talk about it."

"Are we allowed, Rebecca?"

Rebecca remained silent.

"With these issues untouched, or brought up as examples of the 'growing depravity in the world,'" said Jeanne, "do you think anyone would have the courage to acknowledge it was going on in their home?"

Rebecca stared out the side window.

"What about sexual abuse? Do you think someone who's been sexually abused wouldn't enter the convent? In the backwoods, the communities are small, these issues are harder to cover up, they're in your face. But these same problems are in our cities, our parishes, our schools . . . our convents."

Rebecca's hand went down her side to fidget with her rosary beads, but they were gone.

"Until we can talk openly about abuse among ourselves, until we can compassionately acknowledge that some of our own members may have been victims growing up, until we can help them deal with the blame, the guilt, the shame, how can we address abuse in our parishes, in our classrooms?"

"Assuming . . . assuming that there is this problem, right?"

Jeanne sighed. "I don't have the answers, Rebecca. I just wish we—the SCRs—would spend more time studying and responding to these matters than being obsessed with orthodoxy. I wish we would open up to a broader circle of students. . . . We've become comfortable with the upper range of the bell curve. We've become secure with the financial backing of the people who can afford to send their children to a privileged, private school or parish schools that follow our lead with unquestioning deference." Jeanne's voice was rising. "We've become reliant on donors whose money controls our—" She cut off abruptly. Then, almost to herself, "The hinterlands are certainly out of our consciousness."

Rebecca shifted. She wanted to say, *We're forming professionals, tomorrow's leaders, steeped in the values of the Church.* This was their line. But the words wouldn't come out. Jeanne's reflections echoed her own growing, anxiety-ridden awareness.

"Look!" said Rebecca, pointing off to the side of the road, "There's a deer!"

Without turning toward the animal, Jeanne replied softly, "Yes, they're beautiful."

CHAPTER 63

"And here we are," said Jeanne as they passed a weathered sign welcoming travellers to Birchbark.

Scattered homes dotted the winding sides of the roadway for a mile or so before reaching a more condensed centre. At this point, the narrow valley was wide enough for a few side streets forming square blocks. Jeanne turned at one of these streets and, just two blocks in, she was forced to turn again. They pulled up in front of a two storey, clapboard home, freshly painted. Near the walkway that led to the front door a small sign swayed gently on a post: *Birchbark Women's Centre*. Homes were on either side and across the street. Behind the clinic a mountain made a steep ascent. Rebecca had never experienced a town literally cuddled by hills. They gathered their supplies from the Jeep, but instead of entering through the front, Jeanne walked down the side of the house.

"The waiting room will be full at this time and I don't want to intrude—we'll walk through the clinic before we leave."

Jeanne opened a side door near the rear of the building. As they entered, a narrow stairway to the right went up to the second floor. Directly in front of them was a large kitchen-dining area.

"This is used for nutrition classes, food prep for the child care, staff lunches. A group of local women also come to exchange cooking techniques, recipes. They cook together and then enjoy the meal."

Leaving their things on some chairs in the dining area, they walked into a very large porch.

"This porch was added for child care. One side is designed for smaller children and the other for older."

Windows covered most of the wall space providing a bright, open atmosphere and a complete view of the fenced-in backyard play area with the mountain rising behind.

"Whenever the weather permits, the kids are outside."

And so it was today. The porch was deserted. Jeanne opened the back door and walked a few steps down. About twelve children of various ages were playing in the yard or colouring at a picnic table.

"Well, look who's here!" said one of the adults.

Greetings, hugs, and introductions began. The children paused their activities, gazing curiously at the newcomer. To the surprise of both Jeanne and Rebecca, Bev was one of the welcoming party.

"Just making the rounds quickly with a new assistant so I wasn't able to drop by Whitewaters. But we've been looking forward to seeing you today," said Bev as she gave them a hug. "Pam called yesterday and said Rebecca was replacing her for the day." Taking Jeanne by the arm, she continued, "I was thinking, Jeanne, I have an invitation for lunch with Ma Sparks in Cold Creek holler. If you don't mind, Rebecca could come with me," putting her arm around Rebecca's shoulder. "It will give her a broader experience of the people. My assistant can replace her in child care."

Jeanne widened her eyes significantly to Rebecca. "Looks like it is your lucky day!"

Rebecca was thrilled.

"And, Jeanne," said Bev, "we already set up the room for your art session."

"My cup runneth over! Rebecca, come with me just for a brief tour and then you'll be off with Bev."

Back they went through the porch, the kitchen, and up the narrow stairway they passed coming in. This led to a room that spanned the clinic below. The walls were removed, leaving only the supporting beams creating a space for classes, meetings, and other initiatives such as the art sessions. Three women had just arrived and they greeted Jeanne as she and Rebecca appeared at the top of the stairs.

Spread throughout the rooms were easels, stackable chairs, and a few portable tables. As the women poured themselves some coffee or tea at a kitchenette,

Jeanne brought Rebecca to a closet in the back of the room. Its shelves were filled with stacks of plastic containers filled with supplies, and across the bottom shelf was a long row of individual canvases. "We let the canvases dry overnight and then store them here with the names on the side. When the women arrive, they come for their piece."

Jeanne then opened a door at the back wall. "Before we pull out the rest of the supplies, I want to show you the counselling rooms."

They were now standing on the landing of an interior stairway that came up from the office below and divided the space above the kitchen-dining area in half. A consulting room was on either side of the stairway landing. A soft glow came through the curtained window overlooking the porch. It illuminated the quilted wall hangings made by local women and a hanging plant overflowing its pot. Gentle music played somewhere in the background. Rebecca walked over to an open door and peeked in. The same inviting décor, with enough room for two glider chairs, a small, round table between them, and a desk at the back.

Returning to the multipurpose room Jeanne pulled out a number of plastic containers from the supply closet. She piled them up in Rebecca's extended arms, took some herself, and they walked over to the tables. On one they placed the containers with swatches of fabric and sewing supplies. On the other, they placed pieces of poster board, magazines, photos, ribbon, and various sundry items.

As they did so, Jeanne explained, "Not everyone is comfortable with paint and brushes, so we provide other options. The main thing is that the women express themselves."

Several more women arrived, and between the greetings, the veterans of the group helped Jeanne and Rebecca distribute the supplies. Jeanne pulled out a CD player and asked the group, "So what will it be today?" Music filled the room. The women went for their canvases or sat at one of the tables. They quietly began their work and Jeanne began her rounds among the tables and easels. Rebecca caught her eye and waved, then descended the stairs to meet up with Bev.

CHAPTER 64

"Here's a snack for the road," said Bev as they pulled out of the clinic's driveway. "It takes about forty minutes to get where we're headed."

"Where are we going?"

"Ma Sparks."

Bev and Rebecca left Birchbark on the same main road Jeanne had used to arrive there, but they continued away from Whitewaters. After several miles, they turned onto a narrow road, barely sufficient for two cars. Every now and again there was a wider area to allow larger vehicles to pass. Sometime later, Bev drove down an equally narrow, gravel road.

"It's an old coal mining road, but it's still kept up fairly well."

Just the same, their speed rarely went over thirty miles an hour. Down, up, and around—this road followed every contour of the hills and valley. Seldom were they passed by another car going into Birchbark, but when they were, they were enveloped in dust and slowed down even further until the air cleared.

"Dust or mud—I'll take the dust." Bev smiled as they forged ahead. Once again Rebecca was drawn by the beauty: within a meadow of grass and wild flowers a towering sugar maple; ferns and undergrowth hugging the banks of a small river as they wound through a holler. And as they drove, Bev told the story of Ma Sparks.

Ma Sparks was originally Peggy Sparks, a young wife of a coal miner. Jesse was a hard-working man, respected and reliable, and was soon promoted to foreman. So among the mountain women, she was better off. Not only was he employed, but he had a better paying job—and he didn't drink. Peggy was fortunate and she knew it. Her mother had not been so lucky.

Peggy was the eldest of three children. There would have probably been more, but they didn't survive the beatings their mother received before they saw the light of day. Fear pervaded their household. Even when her father wasn't angry, no one knew what would set him off. She and her siblings rarely felt the end of the stick he used so freely on their mother, but they did nothing to provoke it either. Like three little ghosts, they hovered in the background trying to remain invisible. Only when they were far out of earshot, scampering on the hillside, did they release any of their pent-up anxiety or play. Sometimes they would run through the mountain trails until their lungs burned and then drop from exhaustion on a ledge overlooking the sinuous river below. The mountains, Peggy told Bev, had saved her.

Her father's temper and drinking interfered with permanent employment. Had it not been for their mother's resourcefulness, her gardening and canning, life would have become desperate. Peggy quit high school so she could work and help out her mother. She was hired as a domestic for a few hours a week in the home of a wealthy coal mining official. Her reputation spread. Not only did her hours increase in the official's home, but she also took on some tasks in two other households and was able to rent an attic room in one of them. When she could, Peggy went home on the weekends.

During this period, her father decided to do a bit of moonshining in order to indulge his habit more economically. He was no expert. No one knew where he dug up the still, or the cleanliness of the equipment, or what he may have added to speed up the process, but the outcome was lethal. One evening he arrived home with a bottle from a fresh batch, collapsed on his porch, and died before arriving at the hospital.

Without her father, life improved for her family and Peggy could openly share her small wages. Through her job, she met her husband, Jesse. They married: she was eighteen and he was twenty-five. Jesse was already established with a trailer on property left him by his father. He had a strong work ethic, and what's more, he loved and respected Peggy. Four children arrived and the small trailer was replaced by a doublewide mobile home. Compared with her childhood, her life was idyllic. But that was to change.

When her youngest was five, Jesse was killed in a mining accident. Stunned,

Peggy began to break down. She couldn't bear to have her children out of her sight for fear they would not return. School days were torture. The monthly compensation she received was less than she needed for her family's upkeep and payments on the doublewide, but it was enough to exclude her from welfare. Her life, which had been going so well, seemed to be spiralling into the destitution of her childhood. She could not go back there.

Her mother jolted Peggy out of her tailspin. One day while she was weeping, her mother took her by the shoulders, looked into Peggy's eyes, and said, "You can do this. For your children you can do this." This battered, bruised woman had had the courage to go on. Peggy could do no less. She found a job as a domestic, working while her children were in school. But her meagre wage covered the gas in and out of Birchbark and little else. The women's centre had opened not long before and on Saturdays Peggy would drop off her children for a few hours while she worked. There she met Bev.

Bev was sceptical about the compensation Peggy received from the mining corporation, given it was a work-related death. She connected Peggy with a miner's advocacy group. Through their efforts, the coal corporation paid off what remained for the doublewide and increased the pension so her family could at least survive. While her case was pending, another organization supplemented her income with food and clothing. At first Peggy was ashamed but Bev assured her it was only temporary until she got back on her feet. Through counselling, Peggy was able to share for the first time some of the terror she experienced with her father.

With encouragement from Bev, Peggy pursued her GED and scored high. Boosted by her success, she began taking distance learning courses with an eye to obtaining a social service position. The material she studied sparked her curiosity and she became a voracious reader of history and literature, particularly that of Appalachia. She had long discussions with Bev when they met. Bev, in the meantime, had begun to travel into the hollers to meet the local women, hear their stories and, when appropriate or wanted, offer the support of the centre. Being an outsider, gaining trust was a slow process, and locating the small homesteads and communities in the rough mountain roads was difficult. Peggy offered to be her companion when she could.

Bev noticed an immediate change when accompanied by Peggy. Even if she was not always known personally, the women knew about Peggy's husband who was respected among the miners. They had heard her father "was an old cuss of a man" and how Peggy had supported her mama before marrying Jesse. A young widow due to a miner's death, with a household of "young'uns," increased her credibility even more.

Peggy was an intelligent woman, empathic toward her Appalachian neighbours and, as Bev discovered, she possessed a natural gift for social services—willing to assist without being patronizing or developing dependency. As a high-school-dropout mother who went back to school, she gave confidence to other women to do the same.

Through Bev's intervention, Peggy was hired for the centre's community outreach program, providing a listening ear, transportation, early intervention for the women and their children, and connection with other mountain women through the activities at the centre. When Peggy's own truck finally broke down, a grant provided her with a Jeep. As the years passed, she became known as Ma Sparks.

~

"My God," said Rebecca as Bev finished the story.

"My God, is right," said Bev. "These are the people who should be canonized."

By this time, their Jeep had slowed to a crawl as it made its way up a narrow lane off the dirt road.

"She's right around this bend."

Sure enough, a neat doublewide propped up on a cinder-block foundation came into view. Flowers were blossoming near the house and in patches along the driveway. A couple of tethered goats kept down the undergrowth around the tall trees that surrounded the home. A tire swing hung from one of their thick branches. Off to the side, in the back, a dusty Jeep was parked under a lean-to. Beyond that, where the sun came through a break in the trees, a vegetable garden was laid out. As they pulled up to the house, a golden brown hound howled and ran toward their car, its long ears flopping.

Peggy came out the front door, waving.

"Hush now, Molly, these here are friends."

She gave Bev a warm hug, "Just don't see enough of you anymore." And turning to Rebecca, "So you must be Rebecca. Welcome."

"What a beautiful dog," Rebecca said as she bent to rub its head.

"A redbone mutt and a great friend. And Molly keeps the deer away from my flowers and garden."

Chatting, they made their way into the house. The inside was dramatically different from the simple, square, white-and-blue-siding exterior. With the wood-crafted furniture, photos, quilts, and pictures, the interior of the factory-built house had acquired the rustic charm of the Appalachians. The aroma of fresh cornbread and brown beans made their reception even more inviting.

Bev and Rebecca sat at the dining room table, sipping sweet tea while Peggy finished off her meal preparation. At Bev's inquiry, Peggy spoke of her children. Her two eldest were married and now in different parts of the state. She brought over the most recent photos of her grandchildren, two in one family, and one in the other.

"They're growing," said Bev.

"Too fast. Don't see enough of them."

Her two youngest daughters were unmarried, sharing an apartment in Birchbark. One was an elementary school teacher; the other, an intern at the women's centre, working toward a degree in social work. Both had close bonds with the centre, having volunteered there during their teenage years.

"The girls will be coming up this evening. It's our movie night." Then, turning to Rebecca, "Where are your parents from, Rebecca? You don't sound like you're from these parts."

Rebecca told Peggy about her family.

"So you're one of the church ladies, like Bev and Jeanne. Can't get any better than these ladies. The good they do up in these hills."

"There's plenty of good done by many fine ladies, Peggy," said Bev, "you being one of them."

Peggy brushed off the compliment with a wave of her hand and then began to put platters and bowls on the table. "And we are ready!"

Sitting down, she extended her hands to Bev and Rebecca and closed her eyes. Bev took her hand and reached for Rebecca's, signalling with her eyes for Rebecca to do the same.

"Lord, we thank you for this food, for the company of my dear friend, Bev, and Rebecca. Guide us in our journeys, through the dark hollers and the rocky mountainsides, and let your love touch all we meet. Amen." And the meal began.

"This is delicious," said Rebecca.

"Still grow most of my vegetables in the garden out back. It's in my blood, I guess. Mama did it before me. Anyways, it's good to be out in the earth, helping things grow."

Bev asked about some of the women she knew.

"Old Mrs. Spraggins passed on; you heard about that? Her daughter cared for her 'til the end, good woman being over sixty herself. Her mother is in a better place now."

"What about Joyce Belvin?"

"I've been tryin' to get her to the clinic for tests. She says, '*I don't want 'em 'cause I can't afford 'em.*' I tell her they're free and she says, '*Yeah, an if'n there's nothin' wrong, there's nothin' wrong. But if'n they find something,*' I can't afford *fixin' it, so why bother knowin'?*' I'll keep trying."

And so it continued as Peggy passed through one family after another: the child, the job loss, the course completed, the black lung.

"What's black lung?" asked Rebecca.

Peggy exchanged a quick glance with Bev and laughed. "Honey, you really are not from these parts. Like a young sapling just startin' to smell the air and stretch her branches."

"It's a disease contracted from breathing in coal dust," said Bev. "Since mining has been the primary industry in these woods for the past several decades, black lung is common here."

"In the beginning you can hardly tell you have it," said Peggy. "You need an X-ray. Dust starts to build up in your lungs. Then it gets worse and worse. Hard to breath, painful. Sometimes it causes heart attacks. That's what happened to Jesse's daddy."

"Can't the coal companies do something about it?" asked Rebecca.

Peggy shook her head and laughed. "Honey, the coal companies are only interested in money. That's all they've ever been interested in. We're not people here. We're extractors of coal. So some die. . . ."

"There are no laws?"

Bev continued, "Initially, there were no laws to protect the men. As years past and unions formed, some changes came about. However, Rebecca, you have to understand that these are powerful corporations, with a valuable resource—energy. Often they have our government officials in their pockets."

Peggy turned to Bev. "You heard about Col & Tan? Found tampering with the dust-sampling machines again."

Bev nodded. Peggy looked toward Rebecca, "Companies are required to keep the dust down in the mines. The air's supposed to be tested regularly." Back to Bev: "They still haven't paid those fines from . . . what? It's been years."

"Can't the men work somewhere else?"

"Rebecca, Rebecca!" Peggy laughed again. "Let's just gather up the dishes and bring our tea to the living room. Then, Bev, we're going to educate this young lady."

As they got up from their chairs, Bev asked, "Peggy, do you think we can make it down to the old site and back before five?"

Peggy looked at the clock. "I imagine so, if we leave right now."

"Then let's give Rebecca some on-site training. Who knows when she'll ever get the chance again."

Peggy packed the remaining food into containers and placed them in the fridge while Bev and Rebecca cleared the table, leaving the dishes to soak.

"The girls will help me with the dishes tonight. Let's go."

CHAPTER 65

Peggy climbed into the back seat. "No, I insist," she said when Rebecca offered her the front seat. "I want you to see everything."

And they were off, down the dirt road, travelling further into the holler.

"Rebecca," said Bev, "you asked why the men didn't work somewhere else. There is very little 'else.' Most of the land you see around here is owned by outside corporations invested in timber and coal."

"But they're not even using it now."

"Well, they're not letting it go either."

"'Bout a hundred years back or more, some wealthy men in the East heard about our wonderful forests and coal. Most of the land then was owned by small farmers. 'Til then no one gave much consideration of these parts. Some say it was the men who passed through during the Civil War who took note."

"Well, these men couldn't just come in an' log out the place. So some local gents became their middlemen, going to the farmers and buying out the land. Some farmers wanted to sell, seein' the terrain was so rough, roads were few, and farming difficult. But the men buying never told the people its real worth and the railroads they were plannin' to build. So the farmers sold cheap, sometimes as little as ten cents an acre. Others pushed to a dollar an acre. These middlemen got themselves and the corporate bosses mighty rich. The timber companies came in and cleared the hills right out, all the fine, tall trees that'd been here for centuries.

"Then these corporate bosses went after the coal. Now there were still plenty of people who hadn't sold their land and these dishonest locals came up with a scam.

They travelled around the hills near tax time an' told the people they could stay on their land and just sell the mineral rights. Again the people had no idea of the worth and signed contracts for the same pittance. They also didn't realize that the contract gave the company the right to build roads through their property, dirty up their creeks and tear holes in their hillsides. Some were forced to leave."

Rebecca and Bev exchanged a quick glance. Rebecca remembered the first time she had met Bev, the extended table conversation when her eyes had been opened to the realities of the hinterlands. And now to hear it from someone whose family had lived it for generations.

By now, the road had narrowed to one lane and Bev carefully navigated between the pot holes and ruts.

"What these mountains have seen, Rebecca," said Bev. Then looking back toward Peggy, "I've given Rebecca some background on the coal towns."

"Good, because there is plenty to tell." Peggy was on a roll now and there was no abridging her story.

"More and more of the land was gobbled up by the corporations. They came into these hollers and built coal mining towns; we're headed to one now. The coal company owns everything: the houses, the school, the stores, the church building, the doctor's office—everything. And they hire the doctor, the teachers . . . sometimes even the preachers! Can't you just imagine those sermons?—'You all be good, obedient miners, like the Bible says. . . .' There wasn't enough man-power in these parts and people began to pour in from other parts of the US, and foreigners as well. That was tough. When you're new to a country and don't know the language, it's even easier to be scammed.

"The workers are geared up—but not for free. So much a month is deducted from the paycheck. The only housing that's available is from the coal company. They set the price of rent, they determine the quality of the housing, and the maintenance—there's no competition, no other alternative. You want furniture, clothing, anything: it's all at the company store. You can get it at a 'lease.' It's deducted from your paycheck. And at the end of the work period, there's mighty little left, if any. And what the workers receive is not regular American money; no, it's company script."

"What's that?" asked Rebecca.

"It's currency issued by the corporation," said Bev.

"Think of tokens . . . or monopoly money. Script was useless off camp," said Peggy.

"The whole set-up was a racket," said Bev.

"The people are completely dependent on the coal company," Peggy continued. "If they want to quit at the mines, there is no other work because all the other businesses in the town are also owned by the mining corporation. The company bosses control who's hired. You quit or object to the conditions, you can get evicted from your home and where are you going to go?"

"This is unbelievable!" said Rebecca.

"And the worst is what this system does to the people," said Bev. "Nothing beyond the essentials is being invested in the locals—they're merely a means to extract coal. The miners sink deeper and deeper into dependency. They rely on the coal company for every aspect of their lives. Is anything being done to form community leaders, to encourage initiative and creativity? No. Is anything being invested in the community beyond what is indispensable to get the coal out? No. The bottom line is profit for the company with the minimum given to the people to keep them living and docile.

"Some people fell into a pattern of dependency—the company was like a parent figure caring for them and they would do nothing to rock the boat. Others saw the injustice and began to urge others to take a stand, to form unions as was being done in other parts. It took a lot of courage. They were called communists— many were knocked off in 'accidents,' disappeared or killed outright."

Rotting equipment appeared near the roadside, overgrown with the foliage it had tried to destroy.

"Here we come," said Peggy.

The holler widened. Rusty railroad tracks came out of the woods and ran next to the narrow road. Alongside the track flowed a bustling creek. Shortly they were in the midst of a deserted coal town. Bev stopped the Jeep. They got out and stretched their legs. An eerie silence enveloped the holler, broken only by the chirping of songbirds and the rippling water.

"This is spooky," said Rebecca.

The women walked past the company store and other buildings in various stages of disrepair and collapse. Occasionally they went to the windows to peep in. They stopped at an old school building. The steps to the main door were covered with moss and little saplings that had burrowed in the soil blown up over the years.

"The clubhouse is across the way," said Peggy. "It used to house the single men." The railway spawned into four tracks and led, further up, to a complex of structures. "That's where the coal came out of the hills, was weighed and dropped into railway cars waiting underneath. All those houses to the side, they were for the miners."

The wooden structures, uninhabited for years, were in the worst condition of what remained.

"Some towns were larger than this with more facilities; other towns, much worse," continued Peggy. "The houses here had electricity during certain periods of the day, but the women had to go to the pumps for the water. See the little sheds out back? Those are outhouses—no inside toilets here. Obviously, the owners didn't think there was enough money in the mine to invest in a sewage system."

"When the mines were no longer profitable," said Bev, "the companies just pulled out. And since they owned everything, everyone was forced to move."

They walked among the housing still stained with coal dust. Carefully checking the steps before putting down her full weight, Rebecca walked on to a porch and peered in. The house had been stripped of most belongings. A couple of broken chairs remained. A kitchen and living room seemed to be on one side of the house. On the other side, she could see one room, possibly a bedroom.

"Most of these would be four rooms—two bedrooms, kitchen and parlour. Sometimes kids were up in the attic as well."

They walked around to the back. A broken-down lean-to clung to the rear of the house. The outhouse was several yards from the back door.

"That would be a cold walk on a winter morning," said Rebecca.

"You can't imagine," said Peggy. "We had one when I was growing up. In the winter I was afraid my butt would stick to the plank. In the summer, the stench was enough to gag you . . . and the flies buzzing around."

Bev looked at her watch. "We'd better be getting back."

They headed to the car in silence.

"So what's going to happen to this town?" asked Rebecca.

"Just rot, I guess," said Peggy. "After the coal companies pulled out, the community and a few organizations got together with plans to develop some local industry and asked to buy a few buildings, a plot of land. Grants were ready to be given but the corporation refused to sell. I don't know if they even acknowledged the letters. The buildings, as you can see, are just wasting away."

"But what about the government? Can't something be done?" asked Rebecca.

Both Bev and Peggy laughed at this.

"The companies own almost all the land and it seems they have a stranglehold on the government," said Bev. "Coal equals energy—that's a very powerful commodity."

"At least around these parts they haven't started the mountaintop mining," said Peggy, "You know, Rebecca, where they blow off the mountain top and scrape down the mountain for the coal. They throw all the unwanted material down the mountain side, polluting the rivers and destroying the forests. Sometimes I have to stop thinking about it because I feel so helpless. Seems nobody cares."

"I've spent my whole life in the state and never knew any of this," said Rebecca as they climbed back into the Jeep.

~

The three women jostled in their seats as Bev carefully picked her way back up the road, remaining largely in second gear.

"Did you ever live in a coal town?" Rebecca asked Peggy.

"No. My mama did growing up. My daddy, as mean and miserable as he was, held on to the land passed down by his granddaddies. He worked in this mine but didn't live in the town. The mine closed and he just worked odd jobs after that. Jesse's folks held on to their land as well, among the few in these parts."

"Did Jesse work at this mine?"

"No, no, it was closed up by then. He worked at a larger one a ways away. His daddy worked in this mine."

The engine whined as the jeep wound its way out of the holler.

"Never wanted any of my kids to be miners; it was like a curse. As I went ahead with my education, I would talk about all I was learning. I pushed and pushed them to go ahead with their schooling. Didn't want them to leave these hills, but I didn't want them to stay neither 'cause they were trapped."

By the time they arrived at Peggy's it was five and they still had about an hour's drive to Birchbark. After a quick stop, Peggy tried to convince them to have something to eat but they just wrapped up some cornbread in napkins, said their goodbyes and were off. After a few minutes on the dirt road, a car passed them. Bev waved before they were enveloped in a cloud of dust.

"Peggy's daughters. If they had arrived before we left, we wouldn't have been on this road before six!"

"Jeanne usually gets back to the convent by five thirty."

Bev laughed. "She's a good sport. Peggy's going to give her a call to tell her we're on our way."

Rebecca leaned back in her seat. She felt she had been transported to a different world. Whitewaters gave a glimpse in, but these hinterlands were light years from the motherhouse with its wide, polished corridors; spacious refectory and community rooms; stainless steel kitchen and regal chapel. Rebecca was stirred and appalled by what she had seen and heard; unsettled when it failed to lodge comfortably within the beliefs and conventions that governed her life.

"Why did you come to these hills, Bev?"

"I heard about the people and felt drawn, I guess. So did Judy. Our order gave us permission and we've been part of Appalachia ever since."

"Do you ever miss teaching?"

"It's part of what I do."

"I mean in the classroom."

Bev let out a short sigh. "I know your order is committed to teaching. It's a wonderful ministry and I know you love it, Rebecca. Our order was founded to work with the underprivileged, particularly women and children. At that time, there were few schools for the poor, and even fewer for girls. So our primary focus became education. Nursing was added later. Years passed and our schools began to spring up in cities. As all this was happening, education was seen as a necessity for all citizens in the US and schools became available for everyone. Our sisters felt that, to be true to our roots, we had to seek out ways to serve the underprivileged of our own time and new ministries developed. This is one of them."

The Jeep slowed as Bev turned at the intersection with a paved road. "It's smooth sailing from here," she said as she shifted up.

Rebecca and Bev opened the windows they had closed against the clouds of dirt billowing around them on the unpaved road. Dust that had settled in the Jeep swirled a bit before finding its way out. Gritty and sweaty, Rebecca looked forward to a shower. She brushed off some corn bread crumbs from her jeans and realized she had not even thought about her clothes since she arrived in Birchbark. And no one else did either.

"How are Holly and Cody doing?"

Rebecca brought Bev up to date.

"You know she's from this area?"

"I knew she ran away from home and came to Birchbark."

"Her mother died when she was young. She and her brother were raised by her dad. As she got older, she earned money watching over children. One summer she was hired by a couple to give a hand with the household chores and help at their convenience store. Her dad would drop her off Monday morning and picked her up Friday afternoon." Bev looked over at Rebecca. "Do you know the story?"

"Only that she was pregnant and was disowned by her family."

"Her father accused the employer, who hotly denied doing anything. Holly's father wanted to press charges but it required a sworn statement on the part of Holly. Holly refused to tell. The locals began to suspect Holly's father. By not accusing the employer, her father felt betrayed. By not accusing her father, the employer felt his name was sullied by the accusation. She struck out in both cases and to this day, no one knows who the father is."

"Then what happened?"

"She ran away from home, wandered into Birchbark, and got a job as a waitress. As her pregnancy became more apparent, one of her co-workers offered to bring her to the clinic. She began to attend the art sessions with Jeanne. After Cody was born, she completed high school. Jeanne was the first one to draw her out of her shell. From there she went on to counselling."

"Jeanne never mentioned it."

"She wouldn't."

CHAPTER 66

"You drove coming up. I'll drive back," Rebecca offered.

"You know how to drive a stick shift?" Jeanne asked.

"I have an older brother."

It had been some years since Rebecca had driven a standard, but after a jerky start and a few bumps along the way, she found the process returning with little effort.

It was dusk when they drove out of Birchbark, the hills backlit by the setting sun.

"So you and Bev went for a joyride."

"It was an experience. Peggy is amazing. The stories she told."

"She is a quite a woman."

"People remain here and there is so much against them. A losing battle, you know, with the coal companies, the corporations owning so much of the land. Yet they carry on."

"The lure of the land. It gets into your bones."

"I can see how it could happen."

So much had occurred during the day, yet something Jeanne said in the morning continued to gnaw at Rebecca. They were alone now, but how to bring it up?

"Bev said you helped Holly quite a bit. You never mentioned it."

"It wasn't my story to tell. The agency's report gave enough information regarding Cody and Holly."

Looking back, Rebecca could now see the familiarity between Jeanne and Holly, the ease with Cody. Previously, Rebecca had attributed it to Jeanne's overall openness with the children and families.

"Bev said her breakthrough was due to the art program."

"Art expresses the inexpressible. Holly is a brave woman. She's one of the people who make it all worthwhile."

The canopy of boughs over the road now acted like a tent, blocking out what little light there was.

"Take it easy, Rebecca. Deer can hop out of the bushes any time. We'll get home when we get home."

"Jeanne . . . this morning . . . you said something about sexual abuse . . ."

"You were listening."

"So some of our sisters have been sexually abused? Is that what you are saying?"

"Would it surprise you?"

"What did you mean?"

"Only to bring home, Rebecca, that our nuns are not somehow exempt from the domestic violence and sexual abuse in society. In fact, it may be a motivating factor that brings some young women to our doors."

"You really believe that!"

"I know that," said Jeanne softly. "For some people it's easier to leave the big, bad world behind and follow God in the convent. But, sooner or later, running away catches up with you."

Rebecca shot Jeanne a look but the contours of the countryside brought her gaze back to the winding road in front to her.

"It was a grade one class. I taught art to the older students and religion to the younger grades. Of course I used art in my lessons. There was one child, brown hair with bangs, eyes dark and sad. She did what was asked but was quite shy. She would catch my eye when the others were working on their assignments and just look at me. I couldn't interpret it. One day in the spring we talked about love in action. The kids gave a number of examples. Then I asked the class to draw a picture of love in their family. I had the children pass up their drawings. Because I was running late for the next class, I didn't look over the drawings until that evening when I was getting prepared for the next day's lesson.

"And there was her drawing. On the bottom she scrawled, *Daddy loves me.* At first I thought I was reading too much into it; after all, it was done by a seven-year old and she was no Caravaggio. But deep down I knew, and as the awareness took hold, I vomited.

"This child needed help, but what to do? I couldn't sleep that night. The next morning I must have looked pretty bad because the superior asked me if I was ill. After the second day, I became frantic. What was I going to do? Who could I tell? There was a clinic not far from the school. A nurse there periodically came to the school for various needs of the students—you know, the cuts and bruises, and occasional broken bones. Unable to eat, I asked permission to go to the clinic. As usual, I was accompanied, but luckily by an elderly sister and not the superior who was also the principal. I asked to see the nurse, and because she was a woman, I convinced the older sister she did not have to come in with me for the consultation.

"I showed the nurse the picture. She got the wheels moving. A child therapist came to the school with child services. The little girl was, in fact, being abused and the authorities took over."

"What happened to her?"

"She was sent to relatives in another city and I never saw her again. The superior cooperated with it all, but she was offended I didn't come to her first. I just couldn't talk to her about it. Not before, not after.

"I became more and more depressed, lost weight. I found it hard to get through a class, let alone have any interest. The school year ended and I was transferred to the motherhouse *under observation.* Maureen was there for retreat. Although I went through novitiate several years after Maureen, we knew each other quite well. Before Maureen was transferred to Whitewaters, she and I had been stationed together and used to exchange ideas about children, teaching . . . religious life. I trusted her.

"Maureen was shocked at my condition. She had me volunteer for various "retreat chores," you know, gathering and cleaning greens from the garden, sweeping the walkways on the grounds. She volunteered as well—the tasks got us outside together. . . . If Maureen hadn't come for that retreat, I would have probably been sent for shock treatments like Sr. Athanasius."

Athanasius has gone for shock treatments?! thought Rebecca, but she didn't dare interrupt Jeanne's story.

"As we did those chores together, I was able to open up to Maureen."

Jeanne paused and looked out into the darkness enveloping the car. She took a breath.

"I'd been abused, Rebecca, just like that little girl."

Her words confirmed Rebecca's growing realization.

"I'm so sorry, Jeanne." She reached over in the darkness to gently squeeze Jeanne's shoulder but Jeanne pulled away.

"All those years . . . I hadn't forgotten but it was a distant memory, boxed off from the rest of my life, rarely recalled. And when the memory did occasionally surface, it was like a silent, patchy, disjointed montage that had nothing to do with me. I guess seeing the littleness, the vulnerability . . . the sadness of that child . . . I couldn't handle the pain or the shame.

"Maureen was always a step ahead of everyone else. The abuse didn't frighten or surprise her. That, in itself, lifted half the burden. By this time, she had been a number of years in Whitewaters and had some contacts within the learning centre. Domestic violence and sexual abuse were common enough at the centre—counsellors were on hand to help out.

"I managed to share the minimum with the superiors in order to get some help. Maureen knew about this, in fact, she pushed me to do it. She, in the meantime, convinced the superiors to let me come to Whitewaters for a year. I taught art at the school and went for therapy. A year later the superiors could see the improvement . . . but at the same time, I felt they were uncomfortable with my situation. Whatever the reasons, I was sent back to Whitewaters and have been here ever since—thank God."

Rebecca felt honoured by Jeanne's trust, and also frightened.

The road curved suddenly, Rebecca hit the brakes hard to slow down and Jeanne lunged forward.

"Sorry."

Rebecca had never driven without street lights at night. The cavernous gloom shrouded the Jeep's headlights. The road was so dark that she felt she was driving in a tunnel, weaving right and left, up and down, never sure what lay ahead. Her hands tightened on the wheel, her eyes, unblinking, fixed on the road.

"Are you OK?" asked Jeanne.

"Yes. I'm just not used to driving when it's so dark."

"You want me to take over?"

"Stopping would be worse. I'll be all right."

"Just take it slow. Don't try to see so far ahead—you can't anyway."

CHAPTER 67

I t was the last week of school. Maureen watched Rebecca walk down the corridor at a rapid clip. A bystander looking on would have thought she was late for class or behind in her work. But neither was true. The children had only just begun to arrive for class, and all her report cards were completed and submitted. From their morning's conversation, Maureen knew she had planned a day of music and fun.

No, something was churning. Maureen wished she could ease the discomfort, but the path, the perspective, and the decisions were Rebecca's. At this point all Maureen could offer was respect and hope Rebecca would not get mangled by reality.

~

Thursday was the last day of school. Any other year at this time the sisters would wind up their activities, clear off their desks, close down the convent and, by Sunday, travel to the motherhouse for the summer. This year, just ten days after the last day of school, St. Martin's Music & Arts Summer Camp would be in full swing and culminate the following weekend in a parish festival celebrating the anniversary of the diocese. The events planned by the school and parish, and the active participation of so many in the community promised a fun and enriching experience.

Without their honoured guests, Maureen would have seen the festival as a wonderful conclusion of the scholastic year and a celebration of their parish family. Instead, the bishop, Mother, and Petrina added a level of formality, protocol, and pretension that dampened her outlook. Decades had passed since Maureen had been charged with welcoming such an entourage. The superiors expected nothing *personally*, they were assured. However, preferential treatment was a matter of course, instilled from the initial days of formation, done "out of respect for the office." In her younger years, Maureen would have been scampering about, anxious for the superiors' approval. Now she only tired of the charade and planned to provide the hospitality she would offer any visitor.

~

"That's it. The house is as clean as it's going to get," said Maureen.

In addition to preparing for the upcoming summer camp, the sisters had also been giving the convent a thorough wipe down. Although the convent was always neat, none of the sisters had much time or inclination for "deep" housecleaning.

"Nothing like visitors to motivate a spring cleaning," said Jeanne.

"The motherhouse sparkles all the time," said Candida.

"Yes, and they have a host of postulants and novices with little else to do other than keep it sparkling," retorted Jeanne.

Ordinarily lackadaisical toward housecleaning, Maureen knew that Candida would be tweaking their work until Mother Mary Thomas walked through the threshold. So be it. Maureen was not going to give it another thought.

Rebecca took off her dusty apron. All week she, Maureen, and Jeanne, together with parish volunteers, had been busy preparing for summer camp, right up to Saturday afternoon. In addition, the sisters had put their classrooms in order, filed away lesson plans and records, and squeezed in the convent cleaning when they could, mainly in the evenings. And now, on Sunday afternoon, the cleaning blitz was officially concluded.

"Thank God, Candida, you're going to take care of the meals," said Rebecca.

Previously, Rebecca had thought Candida's cooking was a cop-out. Now she considered it a pure blessing.

~

Rebecca was grateful they had been so busy. And tomorrow they would launch their summer camp. Many of the volunteers were parents or past students now in high school. Their ideas and enthusiasm had created a festive atmosphere as crafts were finalized, samples were made, games organized, music chosen, and booths set up. Immersed in her work, Rebecca was diverted from ruminations over the upcoming visitation and the dread that clung to its expectancy. Truly, it was dread.

During her quiet moments at prayer she questioned her apprehension of the superiors. She had always revered them. However, her meetings and conversations were generally within a group. Yes, before the passage from one stage of religious life to another there had been a private interview with Mother or one of the councillors. In these cases, though, she knew exactly what she wanted to say regarding her life of prayer, her experience as a novice, a student, or teacher. It was all done brightly, briefly. Mother and her councillors weren't people with whom she conversed easily and there had been neither the time nor opportunity to find out if she ever could. Henrietta was somewhat of an exception, not that Rebecca had ever confided in her. Yet from the concern Rebecca saw in her eyes and from her gentle pat on Rebecca's shoulder if they happened to cross paths, Rebecca sensed Henrietta was more approachable.

In trying to understand her angst, Rebecca realized that during past visitations, group encounters, and retreats she had been one among many. At Whitewaters, the ratio of visitors to the resident sisters would be almost one to one. And the sensation that Mother was displeased with her during the papal visit only made the anticipation of such close proximity more painful. She would be so glad when it was over and she could slip back into the anonymity and comfort of the past.

CHAPTER 68

C rack!
    The blindfolded child landed a direct hit to the battered piñata and, the children cheering him on, dove for the candy scattering to the ground. Teresa, the mother of Alessandro and Mariarosa, removed the blindfold from the victor and Rebecca took the bat so he could join in the fun.

During summer camp, Teresa had introduced the intermediate children to the art of piñatas. By the end of the week, two had been constructed and filled with treats—one for the grand finale of the Music & Arts Summer Camp and the other to top off the Hispanic dance and music segment at the parish festival the following day.

As the last of the treats were ferreted out, Teresa called over Alessandro and some of his friends to help gather up the mangled remains of the piñata. She pulled Rebecca aside.

"*Gracias, Madre.*"

"Teresa, thank *you*! The children loved making the piñatas and you just saw how much they enjoyed bursting it!"

"Madre, Madre," said Teresa, shaking her head. "*Muchas gracias* for what you did for my children." She hugged Rebecca warmly and then turned and directed her son to the piñata pieces that had blown further into the play yard.

Alessandro had advanced steadily through the tutoring from the retired teacher. Given his progress, he was able to move up to the sixth grade with his class. His tutor agreed to volunteer for another year to ensure he retained a solid footing within his class range. Mariarosa had thrived in grade three and bonded with her classmates. Although a year older than the others, she was comfortable moving on with her friends so Maureen and her parents allowed her to do so.

While Alessandro and his mother chased some flighty fragments across the grassy field, the rest of the children gathered their crafts and backpacks and ran off to the cars that had pulled up in front of the school. Volunteers straightened out the tables and chairs in preparation for Saturday's events.

"It's tomorrow, Sr. Rebecca. Just one more day."

Jacob skipped next to Rebecca as she walked from the crafts booth to the school building with the supplies they would need the next day.

"I've been teaching Spiky all kinds of tricks. You just wait and see. He's gonna win first place for sure."

The dog show was Doug's stroke of genius and a never-ending source of conversation on the part of Jacob and many other children in the school. The chance to showcase their hounds was the highly anticipated event of the weekend. The third grade class had seen numerous pictures of Spiky and heard about him often in class presentations. Had it not been for a couple of other avid dog owners, Spiky would have easily been the third grade mascot.

"What's that you're holding?" asked Rebecca.

Jacob held up his Popsicle-stick craft. "It's a picture frame. And I'm gonna put in Spiky's picture after he wins first place."

"Jacob! . . . ," his mother called from across the playground.

"See you tomorrow," said Rebecca.

"Me and Spiky!"

"Yes, you and Spiky. I look forward to meeting him in person."

"You're gonna love him," he shouted back as he ran toward his mother.

~

"What's going on?" Rebecca asked as she stepped off the stairs that went from the school to the convent.

Maureen and Jeanne had just brought down a folding table and were entering the back door of the convent.

"Doug called from the airport," said Maureen. "He has four guests instead of three. We won't all fit in the dining room so we're setting up tables in the community room."

"You're sure we can't just squeeze in a little?" asked Rebecca.

"You want to snuggle up with the bishop?" Jeanne laughed.

"Eight was going to be tight. Nine is impossible," said Maureen, "with this group."

Rebecca opened the back door and took the end of the table from Maureen as she reached the threshold.

"Thanks."

"Who's the other person?" asked Rebecca.

"We don't know. Most likely, Henrietta. Doug left a message with Candida saying he was leaving the airport with four guests and would be in Whitewaters in a couple of hours or less—that was about a half-hour ago."

Rebecca and Jeanne combined the folding table with the one already in the room, creating a large square. Maureen came from the kitchen with a couple of cloths to wipe them down. The furniture in the community room was rearranged to accommodate the new dining area. Jeanne transferred her easel, current project, and supplies to the school art room. Chairs from the dining room were brought in and a couple of similar tablecloths were found.

"When the table is set, no one is going to notice the different fabrics," said Maureen.

"Should they? This isn't the White House," said Jeanne.

Rebecca set out the plate settings according to Candida's specifications and Maureen arranged the place cards: the bishop and Mother would sit on the side facing the patio; there was more room behind their chairs. Doug, Petrina, and the mystery guest would sit across from them. The four from the community would sit at the table ends where one's knees were most likely to bang against the legs of the folding tables: Jeanne and Rebecca on the far side of the room, and Maureen and Candida closest to the door leading to the kitchen.

"Jeanne, would you find something to dress up the centre of the table, and Rebecca, you and I can finish setting the table."

Candida popped in and out to see the progress of the new dining arrangement and relaxed when the tablecloths transformed the work tables into elegance. Her dining room table had been prepared since noon.

Jeanne laid a wide strip of red ribbon down the juncture of the tables. She placed two thin red ribbons on either side, cut their ends diagonally to follow the angle of the large, centre ribbon. A clay sculpture from the art room was set on the ribbon. Two roses in full bloom were clipped from Candida's garden, set in glass desert bowls, and placed on either side of the sculpture.

With the centrepiece, the dishes set, the napkins fanned out in the glasses, the room itself was transformed.

"Jeanne, you are the Jedi of table decorations," said Maureen.

Rebecca glanced down at her dusty cuffs and the scuff marks on her habit from the day's activities. "I better go freshen up."

"Good idea. They're due to arrive any time now."

∼

Rebecca washed up and changed into a clean set of garments. She was adjusting her veil when she heard the horn honk. She ran down the hall and through the community room, skirting the newly placed dining tables. No one was in the convent. She flew out the back door and saw the rest of the sisters walking toward Doug's SUV. She caught up with the others just as Doug opened the front passenger door for the bishop. Maureen opened the back side door and assisted Mother Mary Thomas, followed by Petrina, then . . .

"Pistós? Pistós!" Rebecca whispered to herself. By now, she was standing next to Jeanne.

"Looks like someone's getting groomed," said Jeanne, raising her eyebrows.

In the meantime, Maureen had greeted the bishop and turned her attention to the sisters.

Candida knelt before the bishop, kissed his ring, and beamed. "Welcome, Your Excellency." Rebecca did the same.

Jeanne shook the bishop's hand. "Welcome, Bishop," she said politely. And turning to Doug, "Thanks for being the chauffeur."

Greetings among the arriving sisters and the Whitewaters community were exchanged as the bishop and Doug looked on. It was very welcoming, smiles on the faces of all. Rebecca felt her every gesture wooden, performed. She knew what was expected and did it. She was there and she was not there.

∼

Doug accompanied the bishop to the rectory. The local sisters led their guests through the front door to their rooms, dropped off their luggage, and left them so they could freshen up before supper.

Candida needed no help in the kitchen. Maureen had given a hand during the afternoon: there were no pots to wash, no counters to wipe. The serving dishes were warmed and the food was ready to be transferred as soon as Candida was given word. Rebecca wandered into the community room. Petrina was in the office calling the motherhouse to report their safe arrival. Maureen was with her, sorting through the various letters and communiqués Petrina had delivered from the motherhouse. Jeanne was nowhere to be seen. In an attempt to feel occupied, Rebecca straightened up a knife and napkin on the table that didn't need straightening.

And so came that awkward moment when everything is ready, but nothing can begin. Waiting with nothing to do. That moment when one desires to fade into a picture on the wall but instead idles without purpose and without being able to relax. That moment when one has nothing to say but must be available to converse. And conversations where—without conscious intent—one avoids what is most pressing and finds topics that keep the exchange afloat and safe.

Mother's voice and dominant footsteps came down the hallway toward the community room. Rebecca stiffened and rebuked herself for it.

"So we've moved the dining into the community room," said Mother as she emerged into the room and began to scrutinize the table setting. Pistós was close behind.

"Yes, Mother. We thought there would be more room."

"Hmm." Mother continued to walk around the table, making slight adjustments. "Where are the wine glasses?"

"We don't have any. We thought we would just use our nicer beverage glasses, one for water and one for whatever beverage was served . . . We also have juice glasses . . . And we do have wine. . . ."

Pistós smirked behind Mother's shoulder.

"Of course, we'll be serving wine!" said Mother impatiently. "Sr. Mary Maureen should have known that, with His Excellency as a guest. One phone call! That's all it would have taken. One phone call! We could have brought the wine glasses from the motherhouse if they're not to be had in Whitewaters."

Rebecca wished Maureen was present to explain their arrangements. She was aware of the general plan but was probably missing some important details.

Her comments were only creating trouble. "We do have the wine . . . in the kitchen. . . ."

"We should have arrived earlier," said Mother as she walked through the community room toward the kitchen, Pistós again on her heels.

Rebecca followed at a distance. As she rounded the corner facing the kitchen, she saw Mother and Pistós looking over the empty dining room table.

"Yes, this would have been much too crowded," she conceded and moved on to the kitchen.

Rebecca stopped at the kitchen door. Candida was obsequiously presenting Mother every dish.

"Hmm. Yes, this will do. The mashed potatoes look a bit dried. How long have they been sitting here?" And not waiting for an answer, "Add some milk and butter. Now the beans. Really, to have them already warming. It would have been far better to put them on when the soup is being served."

"Yes, that would have been better. But they've just finished cooking. Sr. Mary Maureen wanted everything ready . . . so we could all eat together."

"Serving is also a virtue."

Candida continued to smile, but her effervescence was diminishing. Rebecca knew she had been planning each meal for weeks, going over the menu with Maureen to make sure every detail was perfect and all the ingredients were on hand for the weekend.

"I understand you have wine," stated Mother.

"Yes, yes, we do," said Candida. "Both red and white."

"Where is it?" said Mother, glancing around.

"In the refrigerator."

"How long has it been there?"

"A couple of days."

"Oh, for heaven's sake! It's been over-chilled! Take it out immediately!"

Pistós whipped four bottles of wine out of the refrigerator.

Mother picked up a bottle and pulled back her head to focus on the label.

"Hmm. Merlot. His Excellency prefers red zinfandel." She examined the other three bottles. "Hmm. Another merlot and two of chardonnay." Shaking her head, "Just one phone call would have been sufficient."

Then, choosing one bottle, "Sr. Miriam Pistós, open this bottle. You'll be serving the wine. I'll have Sr. Mary Maureen purchase the red zinfandel for our other meals."

While Mother chose the wine, Candida pulled a corkscrew from a drawer. She handed it to Pistós with a smile.

"And the napkin?" asked Pistós.

"Napkin?" said Candida.

Pistós glanced at Mother, "For serving the wine . . . to wrap around the bottle . . ."

"Of course," said Candida as she walked to another set of drawers in the large kitchen. Candida handed Pistós a napkin; however Pistós preferred to look through the drawer before making her selection. Mother, in the meantime, was questioning Candida about dessert. The doorbell rang.

"His Excellency, I'm sure," said Mother. "Sr. Miriam Pistós, bring out the wine when you've removed the cork. And, Sr. Mary Candida, please gather together some suitable glasses."

"They're right here on a tray, Mother." Candida lifted a clean dishcloth off a tray of glasses.

"Hmm." And Mother departed with haste for the front door, passing Rebecca who had receded from the doorway into the dining room.

Maureen and Petrina, also responding to the bell, arrived at the entrance to the tiny foyer with Mother. They made way so she could open the door, greet the bishop and Doug, and usher them into the community room. Rebecca followed after all had entered, hovered near the entrance, and watched Mother and the bishop converse near the dinner table with Petrina and Maureen listening nearby. Jeanne came in and stood alongside Rebecca.

"Where have you been?" whispered Rebecca.

"Dusting the parlour."

Doug, who had been flipping through a periodical on the bookcase came to stand with them. "When have these walls witnessed such distinction?"

"Not since I've been here, for sure," said Jeanne.

"Should we attribute the honour, then, to Rebecca?"

"Oh, I hardly think I'm worth all the fuss," Rebecca quipped.

"Worth? How do we measure worth?" said Doug under his breath.

∼

Maureen waited for a break in the conversation between Mother and the bishop and then interjected, "Supper is ready. Perhaps we could be seated." Turning to the bishop, "Bishop Patterson, your place," she said as she led him to the head of the table. "And Mother, right next to Bishop Patterson . . ." Turning to Mother, Maureen noticed her pique and followed her eyes to the other side of the room. Jeanne and Rebecca had pressed against the patio windows to make way for Pistós entering with a tray of glasses and a wine bottle.

"Sr. Pistós, Sr. Candida and I will be serving," Maureen said gently but firmly. "You've had a long trip. Relax and be seated."

Jeanne reached for the tray to return it to the kitchen. "There must have been a misunderstanding."

Pistós glanced at Mother, who was clearly displeased, but Pistós relinquished the tray to Jeanne when, with a slight jerk of her head, Mother gave her acquiescence. Maureen, perplexed, watched the unspoken exchange and then continued to direct the guests to their places. Jeanne slipped back into the room and Bishop Patterson said grace.

"Make yourselves comfortable," said Maureen and left for the kitchen. When she arrived, Candida was assailing the potatoes with a masher.

"Candida, what are you doing?"

"Mother wanted more milk and butter in the mashed potatoes."

"Mother?"

"She came to look over the meal before the bishop arrived."

Candida continued to mash and mix without looking up. The pot handle slipped from Candida's hand as she pushed with the masher. The pot spun across the counter and the masher flew out of Candida's hand. Maureen pushed the pot toward the wall, keeping it from falling off the counter. The masher clattered to the floor.

"Oh, my goodness!" exclaimed Candida as she turned in a frenzy for paper towel. Maureen intercepted her, and took her by the shoulders.

"Candida, stop." Maureen could feel Candida trembling. "You have done a fine job with this supper. Your potatoes were—and are—perfect. Do you understand?"

Candida nodded and wiped away the tears that welled in her eyes.

"Now you and I are going to go out there. You bring the water pitchers and I the wine and we are going to do just fine. Is that clear?"

Candida nodded again and took a deep breath, "Mother said you should have called about the wine . . . and we over-chilled it."

"Mother should be grateful for what is put in front of her, as St. Paul says . . . and as she so often reminds us."

Candida pulled off a couple sheets of paper towel, picked up the masher, and began to clean up the potato that had splattered on the floor. Maureen covered the pot of mashed potatoes and returned it to the oven where they had been warming. Pistós appeared at the kitchen door.

"Mother would like to know if you need any help?"

"Pistós, we're doing just fine. Return to the table and enjoy the company. I'm sure there is a lot you could learn about Whitewaters."

~

Within a couple of minutes, Candida and Maureen returned to the community room, Candida with two pitchers of ice water, sprigs of mint floating on top, and Maureen with two bottles of wine. Candida set the pitchers on the table and then took one of the wine bottles from Maureen.

"We have white and red wine, Bishop. Which would you prefer?" And they made their way around the table. When they finished, Maureen said, "We'll keep the wine on the table. Please feel free to serve yourselves throughout the meal."

And so the dinner began. Those from Whitewaters made inquiries regarding the upcoming celebrations in the diocese and the bishop and Mother were most obliging in relating the details of the year-long initiative. The planning had absorbed their attention for over a year and the celebration would continue to do so for yet another. With Petrina and Pistós prompting the guests of honour regarding some aspect or other, the topic was sustained for most of the meal. Being so pleasantly indulged and with the meal tastefully served, Mother mellowed to her general disposition.

As the conversation became securely centred on Mother and the bishop, Rebecca began to relax. Her pulse surged when the conversation veered to the papal visit, but the bishop happily related anecdotes of his encounters with the Pope, and Mother added her reflections with nary a glance toward Rebecca. Just the same, Rebecca avoided looking at Petrina and Pistós.

~

The last of the dessert was eaten, the coffee and tea refilled, and the conversation was tapering off.

"So tomorrow will be a busy day," said the bishop.

"The confirmation ceremony begins at eleven," said Doug. "And as you know, pictures follow."

"Yes, indeed"—the bishop chuckled—"the bane of my profession."

"After the ceremony the parish festival begins. A barbeque dinner will be served at two. You and Mother will be the guests of honour."

Mother smiled.

"Bishop, we were hoping you would throw the first pitch at the softball game later in the day."

"I would be delighted," said the bishop.

"We'll have various activities going on throughout the afternoon. I'm sure you're going to enjoy the lineup of local musicians."

"We're expecting a larger crowd than usual," added Maureen. "Families are coming in from the hollers further away—the missions Doug visits monthly. And we have a good number of non-Catholic families joining in the celebration—their children attend our school."

"Very good, very good," said the bishop.

"We're quite pleased with the support and cooperation from the community, given the small Catholic population," added Doug.

"Yes, well, as I often say, let us work hard to get to heaven and bring as many souls as possible with us."

Doug shot a glance at Maureen.

The bishop rose. "And we'll conclude this lovely evening with a prayer of thanksgiving. In the name of the Father . . ."

As parting comments were exchanged, Rebecca quickly gathered some dessert dishes and made her way to the kitchen. She rolled up her sleeves, filled the sink with hot, soapy water, and dove into the dishes, relieved at last to be out of sight and occupied doing something useful.

Jeanne followed with a stack of cups and saucers. "My, my, look who's already at the sink." She brought over a couple of aprons and handed one to Rebecca. "You'd better put this on if you want to remain invisible."

"Gosh, I completely forgot," said Rebecca as she donned the apron and tied the strings.

Jeanne looked at Rebecca as she put on her own apron. She rinsed as Rebecca resumed washing.

"They don't warrant your fear, Rebecca."

Rebecca kept on washing.

CHAPTER 69

Rebecca wiped off her hands and hung her apron on a hook in the kitchen. The day had begun with morning prayer and adoration, followed by brunch with the bishop and Doug. The confirmation ceremony would start in just over an hour. Although Rebecca did not prepare the youth for confirmation, she had been asked to help greet and seat those being confirmed with their sponsors. They were to arrive an hour early in order to have a brief rehearsal. Since several to be confirmed were coming from a distance, a rehearsal earlier in the week would have been too inconvenient.

"Here is a note for you," said Maureen, passing Rebecca an envelope. "It came with the mail from the motherhouse. I didn't have a chance to give it to you last night."

Rebecca recognized the handwriting immediately. "It's from my mother."

Dear Sr. Rebecca Marise . . .

Her mother always used her religious name and title, even when she was at home for a visit—something her father found humorous and never imitated. Rebecca looked at her watch, pocketed the letter, and walked out the back door.

"Sr. Rebecca!" shouted Jacob, waving with one hand and pulled forward by a brown hound on a leash. "Dad, it's Sr. Rebecca!"

Well, thought Rebecca, *if it's not the infamous Spiky.*

Jacob's father waved as he walked at a slower pace behind his son and his pet. Jacob reached Rebecca and knelt next to his dog, pushed down his rear, and held him firmly around the chest.

"Spiky, meet Sr. Rebecca."

Jacob held up one of his paws so that Sr. Rebecca could shake it.

Rebecca stooped to greet the dog.

"I've heard a lot about you, Spiky. I'm glad we've finally met."

To Rebecca's amusement, there wasn't a thing spiky about Spiky. A mutt of unknown vintage, Spiky had floppy ears, wavy brown hair, and a curled, constantly wagging tail.

Jacob's father joined the little circle and Rebecca stood to shake hands. Rebecca knew that his eldest son was among those to be confirmed.

"We wouldn't be able to return home after the ceremony for Spiky, so we brought him along with us now. We're planning on leashing him in those trees beyond the playground with some water." He raised a bowl and a plastic milk container of water.

"You're well prepared! I'll see you in the church."

Jacob and his dad climbed the stairs to the school grounds and Rebecca continued to the front of the church.

~

Petrina stopped in the small foyer near the superior's office and opened the linen closet. With more time and less on her mind than Mother, Petrina was always on the alert for some irregularity. To remain faithful, religious life had to be carefully monitored, deviances nipped in the bud. Petrina believed she had the acuity to discern aberrations before they surfaced. Since her arrival, her gaze had never rested, observing, scanning for signs of that something that eluded her. She picked it up in the sisters' demeanour, and yet it was always just out of reach. Diplomacy had never been her strong suit and her misgivings regarding this community made her peevishness more pronounced. While fawning and obliging with Mother and the bishop, outside their presence a smile never graced her lips. With an hour before the ceremony, Petrina intended to make a closer examination of the convent. She was about to look over the community supply closet when Mother came from the dormitory wing accompanied by Pistós.

"Sr. Mary Maureen is giving us a tour of the school and church grounds before the ceremony. Then we visit the rectory and accompany the bishop to the church for the confirmation."

Petrina closed the door and followed Mother.

CHAPTER 70

"Can I have your attention, please," said Doug. He tapped the microphone a few times. "Your attention, please." The crowd began to quiet.

"Thank you for coming out today for our parish festival."

Doug now had their attention.

"With this festival we celebrate the anniversary of our diocese and we thank God for our parish family and the community of Whitewaters. And what a beautiful day we have been given."

The crowd hooted their assent. Had it rained, they would now be squeezed in the church hall. Instead, the tables were comfortably spread throughout the school playground under blue skies with puffy white clouds.

"For those who have just arrived, I would like to introduce our guests who have travelled all the way from Slandail to celebrate with us. Bishop Patterson—" Doug was cut off by applause. "And Mother Mary Thomas, the general superior of the Sisters of Christ the Redeemer, together with Sr. Mary Petrina and Sr. Miriam Pistós."

Mother waved and smiled to the applauding crowd.

"And now Bishop Patterson will lead us in thanksgiving for our meal."

Doug handed the microphone to the bishop standing next to him and then moved off to the side among the parishioners who stood ready to serve the meal to the main table.

"Before I bless this meal, I want to thank you for the very warm welcome you have extended to me, to Mother Mary Thomas, and the visiting sisters."

The crowd applauded and the bishop smiled broadly.

"In welcoming me, you not only have given me personal pleasure, but you have welcomed, above all, Christ, whom I represent. For those of you who may not be of the Catholic faith, I am the chief shepherd of our diocese in communion with the Pope, the Vicar of Christ, successor of St. Peter."

What the hell! thought Doug.

The bishop shifted his weight to his other foot. "You might wonder, 'What does a bishop do all day? What is a bishop's job?' My job is to teach the Gospel, to govern the diocese in the spirit of Jesus Christ, and to encourage holiness of life— we're here on earth to become saints!"

Jeanne looked at the bishop in disbelief. Maureen walked next to her. Listening to this during the confirmation ceremony had been painful enough, but here, at a barbeque, open to the entire community? It was altogether mortifying.

"We are at a turning point in history. We are living in a culture hostile to Christ. All of us are called to work toward our salvation in Jesus Christ and defend the dignity of human life at all its stages. It is a joy to look out at all of you here with your families—families open to the gift of life, honouring the sacred gift of holy matrimony. . . ."

~

Jacob was not interested in the bishop's job or his reflections on salvation. The savoury aroma wafting from the grill fixed his desire to be at the front of the buffet line. However, that prospect seemed remote.

Spiky had not been happy leashed to a tree with a bowl of water and expressed his disapprobation with intermittent howls throughout the ceremony. He only quieted when he saw Jacob running toward him after the confirmation. The dog show was the first event following the meal. As the time for the barbeque neared, several more families arrived with dogs and, following the example of Jacob's father, leashed their pets to the trees. All seemed well until Jacob was called by his family to join them at the table. When Jacob made the least move toward the dining area, Spiky alternated between howling and yapping at the other dogs.

Jacob's father noticed that a couple of families had hounds dozing near their tables. As a concession to quiet Spiky during the meal, Jacob's family chose a table on the fringes of the dining area, brought Spiky out of the woods and planted Jacob next to him, leash in hand. Spiky wagged his tail contently and settled, at last, near his young master.

When Doug introduced the bishop, Jacob's family and the people nearby walked closer to the head table for a better view of the prelate. Jacob remained at the table with Spiky, straining for a better view of the buffet tables laden with his favourite foods. They appeared light years away.

As the bishop rambled on, Jacob's plan took form. He tilted back his folding chair and placed the looped handle of Spiky's leash under one of its legs.

"Stay," he whispered into the dog's ear, pushing down his rump. Then stealthily he made his way to the buffet.

Jacob was not the only one drawn by the aroma of the barbeque chicken. Unattended, Spiky edged away from the table. The folding chair tipped up, releasing its fragile hold on the leash. Sniffing his way to source, Spiky made his way under the tables toward the platters of barbeque chicken on the buffet table.

~

"A few months ago I had the pleasure of meeting the Pope in person. I'm sure you followed the Pope's travels while he was here in the United States. What a magnificent expression of fai—"

The bishop's speech was stopped short by clatter from the buffet table.

"Stop that dog!" hollered a person from the side.

Others joined in, "There he goes!" "Over there!"

Jacob, standing near the paper plates, watched the whole scene with horror. "Doggone!"

Covered with sauce from the shower of chicken that fell on his back, Spiky panicked and charged away but not before he snatched a couple pieces. Up he charged toward the head table. A large man pounced for the racing dog. Avoiding the lunge, Spiky veered into Petrina, stumbling against her habit-clad legs. Petrina yelled out in surprise and to her great displeasure saw the bottom of her habit streaked with the deep brown sauce that covered the chicken. Spiky was back on his feet in a flash and headed toward the open grassy field beyond the dining area, the chicken secured in his jaws, his leash whipping wildly in his wake. A hound that had, until then, been dozing peacefully among the trees, bolted. Barking voraciously, it joined in the chase. Other dogs tied to the trees, barked and strained against their leashes. A few broke free. A dozen children—Jacob in the lead—were trailing the speeding dogs.

As the chase began, local musicians, ready to entertain during the meal, chuckled and struck up a jig. The people laughed in response and a group began to clap to the beat. Jeanne looked at Maureen with amusement. "There is a God."

But Maureen didn't stay to enjoy Jeanne's humour. She scooped up some fallen chicken, scrambled through the tables, and jogged toward the racing dogs. As she left the dining area, she heard the bishop say over the amplifiers,

"We better get to that chicken before the dogs finish it off!" and the people laughed again.

A group of adults formed a loose net to prevent a re-entry into the dining area. Maureen called to a couple of men and gave them some chicken. Together they closed in on the dogs, keeping them in the far corner of the field. Distracted by the chicken they were offered and tuning in to the commands of their owners, the dogs were lulled into submission and rewarded with the meat. Without the threat of having his coveted morsels stolen, Spiky plopped to the ground, dropped his chicken near his jaws and heaved to catch his breath. Jacob was soon at his side.

~

The bishop was into his address when Rebecca brought out a Jell-O salad from the refrigerator in the school. Holly, helping Kim at the buffet line, took the dish, placed it among the other bowls, and pointed to the table where Cody was standing with Leah's family. As Rebecca arrived at the table, the rampage broke loose. A hound lounging near his young owner jumped to his feet, let out a series of shrieking barks, and pulled to free himself from his master's hold. The chaos frightened Cody and when the dog began to bark and lunge, Cody imagined that he was the target. He leaped toward Rebecca, grasping at her shoulders to get out of harm's way. Inadvertently, he took hold of her veil, pulled to lift himself up, and yanked off her headgear. Rebecca lifted up Cody and stood him on her chair. He buried his head in her shoulder and clung to her tightly. Keeping herself between Cody and the dog, she explained that the dog was not after him and pointed to the chase going on in the field. As the hound settled, Cody picked up on the amusement of the crowd and turned to enjoy the dog chase with the rest of the spectators. He relaxed his grip around Rebecca and she was able to disengage her veil and coif from his clenched fist. For the people nearby, it was the first time they had seen any of nuns without their veils. The children stared in wonder while the adults turned away out of respect. As Rebecca untangled the coif from the veil, she noticed Pistós watching her through the crowd. Rebecca put back on her veil and turned her attention to Cody. The chase was over. He jumped down from the chair and, with Leah and her family, went to the buffet line. But he made sure to steer his course away from the hound.

~

Seeing the other dogs subdued and secured firmly on leashes, Maureen left the pack and approached Jacob.

"Spiky didn't mean to cause trouble, really, Sister," said Jacob as he knelt near his dog, hugging him tightly. Fortunately, his mother had had him change from his Sunday best to a tee-shirt and jeans for the barbeque. The evidence of Spiky's guilt was smeared all over Jacob's top. Meanwhile, Spiky chomped hungrily on his hard-earned loot, oblivious to his owner's humiliation.

Maureen, winded from her romp, could only smile at Jacob's pathetic expression. "Looks like Spiky made it to the dinner line before you."

Jacob relaxed. "Spiky is the best dog ever."

"I'm sure he is. Jacob, give me your tee shirt. You stay here with your dog until I come back." Turning to one of the men who helped stay the rampage, "Roger, would you go to the kitchen and get a wet cloth so we can wipe off this dog?"

Jacob's father came sprinting across the lawn, and from his expression, Maureen could tell Jacob would not make out as easily with his dad as he had with her.

"I'm so sorry . . ."

Maureen took him by the arm, "There was no harm done. Don't be too hard on him."

"Blasted dog. I swear it has a brain the size of a pea."

"Well, we couldn't have paid for that entertainment. Let it go."

Maureen walked back through the grass to the booth selling festival tee-shirts. "Do you have one this size?" she said with a smirk, holding up her soiled sample.

"Ha, ha! I see you caught the culprit!" The woman passed over a fresh shirt. "Great show, Sister, great show!"

Jeanne met up with her as she left the booth. "Quite the sprinter, Maureen."

"I've always told you, elementary school trains you for a triathlon."

"Can you imagine the scene if all the dogs got loose?" Jeanne said with a laugh.

"Maybe we should have thought of portable kennels."

"And missed that performance! Come on, Maureen!" Jeanne took the tee-shirt from Maureen, "I'll take care of this. You better go settle some feathers at the head table."

"Great."

~

Bishop Patterson found the dog chase amusing and Mother followed suit. Petrina was not so easily assuaged. Dogs at a parish picnic! The bishop's address interrupted! It was uncouth and disrespectful. Her irritation over the dishonour to the prelate and superior general would have been considerably less had it not been fuelled by her skirmish with a wild dog and her soiled habit. She made no attempt to hide her displeasure to the several concerned parishioners who tried to assist her.

"I'll be *fine*." She grabbed some napkins and knelt to soak out the grease and sauce. Ignoring all around her, she continued to mutter incoherently, "The likes . . . disgustful . . ." The good Samaritans backed away.

Pistós, having made her way to the head table, knelt near the councillor. "Sr. Mary Petrina, what happened?" she said with concern.

With Pistós, Petrina's vexation came flowing out. "Have you ever witnessed anything like this?" she said as she continued to dab her habit. "Dogs at a parish festival? . . . When the bishop and Mother are guests of honour? Ludicrous! Disrespectful!"

"It's Whitewaters," said Pistós as she surveyed Petrina's oil slick. "What do you expect?"

"A little more from our sisters here!"

"Yes, well, that's another matter." The two nuns looked at each other knowingly. "I just saw Sr. Rebecca Marise. A child ripped off her veil."

Petrina looked up horrified. "Unbelievable!"

"And her hair was cut . . . styled . . ."

"Whitewaters . . . the lot of them." Petrina stood up stiffly, her jaw hardened. "I knew they would be nothing but trouble."

"Sr. Mary Petrina, I heard you had a mishap," said Maureen as she approached the two visitors.

"*I* had a mishap?" said Petrina sharply. "I believe the responsibility lies elsewhere." With Pistós at her heels, she turned toward the head table to take her seat next to Mother.

~

As the meal was winding down, Doug sought out Rebecca.

"We'd better get started with the dog show before we have another side act," he said with a smile.

As Doug announced the dog show, Rebecca, together with other volunteers, began to gather the contestants to the far side of a roped-off ring. The musicians, exchanging smirks, continued to play on their makeshift platform, ready to switch to an appropriate tune should the hounds necessitate one.

Dogs and owners, classmates, friends, parents, and a host of children made their way toward the ring. Doug took the microphone to emcee the event. He and two other parishioners were the judges. The bishop and Mother were given ringside seats. Petrina, who had had more than her fill of the dogs, went to the convent to rehabilitate her habit.

As the contestants arrived at the ring, Rebecca and the volunteers lined them up with a suitable distance between each one. Outside an occasional snap and snarl, the animals seemed more intent on sniffing. Rebecca remained close at hand to keep it that way.

Jeanne and Maureen stood with the crowd gathered around the ring and exchanged comments with the parents and children. Eventually, Pistós joined them.

"So, how are you enjoying the festivities, Pistós?" said Jeanne.

"I would appreciate it if you would call me, Sr. Miriam Pistós or Sr. Pistós at the very least."

"So, how are you enjoying the festivities?"

"Well enough," Pistós conceded. "With better organization, the day could be going more smoothly. . . . Dogs at a parish barbeque?" she said, shaking her head.

Jeanne, whose tolerance for pretension was minuscule at the best of times, reached her threshold. She turned to Maureen. "I see some parents I need to speak with." And she walked away.

~

The dog show was the main attraction for the children and a comedy for the adults. Sixteen dogs took turns strutting around the ring, some willingly, others with continual encouragement, and a few with a short, tight leash. The tricks were a delight. Some of the animals were truly clever. Others could pull off a few stunts. Spiky, however, was in a class all his own. Despite the high hopes created by Jacob throughout the year, Spiky could actually perform but one trick, albeit, with several variations: he stood on two legs in an attempt to reach a treat held over his head, he walked around in a circle in an attempt to get a treat held in front of him, and he found a treat in the grass which was "hidden" as he watched. The best was saved for last. Jacob lay on the grass, put a treat on his belly button and Spiky lifted his tee-shirt with his snout and ate the treat. The audience hooted and clapped.

Despite Spiky's low performance in all areas, the third grade students rallied behind Jacob's treasured pet that they had grown to love, sight unseen, from Jacob's ceaseless adulation.

Then came the moment of judgment. Award after award was conferred. Doug and the other judges had been quite creative in formulating a host of categories and it seemed every pet would be recognized.

Jacob and Spiky alone remained in the ring.

"And now for the last award." Doug paused and looked at the audience. The eyes of many sparkled with amusement. What kind of award could the judges have come up with for this dog?

"The final award goes to Jacob and Spiky for . . . *the Most Loved Dog*."

The audience applauded and cheered as Jacob walked around the ring, leading Spiky and waving his certificate.

"That boy is a born comedian," said Maureen affectionately. But when she turned toward Pistós, to whom the comment was directed, she was no longer there.

CHAPTER 71

Pistós walked into the school gym and looked around to get her bearings. The mediocrity of the dog show could only be matched by grammar school Christmas concerts, which she was sometimes obliged to attend. She had long ago come to the conclusion that these events could only be appreciated by mothers and grandparents. And since she was not obliged to watch these pets exhibit stunts that any dog would do in a walk around the block, she decided to move on to something that *did* interest her.

She ignored the banter-filled conversation of the barbeque cleanup crew and pushed against the doors leading to the school. They were locked.

"Sister, can I help you?" asked a woman who came out of the bathroom.

"Oh, I was just going to the school building."

Recognizing Pistós as one of the visitors, the woman said, "We keep the doors to the school locked. Do you have a key?"

"No . . . no, I don't. I guess I'll have to wait until later." Pistós turned to leave.

"Wait a moment, I'll see if Frank is around."

Presently, Frank ambled toward the doors. "Annie tells me you got locked out of the school." He pulled out a huge wad of keys as he neared the door.

"Are you from these parts?" he said as he searched through the clump.

Pistós chafed under his familiarity; however, needing his assistance to enter the school, she did not want to slight him either.

"No. Just visiting," she said dryly and stared through the glass pane in the door to the corridor beyond.

"Well, there you are," said Frank as he opened the door for her.

Pistós nodded slightly as she passed through. "Thank you," she said without looking in his direction.

~

Pistós flicked on the hallway lights. This morning after brunch Maureen had given them a quick tour of the school. Now, alone, she was able to take her time, to observe without being observed. Her heels echoed in the deserted hallway. She felt strangely excited.

Pistós wasn't sure of her role at Whitewaters. "Assisting with the visitation," as she had been told, could be broadly interpreted. It might mean meal preparation while the sisters of the branch community held meetings with the superiors. However, Pistós was not recognized for her culinary skills. Rather, she was highly intelligent, articulate, obedient, and above all, a resolute adherent of the SCRs and the Catholic Church. She stood out from her peers the day she walked through the convent doors: twenty-six, an MA in theology, summa cum laude, from a college SCRs supported, with a published paper.

The murals captured her attention. They were good. Excellent, really. It was unfortunate they were not in one of their larger schools where more people could admire them. She made her way down the hall and up the back stairway. The rooms on the first floor held no interest beyond what she had seen that morning. But libraries always intrigued her. A theology professor once told her class, if you want to know a person, check out his collection of books. The same could apply to an institution, she reasoned. And she found her theory substantiated among the SCRs. Their strong, united sense of identity could be seen in the libraries she perused when she had the opportunity to visit one of their communities.

Pistós hadn't been asked to check out the library in Whitewaters . . . or anything else, for that matter. In fact, she hadn't intended to return to the school that afternoon. But the opportunity presented itself . . . and here she was. And she knew the superiors were pondering the future of Whitewaters.

Pistós opened the library door. The heat of the afternoon sun compounded the stale air of the closed library. She passed the librarian's desk, walked through some shelves behind it, and pulled a couple of cords that opened two of the windows that lined the top of the back wall. The muted music, chatter, and laughter from the festival below amplified and filled the room together with the cool, fresh air. Pistós glanced at the shelves nearby and saw she was in the teachers' resource area.

"What have we here?"

~

Petrina muttered under her breath at the ironing board. She had succeeded in removing the grease from her habit with a tip from Candida, although Candida would never know. When Petrina left after the meal, Candida followed her, giving several suggestions and even offering to clean the habit herself. Petrina dismissed her before they even reached the stairway down to the convent. A towel and blow dryer removed most of the dampness. Now she just had to deal with the wrinkles. When she glanced at her pocket watch and saw how much time she had wasted with this escapade, she seethed again.

Whitewaters had long been her scourge. Many years before, when the novelty of Whitewaters was waning, she had warned against a community so far removed from the others, with limited supervision, and missing the reunions at the motherhouse during the school year. When Sr. Mary Maureen was made superior, she sensed there would be trouble, especially with Sr. Mary Anita as part of the community—she had never trusted the two of them. Sr. Maria Jeanne—who really knew what was going on with her?—almost sent to a mental institution. And Sr. Mary Candida! Sr. Mary Candida! She couldn't sniff out a skunk if it lifted its tail right in front of her. It was a bad mix. She'd sensed it all along.

CHAPTER 72

The sixties were alarming to be sure. While some religious orders cheered as the documents of Vatican II churned out, the SCRs viewed them with ambivalence. Vatican II, an ecumenical council, was an international gathering of bishops with particular authority over the universal church. It was convened by a Pope. But the documents, while not breaking with the past, were asking for an unprecedented degree of revision. The council seemed to put into question many of their long-standing customs.

Many of the SCRs in the sixties had never travelled outside the state. At that time, their high school for girls had dorms for boarders and within the dorms was a special wing for young women inclined toward religious life. At graduation, most of their incoming candidates crossed the threshold from this distinguished dorm into the postulants' wing.

From the SCRs perspective, the push for change in other religious communities was excessive and disrespectful, fuelled by theological confusion and the venom of angry women. And so they resisted the pressure to "move with the times." Their hesitation and caution were vindicated by the seventies. Large numbers of nuns who "moved with the times" were moving right out the convent doors. Traditional apostolates, especially teaching, were abandoned.

Anita, Maureen, and Jeanne had witnessed it all. Young, isolated, and limited in their access to information, they followed the events through the eyes of their superiors, and the priests and bishops who delivered their sermons. What times! Yet, as they were reminded, the Church had suffered through worse.

This, too, would pass.

Not all the SCRs were as trusting of their superior's judgment. Vatican II required religious orders to rewrite the constitutions governing their communities, retaining the essentials and eliminating the obsolete. As the SCR's constitutions were being revised, a few of the sisters questioned certain customs and strictures. They wanted greater access to information, more participation in decision-making, increased contact with their families, and a broader education open to intellectual inquiry. Whether their concerns were stated publicly or whispered to other sisters, their notions were promptly reported to the superiors. Eventually, these sisters either settled back into the status quo, convinced they had been tempted and confused, or they left. But in one particular case the challenge came from a highly respected member of the community.

Sr. Mary Patricia was the mistress of the student sisters—those sisters who had finished novitiate, had not yet made final vows, and were completing their education to become teachers. She was also a history professor in their community college. Both positions she had held for years.

As happened periodically, Sr. Mary Patricia, a gifted presenter, was asked by Mother Ambrosia to give a series of lectures on the history of the Church during the sisters' ongoing formation sessions. The iron and bamboo curtains were still firmly entrenched at the time. Sr. Mary Patricia's lectures were to examine totalitarian governments and their relationship with the Church. Most thought her lectures would be an elaboration of current situations where the Church was under a communist regime.

Sr. Mary Patricia initiated her lectures with a description of highly centralized power structures throughout history, ranging from ancient kingdoms and dynasties to more recent dictatorships. She pointed out some accomplishments of these regimes: roads, trade, cities, and the illusion of stability—illusion, yes, for compliance derived from coercion and silencing opposition, she pointed out, can only be a delusion. In the second session, she examined the tactics which kept these governments in place and the heavy toll they had taken on vast segments of the population.

In the third session, Sr. Mary Patricia plunged into Church social teaching. According to the Popes and the Council fathers of Vatican II, who pinned the documents on social justice, all governments, institutions, and organizations should be accountable to their constituency and promote subsidiary in governance. They should be open to examination, assessment, and modification so that basic human rights are upheld and all persons are allowed to develop fully, exercising their ability to think critically and choose freely. Trust and collaboration among people are built on respect and transparency in policies, procedures, finances, and relationships.

Sr. Mary Patricia questioned, could these principles, considered so essential to the well-being of individuals and society, not also be applied to religious organizations as well, including religious orders?

~

Although no reference was made to the SCRs, and most sisters calmly took down notes as usual, Mother Mary Ambrosia and her young assistant, Sr. Mary Thomas, were disturbed. They considered Sr. Mary Patricia's presentation a veiled affront to their constitutions and traditions, all approved by the Church, all aimed to promote the holiness of their members.

It was pride. Pride brought down the best. Worse yet, Sr. Mary Patricia was a professor in their college and entrusted with the formation of the younger sisters. What had she been teaching *them*? How had she influenced their thinking— their very commitment to Christ? Within a few days Mother's misgivings had crept through the community. Previous esteem chilled to reserve and caution.

The following week Sr. Mary Patricia was sent to a branch community to substitute for an ailing sister. After she left, her belongings were packed up and her files, notebooks, and personal material read. Her temporary substitution became a permanent assignment and her personal effects were forwarded. From that time on, before lectures were given by their sisters, the outlines were reviewed and the books cited were approved by the mother general with the assistance of an appointed delegate.

Meanwhile, all the young sisters were asked to turn in their notebooks from the classes and formation lectures of Sr. Mary Patricia and these were given to Mother Ambrosia. Sr. Mary Thomas examined them scrupulously.

Although nothing was said publicly, the proceedings became known and sent shock waves through the small congregation. Reactions varied from "I always thought there was something fishy about her," to disillusionment and outrage. That year, half of the student sisters left or were asked to go. Those who remained did so under the tutorage of Sr. Petrina. Their numbers dwindled further before perpetual profession.

~

Anita, Maureen, and Jeanne were in disbelief. Sr. Mary Patricia? Of all their formators, she had been the most insightful, the most receptive, the one in whom they easily confided even years after their perpetual profession. Why had Patricia's presentations so deeply disturbed Mother Mary Ambrosia and her government? Maureen went back to her notes. Through her family, she obtained copies of the books Patricia had referenced and began her clandestine research. From Mother's reaction, Maureen saw that Patricia had questioned the SCRs highly centralized government, the minute control the superiors exercised over members, the isolation and seclusion of the sisters, and the one-way accountability—the sisters accountable to the superiors regarding every aspect of their lives but not vice versa.

~

When Patricia arrived for the annual retreat in the summer, she was greeted with civil distance. The sisters gave a quick hello, a silent wave, or a glare. She was avoided—brusquely by some, suavely by others—but avoided just the same. Maureen was scheduled for the same retreat. One day as she walked the grounds in silence, she saw Patricia moving toward a little grotto. This was her chance. When Maureen arrived at the grotto, Patricia was sitting on a bench jotting something in a journal.

"It's so good to see you," said Maureen.

"Not everyone would agree with that."

Maureen sat next to Patricia. "I read the books you mentioned in your lectures."

Patricia shot her a glance. "You know that we're mostly likely being watched."

"I don't care."

"And you're breaking the silence," she said, raising her eyebrows.

"How can you stay in this congregation," Maureen said with urgency, "knowing what you know, being treated as you are? How can *we* stay?"

"Do we do more good in or out? Do we work toward a mature following of Christ in or out?"

"Following of *Christ*? Our community is being run like a dictatorship."

Patricia gave Maureen her full attention. "I'll be honest with you. I've committed my life to God and the only reason I remain is for him. I believe in the value of a community of women . . . all of us . . . (making a circling gesture) joined by the love of Christ to serve others. But the way we live out our commitment has to mature . . . and it won't happen overnight." Patricia closed her journal. "Do we have the patience?"

As if on cue, they heard gravel crunch underfoot and a sister appeared in the grotto.

"Mother Mary Ambrosia would like to see you, Sr. Mary Patricia."

"Tell her I'll be right along."

The sister turned reluctantly. She stayed near the entrance of the grotto, pulled out her rosary, and began fingering the beads.

Patricia nudged Maureen and they walked off together.

"Perhaps I pushed too hard in the lectures. The superiors . . . I underestimated the depth of their fear." They slowly walked across the large expanse of grass and trees toward the motherhouse.

"So where do we go from here?" asked Maureen.

"Where do *you* go from here? I have no idea. That's between you and God." She put her hand on Maureen's shoulder. "We're in uncharted waters."

∼

A couple of days later, Maureen's uncharted waters flowed into the office of Mother Ambrosia.

"I hear you've been speaking with Sr. Mary Patricia."

"She was my mistress as a student sister."

"You are aware that silence is a very important component of a retreat."

"It was personal, spiritual conversation, Mother. I always understood spiritual colloquies with our superiors or past mistresses were permitted."

Maureen was perpetually professed and could not be sent home without grave cause. And there was nothing about her life even remotely troublesome— she was an exceptional teacher, dedicated to prayer, and a giver in community.

However, there *was* something in her attitude, in her connection with Sr. Mary Patricia. . . .

"Sr. Mary Maureen, we've decided to transfer you to our missionary outpost—Whitewaters."

Maureen never crossed paths with Patricia again. After four years, Patricia's uncharted waters brought her to another congregation. It was never announced, but the news circulated until it was whispered even in the misty mountains of Whitewaters.

~

Despite the admonitions that personal concerns and difficulties be shared only with the superiors and mistresses, Anita and Maureen trusted and confided in each other. Their training, education, and assignments had tossed them together throughout the years and they discovered that they had a common passion for the development of childhood education and a common vision for the future of religious life. Both felt they were called to work from within toward change and were heartened by what they saw as a movement forward. Henrietta, known for her moderation and goodness, was placed in formation. Their schools became more racially integrated and newer methods of education were being explored. They just had to be patient.

As the novelty of Whitewaters waned, Mother Mary Thomas, now superior general, saw new mission fields in the larger cities of the state. Anita heard from Maureen that the mission outpost was downsizing and many transfers were anticipated. Anita let it be known to Henrietta that she was willing to be a Whitewaters missionary. Although Maureen was still viewed with some reservation, Mother Mary Thomas could not but recognize her total commitment to Whitewaters, her attention to prayer, her welcoming presence in community, and her organizational skills. The community was reduced to three—Maureen, Candida, and Anita— and Maureen was appointed superior. Not much of a risk in Whitewaters. When Jeanne went through her crisis a few years later, Maureen was in a position to assist her.

CHAPTER 73

"C atching up on your studies?"

Pistós startled. The noise and conversation passing through the windows had buffered the footsteps and tinkling rosary beads that came down the corridor and paused in front of the opened library door.

"And during a parish festival. You have quite an appetite for learning,"

Pistós regained her composure. "I try to keep myself occupied."

Jeanne walked toward Pistós and glanced at the books she had stacked on the librarian's desk. She set down the percussion instruments she was returning to the music room. "I thought you might be more interested in expanding your understanding of the mountain people, seeing you made the trip to Appalachia."

"We each have our own interests."

"And what would yours be, exactly, here in Whitewaters? The people don't appear to have aroused any curiosity."

Pistós continued to scan the shelves but her previous intensity was flustered. Jeanne picked up the stack of books and began to read off the titles: all pertained to theological or moral issues.

"Pistós, let's not play games. Why are you here?"

"I've been asked to assist the superiors," Pistós replied coolly, riled again by the absence of *Sister*.

"And going through the library books is part of your assistance?"

"Libraries captivate me." She continued to scan the shelves.

Jeanne set down the books. "Please close the windows when you leave and shut the door." She picked up the musical instruments and walked toward the hallway. At the door, she turned back to Pistós. "Evening prayer begins in fifteen minutes."

Pistós's shelf gazing stopped when Jeanne left the room. The insolence of these sisters! She straightened out her selection of books, banging them on the desk. No wonder the superiors were concerned. A rousing grand finale rose from the band outside, accompanied by clapping and cheers. But Pistós barely heard it. Her mind was fixed on more serious matters.

CHAPTER 74

Sunday Mass, the diocesan anniversary liturgy, was finally drawing to a close. Rebecca knelt next to Candida at the far end of their designated pew close the side door of the church. Never before had she admitted to herself how tiresome she found the bishop. Buoyed by the packed church that spilled out the doors, the bishop's pleasure with the Whitewaters parish of St. Martin de Porres swelled into a sermon where one forgot the beginning and lost hope of an end. His exuberance might have been deflated had he realized that the crowd was largely the result of cancelling the usual Saturday evening Mass as well as the mission services in neighbouring communities. And it didn't take much for the modest church building to reach standing room only.

As the eleven o'clock service hit twelve noon with the bishop still preaching, many a parent wished they had found a babysitter, or at least, were among the group outside where the children had more freedom to play. But now the choir broke into the concluding hymn, and the inconvenience would soon be forgiven as the parishioners enjoyed their home-baked treats during the informal reception that followed.

Rebecca joined the singing until she noticed Candida spiriting away to finish preparations on the celebratory turkey dinner. She genuflected and squeezed through those who hovered around the door. Greetings from schoolchildren and parents clustered around the side of the church obliged her to exchange a few words and prevented her rapid retreat to the convent kitchen. With a final wave she was back on track, making her way to the refuge of usefulness.

"Sr. Rebecca Marise," called a voice from the general clamour.

Rebecca turned to see Pistós approaching in her measured pace, the model of decorum.

God forbid she quicken her steps, thought Rebecca as she waited for Pistós to catch up with her.

"Off so quickly?"

"I'm helping with the dinner," said Rebecca as she resumed walking. "Aren't you staying for the reception? The women in the parish baked their very best for the conclusion of this celebration."

"I'm sure I won't be missed."

Rebecca was sure as well, but kept this to herself.

As far as Pistós was concerned, there was no reason for her to mingle at the reception, certainly not for the company. Nor was she tempted by the array of cakes, pies, and cookies—she rarely ate outside a meal. Abashed by the commodious figures of many sisters, Pistós carefully monitored her intake. It all boiled down to mortification.

"You've been here . . . how long? A year?" asked Pistós.

"That's right, almost a year." Pistós already knew exactly how long Rebecca had been there, probably to the day. Irritated, Rebecca quickened her step.

"So what's your impression?"

This was exactly the type of conversation Rebecca wished to avoid. "Impression?" she said without stopping, reaching the back door of the convent.

"Yes. Whitewaters is known to be unique. What has been your experience?"

Pistós' cattiness tipped Rebecca's usual reserve. She stopped abruptly and faced Pistós.

"What has been my experience? In this *unique* setting? *This*?" she said, gesturing widely. "The sisters are thoughtful, kind, and passionate about teaching. They love and respect the people of Whitewaters. They have bent *backwards* . . ."

The force of her words startled Pistós and flustered Rebecca herself. She turned and disappeared into the convent. Pistós glanced at the withered leaves cornered under the stairway that led to the school, the embedded grit in the grooves of its roof, and the dusty garbage bin nearby. She grabbed her garb closely about her to avoid getting dirty and returned to the reception.

∼

"Quite nice . . . delightful, the entire weekend," said the bishop. Maureen set a serving of dessert before him. "Great work, the DVD . . . it was excellent."

After their supper the previous evening, Doug played a DVD prepared by a group of the parishioners on the history of Whitewaters parish. The DVD, together with an attractively bound written account, had been presented to the bishop by the president of the parish council.

"The parishioners worked hard gathering the photos and documents. Took several months. And now we have an historical presentation on our parish as well as a chronicle of events with supporting documents and photos."

"The work is quite impressive. Invaluable for the archives. I looked over the chronicle briefly last night. Quite impressive."

Maureen and Candida served the coffee and tea.

"Wonderful weekend," said the bishop, stirring the sugar in his coffee.

The weather couldn't have been better, the people friendly, the events well attended, and he had been surrounded from start to finish by the attentive care of his favoured group of sisters.

"Wonderful weekend," repeated the bishop. Mother beamed beside him.

Candida and Maureen set the teapot and carafe of coffee on the table and sat down with the others.

"So Whitewaters has had the honour of opening the diocesan anniversary celebrations," Maureen commented.

"Yes . . . well . . ." The bishop hesitated then smiled. "We don't want to neglect our mission outpost."

"And what's next on your schedule?" Candida smiled broadly.

"We're having a statewide pro-life convention in the capital," said the bishop, "And I'll be giving the keynote address."

"I read your statement on pro-life issues, Bishop. You were quite eloquent," said Jeanne.

"Thank you." The bishop nodded at Jeanne and took a sip of coffee.

"His Excellency has always been a strong advocate on behalf of life." Mother nodded.

"What will your topic be?" asked Pistós.

"I'll be addressing the sacrosanct value of human life from the moment of conception until natural death."

Jeanne took a breath. "So I imagine you'll be addressing the law permitting capital punishment in our state."

Everyone turned their gaze on Jeanne. "You did say until natural death," said Jeanne politely.

"No, capital punishment will not be addressed at this time," said the bishop calmly, exchanging a quick look with Mother.

"Yes, I've noticed in your pro-life statements that capital punishment is rarely mentioned," said Jeanne.

The room chilled. Even Maureen looked surprised.

Mother opened her mouth to speak, but Jeanne continued on.

"It seems to me, living here in the heart of Appalachia, that there are other life issues also overlooked."

The bishop put down his fork and turned to Jeanne, "To what are you referring?"

"To mention one, mountaintop removal to mine coal. Mountains are literally being blasted away, the unwanted rubble sent down the mountainsides into the valleys, polluting the environment, suffocating hundreds of streams, endangering human life, and destroying homes and communities. Is this not also an attack on life?" Jeanne asked. "Are we to support political candidates who allow this practice to continue unabated while it presents such a threat to life? In your article you said no Catholic in good conscience could vote for candidates who are against human life."

"Really, Sr. Maria Jeanne," said Mother, in a mix of civility and sharpness, "this is an inappropriate subject to bring up at table."

"It's quite all right, Mother," said the bishop, leaning back in his chair. And turning to Jeanne, "I believe we are treating two different issues, Sister . . . Sister . . ."

"Jeanne," said Jeanne.

"Yes. Sr. Jeanne. As I was saying—abortion, euthanasia, and stem cell research, which I discuss at length in my statements, are direct attacks against human life. Mountaintop mining is not."

"It *is* for the people in the area," said Jeanne. "*They're* breathing the polluted air, drinking the contaminated water, living in houses whose foundations have been damaged by the blasts, forced to move away from communities that they have been a part of for years, if not generations."

"Yes. . . . Well, those of us familiar with intricacies of moral theology and natural law know that we cannot put mountaintop mining and the pro-life issues in the same category. We're discussing apples and oranges."

"How so?" asked Doug. Mother straightened in her chair and impatiently waved away Candida as she made the rounds with the coffee and tea.

The bishop added some sugar to his fresh coffee and began to stir it. "Abortion and euthanasia are moral absolutes, clear attacks against the good of man and contrary to the principles of right reason and natural law." He lifted his cup and took a sip between his sentences. "On the other hand, how we go about mining is a public policy that the Gospel message does not treat directly. There can be a variety of opinions from very principled and educated people. To go into particulars regarding mining is not within my domain as bishop. That's for the secular sector to debate."

"You've been reading Wilson," said Doug.

A slight jerk of his head indicated his surprise, but he continued in a philosophic tone, "You're familiar with his writings?"

"I believe everyone in this room is familiar with his thought." Well, he was sure of at least three from Whitewaters—but he wanted the bishop to know that there were some listeners who knew he was evading the human fallout of mountaintop mining and parroting a prominent conservative thinker. Rankled by the bishop's patronizing tone, he also wanted the bishop to realize that knowledge of "the intricacies of moral theology and natural law" could be found among the "grassroots," even in the backwoods of Appalachia.

"I wonder," said Jeanne, "why we're so cautious about addressing the atrocities of mountaintop mining when we are fearless to take on abortion. Are we afraid of the corporations? Or the good Christians who are becoming rich on the profits? By speaking out, do we risk losing donors for our churches, our schools, our programs? It's always puzzled me. As you've said, it's complex. . . . I can only imagine."

"This has gone far enough!" said Mother Thomas, as she rose to her feet. "Bishop Patterson is a great friend of our sisters and an outstanding prelate. A guest in our house! He will not be insulted!"

"Mother, there is no intention to insult—" began Jeanne.

"This is a very important issue for our people here in Appalachia—" broke in Doug.

"The conversation is ended!" said Mother with a glance and a tone that silenced them all.

The bishop calmly sipped his coffee.

"Your Excellency, I apologize for the impropriety."

"No offence taken, I assure you," said the bishop, setting down his coffee cup.

"We all have an early rising awaiting us tomorrow, so I suggest we close the meal. Your Excellency, would you lead us in grace after meals."

The prayer completed, the bishop thanked the cook and walked to the front door with Doug and Mother Thomas.

~

Rebecca, shell-shocked, immediately began to gather the dishes so she could escape to the kitchen.

Mother was back in seconds.

"Be seated."

The nuns resumed their seats.

"Words cannot express my displeasure. The impertinence! The pride! The audacity!"

The silence that followed seemed interminable to Rebecca. Never had she seen Mother so angry.

Jeanne broke the silence. "Mother, there is no need to detain the others. I'm—"

"You've said quite enough for the evening, Sr. Maria Jeanne. Yes, quite enough," she said softly and leaned back in her chair.

The silence continued for several more moments.

"There will be some changes to tomorrow's plans. Sr. Miriam Pistós, you will return to the motherhouse by plane with me and the bishop, as previously planned. Sr. Mary Petrina, you, instead, will remain with the community as they close the house tomorrow, and drive back with them the day after. We will now go to the church for night prayers, and when we return, we'll go about our duties under the grand silence." Mother turned toward the darkening sky. "And why are these blinds always left open? Even at night!"

"So we can see the stars," said Jeanne, more to herself.

The comment was lost on Mother as Pistós strode to the window and lowered the blinds.

CHAPTER 75

"What were you thinking?" said Maureen impatiently as she and Jeanne dragged the folding table to the school hall. "Now they'll close us down for sure."

"They were already going to close us down and you know that."

"No, we didn't know that for sure."

"Well, now we do."

The two sisters reached the double doors leading to the gym. Maureen leaned her side of the table against the wall, but instead of unlocking the door she turned to Jeanne.

"How can you be so cavalier about this?"

Jeanne threw up her hands. "Cavalier?!" The table crashed loudly on the floor. "For years we've put up with the nonsense we witnessed tonight hoping for change. And have things improved? " She gestured emphatically. "If you ask me, we're going backwards . . . and fast. Mother, ordering us to silence . . . even Doug! And we *sat* there like mute sheep. Who gives her the right? Who gives *her* the right? We do, just sitting there like frightened children, blaming ourselves for upsetting the 'holy of holies.' Are we ten years old, Maureen? Never mind, we wouldn't treat *our* ten-year-olds that way! And the bishop sipping his coffee through it all . . . what a joke! Like some benign philosopher."

"He did manage to keep his composure."

"Sure! That's easy when you have a pit bull at your side! What a farce! And *we* sit there, sucking it up." Jeanne shook her head. "And this is *God* speaking to us? Positively bizarre!"

Jeanne leaned against the wall and the two women stood in silence for some moments.

"I had no intention of confronting the bishop tonight . . . really," said Jeanne softly. "He can be so pompous, so condescending . . . and so ignorant. Living within his cocoon of lackeys, just like Mother. Rarely contradicted, swiftly defended when they are, bolstered by their positions—*the representatives of Christ*. Sweet Jesus." She sighed. "They feel invincible, I suppose." She waved her hands half-heartedly to the left and right. "The bulwarks of the truth, defenders of the faith. . . . It's one thing to observe it from a distance, it's another to dine with it. I'm so tired of the charade. . . . Sorry I dragged you all down with me."

"You didn't drag us down." Maureen sighed. "You said nothing wrong, nothing at all. And you're right. Transferring us out of Whitewaters was already in the works. You just helped close the deal."

"Now what?"

"You're in the arms of Christ," said Maureen.

"Don't give me that pious crap."

"Really, you are. Look up."

Jeanne glanced up at the mural in the wall. She was among the little children embraced by Jesus.

"All for the love of Jesus," said Jeanne, smiling in spite of herself.

"Come on, we still have another trip." Maureen unlocked the doors and they returned the table to the hall. As they walked back down the corridors, Jeanne let her fingers glide across the wall.

"I'm going to miss this school, the children. Do you really think they'll close it down?"

"The convent, for sure. The school . . . who knows?"

"I'll tell you right now, Maureen, I'm not going to live in a community under the surveillance of Mother's minions."

"Think of the children."

"The children don't need this garb."

~

With the clay sculpture and other items from the art room in tow, Maureen and Jeanne had just begun their trek down the corridor when the outside door closed.

Both turned to see Pistós approaching.

"Mother would like to know why you are not in the kitchen helping with the dishes."

"As you can see, Sr. Miriam Pistós," said Maureen, "we're returning items to the school."

"Mother thinks that can be done tomorrow."

"Well, you can inform Mother that it's already done."

Maureen and Jeanne continued down the corridor.

"I'll help," said Pistós as she approached the sisters.

Maureen stopped and turned toward Pistós. Jeanne paused as well, eyeing the two curiously.

"Pistós, Jeanne and I are perfectly capable of finishing this job by ourselves. Why don't *you* return to the kitchen and give a hand with the dishes?"

"Mother will not be pleased," said Pistós.

"She should be displeased," said Jeanne. "You just made us break the grand silence."

Pistós regarded Jeanne briefly then walked back down the corridor and out the door. The two nuns continued down the hall.

"We're in trouble now," said Maureen.

"You don't piss off Pistós."

"Jeanne!"

"Pissed-off Pistós has a nice ring."

"Jeannnne!" Maureen said, shaking her head.

Maureen flexed her fingers after setting down her box. "I wonder how Rebecca's doing."

"Silent and frenetic."

"Too much reality."

"We've all had to deal with our dish of reality." Jeanne put her hand on Maureen's shoulder. "We can't protect her."

"It's sad. She's authentic."

"Yes, she is."

CHAPTER 76

A bell clanged loud and harsh for many seconds. Rebecca started and grabbed the mattress. She instinctively reached out toward her alarm clock then realized the clanking, once again, was coming from the hallway. Petrina had assumed the duty of the wake-up bell since her first morning at Whitewaters, resurrecting, unbeknown to her, a relic decorating a hallway niche that had ceased rattling the sisters to consciousness years before.

Five o'clock. Rebecca had, at last, drifted off to sleep, but her lethargy confirmed that it could not have been for long. Mechanically, she went through her morning prep, donned her habit, and made her way, bleary-eyed to the church for Mass with the bishop.

In the wee hours of the morning the bishop's verbosity waned to a trickle and in less than a half-hour Doug and sisters were outside the church for the parting of Bishop Patterson, Mother, and Pistós. Candida had packed some sandwiches, fruit, and cookies for the long trip to the airport but Doug balked when she brought out the large thermos.

"We'll pick up coffee on our way out of town," he said, foreseeing the spills as the coffee and cream were divided into an odd assortment of mugs—none of which would fit into the car's cup holders.

The leave-taking was awkward and perfunctory. Mother's fury had iced over to merited disregard. The bishop was more discreet. However, his profusions regarding the mission outpost had simmered down to a modest acknowledgment of the hard work of the parishioners. And by the time he arrived at his residence, he would absently pull out the envelope with the Whitewaters DVD and documents, forward it to the archives, and leave it on his assistant's desk without a word.

~

Petrina and the community sisters returned to their prayers and then ate their breakfast in silence. Rebecca had become so accustomed to their usual morning planning session that she had practically forgotten the breakfast silence she had observed for years at the motherhouse. This morning, however, Rebecca welcomed the practice as she sipped her coffee and ate a piece of French toast that Candida had prepared.

When Petrina finished eating, she stood and walked to a small bookshelf built within the wall at the back of the dining area. There was nothing unusual about a bookshelf in the dining area—in every SCR convent there was a similar arrangement that contained books for spiritual reading during meals. What made this bookshelf strikingly different was the scarcity of books and the generous audio collection. A CD player on the bottom shelf was obviously a permanent fixture and Petrina shook her head as she followed its cord, lengthened by an extension, trailing down the wall and along the baseboard to an electrical socket.

With all their meals over the weekend served in the community room, Rebecca figured that the spiritual reading nook had slipped her notice. On the top shelf was the recommended reading matter found in every SCR dining room: a collection of spiritual writings of the saints and papal documents. They stood, fading and aging, like sentinels ready for duty but never called upon. On the middle shelf were the audio books.

Rebecca stopped chewing as Petrina selected several and turned toward Maureen, reading the jackets: "*To Kill a Mocking Bird*? *The Lord of the Rings*? *Grapes of Wrath*? Graham Greene, Charles Dickens, Flannery O'Connor???"

"They're classics and quite inspirational," said Maureen.

"I hardly need to be told what is a classic, Sr. Mary Maureen. That does not make them suitable for spiritual reading."

"I think St. Ignatius of Loyola would differ. What's his famous quote? *Finding God in all things*? The arts can be an encounter with the divine."

"St. Ignatius also knew how to obey and not one of these books is on our recommended list for spiritual reading."

The last bite of toast stuck in Rebecca's throat. She remembered her own initial uneasiness with the audio novels. Over the weeks and months, she not only grew accustomed to, but enjoyed them. Now she felt like a co-conspirator in some subversive plot.

"Sr. Mary Petrina, there is nothing wrong with the content of those books," said Maureen calmly.

"And who makes you the judge to decide what is best for spiritual reading? Our superiors have the graces to determine what is suitable and what is not."

Jeanne shook her head slightly and moved back in her chair. "We have a lot of work to do today. Perhaps you can continue this discussion with Maureen—"

"There is no *discussion* to continue," said Petrina with an edge. "And as a sign of respect, the title *Sister* is to be used at all times, Sr. Maria Jeanne. In the name of the Father," said Petrina sharply as she lifted her hand to her forehead, "and of the Son . . ."

The others rose to join in the after-meal grace.

~

Petrina's proclivity toward housework lay in monitoring its outcome, having long ago left the actual task to the youngest members. Although in this community the seasoned sisters were by far the majority, Petrina was so accustomed to more consequential responsibilities that during the morning's ablutions she remained in her room with an undisclosed task. While this raised the eyebrows of Maureen and Jeanne, they were relieved to have Petrina out of sight for a couple of hours.

Since the sisters had scoured the convent before the celebration, it didn't take long to prepare it for their summer absence. By noon the common rooms were swept and dusted, the bathroom gleamed, the kitchen cupboards had been sorted, the refrigerator and freezer cleaned, and the food divided as to what would be given to Doug and what would accompany them on their trip the next day.

Packing their personal effects after lunch was more of a challenge. While nothing had been said or even hinted by Mother, Maureen and Jeanne knew that the likelihood of the SCRs returning to Whitewaters was slim. And with Petrina travelling with them, the rear passenger seat would have to be pulled out of storage and reinstalled in the van, limiting their luggage space.

~

Rebecca unzipped her suitcase and opened it on her bed. Someone knocked lightly on her door.

"Maureen!" Rebecca said in hushed surprise.

Maureen walked in and shut the door behind her.

"Why don't you sit down, Rebecca?" she said softly.

Rebecca sat on the only chair in the narrow room and Maureen leaned on the sink near the door. "How are you doing?"

"Doing?"

"How do you feel about Mother's visit . . . about last night's meal?"

"I don't know. I'm really tired."

"You worked hard this past week . . . did a wonderful job. The people here love you."

Rebecca was momentarily confused. The summer camp and parish festival were so far removed from her thoughts that Maureen seemed to be discussing an event from the ancient past. "Oh, that . . ."

"Rebecca?"

"She's so angry. . . ."

"You've done nothing wrong, Rebecca."

It didn't seem that way. Mother had barely acknowledged her when she parted . . . had barely acknowledged any of them . . . in marked contrast to her treatment of the bishop, Petrina, and Pistós. When Mother came into the kitchen the evening before and discovered that Maureen and Jeanne were returning things to the school building, she scolded Candida and herself as if they had ordered the two to go. Just the memory caused her skin to prickle. And then her own impatience with Pistós after Sunday Mass. If only she had held her tongue— Rebecca was sure Mother had heard all about it. Her stomach tightened.

"Rebecca, look at me."

Rebecca turned her weary eyes to Maureen. "You are a remarkable teacher and have been a blessing to our community and the people here. Do you understand me?"

Tears welled in Rebecca's eyes. Maureen's words only deepened her perplexity and increased her trepidation. . . . She could not explain it. Deep, nameless, ambiguous dread.

"Rebecca, most likely, you will not return to Whitewaters, so pack up as much as possible."

Rebecca nodded and Maureen left. Packing her personal things took no time at all—a few changes of undergarments, her Sunday habit, a family photo, and a couple pairs of shoes. She reached the bottom shelf. Tucked in the back was the outfit she had used in Birchbark. Her heart quickened. She knew she could never use them again, yet she placed them on the bottom of her suitcase and covered them with her other garments. In twenty minutes her clothes were packed. On the floor at the end of the bed was an open box which she had already begun to fill with a selection of her books, but after Maureen's comments, she decided to revise it. She had some items in the school building she did not want to leave behind. Rebecca quietly opened her door and padded softly down the hallway.

~

A few shafts of lights shot through the glass panes in classroom doors, illuminating the corridor but not dispelling the shadows. Rebecca entered the third grade classroom and opened the windows. She remained for a few minutes, gazing at the hills and valley that never ceased to captivate her. A psalm came to mind that she often recited during the liturgy of the hours and she whispered,

My heart is in anguish within me. . .
fear and trembling come upon me. . .
O that I had wings like a dove!
I would fly away and be at rest.

The prayer brought no consolation and the beauty before her only increased her sadness at parting. She turned toward the back of the classroom. Above the children's coat hooks, were storage shelves where Rebecca kept a couple of empty boxes. She brought one to Anita's filing cabinet—she had reorganized it over the year and made it her own, retaining a good deal of Anita's reference materials. Going through the files transported Rebecca to a different space. She could feel the children around her. She re-experienced her initial anxiety, her enthusiasm, concern, and joy as she grew to know and love the people of Whitewaters.

"Why aren't you with the others?" said Petrina from the doorway.

Rebecca stiffened and rose instantly, blindsided. The renewed dread rocked her composure and sent currents down her arms and out her fingertips. She felt inexplicably guilty.

"I understood we were to pack," said Rebecca, unsure of herself.

"And you're not in the habit of informing your superiors when you leave the convent?" said Petrina as she approached Rebecca.

Rebecca said nothing. Truth be told, the sisters spent little time within the convent walls. Their life revolved around the holy trinity of prayer, community, and school, and though one could debate which was more important, school trumped when it came to time. Their ordinary tasks did not necessitate permissions.

"What are you doing?"

"Packing up lesson plans."

"Did anyone tell you to do so?"

Rebecca paused. "I'd like to have them at hand. Whitewaters is a long distance from the motherhouse."

"Yes, it is," said Petrina, looking closely at Rebecca. "To ask permission would have shown some humility." She walked toward the windows with a view of the mountains in full verdure and turned around to face Rebecca.

"How have you found Whitewaters?"

Petrina was a silhouette against the backdrop of the sunlit mountains.

"It's beautiful, truly beautiful. Breathtaking at times."

"I could have read that in a travelogue."

Rebecca, baffled, focused on the slight, wiry nun standing ramrod before her. "I don't know what you mean."

"What has been your experience in this community?" Petrina said.

"Good . . . very good," Rebecca replied haltingly. In all her years with the SCRs, she had been disconcerted by Petrina. And to be in the room, alone and questioned by her, was unnerving.

"You can bring one box," said Petrina.

"Thank you," replied Rebecca as she watched Petrina depart. In the corner of her suitcase lay an envelope of disks containing all her files from the laptop. It made her acquiescence much easier.

CHAPTER 77

Rebecca tried to soften her footsteps as she walked across the shining marble to her designated place in the motherhouse chapel. The lights dispelled the predawn darkness, illuminating the majestic sanctuary with the tabernacle and crucifix at its centre, a statue of the Blessed Mother in a prominent niche to one side and St. Joseph honoured on the other. She passed along the white walls with gilded trim interspersed with saints immortalized in stained glass and the passion of Christ sculpted in the stations of cross. She had been away less than a year and yet felt dwarfed under the chapel's high, arched ceiling that spanned the broad expanse below. Prayers would begin in five minutes and the chapel was filling with sisters, their heads bowed in silence and prayer. Rebecca glanced discreetly down the pews as she walked toward her own, but did not see any of the other sisters from Whitewaters.

"God, come to my assistance," signalled the beginning of prayer and the entire assembly rose in unison. The sisters recited the psalms in flawless cadence, accompanied by bows and gestures choreographed to perfection through decades of practice. Rebecca had been thoroughly charmed by the practice when she entered; now it felt foreign and formal. Although the same prayers were said and the same gestures were made at Whitewaters, the ritual seemed substantially different among the motley group of sisters in the parish church with its worn carpet, dog-eared hymnals, and scuffed kneelers.

∼

The van transporting the missionaries from Whitewaters had pulled into the grounds of the motherhouse shortly before vespers. The sisters had just enough time to bring their luggage to their rooms before hurrying to evening prayer. Due to the number of sisters at the motherhouse, Rebecca was assigned to the guesthouse and shared a room with another perpetually professed sister, Sr. Agnes Marie. She was some years older than Rebecca and, since they had never been stationed together, Rebecca knew her only through passing encounters here and there. Maureen, Jeanne, and Candida were placed somewhere within the leviathan compound of the motherhouse.

Supper followed vespers. As Rebecca entered the refectory, she passed some of her co-novices standing in silence before their chairs, waiting for the grace before meals. None gave even a slight smile or welcoming nudge.

Quit being so sensitive! she scolded herself. *What are you expecting? You're not a princess. You make an annual retreat here every year.*

The meal was served with its allotted portions and the nuns ate, silent and sombre, while one sister read from the latest papal document. Rebecca, with no appetite, willed every bite she swallowed. She became hypersensitive to the cutlery clinking, her neighbours chewing, pouring or swallowing their beverages, chairs grinding against the floor as sisters finished their meal and went to rinse and stack their dishes. *What is wrong with me?*

~

After dinner, the large group of nuns moved in silence to the expansive community hall for an hour of recreation. Once through the doors, the sisters could freely converse. Rebecca walked tentatively into the large hall. Patrick Marian stood with a group of younger sisters, enjoying a humorous conversation. She looked over at Rebecca, gave a slight nod, and continued talking. The other nuns in her circle turned to look as well and then resumed their conversation. Was it her own anxiety or were the sisters shying away from her. She was imagining things. *Quit being stupid*, she said to herself and began to walk toward Patrick Marian.

Maureen tapped Rebecca on the shoulder.

"Anita's been looking forward to chatting with you," she said.

Anita, standing nearby, gave Rebecca a warm hug. "I've heard so much about you and the wonderful work you're doing in Whitewaters. Come over here with Maureen and me and tell me all about your students. How is Jacob? And what about Leah? I was so looking forward to the new class."

"And how are you? How are you feeling?" asked Rebecca.

"Oh, I'm fine. Don't worry about me," said Anita as the threesome settled down into chairs. "In fact, starting this September, I'll be teaching religion to the primary grades in one of the local schools. But enough about me. Now tell me about my favourite school. Rebecca, how did you—"

Thud, thud. The local superior, Sr. Mary Augustine, tapped a cordless mic. "Sisters"—she cleared her throat—"sisters." Everyone's attention shifted toward the front of the hall. On the dais were several chairs into which Mother Mary Thomas and some of her councillors were just settling.

Rebecca tensed and Anita and Maureen lowered their eyes in disappointment.

The local superior continued, "Before we begin the annual retreat tomorrow, we would like to present an overview of the events planned for the diocesan celebrations. Something we can all keep in our prayers. As you know, our sisters have had a key role throughout the planning . . ."

Petrina stepped off the dais and whispered into the ear of the local superior. Sr. Mary Augustine passed the mic to Petrina who delivered it to Mother Mary Thomas.

"Good evening, sisters."

"Good evening, Mother," responded the sisters.

"Everyone be seated."

Chairs were taken from various positions around the room and turned to face the dais. Many sisters brought their chairs from the rear toward the front for a better view. Candida walked by with several older sisters to a section of chairs put in place by a team of smiling younger sisters. Maureen, Anita, and Rebecca were off to the side and, with the sudden movement of chairs, were now among those in the back rows.

During the rumble of moving chairs, Anita sighed and whispered to Maureen, "This celebration is producing an unending stream of information. *What will* we talk about next year?"

Jeanne walked through the rear door and pulled up a chair near the small group. "What's going on?" she said softly.

"Update on diocesan celebrations," said Maureen. Anita raised her eyebrows.

"I was sufficiently updated last weekend. If anyone looks for me, I went to bed early." Jeanne rose and, in the midst of all the commotion, left the room unnoticed.

As the sisters finished repositioning, the room grew silent, everyone focused on Mother sitting in the centre of the dais.

"Isn't it wonderful to be altogether!" exclaimed Mother, smiling at the sisters and nodding.

A general buzz of assent echoed throughout the hall.

"How I look forward to our time together during the summer. What a precious opportunity to strengthen our spirit, to strengthen our union with Christ and each other for another year of service!" Again she smiled and nodded to the large group of sisters before her.

Then, growing more solemn "We can never take our unity for granted. The charism given to us by our founder is a precious gift, entrusted to us to live and pass on to future generations. It has been blessed by the Pope and approved by the Church. It is a proven path to sanctity for those who follow it faithfully. To those who follow it *faithfully*!"

Absolute silence filled the hall.

"I have said it before, I will say it again," Mother continued, raising her voice. "Fidelity begins with the little things. We start to grow lax with the little things and before we know it, our way of life erodes away. Do we need any more proof than the current state of religious life? What orders are dying? What orders are thriving? Fidelity to even the smallest tradition and custom is essential. They all serve the purpose of directing our minds and hearts to God and all our energies to his service."

Rebecca pulled her rosary beads onto her lap and clenched them tightly.

"No one. Is. Above. The Rule." Every syllable was emphatically stated. "And it is the solemn duty of the superiors to see that the Rule is observed. Any questions regarding our constitutions are to be referred to the mother general, whoever she may be, and her council."

Any SCR with some years of experience knew that these lectures did not come out of the blue. Something was amiss. Among the inner circle, there was no doubt of the exhortation's origin or its target. Those outside this circle would speculate until the word spread. The uninitiated would pray, "Is it I, Lord?" as they scrutinized their lives to see if they had somehow failed and been reported.

"The Rule is a gift. Let us live it in humility and with docility to those who have been entrusted with the service of authority. Let us be faithful daughters of our founder and of the Church. Without fidelity, we are like the branches cut off from the vine. We wither and die."

No one stirred. Rebecca could barely breathe.

"And now, if you could turn off the lights, please. Sr. Miriam Pistós has prepared a presentation on the diocesan celebrations."

Mother, and the sisters with her, stepped off the dais and sat in the chairs already prepared for them in the front row. A screen dropped down behind the dais, the lights flicked off, and a projector in standby mode flashed on.

Rebecca looked at the screen but saw and heard nothing. After a few introductory slides, the other sisters began to respond to the presentation. Pistós could be humorous and received some laughs for several well-timed remarks. The final event, Pistós announced, would be a solemn liturgy at the cathedral and a concert featuring the diocesan choir as well as several numbers sung by the SCR choir. The last item had been a closely guarded surprise. "Ohs" and "ahs" filled the room, then applause. Whitewaters was never mentioned.

~

When the presentation ended and the sisters began to exit for night prayer, Maureen squeezed Rebecca's shoulder. She turned, her eyes distant and veiled. Maureen's own heart welled with sadness and longing.

What is better? To cater to blind idealism? Is that respect? Or is it to challenge, to open, and to stretch?

Seeing the suffering in Rebecca's eyes and knowing the censure she would face, Maureen was no longer sure.

CHAPTER 78

The annual retreat would extend for eight days under the veil of the grand silence. Rebecca longed for this time of withdrawal and solitude as "a deer longs for flowing streams." Surrounded by other nuns, this solemn silence protected her from all but the most necessary and urgent communication. What Rebecca wanted most was to disappear within the multitude of the identically clad and fade out of the superiors' consciousness.

For the first few days, it appeared her desire was fulfilled. And Rebecca did all in her power to assure its continuance. She arrived for all the prayers, sermons, and meals with just enough time to inconspicuously slip into her assigned seat and then withdrew quickly when they finished. She used her room only to sleep— no privacy in her shared room. During the times of personal reflection she sat in a corner of the chapel balcony—visited only by infirm sisters during community prayer—or she burrowed herself in a cove of bushes and trees that sheltered an old metal bench, out of sight and rarely used. Though she longed for more, there were few hours slated for personal reflection. Their schedule was laden with the liturgy of the hours, the Mass, adoration, benediction, the rosary, Stations of the Cross, and two retreat sermons. While present for all, Rebecca felt disconnected. She remembered the retreats of the past, how the sermons filled her with ardour and resolve. Today she sat, pen poised for notes but doodling a border instead.

"Do you long for heaven?" the retreat master queried. "Heaven is not some far-off place for some later date. It is here," gesturing to all of them sitting in the chapel. "You have made the ultimate sacrifice: leaving home; the option of

410

directing your own life, the possibility of a good job, wealth, family—you have left all to follow Christ in poverty, chastity, and obedience. You have not waited for death to begin living in heaven. You have begun it here and now!"

What Rebecca had experienced within the last week was hardly her image of heaven. And when it came to sacrifice, her thoughts turned to Holly's decision to raise Cody despite her sexual abuse and Peggy's decision to move through her childhood trauma and educate herself in order to provide for her family and support the mountain women. Their commitments were just as self-giving as her own—perhaps more. Although she herself didn't personally own property, she mutually possessed the SCR's spacious lakeside grounds, their multiple convents, and was secure of room, board, clothing, employment, and medical treatment until she died. How *ultimate* was her sacrifice, really, considering the sacrifices of the people she witnessed in Appalachia?

Rebecca tuned back into the sermon. " . . .the saint declared, 'Oh, that everyone would enter the monastery!' A novice asked the saint, 'If everyone joined a monastery it would be the end of the world.' The saint beamed and looked heavenward, 'And what a glorious end of the world that would be!'"

Rebecca toyed with her pen, then returned it to her pocket, and closed her journal. Eventually, she no longer heard the preacher.

～

After breakfast, near the end of the retreat, Rebecca walked toward her private cove. The sky was open and blue, the lawns green and lush, the flowers in bloom. Although the temperature was rising, the heat was not yet oppressive and would be even less so in the shade.

"Sr. Rebecca Marise," she heard from behind. Rebecca turned to see Henrietta approaching and cringed. Averting this encounter was impossible—the grand silence did not apply to tête-à-têtes with the superiors. She waited until Henrietta caught up with her.

"My, my, what's the hurry?"

"It's a beautiful day."

"Yes, it is a lovely day. Let's go for a walk."

Rebecca's heart sank, yet she showed no sign of resistance or displeasure as she continued down the path with Henrietta.

Henrietta was different from the other councillors. She was the youngest in the council—early fifties—and exuded a certain receptivity and warmth toward the younger sisters. Her small gestures of appreciation and encouragement meant a lot to Rebecca. Of all the superiors, she would have been the easiest to confide in, but Rebecca had never done so. Monthly until perpetual profession, Rebecca had been obliged to meet with her mistress of formation, and annually as a professed sister she met with Mother or one of her delegates—generally one of her past mistresses. During these colloquies, as they were called, Rebecca did not have a whole lot to say. She got along with others, valued prayer, and was committed to the SCR's mission of teaching. Outside of acknowledging common faults and shortcomings (which she told rapidly, sporadically wiping her sweaty palms on the sleeve of her habit), outlining areas she sought to improve (everything written and rehearsed over and over in her mind), and relaying the ordinary challenges of new teachers, Rebecca had little else to say. Looking back, her previous communications seemed petty and irrelevant. She didn't have a clue about what she would say if Henrietta expected this walk to be her annual colloquy.

"So, you've been one of our missionaries this year."

"Yes."

"I hear from Sr. Mary Maureen that you are an excellent teacher and were a wonderful asset to the community. I want to thank you for going to Whitewaters on such short notice."

Rebecca was speechless. Outside her experience of Whitewaters, Rebecca had never been thanked for fulfilling an assignment, never acknowledged as an excellent teacher or as an asset to a community—nor did she ever expect it. But today, after her recent experience with Mother, Rebecca was anticipating censure, not praise. Confused and disarmed, she fought back tears.

"Sr. Rebecca Marise, are you OK?" asked Henrietta softly. Rebecca could not speak and continued to look down at the path. Henrietta took her gently by the elbow and walked with her in silence until they reached a little bench, set off by itself, overlooking the lake.

The gentleness of her touch, the kindness in her voice, the sensitivity of her silence at last unlocked Rebecca's tears. She did not sob, yet the tears trickled down. She brushed them away with the back of her hand but could not hide them from Henrietta.

"The sisters do good work at Whitewaters."

"Yes . . . yes, they do," said Rebecca, glancing toward Henrietta. Henrietta was looking at her, her brows slightly furrowed; her eyes concerned and kindly.

"The people there love them. . . . I've learned a lot this year."

Some moments went by in silence.

"Yes, we have gifted sisters in Whitewaters. . . . What have you learned while you were there?"

Rebecca let out a little sigh. "The children are more diverse than in our other schools." Rebecca looked out to the lake, "Coming to know them . . . trying to help them learn . . . to help them believe in themselves . . . to understand and respect each other . . ."

"You were doing that before you went to Whitewaters, weren't you?" asked Henrietta gently.

"It's different . . . we can do so much more there. . . ."

"So much more?"

Rebecca told her about Alessandro and Leah and Cody and Jacob, about transitioning the lessons with music, about the math chips, and the games she used to assess the children.

After the brusque treatment of Mother, Petrina, and Pistós, it was a relief to talk to a superior who appreciated the sisters of Whitewaters and the teaching methods they used. She began to relax, and as she relaxed, the perplexities she harboured in her heart began to surface.

Rebecca cleared her throat. "Why . . . why don't . . . why don't our other schools have such a wide range of students . . . like Whitewaters?"

"Well, every area has its own needs."

"Somehow Whitewaters seems more . . . open."

Both nuns looked out at the placid lake. The sun was moving overhead and the shade from a nearby tree disappeared.

Cautiously, Rebecca continued, "We try . . . at Whitewaters . . . to keep abreast . . . of issues . . . of problems . . . you know, like abuse . . . domestic violence. . . . It's a big problem . . . more than I ever imagined. . . . There's a nun, Bev, who works with women . . . you know, women who have been abused. I went to a seminar. . . . She was the speaker. It's an important issue . . . for us to know about."

"There are many charisms in the Church, many apostolic works. We admire the others and are faithful to ours." Henrietta eyed Rebecca closely but her voice remained calm and soft.

Rebecca stammered. "Yes . . . yes, I understand that. It's just that . . . our children . . . some are affected by it. You know, in their families. . . ."

"Sr. Rebecca Marise, we can't solve all the world's problems." While her voice remained kind, a lilt of patronizing amusement came through.

"But we *need* to be aware!" Rebecca halted; she had not intended to speak so empathically and lowered her voice. "We need to be aware . . . to help our children when we can, Henrietta."

"I see you're concerned," said Henrietta, reverting to her previous tone.

Again, Rebecca looked out at the lake following a kayak plying its way across the water. "Bev . . . she doesn't wear a habit."

"You know that not all sisters do."

"Yes," said Rebecca quietly. "She's good . . . She's a very good nun."

"She very well may be." Henrietta turned toward Rebecca. "There are some sisters who would like to wear a habit but their order no longer has one."

"She doesn't want to wear a habit, Henrietta," she said with a sigh. "It could even hinder her work."

"You seem to know her quite well."

"She passes through Whitewaters on occasion."

The convent bell tolled solemnly.

"It's time for the retreat sermon," said Henrietta. "We'd better be heading back."

"Thank you for this time, Henrietta."

Henrietta squeezed her shoulder. "You should hurry along or you'll be late. I'm making my retreat in August."

Rebecca quickened her step. She arrived in the chapel moments before the scheduled sermon and knelt silently, head bowed, with the many sisters already congregated. The retreat master entered the sanctuary and knelt at his prie-dieu, the signal for the organist to intone "Come, Holy Ghost." Rebecca's tears began to well again, but she held them back. Henrietta had been so understanding, so kind . . . and valued the sisters of Whitewaters! Why had she waited so long to speak with her? She would clarify things with Mother.

~

Had Rebecca sat across from Henrietta, rather than facing the lake, she might have been less sanguine. Every time Rebecca, naturally and habitually, used a sister's name without the title, Henrietta grimaced. And when Rebecca said the habit could be a hindrance, Henrietta's brows furrowed so deeply they almost touched.

CHAPTER 79

Henrietta entered her room and resisted the temptation to take off her veil and coif. These were her hours of work and the habit was worn at all times. She walked to her private bathroom—a perk for the members of the general council—and turned on the cold water. After wiping her face and neck with a cool washcloth, she held her wrists under the cold running water for several minutes. An interior door led from her room to an adjoining office. She sat down at her desk and pulled out her journal. She had nothing to write, but somehow by being poised to do so she sometimes calmed herself to reflection. It also gave the appearance of occupation should Mother or another councillor walk through the door.

Mother was in an uproar on her return from Whitewaters. Within an hour of her arrival she called together her council and vented her displeasure openly and at length. Being the councillor who over the past few years had carried out the visitations in Whitewaters, Henrietta was tainted by association and stung by the implication of complicity. Not using the title "Sister," audio novels for spiritual reading, haircuts under the veil . . . How long had this been going on? Had she noticed anything amiss during her annual visits? Henrietta explained that she had focused on the community's prayer, their common life, and their dedication to the apostolate. On these points, all seemed in order. Although under the present circumstances she didn't mention it, Henrietta had also been impressed with the school's overall management and, in particular, the teaching methods they had adapted and honed.

The Whitewaters sisters, always candid, had shared their concerns and hopes regarding the SCRs. But this Henrietta did not include in the reports. She was sympathetic to their concerns and secretly shared some of them herself. However, when Mother related Jeanne's attack on the bishop, Henrietta was aghast. So aghast that it did not occur to her that Mother's report might be overwrought. *No, this was too much!* The thought of her previous sympathy alarmed her. By the time the sisters from Whitewaters arrived at the motherhouse two days later, Henrietta's alarm had dulled the memory of her affinity and was directed entirely at the community. She bitterly regretted having suggested the transfer of Sr. Rebecca Marise to Whitewaters and had decided to speak with her to assess the damage—and damage there was. Sr. Rebecca Marise. Such a promising sister, such a gifted teacher.

Now as she sat with her pen poised, Henrietta bowed her head in self-reproach but this, too, shifted by degrees into anger toward the sisters of Whitewaters. She had trusted them with a young, propitious, perpetually professed sister. And what had they done! Their pride and arrogance! Thinking they knew better than the bishop, most likely, the Pope himself! Mother was right. It begins with the little things, questioning traditions, their long-standing traditions. The little things . . . probed, challenged, set aside. Traditions, slowly eroding until one defies the very authority upon which religious life is approved, safeguarded, and perpetrated. Disregard the little things . . . and before you know it the essence of religious life is threatened. Mother was right. Henrietta was touching first-hand the truth herself. She thought of their rhythm of prayer, the hundreds of schoolchildren they taught, the focus and unity that propelled them forward. Their true founder is the Holy Spirit, Jesus Christ is their spouse, and he continues to guide them through the superiors, the bishops, the Pope, all given the grace and light for their offices. Trust and obedience *are* the keys.

Henrietta closed her journal and picked up a pad of paper. She jotted down notes, preparing herself for the council meeting scheduled that day to discuss the situation of Whitewaters.

CHAPTER 80

Maureen walked up the stairs to the quarters of the general government. It was unusual to be called to a council meeting during retreat; however, with Whitewaters on the line, Maureen was not surprised. She had lost all hope of their continuance in the mission school, and any other alternative regarding her future was disheartening. During the retreat master's sermons, Maureen blocked out the pious exhortations she had heard ad nauseam. She closed her eyes, placed her palms open on her lap, and wordlessly lay bare her heart to God. She had no clue what the future held, no idea how to respond. In the depth of her heart she trusted that God loved her and that a life lived in love, however bleak the terrain, however useless one's efforts appear to have been, was never in vain.

Now, climbing the stairs she suddenly felt the weight of her age. Active, committed, healthy, she rarely considered her sixty-five years. *My God, sixty-five.* She had believed in the ideals of religious life; she believed God had called her to this life; she believed structures could change; she opted to work for change from within. *Sixty-five.* Over forty-five years in the convent. Oh God, where was she now? What had really come of her life? Had she been merely a tool, a cog in the wheel, maintaining the facade of an ideal that never existed, could never exist, that was rotting within? *Sixty-five.* Had her life been a futile attempt to salvage the unsalvageable?

Maureen stood on the landing and opened the door to the corridor of the general government wing. She was surprised to see Jeanne standing outside the door to the council room.

"So, you've also received the summons," said Jeanne. "I thought I was going solo."

"When did you find out?"

"I was informed after breakfast. How about you?"

"The same."

They stood in silence for a few moments.

"How long do you think they'll keep us waiting?" asked Jeanne.

"Who cares. We know the outcome. We won't be going back to Whitewaters."

Neither could have imagined what awaited them when the council door opened.

~

Mother sat at the head of the long square table. The full council was present: four councillors, the secretary, and treasurer—three sisters on either side of the table. Petrina sat on one side of Mother, Henrietta on the other. Maureen and Jeanne were directed to two empty chairs at the end of the table. The sombre expressions on all faces marked the gravity of the situation. Not a word was said as Maureen and Jeanne took their seats.

Mother began without introduction or greetings. "Our presence in Whitewaters has been under review. Invitations have come from other dioceses requiring us to assess the placements of our sisters."

Maureen tensed. Although leaving Whitewaters was expected, she braced herself for the finality of the decision.

"The convent in Whitewaters has been officially closed."

Jeanne let out a sigh, put her elbow on the table, and rested her forehead in her hand. Maureen put her hand on Jeanne's other arm. The other nuns remained as they were, upright with their hands in their laps, the secretary's pen idling on the pad before her.

"Sadly, we have come to discover, all too late, that the sisters in Whitewaters have taken liberties with the rules of our congregation as well as the directives of the Church for religious life . . . and seriously disillusioned one of our newly perpetually professed sisters."

Maureen and Jeanne looked up simultaneously, caught off guard by the accusation.

"What?" exclaimed Maureen.

"Sr. Rebecca Marise Holden," replied Mother.

"*We've* disillusioned Rebecca?" said Jeanne in disbelief.

Petrina shifted in her chair.

"*Sr. Rebecca Marise*," said Mother. "We use the title *Sister* among ourselves. We always have, Sr. Maria Jeanne, to honour each other's consecration to God, as you well know. And yet you have taken it upon yourself to dismiss this tradition, using a merely secular form of address. Quite a common practice in Whitewaters, as I understand," glancing at Petrina.

"Among others," said Petrina. "Styling your hair . . ."

"Oh, how is that possible wearing a veil all day?" said Maureen.

"Your hair is not drawn back at the nape of your neck and cut two inches down."

"It's trimmed. Our hair is easier to wash and dry and, I might add, more suitable to our age."

"What does that matter if you are wearing a veil?" asked one of the councillors.

"Precisely! What does it matter how we wear our hair since it is under a veil?" said Maureen.

"We've heard enough on this, Sr. Mary Maureen," said Mother. "There are other concerns. All our teaching methods are reviewed before establishing them in any of our schools. You know this. And yet we have been informed by Sr. Rebecca Marise that you have implemented several practices that no one in the council has ever heard of, let alone discussed. Do you realize how disturbing this is for a younger sister, intent on living religious life seriously?"

"What are you talking about?" asked Maureen, bewildered.

Mother looked over at Henrietta.

Henrietta looked at her notes in front of her although she had no need. "Math chips, music to transition class periods . . ." and she continued with several others.

Maureen and Jeanne looked at each other. "Rebecca? Disturbed by these methods? That hardly seems possible—" Maureen was interrupted by Henrietta.

"I have spoken with *Sr. Rebecca Marise* myself. She is very upset."

"I find this rather perplexing. The methods you've just stated are very effective," said Maureen. "Our children have responded extremely well to them. Rebecca herself has used them with wonderful results. All of you are well aware that our student body is different from our standard schools. This has been a given from the beginning of our mission in Whitewaters. Our children sometimes require different methods. And our methods have been used openly during all our visitations. This has never been an issue before."

Henrietta kept her eyes fixed on her notes.

"Have you ever brought your methods before the council for review?" asked Petrina.

"Oh, Maureen," interjected Jeanne. "Let's be honest! *Any* of the methods we use would be effective in *all* our schools. This isn't about teaching methods. It's about control."

Petrina glared, Henrietta was appalled, and the others looked on dazed. Maureen sank back against her chair.

Mother, surprisingly, remained calm. Too calm.

One of the councillors said, "We've been informed of your disrespect toward the bishop during Mother's visit, Sr. Maria Jeanne. And your outburst right now only confirms—"

"To disagree is disrespect?" replied Jeanne.

"Interrupting is disrespect," said Mother sharply. "The bishop speaks in the name of Christ and his Church. Your audacity is merely a sign of pride and a clouded intellect."

Petrina stood up and walked to a credenza behind Mother. She brought back a stack of books and placed them on the table. She resumed her seat and said, "These books were all found in your school library. It's no wonder your intellect is muddled, as Mother so aptly pointed out. None of these books have been approved for our communities."

"Sr. Mary Maureen," said another councillor, "you were the superior of the community. Why did you permit these books to be purchased for the library?"

"You've always said the superior has the grace for the office," replied Maureen softly. "The books seemed perfectly suitable for the intelligent, discerning minds that are cultivated among the sisters and staff at St. Martin de Porres."

Murmurs and an exchange of glances took place among the council. Mother shook her head slowly in disbelief.

"It has also come to our attention," said Henrietta, growing more emphatic, "that you've introduced secular dress into your community. This is unquestionably contrary to our traditions and the teachings of the Church. The Holy Father has repeatedly exhorted religious to wear a habit."

Jeanne replied, "I wear secular garb only when serving in remote mountain communities. The people there are wary of the Catholic Church. The habit would be an impediment — at best, a distraction."

From the shock registered on the faces of everyone, including Mother, it was obvious that this was news to them all.

"This is far, far worse than I imagined," said Mother. "No wonder Sr. Rebecca Marise has been so disturbed. Is it any wonder?"

"Rebecca, disturbed?" asked Jeanne. "What makes you so sure Rebecca is disturbed by us, by her life at Whitewaters?"

"Rebecca has told us everything," said Henrietta, "including Sr. Bev."

"Bev? What does Bev have to do with anything?" said Maureen.

"The sister *you* introduced into your community," interjected Mother. "This sister who promotes secular dress—who has already infected you both," said Mother with a flick of her wrist.

"Bev?" said Jeanne in disbelief. "For your information, Bev is one of the most self-giving, generous, intelligent, compassionate sisters I have ever encountered. Ever! This . . . this meeting is ludicrous . . . beyond ludicrous." She threw up her hands. "You? Representatives of *Christ*? This life is a joke. To think I actually believed in it at one time . . . believed in *you* at one time." Jeanne stood up. "I'm done. Fill out the papers, whatever is necessary. I'm leaving." And she walked out the door.

"Jeanne!" exclaimed Maureen and followed her down the corridor.

~

The empty tile-covered corridor echoed her footsteps, the tinkling of her rosary beads, and the swish of her long skirts, increasing her awareness that, rather than arriving among the last for the morning retreat sermon, she would be late. Rebecca quickened her pace. Then, from an adjoining staircase just ahead, she heard a familiar voice. She slowed down as Maureen and Jeanne walked into the corridor. Seeing Rebecca, both stopped abruptly. Rebecca was about to greet them when she was silenced by the expression on their faces.

"What?"

"*What*?" echoed Jeanne. "That's the question on our minds, too." She walked away.

"Maureen, what's going on?"

Maureen looked down the corridor. This was not a conversation for the hallway.

"Come with me a moment, Rebecca." Nearby was a small dining room used to serve guests who were not permitted in the sisters' refectory. Maureen opened the door and glanced inside. The blinds were lowered, the windows closed, and the polished table empty: all signs that the room was not scheduled for imminent use. She entered and Rebecca followed closing the door behind them.

Maureen walked to the far end of the room and pulled out a couple of chairs. Rebecca sat down, baffled. The room was dim, warm and stuffy but neither lifted the blinds or opened a window.

Speaking softly, Maureen began, "Rebecca, Jeanne and I just came from a meeting with the general council. I'm sure the announcement will be made shortly . . ."

Every muscle in Rebecca's body tightened.

"The Whitewaters' convent will be closed. Immediately."

Rebecca froze. From her reaction, Maureen could tell that she knew nothing of the decision.

"You had to have sensed something, Rebecca. During the visitation . . ."

"But I spoke with Henrietta!" Maureen motioned for her to keep her voice low. "She really admires all of you at Whitewaters. She told me so! I thought she would help Mother and the others understand."

It was Maureen's turn to be bewildered. "She told you so?"

"Yes! I told her how much I had learned . . . not just about teaching, but about so many other issues . . . all I learned from Bev . . ."

"Rebecca, you have to be honest with me. Henrietta said you were upset . . . disturbed by your experience in Whitewaters."

Rebecca's face enflamed. Perspiration trickled down her back. "Yes, I was upset by what happened at Whitewaters during our last weekend, but I didn't say anything about Mother or Petrina . . . or Pistós. Are they closing the convent because of me?"

"No, Rebecca."

"I . . . I asked why our other schools weren't more like Whitewaters. Henrietta was so understanding. She must be just as disappointed as we are about the decision."

Maureen leaned back in her chair. *Henrietta, Henrietta.* During the council meeting Maureen was tempted to list the number of times the teachers at Whitewaters had demonstrated particular teaching methods during the visitations—methods that Henrietta encouraged them to develop and use. Maureen could have quoted back some of Henrietta's sage words when they spoke openly of their concerns and hope for change.

But over the years Maureen had witnessed the power of that singular emotion:

fear. The blinding, deafening, paralyzing power of fear. Confronting Henrietta would have been futile. Awareness had already been smothered. Maureen looked at Rebecca, flushed and wide-eyed. She deserved the truth.

"Rebecca, Henrietta is under the impression that you're disturbed by Whitewaters . . . disturbed by our teaching methods, disturbed by Bev's visits, disturbed by our haircuts, disturbed—"

"This can't be true! I tell you, Maureen, she was supportive and spoke so well of all of you at Whitewaters. You must have misunderstood!"

The sound of footsteps clicking down the corridor interrupted the conversation. Petrina and a couple of the other councillors exchanged comments as they approached the dining room. Rebecca turned toward the door but the voices passed by. Maureen knew the drill all too well. Rebecca had been noted missing from chapel and Mother had been informed.

"We can continue this conversation another time. You better go."

"What about you?"

"I'll be along."

Rebecca walked quietly out the door, closing it behind her.

Maureen pulled up the blinds, opened the windows and returned to her chair. Let them hunt.

~

The retreat master stood at the podium, delivering his carefully drafted reflection. Rebecca, perturbed, slid into her pew amidst the silent, seated, attentive nuns. Externally, she melded among the dozens of like-garbed women, yet Rebecca never felt more estranged. The preacher's voice was white noise to her racing thoughts.

Could Maureen be right? No, she must have misunderstood. . . .

But what if it were true? Maureen would never invent such a story.

Despite the air-conditioning, Rebecca's cheeks flushed and her heart pounded like a woman on the run. *Maybe if she went to clarify things with Henrietta . . . But would she just get Maureen and Jeanne into more trouble? . . . Maybe she wasn't seeing things right . . . Maybe she was going crazy . . . Maybe she . . .*

Her eyes focused on the crucifix, the symbol of their submission and sacrifice. *And the curtain of the temple was rent in two.*

Like a slide-show the images flicked by: Mother in the kitchen with Candida,

Mother silencing them with her anger at their last meal in Whitewaters, Petrina scowling at the parishioners during the barbeque, Mother's smugness and condescension at the Pope's rally. The frames went on, right to the orientation following her entrance to the SCRs when, together with the new postulants, she had been told not to tell her parents that their letters were read because, "they wouldn't understand its importance to assist the young sisters in formation."

Reality.

Blunt, harsh, wide-eyed reality.

Deep down she knew.

Yes, Rebecca, you've known, and known for a while.

It was an illusion. An elaborate, pious, idealistic phantasm. From the distance of a rank-and-file nun, obedient, devout, and dedicated to teaching, the illusion could remain intact. Experiencing the inner realm up close exposed the cracks in the veneer.

She had seen, she had heard, she had witnessed, but until this moment, Rebecca could not face it. The meaning of her existence, the purpose of her life hinged, utterly, on belief. Doubting endangered every ideal she had ever embraced.

But it was so. She knew it in the sinews that knit her together, in the blood that coursed through her veins. Her being screamed out the truth . . . and it was terrifying. As Mother's clay feet crumbled and her image toppled over, so did the councillors', and then the bishop's in a domino effect that led, at last, to the Pope. And as his image disintegrated, to her horror, came the ultimate disillusionment—God himself.

The sermon must have ended because the nuns, as one, knelt, recited a prayer, sang a hymn. Rebecca mouthed the words by rote, joined her hands, bowed her head, and left chapel with the others. She felt outside her body, devoid of all conviction and emotion, observing herself going through the motions, dark and hollow like a blown-out Halloween pumpkin with an empty smile carved into its face.

CHAPTER 81

The last day of retreat. Afternoon benediction. Prayers for the plenary indulgence. The retreat master's final blessing.

"Mother would like to see you," said Henrietta as Rebecca departed from chapel.

Rebecca, numb, turned toward Henrietta and, with a mask of acquiescence, smiled and followed her up the staircase.

Go in. Get out. With as little talk as possible, as pleasantly as possible, she told herself.

Henrietta tapped on Mother's door and entered. Mother finished off something she was writing and raised her head as they neared. She motioned for Rebecca to sit in a chair in front of her desk and Henrietta sat in another to the side. Mother put down her pen and put both hands on the desk.

"So you have come to the end of your retreat."

"Yes, Mother," said Rebecca softly.

"It is always good to have the time to pray, reflect, and enter into deeper communion with our Saviour and Spouse, Jesus Christ."

"Yes, it is."

"We are truly blessed to have this privileged time each year."

Rebecca unfolded her damp hands and rested them on her habit.

"I and the sisters of the general government have prayed together regarding the annual transfers. For this upcoming school year, Sr. Rebecca Marise, we have decided to send you to St. Stephen's school and convent."

"Thank you, Mother," said Rebecca in her same calm tone.

Mother leaned back in her chair, her eyes never leaving Rebecca. "You don't seem surprised . . . or disappointed to be leaving St. Martin de Porres."

"You've always told us that we should be ready to leave our posts at the request of our superiors, like a bird on a branch."

"I can see you've made a good retreat." Mother swivelled in her chair, allowing Rebecca to see the afternoon sun glimmering through a tall, leafy tree rising past the office window. "Sr. Rebecca Marise, as we go through life—and this can happen even in religious life—we encounter certain situations, particular behaviours that are not edifying . . . disturbing, in fact. Behaviours contrary to our Rule. Behaviours and attitudes that disregard the teachings of Christ and his Church. In such cases, we need to recall the words of St. Paul to the Galatians."

The oft-repeated quote was so familiar that Rebecca could have mouthed what followed.

"Remember, the Galatians had been doing so well. But Paul discovered that others were upsetting them, distorting the Gospel that he had preached to them. Paul told the Galatians that if he or (raising her voice) *even an angel from heaven* should proclaim a gospel contrary to what he had proclaimed, that person would be accursed!" Mother pointed her finger emphatically toward the heavens as if invoking the veracity of her statement from the saint himself.

"Imagine, St. Paul stating that if *he, himself*, should teach something different! The great apostle Paul!"

Rebecca felt like Dorothy watching the small, arrogant "professor" work the panel of levers to create the wizard of Oz. The curtain had been pulled back, and with that, all previous awe and respect had vanished.

Mother leaned forward. "This is the fidelity we need in our times. The world may go astray. People within the church itself may clamour to modify, to conform to the deviance of our times—the Church's greatest enemies are within—but we must stand firm regardless of how we are judged. God has always worked through a small remnant of faithful followers."

Mother sat back in her chair and glanced at Henrietta—a sign that the meeting was over.

"Sr. Rebecca Marise has some good news," said Henrietta. "Her new little niece will be baptized tomorrow."

"My brother's child," acknowledged Rebecca.

"How lovely. Is it his first?"

"No, he and his wife have three other children."

"What a wonderful family," said Mother to Henrietta. "It's refreshing to hear of a good, Catholic couple so open and welcoming to the gift of life."

"As we discussed sometime back, Mother, Mrs. Holden asked if Sr. Rebecca Marise could be present for the baptism—her brother and his family have come all the way from California." Margaret Holden had relayed everything to Rebecca in the letter she received shortly before leaving Whitewaters

"Yes, yes . . . I recall." Then turning to Rebecca. "So you'll be leaving tomorrow morning."

"Well, due to distance," interjected Henrietta, "her mother requested an overnight stay."

"Yes, quite right. So you'll be leaving this evening."

"Yes, Mother."

"Well, give your mother my greetings and let your family know that they are all in our prayers on this blessed occasion."

"I will."

Henrietta stood and Rebecca with her. To Rebecca's surprise, Mother also arose and accompanied them to the door. With her hand on Rebecca's shoulder she said, "Obedience and fidelity keep us on the path to God. Never forget that."

~

Rebecca knelt on the floor and pulled her suitcase from under the bed. She grabbed her backpack and placed it by her side. Although a metal wardrobe stood near her bed, Rebecca had only unpacked what was necessary for her week of retreat. She opened the suitcase, put her hand under the layer of winter undergarments, and felt the folded slacks and blouse and the packet of disks. She drew them out, put them rapidly in her backpack, covered them with a sweater and pushed the suitcase back under the bed. From her wardrobe she added a pair of sandals, some underclothes, and a tiny bag of toiletries. She then slipped into her Sunday habit and hung her weekday garb on the rod. Reaching into one of its deep pockets she drew out an envelope: *To Mother Mary Thomas*. She put it on one of the shelves, closed the wardrobe, picked up her backpack and walked out of the room.

Supper would be served in ten minutes and her father was due to arrive soon after. Rebecca went to the main entrance to alert the nun on reception duty of her family's pending arrival. To her surprise and relief, she heard the voice of her father and brother conversing in one of the parlours with the sister. Rebecca walked to the entrance of the room.

"Rebecca!" said her father, rising.

"I was on my way to call for you," said the sister, smiling. "Your family just arrived."

Rebecca and her father embraced. Fighting the urge to weep, she turned to her brother who rose to greet her and gave him a brief hug.

"It seems we arrived too early," said her father. "You haven't eaten supper."

"Oh, I'm not hungry," said Rebecca. "I can eat when we get home."

"I'll notify Mother that your family is here," said the sister.

"I just finished speaking with Mother and Sr. Henrietta. They both know that I'm leaving."

As the sister returned to the reception office, Rebecca lifted her backpack, "This is it. Let's go."

Her father and brother, Rob, followed her out the main entrance. Rob took the backpack from Rebecca.

"You travel light," he quipped.

"Next to nothing."

In less than a minute they were loaded and driving out of the convent grounds.

"Mother said that we will serve your family supper in the guest—" The smiling sister stopped as she entered the parlour and looked around. She was speaking to an empty room.

CHAPTER 82

"Sr. Rebecca Marise, you've barely eaten," said Margaret Holden. "I know you practice mortification, but you must have a little more of this fruit salad. Gail . . . you remember Gail from the parish . . . she came across this *scrumptious* recipe. I insisted that she pass it to me for this dinner. She only gave in because you were coming. Here have another spoonful."

Rebecca stood to clear the plates and cutlery. "No, thanks, Mom."

"I don't want Mother Mary Thomas to think we didn't feed you when you return this afternoon. You do look a little peakish. . . . Where did Rob go?"

"He's down in the basement with the kids, catching up on a baseball game . . . Rebecca, just leave the dishes in the sink," said her father as Rebecca walked toward the kitchen. "We'll take care of them later. We see so little of you."

Margaret followed her into the kitchen with bowls of leftovers. "Out, out. You heard your father. When Judy finishes nursing Emily, I'll bring out the cake. Everything is all set."

Rebecca placed the dishes in the sink, ran some water over the mound, and returned to the dining room.

"Let's move to the living room," said Robert. "We'll be out of your mother's way. You know how she is when she has a special meal going." As he and Rebecca settled into more comfortable chairs, he said. "By the way, when exactly do you need to get back?"

"Dad"—Rebecca bit her lip—"I'm not going back."

Robert paused, staring at Rebecca, trying to process this unexpected piece of information.

"You're not going back to the convent? . . . Ever?"

Rebecca looked away out the window. "I don't know how to tell Mom."

Rob strode in, "The Cubs are losing. Down seven to nine."

Neither responded. Rob sat on the couch and put his feet on the coffee table.

"Wait until after the cake," said Robert, not even glancing at Rob.

Rob looked back and forth between Rebecca and his father. "What's going on?" Rebecca continued to stare out the window. Robert let out a sigh.

"Rebecca's leaving the convent."

"What the hell?" Then lowering his voice, "Mom's going to flip."

"You think so?" said Robert, annoyed.

Margaret called from the dining room, "Rob, has Judy finished nursing?" And turning into the living room, "Get your feet off the furniture! How many times . . . ?"

"Mom, I have stockings on." He moved his heels back and forth across the surface. "Consider it polishing."

"Put your feet on the floor this instant. How do you expect to teach your own children?"

"OK, OK, they're off. I'll go see if Judy is ready."

~

The baptismal cake was covered with fondant, carefully piped, and topped with an exquisite white-chocolate lamb.

As Margaret cut the first piece, Judy said, "Thank you, Margaret. You outdid yourself with this cake."

"It's a big day. Emily became a child of God."

"What was she before?" Rob said.

"Emily, is now *indelibly marked* as a child of God and filled with sanctifying grace. You need to study your catechism," replied Margaret, annoyed.

Judy glanced at Rob who winked in return.

"I want the lamb," cried out Brian, who had just turned six.

"No, it's for me!" replied Kristen, seven.

"You can share," said Judy.

Margaret served herself last and ate a couple of bites. "Carrot cake—I just love it." She turned toward Rebecca. "You're awfully quiet. What's wrong with the cake? Everyone else seems to be enjoying it."

"It's fine, Mom. I'm not hungry."

"You've eaten next to nothing since you arrived. Are you feeling OK?"

Everyone focused their attention on Rebecca.

"I'm sure Mother Mary Thomas would allow you to remain another day if she knew you weren't feeling well enough to travel back this afternoon."

A breathless vacuity wreathed among the gathering, sucking the life out of the light banter that Rob and his father had tried to maintain. Even the children looked up from their dessert.

"Mom, I won't be going back."

"What?" Margaret's fork remained poised in her hand over her plate of cake.

"I'm staying here."

"What do you mean, *staying here*?"

"I'm not going back to the convent. I'm staying home."

"You'll do no such thing!" Margaret set down her fork with a clank. "Robert!"

"If Rebecca chooses to remain here, it's her choice."

"She's taken *sacred* vows!"

"OK, kids. Take your cake to the basement," said Rob.

Picking up the seriousness of the mood, the children cleared the table without comment and went downstairs. Caitlyn, now nine, placed her plate on a table and quietly made her way back to the top of the stairs. Kristen followed suit. Brian looked up at his sisters, and then at the unattended desserts. He added a hunk of cake from Caitlyn's dish to his plate and climbed back up the stairs, eating his dessert as they all listened behind the closed door.

"You have made a solemn commitment to God himself! You don't just quit!"

"If Rebecca is leaving, I'm sure she has good reason," said Robert.

"Well, I would like to hear it," said Margaret.

Rebecca sighed. "I don't want to talk about it.".

"Don't want to talk about it! And you expect to remain in this house?"

"It's her home, Margaret!"

Margaret, exasperated, turned toward her husband. "If Rob decided to leave Judy and their children, would you just let him back. Without any explanation?"

"Don't drag us into this, Mom."

"You stay out of this, Rob!" retorted Margaret and turned her attention back to Rebecca. "I received special permission from Mother Mary Thomas for you to come for Emily's baptism, not to run away from the convent." She paused. "To think she might think *I'm* involved in some way. Sr. Rebecca Marise, this is a disgrace."

"Margaret, calm down. Can we try to understand and support—" said Robert.

"I will not support a person who defies the vows she made to God! And uses a family baptism as a ruse to do so! Imagine how this will appear to the parish— to all who know Sr. Rebecca Marise and think so highly of her. How will I ever face the sisters again?"

"Mom, is this about you, or Rebecca?"

"Rob, that is enough!" said Margaret incensed. "You are religiously obtuse. You don't have a clue about what is going on. Don't think I didn't notice Caitlyn's early arrival. Always cutting the corners."

"For Christ's sake!"

"So now you use Christ's name in vain!"

Judy sighed and stood up. "If you recall, Margaret, Rob and I were engaged for over a year. We were a committed couple."

Margaret had no inhibitions reprimanding Rob; however, she was reticent to directly challenge his calm and thoughtful wife. Judy went to join her children in the basement only to be met on the staircase by three wide-eyed listeners.

"Margaret, Rebecca is remaining at home when and for as long as she likes."

"I'll have you know this is my home, too!"

"Just stop!" said Rebecca. In a hushed voice, she continued, "I'm not going back, Mother. I don't care if I have to sleep on the sidewalk."

Margaret stood. "I'm disgusted with you!" She picked up the car keys near the back door and walked out.

"Dad, I can't go back." Her body shook with emotion.

"Rob, get me the phone."

"I don't want to talk to them. I left Mother Mary Thomas a letter in my room."

"Good God."

Robert took the phone from Rob, selected a speed dial, and pushed.

~

Margaret sobbed, surrounded by the three SCRs at the parish convent. "I can't reason with her." One of the sisters offered her a box of tissue. "I don't know what to do."

The parish school sisters were her dearest friends. Although one or another was transferred every year or so, Margaret easily accommodated to the newcomers and they were warmed by her fresh baked goods, willingness to volunteer for any need, and her unbounded support of all they did.

"We'd better call Mother."

Margaret sobbed anew. "She'll be so disappointed."

The superior of the house asked the other two sisters to leave and brought over the phone they kept in their small parlour. She punched in the number by heart and with a few terse comments, had Mother on the line.

"Mr. Holden's already called? . . .Yes, yes, she is right here." The superior passed the phone to Margaret.

"I'm completely baffled. . . . No, sign at all . . . She won't say . . . Yes, Mother. . . . Yes, Mother. . . . Yes, Mother. . . . I'm so terribly sorry. . . . I never would have asked if . . . Of course, Mother, we appreciate it."

Margaret set down the phone. "Mother is such a wise, good woman."

CHAPTER 83

The full council was assembled in the conference room. Mother's eyes welled with tears. "The sacrifices we have made to maintain our mission at Whitewaters for all these years and this is her response?" Mother held up Jeanne's letter requesting a dispensation. "And look at the effect she had on Sr. Rebecca Marise. Her mother is beside herself."

"I'm so sorry I ever recommended her to go to Whitewaters," said Henrietta.

"We should have closed that convent years ago," replied Mother. "Too far removed . . . Much too far removed. Rome would have been closer."

"Those wild, twisted mountains—the demons that wander there," said one of the councillors who grew up along the coast.

"The demons were lurking in our midst," said Petrina.

"Two dispensations . . ." began Henrietta. She shook her head sadly.

"Two of our daughters," said Mother, wiping tears from her eyes. "And what will befall them now? We can only hope and pray."

Seeing Mother grieved as she was affected them all and for a while no one said a word.

"There is nothing more you could have said or done, Mother," said another councillor. "How often have you exhorted us to be faithful to our Rule."

"Yes," said Mother, wiping away a final tear. "At some point each sister must stand on her own two feet. And how clever the devil is in turning us from the path of sanctity. How well he knows the power of a consecrated soul at prayer and in the classroom. If we allow him to wile his way into our thoughts, lodge his pride into our hearts . . . The consequences are before us." Mother pulled out a carefully ironed handkerchief and blew her nose.

"'Discipline yourself, keep alert. Like a roaring lion your adversary the devil prowls around, looking for someone to devour . . .'" quoted Petrina.

"'Resist him, steadfast in your faith,'" said Henrietta, finishing the familiar scripture passage from night prayer.

Mother regarded her council, "We have been warned by the saints, warned by our founders, warned by the Pope. No one is free from temptation—obedience and prayer are our only surety."

～

"You *will* see them. They're my guests," said Margaret emphatically. She wiped the kitchen counter to avoid looking at her daughter. The sight of Rebecca with her natural waves and dressed in a blouse and jeans sickened her.

"You'll be entertaining them alone."

Robert, at work, was not on hand to avert this new round of attack. Rob and Judy had gone to the recreation centre for a few hours in an attempt to remove the children from the Arctic cold front that had settled in the family home.

Under advisement from Mother, Margaret had said little to Rebecca over the past two days, waiting for the visit from Henrietta and the local superior from the parish. Since, from Mother's perspective, Rebecca had already confided in Henrietta, she reasoned Rebecca might do so again and a young vocation could be saved. Margaret kept the impending visit to herself. No one else in the household seemed to understand the seriousness of the matter. The sisters were due to arrive in a half-hour and Margaret had hoped Rebecca would change into her habit for the occasion. But Rebecca refused to even see them.

Margaret took the soft scrub from under the sink and began to clean her spotless stove. Her relentless cleaning, however, wasn't enough to still her churning indignation. She turned abruptly. "Do you have any idea of what you are doing? You just made perpetual vows a year ago!"

Rebecca edged toward the passage to the dining area. "You stay right here, young lady. I've held my tongue long enough! Is this how we raised you? Would you run out on a marriage at the first difficulty! Do you think life with your father has been a picnic?"

There's two sides to that story, thought Rebecca.

"And raising you kids? Do you have any idea of the sacrifices I've made? We keep our promises, Rebecca."

Although she trembled before this tirade, Rebecca would not be cowed into submission. She had no desire to discuss her decision with anyone, least of all, her mother.

"We stand by our word. Especially when we have made a solemn commitment before God himself. Do you realize that in flouting your sacred vows you are imperilling your immortal soul?"

Rebecca continued to move slowly toward the dining room. "I don't want to discuss it."

"I am your mother. I have a duty before God to recall you to your senses. Your eternal destiny is at stake. Do you realize that at this very moment you could be in mortal sin?"

"Mother, I'm begging you to stay out of this." Rebecca hugged her arms to keep her hands from shaking. "I will *never* go back. Ever. And your ranting only strengthens my decision." Rebecca left the kitchen and ran out the door. She darted down the sidewalk, aimlessly turning and veering down one street after another.

～

The afternoon heat and humidity still lingered in the air; however, a breeze had picked up and drew a number of sisters outdoors for their community hour. Maureen and Anita sat next to each other on a bench, watching the sisters at the picnic tables laugh and jest as they played cards or board games.

"It's like nothing has happened," said Maureen.

"Many may not even be aware," replied Anita.

"I doubt that. Mother announced the closure of Whitewaters this morning and not a peep from the sisters. . . . Jeanne is leaving tomorrow."

"She has permission?"

"Pam's coming to pick her up. Mother will be just as happy that she's gone—with or without permission."

"I don't know," said Anita. "Mother seemed rather distraught this morning. She came to the infirmary to ask the senior sisters to pray for a special intention."

"I'd wager most of Mother's dejection is rooted elsewhere. She was humiliated when Jeanne dared to challenge the bishop—you missed *quite* the dinner conversation. It could be interpreted as a mar on our stellar reputation."

"You don't think Mother cares at all?"

"Perhaps at some level . . . wayward daughters leaving. But I can guarantee you, the only lesson learnt will be the need for stricter regulations."

"Closing Whitewaters . . ."

Sr. Mary Augustine, stocky and as driven as ever, came to join them. Maureen smiled and said, "Anita, I would like to introduce you to my guardian angel."

Augustine's ruddy complexion went crimson.

"I have to hand it to you, Augustine, you are quite tenacious . . . and very good. But for this evening Anita and I would like to be alone."

Irked, Augustine got up and walked back indoors.

"You've become quite bold."

"We have nothing to lose, Anita. Let's go for a walk."

They strolled together in silence, down the paths and around the trees that had been their life for over forty years.

"What will Jeanne do?"

"Agencies are looking for people like her . . . willing to work in the hollers."

They walked on in silence.

"What were we thinking?" said Anita, almost to herself.

"We were hoping."

"Some of these younger sisters are more entrenched than Mother," said Anita.

"Or just trusting . . . or infatuated."

"It's amusing—and frightening—to see them surrounding her like chicks around a hen, giggling and chirping, 'Mother, Mother, Mother.'"

"She enjoys it," replied Maureen.

"And, sadly, likes to keep them that way."

"It's not just Mother. Bishop Patterson certainly relishes the pampering and favour he receives," said Maureen.

By this time they had reached the lake and sat on the benches that surrounded the burnt-out barbeque pit.

"Are we hypocrites to wear this habit when we no longer swallow Mother's vision of religious life?" Maureen's voice cracked.

"I don't know." Then, shaking Maureen's shoulder, "You want to go naked?"

Maureen laughed through her tears. Then, serious again, "God, I feel shackled and gagged. How have you survived this past year?"

"I don't think long-range anymore. Life has become very, very simple. I just live each day as it comes."

"Sounds defeatist."

"Not really. My life didn't go as I had hoped and I can't change that. Now I just make the best of what I do have. No one can take away God's respect."

Maureen stood up and walked toward the shore. "I suddenly feel so old."

Anita got up and walked with her. She picked up some flat stones on her way to the lake and when they arrived at the edge, she began to skip them across the surface.

"You were always the best at this," said Maureen, taking a few stones and joining in.

"How's Doug?"

"With the priest shortage? He has nothing to worry about. And, as you know, Whitewaters isn't the most popular destination—off the beaten track with mission churches scattered all over the hollers. I predict the bishop will keep him planted there."

"Have you heard from Rebecca?"

"No. Jeanne is going to try to call her." Maureen threw a stone. It skipped once and sank.

Both turned at the sound of gravel crunching underfoot.

"Pistós!" said Anita, "We've been expecting you."

CHAPTER 84

Robert picked up his office phone.

"Dad, it's not going to work—Rebecca staying here with you and Mom," said Rob in a hushed voice. "You have to hear the way Mom talks to her—when she talks to her at all. Her icy silence is even worse."

"I hear and see enough."

"Well, then, imagine that all day long."

"It was a shock to your mother. She'll get over it."

"Not any time soon. Dad, you've got to see that. God, she even had the nuns over today."

"What!"

"Rebecca refused to speak with them and left the house. Mom's been fuming from the moment we came home with the kids."

Margaret's religious views had grown more rigid as the years passed. Robert learned to avoid conflicts by keeping his thoughts to himself. Watching his daughter's growing interest in the SCRs unsettled him. When she told him she was entering, he advised her to wait, finish college, gain more experience. But Rebecca was decided, supported by the advice from the SCRs and encouragement from her mother. He was left with the only option available—respect her decision. Now, as much as he wanted to believe that his wife would calm down and be more accepting, he, too, was having doubts. Never had he seen Margaret so bitterly unyielding toward their children, not even when she was disappointed by Rob as he sputtered and backfired toward adulthood.

"Where's Rebecca now?"

"Here. She walked in about thirty minutes ago."

Robert pressed his eyes to hold back his tears and growing frustration.

"Dad, if she wants, Rebecca can come to live with us in California until she gets on her feet. Judy agrees completely."

Although Robert saw the wisdom in the proposal, his disappointment and anger toward Margaret mounted. Rebecca was being forced to leave her home and his support because of Margaret's irrational and vehement opposition.

～

That evening, Margaret left the house to attend adoration and benediction at the parish. The rest of the adults met in the living room to discuss Rob's proposal.

Rebecca could see the impossibility of remaining at home, but neither did she want to impose on Rob and his family.

"You won't be imposing. Besides it won't be hard for you to find a teaching job. You'll be on you own in no time," said Rob.

"I appreciate what you are trying to do . . . but I don't want you tangled up in this, Rob. Mom will—"

"To hell with Mom!" said Rob, pushing back in his chair.

"Rob, Mom adores your children. Do you want to ensnare them in this hoopla? And Dad will be caught in the middle . . ."

"Don't worry about me" said her dad.

"It's not worth it," said Rebecca, raising her voice. "And besides, I want to be by myself. I need to be by myself and away from here."

"Where?" asked her dad.

"I don't really care. And I don't want to teach."

"Rebecca, you love teaching!" he said.

"I can't right now." Rebecca looked away and pushed back her hair from her forehead. "You're both with insurance firms. Is there an opening in some branch? Entry level? There has to be something that doesn't require an MBA."

～

Both Rob and Robert worked for large insurance firms that branched throughout the States. By Friday, one of Rob's connections hit upon several openings. Resumés were emailed, weighted with references from colleagues. One branch, in a Midwestern city, responded and set up a telephone interview for Monday the following week.

Rob and his family were booked to leave for California on Saturday. On Friday Judy took Rebecca out, Emily in tow, to buy some clothes and a suitcase. Robert left work early and was home when they returned mid-afternoon. Margaret had yet to be informed of Rebecca's plans and it could be put off no longer.

"You want an ice cream cone?" Rob shouted down the basement stairs. His children came running into the kitchen calling out their favourite flavours.

"Let's see what Mom has in the freezer."

Commotion in the kitchen brought down Margaret from her activities upstairs.

"I'll take care of it."

"Mom, I can scoop out ice cream!"

Margaret didn't reply but simply went to the cupboard to find the cones and took the scooper from Rob. The children were served and skipped under a tree in the backyard licking their treat.

Margaret returned the ice cream to the freezer and wiped the counter. Rebecca and Judy were sipping iced tea and Rob and Robert nursed beers around the kitchen table.

"Why don't you come and join us, Margaret," said Robert. "Would you like something to drink?"

"I might." She filled a glass with ice cubes and water from the dispenser on the fridge but remained standing, leaning against the counter.

"Mom, I've applied for a job at an insurance firm. It looks promising."

"Insurance firm? What would you be doing at an insurance firm?"

"Enrolment rep."

"Enrolment . . . isn't that . . . ?"

"Data entry, Mom."

"Data entry!"

"Most likely in the Midwest."

Margaret set her glass down on the counter and looked at the faces of the rest of the family seated at the table. "I see all of you knew this except me."

"I'm telling you now."

"A little late. Always some scheme brewing in the background. I'll never be able to trust you again."

"For God's sake, Margaret!" exclaimed Robert. "We never know how you're going to react."

"And I never know what's up your sleeve! Go, Rebecca! Your mind is made up. Run away from your responsibilities! You can't even face the nuns to tell them you're leaving! I know the whole story—the letter you left behind. Cowardice! Is this how we raised you?"

"Margaret, enough!" Robert stood up, adamant. "This is the end of any discussion about Rebecca's decision. I don't want to hear another word. Not another word."

"I've said all I need to say."

"That's a relief," said Rob, only to be silenced from further comment by the glares he received from Judy, his dad, and his mother.

~

"Rebecca, the offer is open," said Judy as she hugged her goodbye. "You're always welcome in our home."

"Thanks." Rebecca kissed Emily and handed her back to Judy. She turned to hug her nieces and nephew before they climbed into the rented minivan. Robert watched from the lawn with Rob.

"She puts up a good show with the kids," said Rob.

"She's a ghost of herself," replied his father.

Margaret came out the door with a bag of fruit and snacks. "Judy, just a little something for the trip."

"Mom's been pretty hard on her," continued Rob. "Maybe after some time away . . ."

"That's the issue—being kept away."

CHAPTER 85

The sun was setting and the trees cast long shadows over the sidewalk and lawns, making the humid evening air more bearable. For a long time Rebecca and her father walked in silence. Tomorrow he would head back home.

Rebecca had secured the enrolment rep position and, a week after Rob and Judy left, she flew to the Midwest with her father. She had no bank account, no credit or insurance history, no savings or income, no debit or credit card, no furniture, and just a handful of clothes. As far as her financial, tax, and insurance records were concerned, she had been nonexistent for the past nine years. Renting a car would have been impossible, let alone an apartment. She set up an account at a local bank and, with her father's backing, procured a furnished bachelor suite near a bus route. That afternoon they had completed the walk-through, received the key, and stocked the cupboards and fridge with groceries. The next morning, after her father left for the airport, Rebecca would move in.

"Dad, you've been so good to me. I'll pay you back for everything."

"Rebecca, that should be the least of your worries. Don't give it a thought."

"I'll pay back everyone—Rob and Judy, the sisters for my education."

"You also gave to the sisters, don't forget that."

"I don't want a handout."

Robert looked at his daughter, aching to understand.

"I know you don't want to discuss this . . . and you don't have to. But you know you can tell me whatever you want, whenever you want."

Rebecca kept her eyes to the ground as they continued to walk.

"Dad, don't get offended. Promise me."

Her father put his arm around her shoulder, "Just let me know what's troubling you."

Rebecca looked ahead.

"You're not really into God, are you?"

"A little differently than your mother. But I believe in God."

"You don't believe in the Church."

"Let's just say, I never took the Church as seriously as you and your mother."

"But you go to Mass every Sunday."

"It's important to your mother. I respect that."

"So it's a façade."

"It's peaceful . . . something we do each week together. Your mother has her reasons and I have my own."

Rebecca kicked a pebble off the sidewalk. "I can't live that way. It's lying."

"Well, for me, believing in God is a lot more about how you live and treat others. And if I bend to please your mother an hour a week—it's just part of life. I take from Mass what I find inspiring and leave the rest."

Again they walked in silence.

"It's all a charade . . . March to the beat of the drum, accept everything with trust. . . .It's idyllic, inspiring . . . unearthly. Only blind faith holds it all together. Once you begin to question, the underside appears—knotted, tangled, ravelled, fleeced. The distortion, the control . . . an utter certainty that's . . . that's . . . downright arrogant, even mean. And it's all in the name of Jesus."

Rebecca let her fingers run across some bushes that bordered a lawn.

"As you see it, you realize you knew . . . deep down you saw it long before."

Her voice cracked and her eyes filled with tears. "There's no God. The Pope? Infallible? Enforcing that structure, backing up Mother? . . . He is a man . . . fallible and limited, like all of us. . . . We want our lives to mean something . . . we create illusions. We're caught up in a vortex of desperate faith . . . so desperate we lay our minds at the feet of others. There's nothing, not really. Nothing but oblivion."

~

Tears rolled down her father's face. Rebecca's despair was beyond anything he had imagined. He was only grateful that she had trusted him enough to share it.

They continued to walk in silence, his arm around her shoulder; her arm around his waist. The occasional passersby diverted their eyes, leaving the mourners to their grief.

What had they done to her? . . . What had he done to her?

CHAPTER 86

Rebecca turned the key and opened the door to her tiny suite. Her father hadn't been happy with it, but Rebecca refused to see anything that would exceed her ability to save from her limited income.

She set her suitcase near the entrance and locked the door. She crossed the room, lifted a gritty slat of the mini-blinds, and looked out her only window into a row of scanty backyards, some ground down to mud by their high-strung dogs. Footsteps pounded overhead and a door slammed. Startled, Rebecca turned. Next to her was a worn sofa bed, pocked and spotted with stains that chronicled its long history. It was encircled by a rug bearing bleach marks from some overzealous renter of the past. The heat in the closed room was stifling. Rebecca pulled up the blinds and attempted to open the window. The aged wooden frame, swollen with humidity and heat, refused to budge.

She struggled for several minutes. Her head began to spin, she groped for the couch, and sat with her head in her hands. Still dazed, she opened her eyes. Just beyond, in front of the kitchenette, were two chairs on opposite sides of a Formica topped table. The metal legs, laced with fine lines of rust travelling up the scratches, began to swirl and dance around the room. Before her head touched the sofa cushion, Rebecca blacked out.

PART THREE

CHAPTER 87

Andrew lingered in the airport terminal watching the line of travelers trudge slowly through the serpentine course leading to the security entrance. When Rebecca passed out of sight through the glass doors, he wandered aimlessly through the labyrinth of airport kiosks and shops, surrendering the hope that she might change her mind. It was only a week ago that she'd divulged her plan.

"What if they're right?" Rebecca had said, her voice low.

"How can you say that?" asked Andrew, astounded. "How can you even imagine that?"

"I'm just telling you what I feel when I think back. It gets confusing. . . . Why do I avoid my mother? Why can't I just let her believe what she wants to believe and remain in peace?"

Rebecca looked over at Andrew as they walked through the park that bordered the river. "It's become clearer to me during these past weeks, telling my story to you. Dealing with my mom brings up that nagging, haunting fear, 'Maybe she's right.'" Then dropping her voice, "God, look what's become of my life."

"You survived. Give yourself some credit."

"I'm afraid I'll just drift, that I'll never be happy."

"What's 'happy' anyway? Being under the illusion that you know all the answers?" Andrew stopped and looked at Rebecca, "Do you really believe that a loving God would have wanted you to remain in that system . . . would have wanted you there at all? Your dad was certainly apprehensive. Why do you focus on your mother?"

Rebecca looked off and shrugged. "She embodies my fear?" Then she shook her head. "It's absurd, I know. On one level, I reflect on what happened and I'm confident in my decision, yet, slithering deep down are doubts and fear. Some nights, I break out in a sweat. It's gotten worse since I started talking to you."

"I'm glad I've been so helpful," said Andrew wryly.

Rebecca put her arm through Andrew's as they walked, "I'm just telling you how it is." Both remained silent as they continued on.

"I need to go back," she said at last.

"You want to re-enter that convent?" exclaimed Andrew, his surprise breaking through his usual unflappable demeanour. Unbeknown to Rebecca, it masked his near horror.

"No!" said Rebecca, sounding just as surprised that he would think she would even consider it. "I left feeling betrayed, angry, disillusioned. . . . I need to go back and see with my eyes now. I need to discern with my experience now; to understand from my perspective now. I need to find peace—and purpose."

Rebecca resigned from Secure Star—that was no surprise—and booked a flight back East.

Andrew had no idea who he would encounter when she returned.

CHAPTER 88

S ally hung up the phone. At last she knew the truth. Members of Centre City Christian Fellowship, led by Chuck Blaston, hired an auditor to examine the church's finances, and it was true—Rev. Martin had gambled on real estate with church funds. His initial success in flipping a house netted him a handsome bundle and made him bolder. He purchased another house, "borrowing" the down payment, as he had done before, from the church coffers. This time the resale was sluggish and he needed to unload the house quickly. He knew Don was unhappy with his rental and interested in purchasing a place of his own. So Rev. Martin "tipped off" Don about a property of "an old friend" that was going for a good price. Claiming to be the third-party mediator of his friend and having Don's implicit trust, Rev. Martin handled all the transactions. He was able to return the borrowed funds without detection but, selling at a loss, he also had to forfeit most of his profit from the previous sale.

The narrow escape dampened Rev. Martin's urge to invest in such a risky manner. His resolve weakened when the housing market heated up. With a gap of a few years to dull the memory of his near miss, Rev. Martin again used church funds for a down payment. Shortly after his purchase, however, a major manufacturer in the region announced an unexpected downturn resulting in numerous layoffs. The housing market deflated. To cover the missing funds and give himself more time to recoup the money Rev. Martin padded the records of church expenditures. But Chuck Blaston became suspicious and, when confronted, Rev. Martin confessed. Rather than wait for a full audit and complete disclosure from Rev. Martin, Chuck felt impelled to inform to his fellow members not only of Rev. Martin's misuse of church funds but Don's suspected complicity in the scandal. A few weeks later, now as the new pastor, he urged his members to ignore the rumours implicating Don (without stating he had started them). In the final report, he said, the auditor was reasonably certain that neither Don nor the first buyer were aware of any wrongdoing.

"I'm truly sorry about the accident . . . about Don," said Betty as she finished the story.

Betty was the only church member who had broken through Sally's impasse with Centre City Christian Fellowship. After Don's death Sally cancelled Betty's after-school services and left her children in the care of the elderly couple next door until she came home from work. Sally wanted no ties whatsoever with the fellowship. However, Betty had always been kind to the children and willing to accommodate delays or unexpected overtime so Sally agree to speak with Betty when she called her that evening.

"If you need anything, just let me know."

"We're fine," said Sally as civilly as she could.

"We miss you at Centre City Christian Fellowship. You and your children are always welcome. In fact, Rev. Blaston asked me to give you his greetings and the promise of prayers from the fellowship"

So Betty had been commissioned to seek out the lost, to inform her that Don had been exonerated and that she and her children could now rejoin the fold. Sally marvelled at Chuck's audacity.

"I really must go now, Betty. Good night."

In the weeks following Don's death Sally struggled to assume responsibility for the household. Sally's distress subsided significantly when, following Andrew's suggestion, she looked into Don's past benefits. As it turned out, she was not as stretched financially as she had thought. During his year with Reliable Trucking Don had been contributing to a life insurance policy. Although he had been laid off, Don's benefits had extended to the end of the month and Sally received a sizable sum. It was enough to keep her family afloat until she could formulate some plan for the future.

CHAPTER 89

"Can you believe the bitch took off on us," said Gladys to Sally during one of their coffee breaks.

"Well, she promised she'd be back."

"What do you have going for the weekend?"

"Nothing much."

"I know you're still angry with the bastards over at your old church, but I'm telling you, there's a good thing going on at South Side."

Sally looked askance at her only remaining friend.

"Look, it's not the hellfire BS you're used to. And it's not always the same people up there preaching. There's this woman—"

"A woman preaching? How did they pull that off?"

"Not all churches are like the tight-assed group you belonged to. Anyway, this lady is amazing. She's got a series going about relationships, and you know my record with guys. Ben's great and I don't want to screw up. I'm going every Sunday just to hear her—God, can you believe it?"

Sally still looked sceptical. "I haven't crossed the threshold of a church since Don's death," she said.

"Just come and hear her once. If nothing else, your kids will be hanging out with mine in the children's programs and you can lean back in the comfy seats and sleep."

~

Caleb stared up at his mother. "We're going to church?" Deborah and Sarah stopped what they were doing.

The only religious practices that Sally now observed were thanksgiving before meals and bedtime prayers. The latter she continued only because her children prayed for their father, "who was now with Jesus in heaven," and it seemed to bring them some peace. Regarding God, Sally wasn't sure what she believed anymore, but listening to her children's tender prayers at night, she had decided to go gently on their beliefs.

"We're going to Gladys's church. You'll see Jeremy, Sasha, and Eliza." At the sound of their friends' names, the children brightened up but Sally sensed their anxiety.

"Will Dad get mad at us if we go?" Deborah asked.

So this was it. After Don's death, Deborah had become the model daughter. Sally never heard a whine or complaint from Deborah's lips and she rallied the other children into compliance if they objected to bedtime or their chores. Sally surmised that Deborah, being the oldest, had sensed more acutely the strain entailed in running the family after the sudden loss of her father. But what do you say to a sweet, dutiful, obedient child—relax and misbehave once in a while? Deborah's question now threw a new light on her behaviour. Her strict father no longer had a limited, physical presence. He was everywhere, watching her every move, right there next to Jesus.

"Deborah, I know that Dad wanted us to go only to the fellowship. But Dad wasn't always right. Sometimes he made mistakes." Sally sat near her children, "Dad can't get angry at us from heaven. I think he is so happy that he stopped being mad and he just smiles at us now."

Her children didn't make a move.

"Let's make a deal. We go to church with Gladys for a few weeks then decide if we want to keep going.

~

The singing was underway when Sally settled in a chair next to Gladys and greeted Ben who had saved their two seats. Gladys was right regarding the woman preacher. Her theme today was letting go of resentments. She even managed to get a laugh out of Sally. The pastor gave a few closing remarks.

After thanking the preacher he said, "You know, sometimes we find ourselves in the middle of crisis, in the middle of a relationship that we have allowed to fester with resentment. We find ourselves disgruntled in a job we hate or swamped by debts that we have allowed to accumulate. We whimper and blame everyone else for our problems. We plead with God to rescue us. We want him to fly in like Superman, grab us by the scruff of the neck and pull us out of our mess.

"God is not a rescuer. God is an empower-er. And the angels he sends to help us are not covered in feathers. They may be the people sitting next to you; they may be debt managers who teach you how to live within your means; they may be friends who encourage you to further your education, to step out of what has become comfortable yet is stifling you. How do you know it's God?" the pastor asked. "You know it's God when you begin to take responsibility for your life and help others to do the same. It's easy to complain, blame, and feel sorry for ourselves. It's another thing to step out in faith, to take responsibility for ourselves, trusting that God will be there to help us—not rescue us—but help us every step of the way. Learn from the past then push forward toward the future. It's wide open and grace filled."

Sally didn't move a muscle.

CHAPTER 90

Rebecca drove from the Crossroad to the outskirts of Whitewaters. The city was small—most would consider it a town—but Rebecca had spent so much of her time within the convent-school complex that she really didn't know her way around. She pulled into a parking lot to consult a map and refreshed her memory. More confident, she headed toward the ridge that overlooked Whitewaters and held so many memories.

The engine automatically shifted to a lower gear as her car climbed the side of the steep embankment. The familiar narrow road turned sharply then the car swung quickly into the main entrance of an upscale condo complex constructed with an alpine motif. There was no sign of the church and convent that had once shared this lower ridge. Rebecca glanced up toward the school but bushes and trees blocked her view. She drove back out to the road, went up to the top level and parked the car. Before her was an array of buildings with the same alpine theme, recasting the ridge that had formerly housed the school, playground, and yard. The upper and lower ridges were so transfigured that Rebecca could not even mentally place the modest buildings that had structured her life for ten months. She walked to a half-moon terrace that extended past the edge of the ridge and overlooked the holler. Before her were the mountains and trees, wisps of mist hovering within and the clouds drifting above the holler—a scene that had soothed, beckoned, and enchanted her since her first morning at Whitewaters years ago. Without this vista she would have questioned her location. But, undoubtedly, this was it.

A door closed somewhere behind her. Rebecca turned. A smartly dressed couple with a young child were leaving one of the units and walking down the road toward the lower level.

"Excuse me," said Rebecca as she approached the couple. "Do you know what happened to the church and school that used to be here?"

The couple looked at each other puzzled. The wife shook her head. "No, sorry, we're from Florida and rent a summer vacation condo here." She took a deep breath and gestured to the hills, "We come for the cool mountain air—never heard of a church and school."

Rebecca went back to the terrace, lingering a little longer with the mountains, watching the clouds slowly glide over the holler. Reluctantly she turned away and walked to the main office below. She asked the young clerk for a list of the churches in town. St. Martin de Porres was still on the list but its new location held little interest for her. Rebecca pulled out of the parking area and headed for Birchbark.

~

"Well, look what the wind blew in," said Jeanne.

Rebecca stepped off the staircase that came up from the side entrance of the Birchbark Women's Centre. "The receptionist in the clinic told me I would find you here."

"You have good timing. The art session ended about fifteen minutes ago."

"I was waiting outside in my car. I saw the women leaving."

Neither woman had moved from the spot where they stood when they had first caught sight of each other.

Jeanne, in many ways, was just as Rebecca remembered her, albeit without the habit. Her hair was a short cut, blown back, a little greyer than before perhaps. And when Rebecca stepped into the meeting room, there she was, in front of her easel, gently dabbing in the details on a painting. Now she stood, her hand suspended, looking at Rebecca as if she had seen her only yesterday and, at the same time, as if Rebecca had risen from the dead. Neither said a word.

"Jeanne?"

Jeanne blinked into the present. She set down her brush, walked toward Rebecca, and embraced her warmly.

Holding her at arm's length, she said, "Rebecca, you look great."

Rebecca regarded Jeanne without a word. Their ten months together at Whitewaters had imperceptibly bonded them together. However, following the debacle at the missionary outpost, each had plunged into very different worlds. Years had passed.

"How long are you in Birchbark?" asked Jeanne.

"I don't know."

Jeanne moved back toward the easel and began to put away her art supplies.

"I'm finished for the day. Why don't you come over to my place for tea?"

CHAPTER 91

"Is mint tea OK?" Jeanne asked from the kitchen.

"That's fine," Rebecca answered from the adjoining room. She rose from the rocking chair and walked toward a windowless wall to admire a painting that was decidedly Jeanne's. She leaned over a round wooden dining table, then put a knee on one of the few chairs that surrounded it to stretch in for a closer look. The squeal from the boiling kettle brought her attention back to the room. In addition to the rocker and dining set, the only other significant piece of furniture was a futon. A motley collection, for sure, yet each piece possessed a rustic character creating a certain kinship among them. This was furthered by the patchwork runner that covered the scarred tabletop and the patchwork quilt that lay over the futon's weary upholstery. A small TV sat on the top of a low bookshelf, but judging from the long cords that flowed from its base down the side of the bookshelf, the TV made the rounds of the room according to need.

Rebecca walked toward the door that opened to the galley kitchen. "Do you need some help?"

"I'm almost done; besides only one person can fit in this kitchen." Jeanne reached into a cupboard. "Here are a couple of mugs"—then taking some cutlery from a drawer—"and spoons."

Rebecca brought the mugs and spoons to the table and was soon followed by Jeanne with the teapot and a plate of cookies.

"Well, you found your way back to Birchbark," said Jeanne after she had poured the tea.

Rebecca nibbled on a cookie. "The school is gone. The church and convent, too. Not a trace is left."

"So you visited the site."

"It was surreal."

"The school closed the year after we left."

"That long," said Rebecca, her voice flat.

Jeanne tilted her head and smiled. "I see you've developed a sense of irony."

Rebecca gave a slight nod, listening intently as Jeanne filled her in. "Doug scrambled to find replacements when he heard the news that the SCRs wouldn't be returning. A couple of teachers came out of retirement to give the parish a chance to recoup. Doug offered me a job but I felt it would only rankle the bishop and threaten the school's future. As it turned out, it wouldn't have made a difference one way or the other."

"So the parishioners opted to close the school?"

"Oh, no! The January after we were pulled from the school, the bishop wrote a letter to the parish. He said the people of Whitewaters would be better served if the focus of St. Martin de Porres moved from education to evangelization. He expressed concern about the Catholicity of the school: the SCRs could no longer provide sisters and there was a limited pool of Catholic schoolteachers to choose from in the vicinity. He failed to consider recruitment. . . . Over the years Maureen had hired young teachers right out of university looking to serve in Appalachia for a couple years. A few of them even married and settled in Whitewaters. But as the events unravelled, it appeared Catholicity was actually a minor issue."

"What happened?"

"The bishop said the diocese could no longer provide for a school that showed no promise of sustaining itself. In reality, the diocese contributed very little to St. Martin's but without the bishop's backing, the school lost its funding from a national Catholic outreach organization. It was impossible for the parish to shoulder the financial burden alone, especially when two full-time teachers and a principal were added to the payroll. So the doors were closed.

"That left both the school and convent empty. As Doug and the parish council met to determine the best use of the buildings, the bishop and some diocesan financial officers were moving ahead with their own plans. Developers had long been interested in the parish site. It's close enough to Whitewaters to benefit from all the amenities and recreational facilities in the area and, at the same time, it's quiet and secluded. The view is spectacular."

"The condos look rather exclusive."

"Five-star exclusive. Yes, a high-end developer made the diocese an offer: in exchange for the ridge they were willing to give a plot of land wedged in a corner of the holler just big enough to house a modest church with a basement hall, a tiny parish office and, in the rear, compact living quarters for the priest—plus a hefty sum for the diocese. Brand new facilities for a small mountain parish? And the parish rid of the responsibility for buildings they did not need? To the bishop and his team, it was a win-win for all involved."

"I'm guessing this didn't go down well with the 'founding fathers.'"

Jeanne laughed. "Nor the 'founding mothers.' They were the folks who had donated the land and shook down every friend and organization they could to build the church, school, and convent. When they realized that the sale was a foregone conclusion, they called for the establishment of a parish endowment fund managed by a parish financial board. In this way, the money from the property could be used to support the parish and its mission churches and develop other forms of service, like a daycare or after-school programs. But the bishop would hear nothing of it. It was his responsibility, he said, to allot church funds where they would be the most beneficial—a comment that nettled the locals. Whether intended or not, he gave the impression that money spent on children in a poor region of Appalachia does less good than in a more affluent region to the east. Needless to say, a number of parishioners are now worshiping in the Episcopal Church. The Episcopalians call them 'AWOL Catholics.'"

"So, how much money did the diocese make on the sale?"

"Given its location and view, the estimated value of the property without the buildings was several millions—at least."

"How did Doug handle it?"

"He didn't. He was furious. Challenged the bishop every step of the way, especially regarding the hierarchy's record of 'pastoral allotment of funds.'

"He dug up the cost of the temporary altars built for the Pope when he celebrated Mass during his last visit—$400,000.00 for one, if I remember correctly—and the altar was used for less than twelve hours! Then he looked into the expense of World Youth Days. Even I was shocked that the amount needed for increased city transportation, traffic control, and security, let alone the rent for the venues, food, and all the rest. Bishops, priests, young people travelling thousands of miles to boost their faith? That can't be done at home? What's the purpose? To get a glimpse of the Pope on a Jumbotron? Ultimately, Doug pointed out, it's the taxpayers and the people in the pews who have to fork out the money for the debts incurred.

"Doug really roused reprobation when he cited the sums of money 'allotted' to pay out the settlements for sexual abuse claims. . . . Well, you won't find him in Whitewaters. He's been transferred to Slandail—chaplain in one of the hospitals."

Rebecca began to fidget. The room was suddenly confining.

"Are you OK, Rebecca?"

"I just need to walk a bit. Can we go outside?"

~

The late afternoon sun filtered through the trees and a stiff breeze kept the mosquitoes from alighting. They walked quietly through the neighbourhood, passing homes built over fifty years ago. Occasionally a person rocking on a porch shouted out a greeting to Jeanne. Passing vehicles tooted, the driver waving a few fingers from the steering wheel. Townsfolk they met on the sidewalk stopped to chat for a few minutes. Eventually Jeanne veered off to a path that followed the river.

"What happened to the children?" asked Rebecca softly.

"They went to other elementary schools."

"Alessandro?"

"He did OK from what I understand. He and his sister stayed at St. Martin's for its last year, then the family moved east to a larger city —both parents found jobs as janitors in a hospital."

"Jacob?"

"You know Jacob. A born entertainer. I meet his mother sometimes when I'm in Whitewaters—she works in a supermarket there. Both her boys are doing fine. She asks about you from time to time."

Rebecca cleared her throat. "And Cody?" Her chest tightened.

"Holly married about three years ago. Had a little girl." Jeanne paused and looked over at Rebecca. "A couple of years ago Cody's class went on a field trip into the mountains. . . . He got too close to the edge, it seems. . . ."

Rebecca stopped walking and stared at Jeanne.

"No one knows for sure what happened. Fell down the ridge to the rapids below. They never found his body."

Rebecca gasped. Searing rage shuddered through her body until, heaving, it gushed forth in waves of unending sobs.

~

Rebecca awoke in a daze and took in the strange environment. Her suitcase lay askew on a chair near the dining table. Jeanne sat in the rocker reading.

"Well, look who woke up," she said as she placed a bookmark and closed the book.

Rebecca closed her eyes and dozed again. After several minutes she awakened and muttered, "How long have I been sleeping?"

"About fifteen hours."

Rebecca sat up on the opened futon, held her head until the fog cleared then shuffled to the bathroom. She gazed at her mussed hair and puffy eyes in the plastic-framed mirror. Every muscle ached, every sensation grated, but worse, her heart was stripped and raw.

Jeanne had the futon up and the coffee and toast ready when she reappeared in the main room.

"How are you feeling?"

Rebecca sank in a chair. "If a two-year-old frowned at me right now, I would burst into tears."

"I want you to stay here and rest—for as long as it takes," said Jeanne.

CHAPTER 92

For the first week, Rebecca did little more than sleep and make attempts at light housework.

"I feel like a slug on your mirror," said Rebecca after a couple days. "Doing nothing and getting in the way."

"Rest," was Jeanne's only response.

By the fourth day, she remembered to recharge her depleted cell phone—a departing gift from Andrew—and checked her messages. She hadn't contacted Andrew since she had landed at the Crossroad, and in his successive voice mail messages, his tone of voice had become increasing concerned. Rebecca had no desire to talk to anyone and only texted to say she was fine.

During the second week she began to take walks along the river for hours on end. Tears flowed as she recalled her days with Leah, Alessandro, Jacob, Mariarosa, and Cody . . . always Cody. She felt she had deserted them—deserted him, left him vulnerable and unprotected. Had his fall been a distracted slip, a simple misfortune? Or bullying that went too far: a shove intended to cause a stumble but sent him over the edge? Or, most painful of all, had he wanted to fall?

And then would come the rage—at Mother's hauteur, her undisputable certainty; at the time, effort, and money to showcase the diocese, the bishop and their congregation during the anniversary year; at so little done to appreciate and preserve a school that not only valued academics but honoured the local culture—a school willing to learn from agencies and leaders in the larger community on how to address the needs and challenges of their families. The sisters and staff at St. Martin's had spearheaded teaching methodologies and attitudes toward the students and their families that could only have improved the SCR schools statewide. Yet the sisters who piloted these programs had been withdrawn and ostracized and the school closed a year later.

Rebecca reproached herself for indiscriminately accepting all she had been taught during her formation years and for repressing her misgivings and doubts. And she was enraged at the Pope and the hierarchy, whose authority she had trusted, for tossing endless laurels at the feet of Mother Mary Thomas. Their commendation augmented Rebecca's belief that Mother's every disposition was the will of God and intensified her guilt when doubts seeped up. She was infuriated at the Pope and Vatican officials who wittingly or unwittingly gave their approval to a style of life that thwarted the individual sister's capacity to think critically and freely in pursuit of goodness and truth. These men, speaking in the name of God—the Pope infallibly, so they were taught—ratified a life-long commitment under church-sanctioned rules that formed an army of young women who did the Church's biddings without question, disposed to view their religious superiors as conduits of the Will of God and assured of eternal salvation, even sainthood, if they were faithful.

Rebecca recalled the many visits of Bishop Patterson and the intermittent visits of cardinals and Vatican officials, all beaming when greeted by the smiles and songs of a multitude of young sisters. The prelates basked in the attention of the coddling superiors, each party enjoying reciprocal fawning and eliciting each other's support. The Stepfordian atmosphere never seemed to give the high-ranking clerics pause. The silent departures of novices and sisters never mentioned; the disenfranchised "unavailable"; the questioning sent to the missions; the spokes-sisters reiterating what they had all heard umpteen times in classes and lectures from superiors and formation mistresses. All this went unnoticed. To the ecclesiastical officials, the SCRs were faithful to the Church, God was blessing them with vocations, and they were wholeheartedly supportive of the hierarchy. The accolades flowed. Yet few, if any, of these prelates would ever buckle down under Mother Mary Thomas's control over the minute details of *their* lives—minute right down to the style of underwear or how much toilet paper should be used for each wipe. And most certainly they wouldn't relinquish their credit cards or stand in line to request permission to obtain a new pair of socks.

~

The extended walks stretched into the third week. Rebecca would lie on the futon until she heard Jeanne leave for the centre. Then she would eat a light breakfast, buy some food at the local store, and set off. In the evening she would return, talk a while with Jeanne, take a shower, and go to bed.

As the days went by, her tears came less frequently and her roiling rage simmered to anger. However, her self-reproach, like a burr, rasped across her memories. She berated herself for her naivety and ingenuousness, for giving scant consideration to her father's reservations, for abdicating her capacity to think and discern. Rebecca's current perspective rendered her unmitigated docility utter lunacy, plunging her to the depths of humiliation that no denunciation from without could have ever conjured.

CHAPTER 93

On that first evening, Jeanne sat silently next to Rebecca near the path on the matted grass and gravel. She wiped away her own tears as Rebecca heaved with sobs for over an hour. For the first week Jeanne worried that Rebecca might require more help than just the rest she had recommended, but as the days went on her lethargy diminished and long walks ensued. When Jeanne left for the centre in the morning, Rebecca was asleep on the futon. When Jeanne returned home, the futon was upright, the house cleaned, and Rebecca gone. The only sign that she hadn't left entirely was the zipped suitcase stowed in a corner of the room. Initially Jeanne had prepared enough supper for both of them, but Rebecca invariably returned in the evening having already eaten. She would inquire about Jeanne's day but kept the conversation strictly to the mundane.

～

One evening in the third week Rebecca had prepared a cup of tea and sat at the dining room table. "What happened at Whitewaters?"

Jeanne looked up from a book she was reading, feeling like she had missed the first half of a conversation. "During the Civil War?"

Rebecca gave out a light chuckle, realizing the suddenness of the question. It was the first time Jeanne had heard her come close to a laugh since she'd arrived.

"During Mother's visit."

Jeanne set down her book. "You were there."

"I missed a lot."

"Is there more tea prepared?"

"A whole pot."

Jeanne returned with a mug and gently rocked in her favourite chair.

"From my perspective, the Whitewaters mission continued as long as it did because it was a convenient way to house Anita and Maureen away from the motherhouse. Both sisters were perfectly capable of managing any of our larger schools, the entire congregation for that matter. But neither looked starry-eyed at the hierarchy or Mother and her council. Nothing disparaging, mind you, but they weren't afraid to question. An oddity, those two. Intelligent, committed . . . seeking, I guess. . . . They didn't fall among the minimalists who were content to coast along or the malcontents who were indiscriminately irritated. Being in Whitewaters opened them to other realities and points of view. They were no longer enclaved within the motherhouse or within the tight circle of like-minded Catholics whose children filled our schools. More than anything, they were constantly exploring teaching approaches and ways of addressing the issues of the children and their families. They wanted more participation in the decisions that governed their lives. Both believed in moderate change from within."

Jeanne reflected for a moment.

"Whitewaters was both a blessing and a curse—they were distanced from central control and given greater liberty in the management of St. Martin de Porres. It created the illusion that the gradual change they hoped for was moving ahead. Henrietta was considered a breath of fresh air. As the years went by, however, it became obvious that St. Martin was an anomaly. Retrenchment was the order of the day. In the last few years, with requests coming in from other dioceses for the SCRs, we knew that St. Martin was threatened. The harbinger of the future came when the developers approached Doug and we realized the value of our property."

"So your 'exchange' with the bishop regarding his pro-life stance had nothing to do with the closure?"

"I think the closure would have happened before you even arrived if the congregation and the diocese weren't so busy planning for the anniversary celebration and then had the Pope's trip thrown in as well."

"As I recall, during our little dinner party, Mother hit the roof."

"Anita's heart attack and my little wrangle with the bishop may have quickened the process by a year or two, but the decision was already in the works.

Jeanne rocked quietly and Rebecca went to the kitchen to refill her cup. She returned to the futon, flicked off her sandals, and curled her feet under her legs.

"If Henrietta was such 'a breath of fresh air' why do you suppose she twisted my words?"

"I have to confess, after Henrietta gave her rendition of your conversation, I thought you were a duplicitous, snivelling brat. It was Maureen who questioned her account. After all, Henrietta also failed to remember the encouragement she gave us in Whitewaters. How Henrietta managed to skew the facts . . . don't ask me. But you'd be surprised how powerful ostracism can be. I've seen the opened eyes of intelligent, educated sisters glaze right over. Who wants to be rejected by the people you love and admire, especially when your whole life is dependent on them? What you did took guts."

Rebecca started. She had never considered herself brave nor did she think leaving the SCRs was courageous.

"Guts? I was a coward for not confronting Mother, for bolting instead of going through the process for departure."

Jeanne stopped rocking and bent forward resting her arms on her knees. "Are you serious?"

"What did you do?"

"You can't compare yourself to me. I had years to mature my views, to consider my options. You, instead, were awakened with a slap."

"You're just being kind."

"Rebecca, did your conversation with Henrietta change anything?"

"It just made matters worse."

"So do you think talking to Mother would have gone any better?"

Rebecca recalled Mother's pious exhortation before she left for Emily's baptism. "No. . . . and I wouldn't have been able to handle her displeasure . . . her anger. My mother's badgering was bad enough."

Jeanne leaned back in her rocker. "So, like I said, you had guts."

"I can't believe I was so gullible . . . so stupid."

Jeanne rocked with her eyes closed.

"We can all be stupid at one time or another. Be grateful you're awake now."

"And I pestered you and Maureen with such drivel."

Again, Jeanne leaned forward amazed. "Rebecca, what I remember is your passion, the way you reached the students . . . your willingness to learn. You were open to different approaches. Rebecca, you're an outstanding teacher. And I know Maureen thought the same. Give yourself a break!"

After a couple of moments Rebecca asked, "Where is Maureen?"

Jeanne looked at Rebecca. "Maureen hasn't been well . . . she's been battling cancer for a few years . . . It went into remission, looked very hopeful, but the cancer flared up again this spring."

Jeanne put her head back and rocked a bit. "Rebecca, Maureen died in June."

CHAPTER 94

Rebecca waited at the deli counter of the grocery store as the clerk wrapped and bagged her sandwich. A woman down the aisle looked at her quizzically but Rebecca recognized her instantly—Ma Sparks. She walked down the aisle to greet her.

"Peggy, it's me, Rebecca. I visited you once at your home with Bev . . . many years ago now."

"Oh, yes," Peggy said, her eyes brightening with recognition, "the young church lady from Whitewaters."

Peggy stepped around the miniature cart she was pushing and gave Rebecca a warm hug. The deli clerk set Rebecca's bagged sandwich on the ledge of the deli counter and took his time to write the price on the paper wrapping. For weeks he had speculated with the regulars on the stranger in town. Other than being a friend of Jeanne's, little could be mined from their reticent customer.

"So are you here to work at the women's centre?"

"No, I'm just passing through." The clerk raised his eyebrows as he wiped the deli counter. "Stayed a little longer than I expected." The clerk acquiesced with a nod as he continued to wipe. Peggy noticed his attentiveness.

"Rod, did Darlene bring in her eggs today?"

Rod jerked his head up, surprised to be addressed directly, and dropped his cloth in a sudsy bucket on a lower shelf. "Sure did."

"Would you fetch me a dozen?"

Rod disappeared to the fridge in the back designated for the "community food distribution": a service the owner managed for a small fee. Peggy was adamant that the eggs from Darlene's free-range chickens were more wholesome than those trucked in from the egg production plants to the east. And she could supplement her neighbour's limited income by passing on a "donation" for the "gift" of her eggs.

"I always get my eggs from Darlene," she said to Rebecca. "Corporations don't need to pinch pennies from mountain folk. Unlike the cities," she said with a grin, "we still have people around here who know how to tend chickens."

Rebecca picked up her sandwich from the counter.

"Looks like you're getting ready for a picnic," said Peggy.

"Just going for a walk."

By the time Rod caught up with the two women, Peggy was chatting with the cashier. He had missed Peggy's invitation to show Rebecca her favourite hiking path.

~

Peggy didn't prod Rebecca's propensity to silence on the drive to her home. She knew the church ladies were no longer in Whitewaters and that Rebecca had left the group. When the church property was sold and the school, convent, and church torn down, speculation and gossip sped swiftly throughout the creeks and hollers. As far as Peggy was concerned, the only good that came of it was Jeanne now working full-time at the women's centre and settled permanently in Birchbark.

~

The groceries unpacked and Peggy's offer of coffee declined, the two women set out for their hike behind Peggy's home. As mosquitoes and gnats swarmed around them in the undergrowth, Rebecca was beginning to regret the impromptu trek. Peggy waved away the pests from her face and said, "We'll be free of these skeeters as soon as we get a little higher and round this hill."

That "little higher and round the hill" arrived a half-hour later. Sweat trickled down their backs and little bumps swelled on their legs and arms where the mosquitoes had feasted despite their efforts to shoo them away. Now, sitting on a rock near the crest of a hill and shaded by the trees behind, Peggy and Rebecca looked down on a couple of homesteads sharing a small holler. In the meadow below goats grazed around the rock and stubble, corralled by barbwire fences, their greying posts tilted nonchalantly in various directions. Small barns and outbuildings clustered near the homes, but they were kept at a distance by the white, slat-wood fences, giving a special distinction to the houses with their yards in the front and their gardens behind. Above and beyond the holler were the overlapping hills in the distance.

High up on the hill, with the fields open below them, a breeze blew freely, rustling the leaves behind them and forcing the mosquitoes and gnats back into the undergrowth. The hike had been worth it after all.

"This is where I come to settle," said Peggy.

"What do you think about?"

"Honey, when I come out here, I don't think about anything. I just enjoy."

After a few minutes Peggy asked, "Would you be able to find your way back to my place?"

The narrow path had been easy enough to follow behind Peggy but there had also been several intersecting paths along the way.

"I have a cell phone. . . ."

Peggy laughed. "Give me a call when you're ready to leave and I'll pick you up on the road near those farms below. Just follow that path on the edge of the field over there," she pointed.

"I could go back with you now."

"No, no . . . I have plenty to do at home today—you gave me a good excuse for an outing."

As Peggy dictated, Rebecca punched her phone number into her cell, then Peggy wandered up the path and disappeared into the brush.

～

Rebecca rummaged in her backpack for some water and pulled out her journal. She was surprised and saddened by Maureen's death, and for a while her mind went over the memories of their time together in Whitewaters and, in particular, their last conversation at the motherhouse. Maureen trusted her, had always trusted her. From the very beginning Rebecca had been treated as an adult, as an equal. Her pen remained poised over her open journal as she considered her time with Maureen. Gradually her mind drifted to the scene in front of her. She closed her journal and pushed every concern from her mind.

The goats lazily chewed the grass, the young ones sometimes scampering off together. A loner, off to the side, stretched its neck through the barbs to munch the leaves of a bush on the other side of the fence. The houses at the far end of the holler seemed deserted. After a while Rebecca saw a tiny figure emerge from one home and bend over in the garden. Occasional trucks and cars sped by to unknown destinations looking like toys on the narrow, winding road below.

The breeze picked up, caressing Rebecca's face and gliding its gentle fingers through her hair. Billowing clouds, swelling and swirling incrementally, assumed bizarre and comic forms and floated past in an aerial parade toward the distant mountains.

Somehow, it all hung together in a balance, the beauty and the mystery: the minute, busy ants, the bleating goats, the wild flowers skirting the fields, the unknown families carving out their existence in a hidden little holler; the sky and the sun and the mountains and the clouds. All of them part of some mysterious whole—some beautiful, good, mysterious whole to which Rebecca belonged. It came to her now, the final words from Maureen as Rebecca left the stuffy, dim dining parlour at the motherhouse, a quote from Julian of Norwich: "All shall be well, and all shall be well, and all manner of things shall be well."

A sense of peace settled within her, a sense of being embraced by Something or Someone much larger than herself. It was beyond her yet she could touch it, allusive yet she could sense it. She stood before it—within it—surrounded and immersed in a loving, mysterious Presence. It was in the bleating goats, the rustling leaves, the woman tending her garden. In this love she felt valued, appreciated, unjudged, trusted. She didn't need to know all the answers, she didn't need to be sure of the future, she didn't have to get it right. Only be open, honest, loving, and seeking.

Could she trust herself? Would she trust herself? The choice was hers, and hers . . . alone. Naked and solitary. The terrifying choice of freedom.

~

Rebecca sat on the back steps of the women's centre and watched the daycare children dart around the backyard, playing with toys or clamouring around the play structure. At times she laughed unconsciously at their antics, caught up in the moment, enjoying their play.

Jeanne watched her from the window of the back porch. She had not seen Rebecca so relaxed since she had arrived.

"Peggy said I would find you here," said Jeanne as she walked out to the stairs.

"So she decided to go upstairs and say hello after all," said Rebecca, turning to Jeanne. "I bumped into her at the grocery store this morning. Took a walk behind her place."

"So she said."

"I'd like to take you out to dinner tonight. Are you up to it?"

CHAPTER 95

Andrew turned on the AC as he drove along the avenue, his windows open until the vents, now blasting hot and humid air turned cool. His cell phone vibrated in his belt.

"Damn!"

Over the past few weeks he could count on one hand the times he had heard from Rebecca—all texts and each as sparse and general as the other. They did little more than assure him she was still alive. Hoping this would be a phone call instead, he swung into a bus stop and flicked open his cell. It was a text: *Will be home soon. One more stop.*

CHAPTER 96

The pipe organ intoned the opening chords and over a hundred nuns and dozens of young sisters-in-training stood in unison and began to sing. The cross bearer was flanked a step behind by two candle bearers, followed by the lector and then the celebrant. It was a Sunday Mass and the six pews in the back, reserved for guests, were packed on both sides of the aisle. Rebecca slipped into the end of the last pew in the far corner. A middle-aged woman huffed as she reluctantly gave up her aisle seat and moved into the pew, causing a domino effect of shuffling feet and readjustments of purses and sweaters as the earlier arrivals squeezed in to make room for the latecomer. The arches above, the polished marble below, the gleaming pews before her, the music, the singing, the gestures, the flowers, the myriad of nuns in their long, graceful habits— entrancing, brilliant—but Rebecca was no longer mesmerized. "In the name of the Father . . ." She went through the motions and recited the responses that came back spontaneously after an absence of several years.

Rebecca's spot at the end of the last pew was hardly appropriate for the purpose of her visit, but her opportunity came during the distribution of Communion. The visiting laity remained sitting or kneeling while the all sisters received the sacred host. They rose for Communion only after the celebrant walked down the aisle to their section. Rebecca scanned the sisters rapidly as they exited their pews, made their way up the main aisle and back down the sides. Although she recognized many, she was looking for only one. Mother Mary Thomas turned sideways and walked toward the centre aisle. The matriarch, so confident and assured, but aging.

No one was invulnerable to time. She found her aversion mitigated largely by sadness and pity. And then Rebecca saw her—Anita—near the back, in the pews designated for the senior sisters on the very side of the chapel where Rebecca was seated. At times, long-standing customs were very useful.

Rebecca smiled weakly at the disgruntled woman whom she had displaced from her aisle perch at the beginning of Mass. Having deferred Communion, Rebecca remained in the pew and tucked in her knees as tightly as she could so the woman could navigate around them as had the rest of the pew's occupants. The dowager was not pleased, Rebecca, however, was not going to let go of her position at the end of the pew. When the final hymn began and everyone was standing, Rebecca slid inconspicuously up the side aisle, past the laity and into the section reserved for the sisters. With the organ blasting, voices rising, and eyes glued to the hymnals, those at the end of the pews barely noticed the young woman slip past. A few pews into the sisters' section, Rebecca reached behind an elderly nun near the aisle and tapped Anita's shoulder. Anita turned, at first blankly, but when the recognition dawned, her face broke into a wide smile. She put down her hymnal and, gently pushing her neighbour forward, stepped out into the aisle to embrace Rebecca.

"I must see you," Anita whispered in Rebecca's ear as she hugged her. "Meet me at the main doors at ten. Can you do that?"

Rebecca nodded and made her way quickly back down the aisle. The meeting was over in seconds. The sisters were still singing and her companion during Mass still scowling when Rebecca walked out of the church.

~

Rebecca beeped open the car door as she approached her rental. It would be a couple more hours before she met Anita.

"Rebecca, Rebecca!" someone called from across the parking lot. A woman jogged through the parked cars followed by a young man at a more leisurely pace.

"Rebecca, I thought it was you!"

Rebecca looked at the woman in jeans and layered tee shirts, her long brown hair streaked with blond, until she recognized Patrick Marian morphed back to....
"Patrick Marian?"

"Well, Jennifer, now."

Jennifer gave Rebecca an extended hug, oblivious that Rebecca barely reciprocated.

"I've never seen you here before."

"Do you come often?" asked Rebecca.

"Every now and then if I happen to be in the area. Like to keep abreast of my old friends—the dears."

"You visit?"

"You know how it is—just for certain celebrations. But in the summer everyone comes back to the motherhouse so you can at least see who's around . . . or not."

Jennifer turned to the young man who had lagged behind and was now loitering a few yards back. "Brett, I want you to meet someone."

The young man came over and put his arm around Jennifer's shoulder. "Brett, this is Rebecca. We were nuns together. She left a couple of years before me."

Brett shook hands with Rebecca.

"Brett and I were married last year—met at a Catholic leadership program. Now we're campus ministers."

"Congratulations."

"Did Sr. Maria Eucharistia get a hold of you? She was going to contact you after she left."

"I didn't even know she had gone."

"Right before me . . . Sr. Mary Lourdes was on the fence . . . I didn't see her today but she could be visiting her family."

Some things never changed. Jennifer should have gone into private investigation.

"Did you hear about the new appointments?" asked Jennifer.

Rebecca hadn't but Jennifer didn't stop for her response.

"Sr. Miriam Pistós is a general councillor—one of the youngest ever! No surprise there. She always was Mother's devotee." Jennifer pulled her shoulders back and pretended to be straightening the back pleats of a habit, then opened her eyes wide at Rebecca.

"Seems to me you made use of that connection."

Jennifer looked puzzled.

Rebecca refreshed her memory. "The Pope's visit?"

"Oh! Now that was something to remember!" Turning to Brett, "You remember: the Pope's final Mass I told you about." Then turning back to Rebecca, "We never dreamed we'd get to see the Pope so close but it turned out that our seats were near the route of the Pope-mobile. What a thrill. When we returned to the motherhouse we were welcomed back like homecoming heroes."

"The closest I've ever gotten to the Pope is the TV," Brett said to Rebecca.

"It's nothing like being there in person, right, Rebecca?"

"Certainly provides different perspectives."

"So what are you doing now? I tried to look you up but you seemed to have vanished."

"I'm on a trip . . . which reminds me . . . I must be going. All the best to both of you." Rebecca opened the car door.

"Oh, no you don't, not without saying goodbye. Brett, give her our campus ministry card from the college."

Jennifer came over to the side of the car and gave Rebecca another bear hug. "Keep in touch."

Brett extended his hand and passed the business card. Then, waving goodbye, Rebecca left them in the parking lot.

CHAPTER 97

Shortly before ten, Rebecca backed the car into a spot at the far end of the parking lot and waited inside for Anita. A few minutes later the nun opened the carved, wooden door of the main entrance and glanced around. Rebecca stepped out of the car and waved. Anita turned in her direction, walked down the stairs and the two met at the corner of the building.

"It is so good to see you. I never gave up hope that you would come," said the older nun as the two embraced.

"Jeanne told me about Maureen. I'm so sorry."

"She would have loved to have seen you before she died but I'm sure in some way, she is with us right now. How is Jeanne?"

Rebecca relayed Jeanne's greetings and news of her work in Birchbark. "She said that she was able to speak with you at Maureen's funeral."

"It was a sad occasion but lovely to see Jeanne again. The opportunities are too few. . . ."

The two walked down a long path skirting the boundaries of the convent property, leaving the motherhouse behind.

"So where have you been since you left? Maureen and I were quite worried, especially when we heard how displeased your mother was."

"Vehemently displeased would be more accurate. . . . My father and brother were supportive and helped me get started." Rebecca briefly detailed her whereabouts over the past years.

"It had to be rough," said Anita, eyeing Rebecca.

"I feel like I've turned the corner."

"Turned the corner?"

"It's hard to explain. Like free-falling . . . not knowing but trusting . . . willing to search without any predetermined goal. . . . Loving . . . seeing the world in all its harshness, and still seeing all the beauty and good as well."

"That's quite a corner. . . . Where do you go now?"

"I don't know. It's still kind of frightening. . . . One thing for sure, I'll believe only what I come to see as worthy of belief, to be honest with myself before Love—that alone."

"God bless you, Rebecca."

Anita plucked a sprig of leaves dangling from a branch and tapped it in the palm of her hand.

"God *has* blessed you. It took me a lot longer. Like a kid on the monkey bars, afraid to let go, afraid of getting hurt. God was prying my fingers off one by one, coaxing me to trust him. You understand, I'm sure. . . . Once you admit certain traditions and rules need to be examined, you've opened the lid to them all. It's easier to keep up the blinders."

"But you did let go. . . ."

"Yes, in time God loosened my grasp. . . . And it was frightening, as it was for you. When the importance of the length of your hair and the height of your hem are emphasized as much as fidelity to your commitment, you don't stop at how relative a dress length is, you question the veracity of the whole system.

"When you question the teaching that missing Mass on Sunday is a mortal sin that can land you in hell . . . I mean, really . . . does a loving God want our weekly worship motivated by fear of hell? And so if I skip Mass, I'm headed for hell just like I would if I committed cold-blooded murder?" Anita voice was rising. "And what about hell? God curtails violence by violence? Is that a loving God?" Anita caught herself and began again in a calmer tone. "Forgive me, I'm rambling now. . . ."

Anita tapped her palm with the sprig and continued.

"When papal teaching has been shown wanting on one issue, you begin to wonder where else it went wrong. And that can get messy—it's hard to sort through the cultural barnacles and traditional embellishments that get latched onto the heart of the Gospels. In the process, the baby can get thrown out with the bathwater. It's confusing and muddy: you need to be comfortable with ambiguity, to allow the possibility of making mistakes and resolving them.

"Extremes are always the easiest—you know: change nothing or anything goes. And so to avoid *anything goes*, the safest position is not to question anything."

Anita tossed the sprig under a bush.

"Sometimes, doctrine is not even the issue—one's authority or one's comfort is at stake. It's complicated, for sure. . . ."

"How can you stay here with what you know?"

"I cast my lot with the SCRs years ago. I loved teaching and still do. We hoped for change—Maureen, Jeanne, and myself. That hasn't happened and it probably won't in my lifetime. But I've spent my life for the children. . . . Perhaps I made a difference in their lives. That's all I hope for."

The two walked on quietly. After some time the path they followed turned back toward the motherhouse.

Rebecca broke the silence. "I want to pay back the SCRs for my education. I don't want to leave behind any debts."

Anita shook her head and chuckled. "Debts? . . . You don't owe anything, Rebecca. You gave wholeheartedly while you were here and, quite frankly, the congregation is doing very well when it comes to donations. You see that new wing over there?"

Rebecca had noticed the large new extension matching the style of the older buildings.

"It was built to house the growing number of recruits—and it was completely paid for before it was finished. Millions. Besides, from what I heard about your mother, you can safely assume that over the years she contributed enough to the congregation to pay for your education twofold. Invest in children, Rebecca. That's all the repayment any of us needs to do."

Anita reached into the folds of her habit, pulled out an envelope, and handed it to Rebecca.

"Before we part: Maureen asked me to give you this letter if I should ever see you. She loved and admired you."

Rebecca took the envelope and embraced the older sister. Anita was still walking to a rear door of the motherhouse complex when Rebecca drove away.

CHAPTER 98

*D*ear Rebecca,
     As I sit with pen in hand, I think of you and reflect on my own life. *The convent in Whitewaters is closed and the school as well. Jeanne left and works now in Birchbark. Anita is kept busy with infirmary duties and, when needed, religion classes in neighbouring parishes. And Candida? You know Candida. Content enough as an assistant cook and even more as a gardener here at the motherhouse. I give a hand as needed at our schools in the city—substituting, reading assistant, and the like.*

Where have the years gone? What have they yielded? Has my life been in vain? I don't know. Life is what it is. The disillusionment and "what-ifs" have long vanished, and with them the bitterness and anger. Somehow I've managed to preserve my integrity and purpose as I live the daily regimen in our motherhouse. Through the despair, I discovered a depth of love that goes below and extends beyond the particulars of life and, at the same time, breathes through them all. The wonder of God's goodness pulsates through my day and opens me to love as I've never experienced it. Feelings of being trapped have given way to the possibility of reaching out, in however small a way, to another. My eyes look afresh at the beauty of spring, the joy of children laughing, the playfulness of puppies.

The adulation laid on the order troubles me. Increasingly, we garner the attention and praise of high-ranking cardinals, priests, and influential laity. No one questions the stringent regulation of the smallest details of our life and the deference of one's perceptions and judgments to superiors in the name of God.

For now nostalgia reigns and there is little more I can do. My concerns are viewed as a lack of faith. So I let it go and turn my gaze to one thing only—to respond in love moment by moment as life unfolds each day. Whatever meaning my life has, whatever purpose it has served, I leave in God's loving hands. For now it is enough to love, to move beyond my pain, even my hopes, and reach out to others as they are, where they are.

Rebecca, you are young and you are gifted. The depth of your disillusionment and anger only reveals the depth of your insight and your potential for compassion. The world is big, the needs are many. We can't allow our hearts to be shrivelled and swallowed by the injustice of others. They know not what they do. Love and forgive. It's the only way to peace and meaning. Life is too short for anything less.

God bless you always.

With much love,

Maureen

CHAPTER 99

Gladys poked her head into Sally's cubicle. Sally had transferred into Enrolment and Gladys had her sights set on becoming an underwriter.

"The bitch is back!"

Sally deflated any illusion Gladys might have had that she came with breaking news. "Yes, Rebecca called me last night, too."

"Are your parents still over?"

"No, they left a couple of day ago. They're coming back for Christmas."

At the end of June, Sally had finally contacted her parents about Don's death. They made the long drive to visit a couple of times over the summer and her children were getting to know their grandparents. Sally's mother urged her to move closer to their home but Sally decided to remain. She was upgrading her education and had opportunities for promotion in Secure Star. Unlike Gladys, men were off her radar. She wanted no interference with her children—for now, they were her life.

"So you'll be at the picnic?"

"Wouldn't miss it."

CHAPTER 100

Andrew leaned against the trunk of a large oak, its ancient branches extending up and out, forming a broad canopy overhead. The sun shimmered through the leaves like a kaleidoscope, mingling and variegating hues of green and forming shadows and shapes on the lawn. Rebecca leaned against Andrew's chest, her forehead near his chin, one arm entwined in his and the other around Emily who snuggled up against her, taking a few minutes from play to sip on a juice box.

"Emily! Come on," shouted Eliza and Sarah, each munching a handful of popcorn. Nigel, putting a couple handfuls in his pocket, was already moving toward his father, who was adjusting the volume on a CD player.

Emily popped up and ran off, handing her mother the empty container as she went.

Judy set the juice box near her lawn chair and laughed. "Mothers: universal coat racks and garbage disposals."

"Andrew and Rebecca! Let's see your butts out here!" hollered Gladys. In a grassy area just beyond the oak tree Gladys and Ben were beginning the line dancing.

"What a mouth!" said Harriet, resting in a lawn chair next to Judy.

"We're keeping your mother company," shouted back Rebecca.

"Like hell you are! Sally and Judy have her under tight surveillance."

"Not anymore," said Sally as she got up from her lawn chair near Harriet and went out to join the dancers. Sasha and Deborah clapped as she arrived and stood on either side of her.

Jeremy, Brian, and Caleb sat close together, their heads touching like conjoined triplets, watching each other's moves on Brian's handheld game. When the music started, Jeremy and Caleb jumped up. Brian watched as his new-found friends joined the rhythmic lines. For a while he continued with his game but when he saw his father, Rob, among the dancers, he dropped his device into his mother's lap and joined the others.

Judy waved the device at Rebecca. "Guardian of the electronics!"

Jeremy took his position in the front with his mother and they led the steps. Caitlyn and Kristen were in their element and, as soon as they got the hang of the steps, began to add extra flourishes while still keeping time. Nigel, at the fringe of the second line near Ben, made up his own moves, sometimes just spinning around and then walking forward in a dizzy saunter.

Andrew chuckled at his antics and then asked Rebecca, "How's Nigel doing?"

"He's in a new program that was developed for kids whose parents had substance abuse issues. Ben is uncertain whether his ex-wife was using during pregnancy or how much Nigel was neglected before he realized what was going on. Gladys seems to think he is interrelating better. . . . That's major coming from Gladys."

"Are she and Ben still living separately?"

"Until Ben gets a handle on Nigel's issues, they both think it's better. Last I heard, they were considering a home with a basement suite where they would have separate living quarters but could still be together."

Rebecca glanced around. "Where did Mom go?" she asked Judy.

Judy pointed down a path behind the trees that encircled their picnic area. "She and her beau went for a stroll along the river." Judy raised her eyebrows.

Margaret had met Cliff on the Christmas cruise eight months before and, from what Rebecca could tell, he had more in common with her mother than her own father had. Cliff lived in Florida and had paid for her mother, Rob, and his family to fly out for a week's vacation at the end of August. Rebecca had missed the invitation while at her Birchbark retreat—with no regrets. Cliff planned to return to California with Margaret so they all decided that on their way back they would to spend Labour Day weekend with Rebecca. Shortly after their arrival, Margaret felt duty bound to tell Rebecca that she didn't approve of "the nature of her relationship" with Andrew. But after making that clear, Margaret managed to be civil during her weekend stay, and Cliff had the sense to remain silent on the issue.

Rebecca felt Andrew's measured pulse on her arm, his breathing gentle on the side of her face, unfathomable a year ago. She whispered to Andrew, "How did you know me?"

"It's a long story," he said.

Rebecca pulled back her head to look at Andrew. "You'll tell me?"

"I will."

Rebecca settled back in the nook of Andrew's arm and he gently squeezed her arms.

The CD player pealed out a familiar song. Judy sang along and Harriet tapped her toes. Several children from other picnic groups nearby walked closer to the line dancers for a better view. With Gladys's encouragement they joined group. The lines of dancers moved together to the beat: forward, to the side, back, forward, side to side. When the song ended, Jeremy let out a hoot. Caitlyn and Kristen ran to Gladys to help pick out the next song, and Jeremy squeezed in near his mother to be part of the consultation. Gladys gave each of the girls a high-five and Jeremy passed on the choice to Ben who squatted near the CD player. Music again filled the air. The proficient dancers followed Gladys easily; the learners, laughing, tried to catch up.

A breeze rustled the leaves, swaying the oak's cupola and refiguring the images cast by the leaves around Rebecca and Andrew like a stained-glass window.

ACKNOWLEDGEMENTS

My parents for instilling in me a love of reading and a desire to write.

My brothers and sisters for their love and support throughout the years and their encouragement as I wrote my novel.

Helen and Colin MacIsaac, the first to read a draft and whose goodness has accompanied me during these past years.

Those who read my novel and whose input was both encouraging and insightful: my sisters Kimi and Nikki; my niece, Lisa; Elaine Parks; Sr. Brenda Dolphin; Corrine Winters; Yolande Gagnon; and Marilyn Potts.

Margaret Downey and Krista Francis-Poscente, who shared their expertise in teaching children, and Chantal Penney, who gave me a glimpse into insurance processing.

My editor, Patricia Anderson, for meticulously reviewing my manuscript and for her confidence in the value of my story.

My cover and interior designer, Erik Mohr, for his beautiful art and his dedication to the project.

My brother, Anthony, for his efforts to promote Terrifying Freedom.

All those who, through the years, have shared their lives, their love, and their thoughts: thank you.

BIO

Linda Smith lives near Calgary, Alberta, enjoying the beauty of Rocky Mountains. For 30 years, she was a member of a community of religious sisters. She currently works in an organization that is dedicated to assisting and advocating for traumatized and neglected children and their families.